Mortal Screaming

The Legend of Hereward
Book Two

Kon Blacke

Dreamsphere Books
Winnipeg, Canada

Published August 2023 by Dreamsphere Books, an imprint of Story Perfect Inc.

Dreamsphere Books
PO Box 51053 Tyndall Park
Winnipeg, Manitoba R2X 3B0
Canada

Visit http://www.dreamspherebooks.com to find out more.

"The universe has a plan for us all even if we never understand it, not even with our last scream or dying breath, oaf."

> *— Abbot Hosho whispering to Lord Hereward after saying his farewells and the knight embarks on his journey with Dorgan to find Oswin.*

"What's fate ever done for me except give me grief? Otherwise, I wouldn't be stuck with a lord who doesn't know his arsehole from his breakfast while I wait on him hand and foot. God, if this is what I have to suffer until the day I die, take me now!"

> *— spoken by Oswin inside the castle's latrines, having been overheard by the scullion boy who'd had to suffer the lord's wandering hands recently.*

"A fate as the lord's bit o' fancy is all I can hope for."

> *— said by the scullion boy to Oswin some days later.*

Oswin in reply: "Then we will flee the Keep together. No one will ever find us. No one! That's fate too, right?"

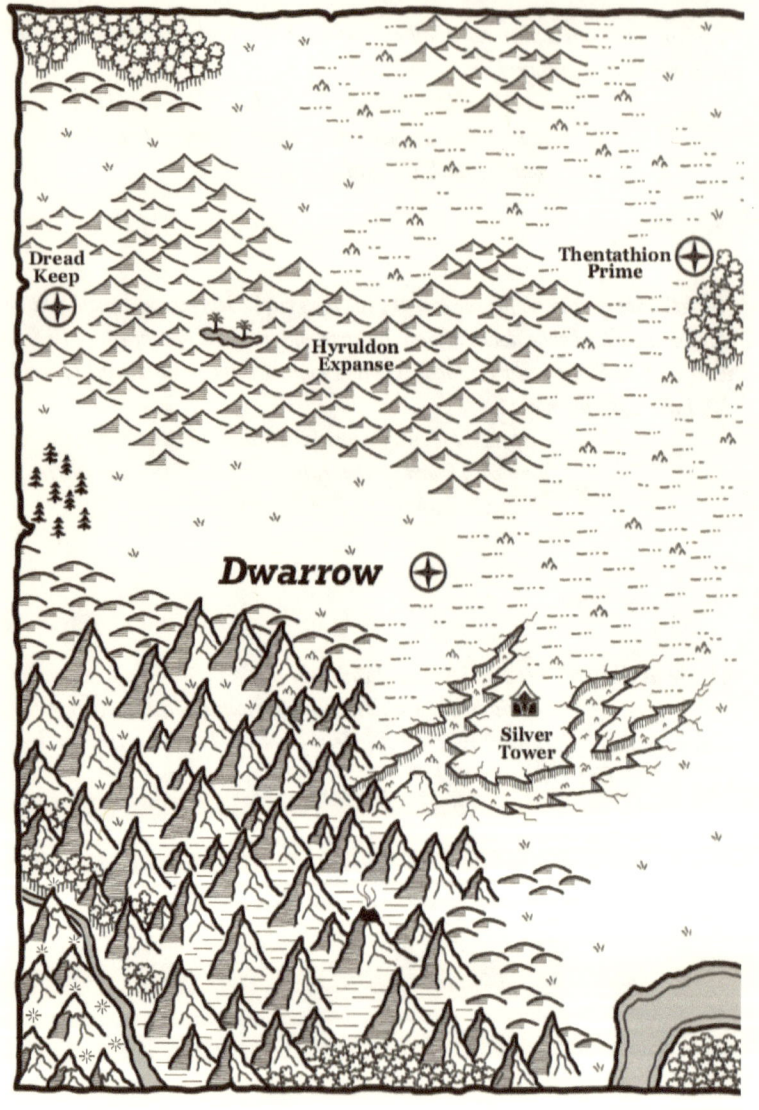

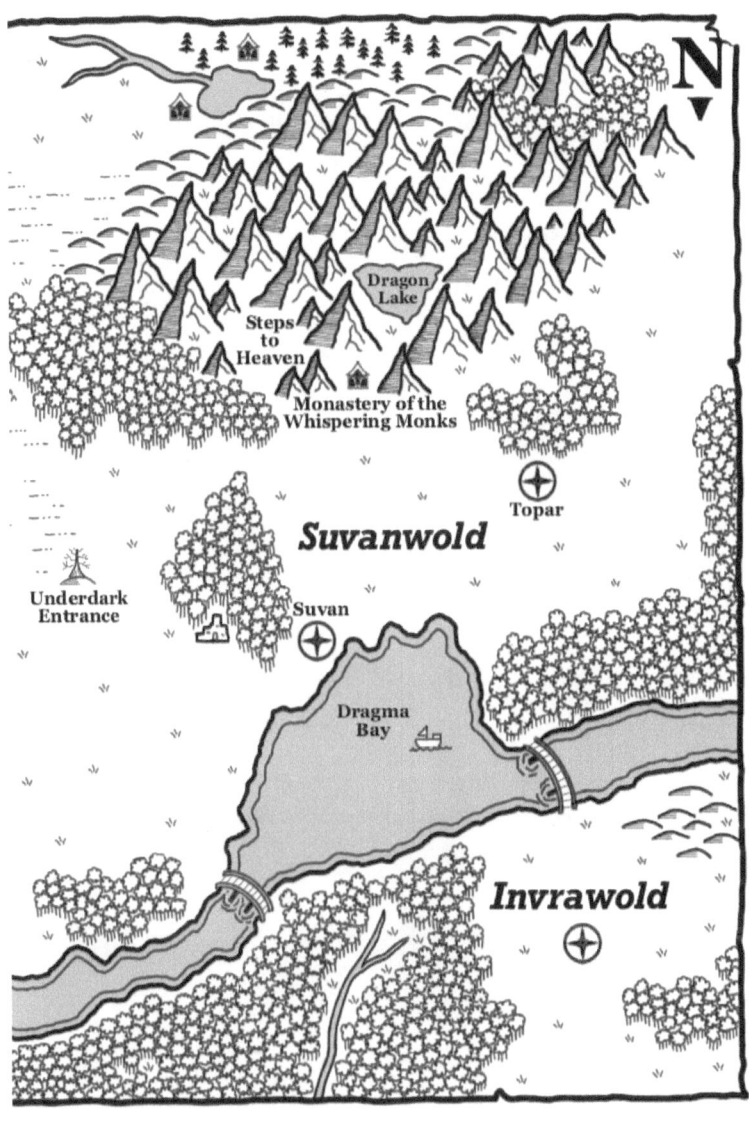

Mortal Screaming

Part One

1
Hereward's Justified Grace

THEY'D FOLLOWED THE THREE bandits to their camp. Wasn't hard to do. The fuckers didn't even attempt to hide their escape after what they'd done; a blind dog with a head cold could have followed them into the woods, they were so careless.

Bad for the men.

Fucking good for Hereward.

Hereward snuck up to crouch behind the thick undergrowth bordering a small glen with his sword hand itching and at the ready, as always. Dorgan, the silver dragon now in human form, was by his side—also, as always.

He liked Dorgan being with him. Loved what they did in bed together even more. It was good to have a companion who fucked as magnificently as he was fucked after spending the day adventuring in the wilds. Loneliness had always been the biggest drawback.

Hereward, after a moment of contemplation, returned his thoughts to the here and now. His hand wandered to the pommel of his sword god. He flexed his thick fingers.

Easy now, my love. Soon. We shall spill their blood soon, his sword god said to Hereward within his mind with her lilting and beautiful voice. *The king's reward will be ours soon too.*

Too fucking right, Hereward replied in thought.

To be truthful, he didn't care about reward, only justice. As such, he remained silent and watching. Only the night sounds of numerous nocturnal animals foraging for food or a mate or both broke the bubble of stillness. Hereward then caught the bandit's conversation, their gloating, and he seethed at what he heard.

"...farmer's daughter were too fuckin' loose," a voice crackled like the open fire the three men sat around, faces aglow in the flickering light, "even though she were as dry's a bone. Hated to have had her all wet n' willin', hey? I might'a lost myself in her insides if I'd thrust too hard."

One man laughed at those words.

But the man sitting next to the speaker on their shared fallen log harrumphed. He then smiled wickedly. "Maybe your cock's just too fuckin' small, Roddic. Ever think 'bout that?"

Roddic, affronted and red-faced now, stood up quickly. He unbuttoned his pants and fished out what was mocked, grabbing it tightly to emphasize its surprisingly large size. With a posturing growl, he barked, "This too small for ya, Fron?" He then flicked his flaccid, vein-riddled appendage onto Fron's cheek a few times before the man could back away in submission.

A large wet mark was left on Fron's stubble, glistening in the fire's light; no doubt what remained of Roddic's orgasm that'd finally leaked out because of his sudden jerking action. Seemed Roddic got what he wanted from the farmer's daughter despite what he'd claimed.

Hereward's face burned in anger, right down his neck. He felt sick to his stomach at the thought of the bandit raping an innocent girl. And for what? A handful of coins? Bile found his throat.

"The bastards," Dorgan whispered with barely a breath.

Hereward agreed. But because of what had unfolded, he realized the fucking bandit named Roddic hadn't taken a piss after he'd ejaculated to clean out his pipe. He knew the men hadn't stopped to rest after fleeing the farmhouse they'd raided until they got to their camp, less than half a league from the farmhouse.

Therefore, the dripping off Roddic's cock was clearly the remaining result of his debauchery. Evidence enough in Hereward's mind they'd pursued those responsible. And the bandits had a lot to answer for: the farmer was dead, as was his wife. Done while they slept in their bed. Both were murdered for their meagre savings and a few trinkets. The daughter was raped and then murdered, brutally so. No doubt, by Roddic. Or all three of them. But Hereward had to be sure before he got his sword god and Dorgan to help him dispense the king's justice while they both searched for Oswin, their ultimate mission. No harm in doing side work getting there, though. Evil needed stamping out. Always.

His hand itched again, and he grabbed his sword, his beautiful god. She was cold to his touch. Cold like her steel heart towards Hereward's enemies. And the men they watched *were* enemies.

Soon, my love.

The bandit's conversation continued to disturb his thoughts as the men hung themselves with their words.

"Sorry." Fron wiped his face, offering a weak smile. "Was only jestin'."

Roddic seemed mollified. "Say dat again, n' next time I'll use me sword instead o' me cock on ya. Got it?"

Fron didn't reply that time, but his eyes turned dark and planning, revealed by the fire's light. Hereward thought the sight delicious; treachery amongst thieves was real. Good. Very good.

The third bandit raised his hand and offered a shallow guffaw, sounding like the grating whelping of a wild dog. "Easy now. You'll get ya share o' the coin despite the fun not meetin' your expectations. Maybe next time it will. Am I right?"

Roddic stuffed his cock back where it belonged and sat back down on the log, brooding. He picked up a twig, snapped it, then threw it into the fire in disgust; a popping noise resulted when it was consumed by the flames. "Weren't much coin," he grumbled. "Hardly worth it."

"I agree," Fron said tentatively, still rubbing his cheek as if the stain Roddic left on him could never be removed. "Two pieces o' silver n' a few coppers each is a jest for all our efforts."

Fron spoke as if breaking into someone's home in the dead of night, raping and then murdering them for good measure, then stealing what little they possessed of any worth was work. Hereward hated them even more. He had to suppress the urge to strike too soon. He needed to know more. The men had to incriminate themselves without a shadow of doubt because his sword god's justice would be swift and merciless. Dorgan placed his hand tenderly onto Hereward's knee as if in understanding. The gods bless him.

The third bandit, as yet unnamed—not that it mattered—changed his tune to one more leering, and, to Hereward's disgust, more sinister. But they were words he needed to hear, really.

"Though you should'a done like I did and stuck the fuckin' son instead o' the daughter, Roddic. The boy was so nice n' tight; it were unbelievably good. I wager the little fucker'll be pissin' blood outta his arsehole for a week now, I've wrecked him good and proper I did." The man laughed at his own words.

The other two didn't.

Hereward and Dorgan didn't see the farm boy in the carnage and destruction the men had left the house. He must have hidden after being raped. Hereward seethed even more, his vision tunneling. A red mist found his eyes. He'd go berserk soon, he knew it. Could feel it to his bones.

Fron spat, "Yeah, if ya like boys ten summers old for ya fun. Should'a killed him though. We killed the others—butchered 'em like pigs. Why not him?"

Dorgan gasped. Hereward's stomach turned again. By the gods, the farmer's son was young. Too young. He couldn't imagine the horror the poor boy had gone through and now he was an orphan thanks to these fucking pieces of shit. The boy's life wouldn't be easy if he could survive without his family's support. Hereward was really fucking pissed off now.

Soon, my love.

"I may go back for seconds." The third shrugged. "Or thirds n' fourths, 'fore I slit his fuckin' throat from ear to ear."

Roddick, obviously still in his mood, offered, "If ya don't mind shit on ya cock from a frightened little boy crappin' himself while ya rape him, then yeah, suppose you're right. But if ya don't kill him soon, I will. Can't have witnesses, can we?"

The third didn't look happy. He stood. "Gonna blow me fuckin' load into the boy's guts as much as I wanna. Only I'll decide when the boy gets to see the halls of his gods. Not you, Roddic, nor you either, Fron. Only me. Hear me?"

A tense moment of silence followed.

Now! Hereward's sword god said deliciously. *Let their blood trickle down my fuller to my quillon to satisfy us both. Only their deaths will do so.*

She was right. The time had come for Hereward's itch to be satiated. He'd heard more than enough; justice had to be done. Without further thought, he grabbed Dorgan and sprang into the clearing, yelling his anger and disgust at the bandits, emotions seething.

His sword god thrummed.

Oh, their shock was the last thing they would remember. Hereward chopped them up into dog meat with ease, not even breaking a sweat. Blood stained the air with its coppery wonder. His god was magnificent, slicing through the bandit's unarmored bodies as though they were made of butter. Hereward made sure Roddic and the third man got a good look at him before there were more outside of them than inside, the fucking cowards.

May they rot for eternity.

When done, there was bloody meat, broken bones, slashed guts, piss and shit everywhere in great oozing, stinking piles scattered around the campsite. The fire crackled as though nothing around it had any bearing on it giving warmth. Which it didn't. Hereward felt a lot better.

Dorgan, his sword dripping blood, stood with his mouth agape.

"What?" Hereward questioned.

"You could have just run them through not hacked them into bits a mouse could eat comfortably. You were like a man possessed."

Hereward methodically wiped his sword god clean of blood and his disgust at what the men represented with the cloak of one of the men—Roddic's, he believed—before scabbarding her with care.

Thank you, my love.

You're fucking welcome.

Hereward threw the cloak into the fire. It roared, flames growing brighter and sparks flittering up within the smoke. Another satisfying sight. He smiled, then snorted. "Gotta make sure there's fucking nothing left of them to sit at the halls of their gods, don't I? They don't deserve any comfort for what they did. Cowards die in fucking shame with only the eternal Circles of the Nine Hells good enough for them."

"Yes, they were evil men," Dorgan agreed.

"You all right, lover?"

"I am."

Hereward embraced Dorgan, holding him tightly. He needed a good fucking hug after having dealt with those bandits as did Dorgan, he knew. But the men's deaths would offer no comfort to the poor farm boy left alone. "We have to go see the lad. Make sure he's looked after."

Dorgan kissed Hereward's lips lightly. "I didn't think that was ever in question."

"Then after that I'm gonna fuck your brains out—killing gets me fucking horny." Hereward shifted his weight as his cock stiffened, harder than the steel of his god, he knew it.

"Me too."

Fuck, Hereward loved Dorgan.

The farmhouse had been ransacked, everything destroyed for the scant few coins hidden under a couple of loose floorboards near the fireplace. The building was dark except for a well burnt down candle left lit upon a rustic wooden table within one of the back rooms: the looted scullery.

Hidden inside the larder, the naked and bleeding farm boy was huddled, looking lost, frightened, and so very alone. He'd been crying his eyes out; his dirty face was marred by clean trails down his innocent cheeks. He'd been through fucking hell, the poor boy. Hereward's heart sank at the sight of him. He wished he'd got to the farm sooner. Much sooner. Although, the boy wasn't crying now even though his expression was no less gaunt and grief stricken.

Hereward knew the boy was in shock. He couldn't fucking blame him. The boy clung onto a shawl, no doubt his mother's. The boy's raped and slaughtered family were sprawled out on the scullery's floor, their faces masks of fear and agony from their death throes, their blood over every surface, including the low beamed ceiling. They really had been butchered like pigs. They'd also been placed there deliberately to taunt the boy. Remind him of what would happen to him the next time the bandits came calling.

Hereward's heart sank even further. He wanted to cry. Actually, fuck it. He did until he could gather himself. It took a few moments.

Dorgan immediately went to the boy, offering his cloak to cover him. There wasn't any reaction. Not even a blink from the boy's bloodshot eyes. He had no chance at sanity with his dead family around him, so they took him outside. Took him into the fresh air away from the stain of blood.

Hereward said quietly, "I'm so sorry." He bit back his emotions again as he knelt beside the boy. He didn't touch him, though. He didn't want to frighten him any more than he'd already been. "We killed the fucking men who murdered your family. You can have the king's reward as compensation, as meagre and meaningless as it is."

No answer. Not even a blink.

"What's your name, boy?" Dorgan asked with a smooth, reassuring voice. Hereward understood the dragon was doing his best, but really nothing could compensate or reassure the boy for what he'd lost. No response. "Is there any family you have around here we can take you to?"

Eternity turned while they sat with the boy, comforting him.

There was no rush.

As dawn's light began to seep into the world, pearling the glorious sky, then turning it to lavender and other pastel hues, the boy finally moved, coming out of himself. No words were said as he registered their presence.

After another age and with trembling lips, all the while holding onto the shawl tighter, he whimpered, "W-Wallace." Thick tears fell from his eyes and ran down to his chin, dripping off it and staining Dorgan's cloak with fat drops. "My...n-name's...Wallace. I've got no...

just wanna…me Ma n' Da n' Sis back. Just wanna…" He broke down and heaved tears; the rest of what he spoke was unintelligible.

Wallace fell into Dorgan's arms.

Dorgan held Wallace, and Hereward held them both. Without second thought, he blurted, "We're going to make sure the boy is safe from now on, that's my oath to him. Poor little thing's been through hell. No one deserves that before they're even old enough to hold a sword in the right way to defend themselves."

"Are you going to adopt Wallace, then?" Dorgan questioned. "As would be your right, under King's law."

"No, I'm not—*we* are."

Dorgan looked taken aback. "How? We're not even a proper couple…*are we?*"

"Can be if you want us to be," Hereward said matter-of-factly and as if a given. He'd consummated his love for Dorgan a few times since they'd left the Steps to Heaven mountains in search of Oswin, doing the king's duty while they did so. Upholding the law at the edges of the wild as it were. It was the right and proper thing to do, anyway. Hereward was a lord. As was Dorgan since they'd been joined by their cocks and swapped body fluids regularly. It was only right and proper to move to the next step with him. Dorgan was his man as he was Dorgan's.

Hereward added, "Wouldn't mind you keeping my bed warm beside me for a lot longer. The rest of my fucking life if you wish."

Dorgan's eyes widened. "Is that a proposal, Lord Hereward?" But Dorgan's expression quickly softened, his greyish silver eyes glistening beautifully. Hereward had learned the look was of Dorgan's love.

Hereward returned it. He smiled, kissing Dorgan square on the lips, Wallace nestled safe and sound between them. "As good as any, I reckon."

"Then I accept. But I want a big diamond ring for my finger to make it all official."

"Oh, you'll get something big all right."

Dorgan's face brightened in the growing light of a new day that'd managed to break the gloom and carnage of the scullery. "Indeed."

"Who…a-are ya?" Wallace stuttered meekly as soon as Hereward parted his affection, knowing full well Dorgan meant his words.

Hereward replied, "I'm Hereward, Lord of the Realm of Suvanwold, protector of the innocent, upholder of the law of King Hurald, and keeper of the speaking sword." He gestured to Dorgan.

"And this here is my lover and companion, Dorgan the Wise of Dragon Lake, son of Brakon the Swift."

The boy nodded in understanding while wiping away more tears. "I'm j-just Wallace. Wallace t-the...farm boy. Son o' Poul."

"Well, just Wallace the farm boy, by the sword god I carry by my side, I'll protect you until my dying breath. That's my oath and my promise, if you accept it."

"Will ya...p-protect me always? Even...even f-from the evil men who'll wanna...*stick me*...with more t-than their swords, Lord Hereward?"

"Especially from them, the fucking bastards," Hereward spat. His disgust returned with a vengeance at the memory of the senseless loss, staining his thoughts. "But I'll do more than that, Wallace, my boy. I'm going to teach you how to wield a sword and defend yourself; then *you* can stick the fucking men who might threaten you instead of the other way around."

"And I will protect you, too, Wallace," Dorgan offered.

"Ya a dragon?" Wallace asked, watery eyes widening.

"I am."

For the first time since they'd arrived, Wallace managed a quivering smile with his tear-wet lips. "Then...I'll surrender myself to...to ya protection, Lords. I have...n-nothin' else, do I?"

Dorgan got up, offering his hand to Wallace. "After we have given your family a proper send off so they can sit within the halls of their gods with honour, you'll join us on our journey, Wallace."

Wallace nodded. Hereward watched peacefully as Dorgan transformed into a silver-scaled dragon, massive and beautiful, to blow his fiery breath upon the farmhouse, turning it into a pyre. But not before Hereward retrieved clothing for Wallace and placed two coins into each of the mouths of those they sent off into the afterlife with their blessing.

All three cried for what had happened until the sun's blazing glory rose above the horizon proper. They continued to hold each other as the house crumpled to smoking ashes, the sky corrupted by the result of the bandit's evil—evil that'd thankfully been silenced.

After the ashes cooled and the day began in earnest, birds chirping excitedly for worms and insects within the bushes, they walked away, hand in hand—Wallace between them—to continue their journey. An important one, for Oswin was vital to ensuring future events unfolded as foreseen as far as Hereward understood it. Abbot Hosho had told him as such. Many, many times. What Oswin's importance was within the Grand Arena of the universe, though, Hereward didn't understand. Then again, he never understood half of what came out of the fucking monk's mouth. He loved the orange robe wearing blind bastard like a father, though. Loved him to fucking pieces.

But to his dismay, and swearing at himself for not considering such a thing sooner, Wallace said, "Ya got all four o' 'em, did ya?"

Dorgan stopped short, offering a glance of horror to Hereward. "What are you talking about, Wallace? There were only three bandits as far as we knew." He then paused, the worried expression deepening. "Wasn't there?"

"Certain as day there were four o' 'em." Wallace shook his head, eyes glassy once more. "One got me Sis. One got Da. One Ma. An'…an' one…he did things to m-me." He began to cry again, but that time with pain in his eyes.

Hereward couldn't believe it. They'd missed one of the fuckers somehow in their haste. "Fuck!"

We will get him, my love. Patience.

Hereward brushed his fingers tenderly over the pommel of his sword god in reply. His hand itched again. *I know.*

"What did the man look like?" Dorgan asked.

Wallace, still justifiably upset, whimpered, "He were the leader o' 'em. Never seen the likes of a man like dat 'fore 'round here. He were t-tattooed all over his face, wore a cloak too. Glowed like he had magic, an' all."

"A fucking darrow!" Hereward snorted. Now his sword hand really itched, right up his arm to his shoulder.

2
Greysen's Unbelievable Punishment

HIS LORD'S HARD COCK, throbbing with excitement, was rammed into the back of Greysen's throat. He didn't gag. He'd become used to it since he was first taken by his lord when he came of age some three summers ago now.

But Greysen's head was held to prevent any premature withdrawal by eager, trembling clawed hands. His lord, demon god of the undead, of bones, of death, and the reaper himself, was about to relieve himself, squirt his thick pungent seed down Greysen's throat. The fluid would then ooze down to his stomach to become a part of him. Greysen relished whatever his lord gave him, that especially. He would die for his lord's love.

But before he could have what he desired, there was business to attend to. He knew it. Greysen, eyes watering, spittle and runny snot lubricating the cock he keenly serviced, wouldn't be able to answer back.

Just the way his lord liked it.

"You disappointed me, A Rúnsearc," Myrkul, his husband and god, rumbled. Thankfully, he called Greysen his "secret beloved" in the language of his kind.

The news wasn't going to be bad, then.

Greysen relaxed a little. As much as he could with a demon's cock, complete with a massively swollen and teardrop shaped knob like a dire wolf's, stretching his lips to the point of cracking, jaw aching, deep inside his wanting mouth.

His eyes wept more tears. Greysen was on all fours before his lord, who sat upon his throne made of bones. The bones of those who had been Myrkul's lovers before Greysen swore his allegiance in matrimony. He relished the idea that he would join them when his time came, his lord sitting upon his polished bones until even eternity died.

Saliva dribbled down his chin to patter in rhythm upon the black stone floor. Yes, he was edging towards the point of agony, but Greysen relished it. He was his lord's vessel to fill.

This time, his lord wanted Greysen's mouth.

When Myrkul desired his anus, rutting him like a bitch in heat, Greysen bled for days. And not only from the scratches clawed in deep furrows upon his back.

But he wouldn't have it any other way. Greysen would let his lord rip him apart while fucking him. He enjoyed the idea of dying in agony and ecstasy underneath his lord, giving his body and blood willingly. If he were truthful to himself, he'd love it if Myrkul strangled the life from him while defiling him. That was his fantasy. And he knew Myrkul would resurrect Greysen so he could own him over and over, again and again for millennia.

Over that time, eons passing, Greysen would think of many ways, ever more exotic, to die for his lord's love. At such a thought, Greysen increased his vigour. Myrkul moaned deep from his throat. He had done well.

But Myrkul hadn't killed him during their sweet bliss together as of yet, no matter how many times he begged for mortal release. How many times had he offered himself for such sacrifice? Too many.

Greysen yearned to be immortal. He would give himself to Myrkul, his lord and husband, willingly and in every way to be so. He would scream in blood until he was snuffed out in the wonderful bliss of death if he had to only to do it again and again. For to be with Myrkul as his immortal husband was to also have absolute power over everyone else.

Another thing Greysen yearned for.

But now he yearned for a different reason; he was close to ejaculating. He pleasured himself while he pleasured his lord, his hand a blur upon his own pulsing, aching erection. But Greysen knew his time wasn't up. Not yet. He had work to do for his lord.

"Do you know why you displeased me?" The booming baritone of his lord's voice was returned to him many times as it echoed through the dark stone chamber of his throne room. A massive room Greysen knew all too well, for it was only here and within his own private chamber where he was allowed. All the other rooms in the Dread Keep were for his lord and his lord only. Aside from the stone, the throne of bones made of past lovers, and the nine twisted dark onyx carved statues representing the torments of Hell, the room was bare. Myrkul never liked clutter; simplicity was beauty. Like sex. Like death. Simple and beautiful.

Two ghoul guards, one on either side of the throne, looked on with disinterest as Greysen, naked as he always had to be, sucked and slurped in reply to Myrkul's words. Greysen's jaw ached unbelievably, but he didn't stop. The noises of his actions joined the echo.

"I shall tell you."

Greysen was very close to orgasm. His heart thumped in his chest, blood rushing, body aching. But he couldn't release until he got permission. To soil the floor before being told to do so would deny him carnal pleasures for weeks. He wouldn't even be allowed to touch himself, his cock caged.

"I am not pleased with the lich generals and their progress. And they are under your command, are they not? Therefore, it is your fault they fail."

Greysen knew Myrkul would have slaughtered the generals who displeased him. He became more excited by such a thought; he desired his lord to slaughter him, spill his blood, then bring him back to life. Not like those generals, though. They would be lost to eternity.

"You may relieve yourself while I think about what you need to do to make up for your failing, A Rúnsearc."

A wave of pleasure burst through Greysen. He shuddered, and before he could stop himself, he spurted his seed all over the black stone beneath him. He'd also clamped his jaw, biting into the hardness of his lord's cock.

A moment of panic surged through him, until his lord responded.

"Hmm…yes!" Myrkul moaned, writhing upon his throne, his balls tightening. "Bite me harder. Draw blood and feast on it. I will also give you my seed to join my blood. Your mouth has pleased me, unlike the rest of you."

Greysen obeyed, the tang and bitter salt of both blood and semen flowing down his throat. When Myrkul had unloaded all he would give, Greysen came off his cock with a popping sound, saliva dripping.

"Speak, A Rúnsearc."

Greysen had to work his jaw to chase away the pain and numbness. He'd been sucking his lord's cock for more than an hour—a quick finish compared with other times. Greysen yearned for more already.

With his voice hoarse, strangely dry considering he could still taste the fluids of his lord around his mouth, he said, "I'm at your mercy, my lord. My body is yours to defile and destroy. My mind yours to ruin. My soul yours to keep."

"Indeed. Now lick up the mess you made. Then kiss my feet in thanks for what I gave you." He could see Myrkul was still aroused, his wet with saliva cock hard and leaking. Greysen's bites upon it were red, and blood still flowed, but Greysen didn't hesitate not wanting to stare even though he couldn't help himself. His lord was magnificent.

He licked up his ejaculate, swallowing it all down when done. He then kissed his lord's feet as he'd been commanded.

"Lick between my toes."

Greysen did so, again relishing what he did with his tongue because it pleased his lord. Myrkul then clicked his fingers, the echo of the sound seemed alive within the throne room's gloom. Greysen sat up but remained kneeling. He hadn't been asked to stand.

A lich lord, an obsequious soul hungry for power, entered the throne room. In the lich's twisted fingers was Greysen's chastity—a golden cock cage with a lock that could only be opened by magic.

Was his punishment to wear his cage? Relief washed over him.

Was that all?

"Put that on my A Rúnsearc, Novane. But carefully. If he is hurt by your hands, you'll suffer the eternal consequences." Novane bowed as low as his undead bones would permit. Myrkul added, "Then get him clothing. The finest you can find. Clothing fit for the beautiful prince that he is to me."

Greysen became confused as Novane slid the urethral insert into him—sealing his cock so he couldn't piss or ejaculate without permission—before caging his cock completely. He couldn't get hard now, either. Not unless released.

Even though the lich's touch was cold like death's kisses, the creature was gentle. Greysen wanted to ask his lord, his husband and god, why he was being caged and clothed but thought better of it. Sure, he was often put into chastity; he had to keep himself clean shaven because of it. But this time, he didn't know why. Yes, only Myrkul could touch him intimately, and he could only touch himself when given permission…but given clothing as well? His whole body given chastity? Greysen couldn't fathom it. Besides, he hadn't worn clothing for years. He'd lost the memory of what it was like to wear them.

"Come to me, A Rúnsearc," Myrkul said once the lich's job was done and it scurried away out of sight. "Come sit on my cock. I still hunger for you."

Before Greysen did so, he retrieved the ornate bottle of lubricant from the hiding place within the bone throne's structure. He poured a good dose of the contents onto his lord's hardness eagerly, his hunger returning too. The sight of such a magnificent cock glistening, begging to be sheathed inside Greysen's body was overwhelming to the point of agony. Greysen's cock swelled in response, but pain shot through him instantly; the cage saw to it that his erection was deflated. It didn't matter. He didn't matter. Only his lord's needs mattered.

With Myrkul's arms wrapping around him, Greysen lowered himself onto his lord's harness. Slowly. Painfully. Beautifully. They were face to face. Greysen kissed his lord's hard lips, his tongue begging for entrance so he could deepen their contact.

His lord gave it.

Greysen moaned as he slid lower and lower until he'd taken all of this lord's length within him. It fucking hurt like hell, as always. So wonderful, he was shaking. Pain ruled his every thought, matched only by his love for Myrkul. He gasped, the sound muffled because Myrkul smothered him within his embrace. His lord's tongue, forked and long, fucked his mouth as much as he was being fucked. He was consumed.

When Myrkul parted their kiss, he grabbed Greysen around his throat with clawed hands, squeezing tightly while he continued fucking him, Greysen's body weight aiding the action. Greysen's eyes watered. His lord's cock was so deep inside him he could feel it pulse within his guts, and he knew his stomach had become distended because of it. He shuddered in agony, gasping even more as Myrkul's hands gripped tighter.

Greysen loved every agonizing moment.

"You want me to strangle the life from you, don't you, A Rúnsearc?"

Greysen could hear blood rush in his ears; his cock hurt even more because of his arousal against the cage, more so after his lord's words. Blissfully beautiful pain consumed him with even greater intent.

He replied, "Yes. I desire it. Kill me while you're inside me. I'm yours eternally; let me begin the journey." Greysen winced as Myrkul thrust and tightened his hold around his throat. His vision tunneled. Yes! This was the moment he'd been waiting for. The promise he'd been given on his wedding day.

Greysen moaned and gasped, but with his voice hoarse, breathless, he managed to add, "I beg you...my Lord. I've waited three years for you to make me…immortal. Kill me. I'm yours…to desecrate and…I abase myself for you."

Unexpectedly, Myrkul released his grip. The sweet fresh air filled Greysen's lungs. He hated it.

"Why?" was all he could manage as clarity returned. He was hurt more than anything by his lord's sudden change.

"You will get what you desire when you have served your punishment. Speak no more and pleasure me with your body."

Greysen, gathering himself, nodded obediently. He wanted his punishment done with so he could become immortal. But he couldn't think of such things now. He had to please his lord. Always.

He moaned and writhed, shuddering with desire. His flesh was racked with pain as he moved up and down his lord's length. For an age, one where ghouls could pass into dusty oblivion, Greysen was fucked and fucked, sweat covering him, clinging and satisfying as much as his lust. His whole body ached, both in excruciating pain and ecstasy. His arsehole was on fire, his guts ruined by his lord's massive cock. But he loved it. Even when his lord's nails raked over his skin, drawing blood. So much blood.

When Myrkul was spent again, Greysen filled from the other end, he remained on his lord. He hadn't been given permission to dismount. Myrkul went flaccid inside him, and Greysen felt relief. He also yearned for more.

"I have thought of your punishment," Myrkul purred satisfyingly, the glow of his double orgasm amazing to witness upon him.

By the Nine Hells he was handsome. Devastatingly so. With his dark, thick hair all over his pasty grey skin, his big, black eyes and twisting horns atop his head, he took Greysen's breath away.

"I accept without question whatever you want to do to me, my Lord."

Myrkul said coldly, "My undead army marches north to conquer all, sweeping all unbelievers aside. They are now entering the fertile and virgin lands of Thentathion, ripe for the picking. I know you liaise with the generals who come to the Keep for your orders, as I have given you that responsibility, but you will not be a part of their victories that honor me. Instead, you will travel further north to Invrawold."

Greysen was shocked but didn't speak his feelings; he hadn't been asked to.

"When you get there," Myrkul continued, still purring, "you will seek a man named Oswin. He is important to my goal. I must have him.

Bring him to me alive. That is your punishment for displeasing me with your sloppy, ill-considered command decision. Did you think I wouldn't notice your error? Your betrayal?"

What?

Greysen was aghast. His stomach roiled. A cold sweat found him, replacing the one of passion from earlier. Before he could think, and rather foolishly, he blurted. "But I can't leave you, my Lord." Hot tears stung his eyes. Not being with his lord was worse than anything...betraying him unthinkable. Unfathomable. Even the cold bliss of death without the promise of resurrection would be better. "I did only as you asked when I spoke the commands to the generals. I've not left you since—"

Myrkul raised his clawed hand to silence Greysen. He didn't seem angered, only distant. Greysen swallowed. His lord reached into the same compartment the bottle of lubricant had come from. He produced another chastity device, this time an anal plug for Greysen to wear, golden as well.

Offering the device to Greysen, Myrkul commanded, "You will also wear this. Always. I will not have you touched by anyone while you serve this punishment for me." Greysen knew the plug would be magically sealed as well, only releasing under certain conditions, like the cage. His lord's next words confirmed his thoughts. "You may only remove it to defecate, as you may only remove your cock cage to urinate—I have made sure of it."

"Y-Yes...my lord," Greysen mumbled sadly, accepting what his lord gave him.

Greysen swallowed his emotions, fought back his tears. Now he knew why he was getting clothing. Now he knew why his lord had spent himself twice within him. Greysen wouldn't be touched by his lord's love for a long time. All because he told the generals to march an hour before Myrkul desired it. What difference would an hour have made?

His punishment was cruel.

The cruelest imaginable.

Greysen hated himself. And after he had been given permission to dismount from his lord's cock and inserted the plug himself, he hated the clothing he had to wear with a passion. The material, no doubt the finest in the lands as promised, itched unbelievably. He wanted to rip the clothing off his skin.

He knew he couldn't.

Clothed, caged, and plugged like an abomination instead of

someone who gave themselves willingly to their lord, Greysen became miserable. An emotion he hadn't felt since he married Myrkul and bound himself to the demon, body, mind, and soul.

He felt worthless.

"Leave my sight," Myrkul boomed, seemingly angered by Greysen's presence all of a sudden. He now ached for a different reason. "Oh, and Novane will join you while you serve your punishment, for only he can release your chastity. The sooner you do as asked, the sooner you can service my cock again. Then maybe I will grant you immortality. Now go. Begone from my sight."

Greysen bowed. "Yes, my Lord." He noted that his lord didn't call him his 'A Rúnsearc' then.

As soon as Greysen's back found the door leading out of the throne room, the world beyond its threshold one he hadn't seen for three years, Myrkul added, voice booming, "Your mistake cost me dearly. Your father is now aware of my army's presence. All because of your impatience and disobedience."

Greysen gasped. "Abbot Hosho?"

"Yes." Myrkul reclined. "Come back before you obtain this Oswin boy, and I will not even bother to defile you in the way you desire. I will rip you to shreds and piss on your corpse, banning your soul to the Void beyond the Nine Circles of Hell where it will never be resurrected. You will be truly dead."

"I will not fail you, my Lord."

"You'd better not." Myrkul smiled, and his cock twitched, still wet from Greysen's attention upon it. "But because you please me, despite your human failings, I will grant you limited access to my magic. You will be able to do so three times. Simply call my name." Myrkul touched himself, as if in memory of Greysen's love shared a moment ago. "No go and do this for me. Serve your punishment to please me even more, A Rúnsearc."

A Rúnsearc.

Greysen loved hearing his lord speak such endearment.

Without word, and another bow, Greysen left the throne room. Novane was waiting for him. "You will fail," the lich spat.

"Fuck you,' Greysen shot in return.

The lich smiled, one thin-lipped and cruel. "Didn't plug your mouth, did he?"

Greysen's stomach roiled in disgust. "Touch me in any way other than you have permission to by our lord, and I'll ensure you'll never be able to piece yourself together for millennia."

His insides still hurt from the fucking he'd received by his magnificent lord, his entrance plugged to add to the discomfort. He grabbed at his stomach. It felt weird to feel clothing there, an emerald doublet covered by a fancy leather jerkin and inlaid with the delicate golden filigree of some sort of delphin design. He also wouldn't get used to wearing pants. But the shoes were the worst; they felt heavy and cumbersome on his feet.

How was he going to breathe being so suffocated? Clothing was the worst chastity of all. Sure, the Dread Keep was warm enough to remain naked, but being outside and clothed was going to be unbearable. Greysen yearned to be in his lord's arms again already; as a result, his cock pressed tightly against the cage to chase away such thoughts. Pain shot through him. His only comfort now.

Novane, his sneering not complete, said, "You'll be begging me to permanently remove the chastity forced upon you before the week's end. Yes, I have been given the ability to do so. I reckon you won't be able to help yourself. You'll displease our lord in the end no matter what I do, human filth."

"I said, fuck you." Greysen spat in Novane's face; the lich didn't flinch. Not even when the globule ran down his nose to touch his thin lips.

He hated to admit it, but the lich was really Greysen's perfect companion while he served his punishment. Of all Myrkul's servants, he looked the most human—aside from Greysen, of course. In life, Novane would have been handsome even if plain with brown hair and brown eyes. Traveling together, they wouldn't arouse any suspicion.

"We shall see." Novane, with a calm, composed gesture, then wiped his face with the back of his hand.

Greysen stormed past the lich, eager to get on with things so he could be in Myrkul's arms and sheath his cock with his body as he yearned. Then, immortality would be his.

3
Wallace's Life Lessons

FOR THE NEXT FEW weeks, while they traveled through the wilds north of the town of Topar, through massive forests of birch, elm, and pine never-ending, and come sun, rain, hail, or wind, Hereward spent every waking moment with Wallace. During which, he taught him swordcraft, stances, defense, and strategy. He also told the boy stories at night, mostly about handsome farm boys who became handsome princes.

"…and the prince married the love of his life, living happily ever fucking after," Hereward concluded, the story done.

He'd tell a new one tomorrow night with a similar plot, perhaps with an added monster or two to slay, but definitely with different character names. Farm boys always made good in his stories to Wallace's delight.

But tonight, Wallace sat in his cot looking puzzled while he clutched his mother's shawl. The frown he often wore when he concentrated marred his brow. 'Wallace's frown' Hereward had named the expression because it was so distinguished for someone so young.

Wallace had his own tent pitched next to Hereward and Dorgan's. The mule that'd pulled Wymond's litter to Gethrene what seemed a lifetime ago now was also with them. Her bed of hay was on the opposite side of Wallace's tent. The boy and the horse got on well. He called her Missy. Stupid name for a horse, but Hereward didn't mind. Wallace was happy.

"I don't git it, me Lord," Wallace declared, brow furrowing deeper.

"What don't you get?"

"I don't git why the prince always marries a girl in ya stories. Why can't he marry a boy he likes? You wanna marry Dorgan; I hear ya doin' sex with him most nights, like me Ma n' Pa used ta do. What if I wanna marry a boy, an' all?"

Hereward was taken aback, and a little embarrassed. Wallace heard them? By the gods. "Um…err…I didn't want to impose anything on you, that's all." But he gathered himself. So what if Wallace heard? The boy should be raised by people in love. He added, cheeks still warm, "I'm just telling the fucking story as it's traditionally told."

Wallace's brow unwrinkled. "Shouldn't have'ta have a boy bein' with a girl as how it's always told. People should love who they wanna love. If dat means a boy gits with a boy or a girl gits with a girl, then dat's all right, ain't it?"

Hereward harrumphed but in agreement. "You're fucking right. From now on, I'll tell it so the prince marries the boy he rescues and comes to love him with all his heart. How about that?"

"Ta." Wallace smiled, laying back down; Hereward tucked him in. But Wallace's frown returned. "But what if the prince likes a boy n' a girl? Or he don't like any o' 'em?"

Hereward sighed in resignation. "How about I just tell the story where the prince kills all his enemies and is as happy as fucking ever for doing it?"

"I'd like that better."

Hereward discovered Wallace was a quick study with his sword lessons. It made him fucking proud. But at the same time, he was upset with himself for not catching the fucking darrow they hunted through the wild forests. Too many hiding places in the woods. Too many nooks and crannies. As such, the leader of the group who'd done unspeakable things to Wallace and his family remained elusive even though the trail was clear; broken twigs, crushed leaves, and footprints only a day or two old. Which meant the fucking darrow hadn't gone to ground yet.

Soon, my love.

I know it. They're hiding close by somewhere. I can feel it. The fucking darrow knows we're on to them. Good. Let them shit their pants. The cunt's going to get a lot worse soon enough, Hereward replied to his sword god as he watched Wallace practice his lunges with a stick fashioned into a dummy sword.

Dorgan had gone back into Topar that morning, the largest village in Suvanwold, to buy Wallace a proper weapon. The boy was ready, the stick no longer sufficient.

He's got good form already, Hereward mused.

A moment after the thought, the sun's light blinked out, and

Dorgan flew down from the heavens like a silver angel in dragon form. He transformed into the beautiful man he was within a blink of an eye. He held a gift for Wallace.

When Dorgan approached, Wallace's eyes lit up, and his wide innocent smile cracked his face delightfully. It was good to see the boy smile. "Ta, me Lord! That's real nice o' ya. 'Preciated an' all too."

"I'm not your lord," Dorgan said humbly. "Just someone who cares for you."

Hereward took the sword before Wallace could grab it.

Wallace shrugged. "Then ya me Pa. Got no others, 'sides from you an' Hereward."

Hereward, testing and approving the short sword before Wallace could hold the weapon, liked what he felt. The steel was no god, but it would be magnificent. Sharp too. He would teach the boy how to use a whetstone to keep it that way. The sword was also a good weight. Perfect for Wallace's size and strength.

But aside from the distraction of new steel to wield, he said, "And who the fuck am I to you pray tell, Wallace, my boy?" Hereward handed Wallace the sword.

The boy accepted the weapon graciously. "Ya me Papa, Hereward."

Hereward was taken aback. "Dorgan and me can't replace your family, even though we look after you now. Just call us by our names; that will suffice."

"Can call ya what I wanna call ya." Wallace swung the gifted sword, and his smile got wider. "Have done, ain't I? Ya me Papa. Dorgan me Pa. I got a Papa n' Pa now. Happy as a pig 'n shit, I am. Never been happier—'cept when I gets the nightmares."

"The nightmares when you remember your parents and sister you mean?" Dorgan asked tentatively.

Wallace nodded. "Ya. When I's 'member 'em."

"They were good people," Dorgan offered even though he clearly didn't know Wallace's family any more than Hereward did.

Hereward kind of felt guilty. Wallace was a good boy. He didn't deserve what had happened to him. Sure, the physical wounds had healed, thanks to Hereward and Dorgan's care, but the emotional scars would be there for the rest of his days.

Wallace brightened, though. "C'mon." He swung the gifted short sword again like he was trying to swat flies with it, chopping and slashing; it thrummed nicely though the air. The blade glinted nicely when it caught the sunlight. Hereward was pleased, but not as pleased as Wallace. "Let's use me sword. Test it out. See how good it is, an' all."

"It'll be a beauty," Dorgan stated.

"And it'll help you defend yourself," Hereward added. "Once you learn your left foot from your right. Sword craft has its roots in where your feet are, not the hand holding the weapon."

Wallace looked down, sticking out his left booted foot. "I painted one o' me shoes red—dat the left, Papa?"

Dorgan laughed. Hereward replied, "It is. But what if you're not wearing your fucking shoes? What then, Wallace, my boy?"

Wallace shrugged, offering a cheeky smile. "I'll paint me feet."

Hereward held Dorgan, kissing his clean-shaven cheek tenderly. "Can't argue with that logic, can I?"

He watched Wallace run to the mock dummy he'd strung up from an overhanging tree branch; the boy prodding the straw-stuffed hessian enthusiastically with his new sword. He even barked out cute yelps with each thrust.

Wallace's footwork was improving, but he had a long way to go. Time and practice would see to him becoming a good swordsman. Not a great one, but good enough to stick any who fucking threatened him competently and with confidence. The rest would be up to Hereward and Dorgan to ensure their oaths to the boy were kept.

And they'd gladly keep them too. Wallace was already like a son to them. Hereward realised he was happy, a rare feeling, and he pulled Dorgan closer. In reply, Dorgan kissed Hereward upon his bearded cheek. His heart pounded. He had so many he loved now. A far cry from when Ealdræd, the mad magician—rotting in Hell with the demon Alquam as far as he was aware—had taken Camdyn and Lord Ayrdon Slade from him. With Abbot Hosho, his brother Beornræd, Wymond, Kieron, Vash, and now Dorgan and Wallace, Hereward had true family. Family not entirely of blood, except for his brother, but of soul and love. The best kind.

"You'd better go join Wallace before he does himself a mischief," Dorgan said, still chuckling. "I'll fix us all our supper."

Before Hereward let go of Dorgan, he said, "You do know Wallace can hear us fuck each other, don't you?"

Dorgan didn't seem concerned, only offering a knowing grin. "The way you growl, I'm not surprised."

"I don't fucking growl all the time." Hereward cast his mind back to the prior night. "Do I?"

"You most certainly do, especially when you're eating out my arse to get me ready for your cock."

Hereward kissed Dorgan, complete with a smacking of his lips. "Complaining, are you?"

"By the gods, no."

That evening, the canvas of their tent flapped almost hypnotically as the wind shifted from the south to the north. Not unusual weather during early Spring within the Eleven Kingdoms. As Hereward was about to drift off to sleep, the salty taste of Dorgan's ejaculate still fresh within his mouth, he heard a noise out of place for the usual night sounds of the forest. He sat up with a start, the cot creaking.

Dorgan stirred beside him. "Probably only Wallace having one of his nightmares again. He'll settle in a moment once he feels his mother's shawl on his skin."

Hereward knew Dorgan's words as true; Wallace would calm soon enough. But he lit the candle by the side of their bed with the striking box, a few attempts required to get a flame going and needed light.

"I'll go check on him, anyway."

After Hereward removed Dorgan's hands from around his chest, he grabbed his sword—always by his side—and dressed in his undergarments. Moments later, he was outside in the frigid air, wishing he'd slipped on more than what he had. He held himself, breath visible in the moonlight cast through the swaying canopy.

He peeked into Wallace's tent, and his blood froze. "Fuck!" Hereward boomed, frightening possums and other night dwellers from the branches above.

Dorgan rushed out of their tent, eyes wide, also dressed inadequately for the weather clawing at them. "What's the matter?" His expression was grim.

"Wallace is fucking missing." Worry stabbed at Hereward as much as the cold fingers of night.

I don't like this, my love, his sword god stated. *Wallace never leaves his bed once you tuck him in for the night. Never.*

Hereward knew those words as truth. Even if the boy needed to answer nature's call in the dead of night, he used the makeshift chamber pot fashioned from a pewter bowl Hereward had provided him. Wallace called it his "really fancy pissin' pot" and enjoyed filling it even during the day when they traveled. Hereward knew the real reason for doing so; Wallace didn't want to wander too far away from them. He was never out of their sight, truth be told. Hereward couldn't blame him, and he missed the boy already. Worried for him even more.

"Are you sure?" Dorgan asked.

"Sure, I'm fucking sure. He's gone. Look for yourself."

Dorgan didn't, obviously trusting Hereward's word. "Then we must find him."

With those words Dorgan became a dragon, crashing through the canopy in a blizzard of leaves falling around Hereward within a blink of an eye. Dorgan would survey the land from the sky; Hereward would search on foot.

We must hurry. Wallace may be hurt.

Hereward's insides roiled. As he scanned the ground for clues, it was then he noticed the tracks. Footprints that caught the moonlight where the ground had become mud from a recent rain. Too many of them.

Worry no longer stabbed Hereward. Anger did. If his boy, his and Dorgan's son, was hurt in any way, even by the merest scratch, those responsible would become feed for the crows and worms. Fuck, they'd be slain anyway, but Hereward would make sure they would never sit at the halls of their gods either way. Never, in eternity. The fuckers.

He rushed into the tent, slipping on his leather battle pants, doublet, and jerkin. Over those, he hastily put on his metal breastplate and then climbed into his boots. A few heartbeats later, he was following the footprints, Dorgan above him blocking out the moon to hide Hereward below.

After an hour or so, becoming desperate and worried even more with each passing moment, Dorgan landed and returned to human form. Hereward kissed his man, pleased to see him.

"What news?" Hereward asked.

Dorgan told of how Wallace had been taken by six men and one darrow spell-caster. The one they sought these past few weeks. The smell of the darrow was the same, he explained. The men and darrow were in a clearing by a stream nearby. Hereward's sword hand itched—no, his whole fucking arm did.

Soon, my love.

"But they have dogs too," Dorgan announced. "The men, I mean."

"How many dogs?"

"A pack of them, more than a dozen. Vicious things they are. Rottweilers, I think."

Hereward knew straight away who the men were and what they were doing in the dead of night. He'd heard of them living within the depths of the forest away from prying eyes where they could get up to no good. They were a criminal gang; but not the kind who stole. These men were far worse.

But why was the darrow with them?

He explained as calmly as he could manage, "These men are fucking dog fighters. Doing it for sport and to gain coin from betting on the outcome. We've gotta be fucking careful."

"Why?" Dorgan looked genuinely surprised. "I can take on dogs with a mere breath, and you can handle the men. Together, we'll deal with the darrow, spell-caster or not."

Hereward snorted, as he did when considering things. "We've got to be careful because these men are going to use our Wallace as practice for their dogs; the fucking darrow no doubt told them where to find him because they want to get rid of the only living witness to their crimes."

"Are you saying what I think you're saying?"

Hereward wished he wasn't. "These pieces of fucking shit use live bait to get the blood lust into their dogs. Gets the animals riled up and aggressive. That then makes for better sport and spectacle too…so they reckon."

"The bastards."

And it was true. Hereward wished it weren't.

As they approached the edge of the clearing, crouching low as was their modus operandi lately, a lot more men had gathered. Another dog fighting gang arrived, more than two dozen men, rough and uncaring looking, bandits and rogues mostly.

All the dogs barked and snarled, straining on their leashes for blood. Any blood. The men chatted loudly above the din the dogs made. The noises of the gathering were deafening. If the men who took Wallace hadn't left footprints, Hereward could have tracked them by their commotion alone.

Soon, even more men arrived. But they held no vicious dogs on leashes. These men were the paying audience, some Hereward recognized as wealthy landowners. No doubt they were out for a night's entertainment. He would wager his left bollock on the fact King Hurald wasn't aware a few of his vassals engaged in such illegal activity. Hereward couldn't wait to bring them to justice.

But for now, he watched, seething, as the scene unfolded.

After plenty of hearty handshakes and the jovial laughter of acquaintances who'd gathered many times for such an event, coins began changing hands as dogs were examined and discussed.

The sport of blood would soon follow.

To Hereward's relief, Wallace was safe. For now. He spied the boy at the center of what he supposed would be the fighting arena, a circle of sand scratched out by the river's bank.

Two other children were with Wallace. Both young boys about his age, if not younger. Their hands were bound, as were their feet. The boys wouldn't stand a chance against the dogs. Hereward spat. He would kill the fuckers who'd taken these boys. Every fucking man, including the vassals.

Hereward swallowed hard. But even amongst the horror of such a sight, pride found him. Of the three boys, only Wallace hadn't pissed himself out of fear. Nor did he cry as the others were.

The men close enough laughed and jeered at the two crying boys.

Wallace wasn't rattled. "Ya just wait till me Papa n' Pa git here," he shouted defiantly, cheeks red with rage as he wriggled to test his bonds.

Hereward felt even more pride. Fuck, his son was magnificent despite the horror he faced. Yet again. But by the gods, he was too young to experience so much already. He'd be as hard as nails when he came of age.

One of the men, a podgy fellow whose jowls moved more than the rest of him, cuffed Wallace across his face. The slap stung Hereward as much as it would have Wallace.

The podgy man said, "Bait don't speak unless told to, hear me, brat?"

Dorgan snarled worse than the dogs. "That one's going to die first." He shifted his weight as he gripped his sword. Hereward couldn't blame him. His sword arm itched even more. He seethed too.

I don't think we should wait this time; Wallace needs us now! I fear the situation will escalate too quickly for you and Dorgan to control. Wallace is in danger!

Hereward tended to agree. The men were already gathering around the makeshift arena, getting their dogs ready. They'd soon be unleashed. Then the boys used for bait wouldn't last long, ripped to shreds as they screamed their final screams. More coins changed hands—the final flutter before the event. Hereward could hear they were betting on how long the boys would last against the dogs. He felt sick to his core. He also couldn't stand it any longer.

Without further delay, Hereward came out of hiding, unsheathing his sword, the sound of the metal being freed ringing in his ears was perfection. Dorgan came beside him.

Hereward boomed, "Which one of you fucking cunts wants to feel the deadly kiss of my god first? I'm taking volunteers before I start choosing!"

"Papa! Pa!" Wallace screamed with joy, face brightening. "Knew ya'd come for me. Knew it!" He'd also wiggled out of his bonds. Clever boy. He was soon running towards them. Unfortunately, one of the men grabbed him. Wallace yelped but back kicked the man in the shins.

The man screamed, "You little shit!" and let go.

Wallace ran again, but was caught once more, this time by podgy man. "Where do you think you're going, bait?" He didn't let go no matter how much Wallace thrashed and kicked.

"I ain't bait!" Wallace tried to bite the man's arm but failed. "Ya'll be bait when me Papa's done with ya!"

That was Hereward's cue. He stepped closer to the man, swinging his sword. His god felt good in his hand as she sliced the air, it's substance trembling in fear in the steel's wake. He only needed to put a few men in her path to really satisfy them both, starting with the podgy man who held his son.

"Stay…b-back…knight!" the podgy man said, the trembles filling his words as much as his jowls jiggled. "Or I'll…c-choke the life outta this…this boy."

"Glad you volunteered." Hereward knew he was wearing his best 'I'm-going-to-fucking-kill-you' smile. An expression that fit him well. "Seems you're the first for my god's vengeance, then. Say your prayers, you fucking arsehole."

Heads fat or thin were all the same to Hereward's god; they were decapitated as easily no matter their size or shape. The podgy man's hit the dirt with a wet thud. Wallace broke free while the body of the man decided what to do without its head.

"Go to Dorgan, Wallace!" Hereward commanded as many men charged at him, shouting and screaming their anger when the podgy man's body joined the rest of him in the sand.

"Ya, Papa!"

"Quickly! Climb onto my back, Wallace," Dorgan called as he transformed into a dragon.

When Wallace got to Dorgan, he cheered, "Git 'em all, Papa! Ya too, Pa!

The dogs tucked their tails between their legs, ears down, as they broke away from their master's hold and fled into the night, yelping as they went. No amount of blood lust would counter their fear of a dragon. The dogs were wiser than the men remaining, that's for sure.

Hereward dispensed with two more men, their thick and coppery blood staining the air as it sprayed from their opened veins. It wasn't a fair fight. Not until Hereward came to the men of the gang who'd abducted Wallace. They'd armed themselves with rapiers, swords, and knives.

"Fucking excellent," Hereward boomed, really enjoying himself as he dispensed his justice. "This is the sort of sport I can really get behind."

Those men didn't last long either, untrained and desperate. One of them had the balls to throw a knife before Hereward slashed him into two without any effort other than a grunt and a fart. The tossed knife didn't come near him, aimed poorly with shaking hands of fear before the man found his death by the cold, hard steel of Hereward's god.

I'm loving this sport too.

"Knew you would be, my love!" Hereward replied to his god out loud.

He felt the heat of Dorgan's fiery breath as his lover burnt any who tried to flee the clearing. Wallace kept cheering. The vassals cowered on the ground, prostrating and blubbering as others with less standing than them stood to meet their fate. Hereward dispensed with them all; rich heads, poor heads, all were the same in the end.

The carnage he left as he sliced through them effortlessly, his sword god thrumming beautifully, was a thing of magnificence. His adrenaline pumped through him. And because Dorgan had his back during the easy fight, not needed other than to ensure Wallace was safe, he'd be even more horny later; Dorgan wouldn't know what hit him.

Hereward finally came to the last man standing.

Without mercy, because the man deserved none for what he'd done despite his pleading, he sent his sword into the man's guts, twisting it and slicing upwards, blood gurgling from the poor bastard's aghast mouth as his life left him as quickly as his insides did. A good sight.

Hereward wiped clean his god with the man's tunic once the deed was done, pleased he'd only suffered a bloodstained boot for his efforts.

Although, his mood changed dramatically when he got to the center of the sandy makeshift arena.

There, the darrow waited, holding one of the boys who'd been captured with Wallace. The poor boy was trembling and crying; the other boy was dead at the darrow's feet, eyes blank and staring up into the canopy. He was surely killed by magic, for the darrow held no weapon in their other hand.

Hereward's stomach churned. He hated magic. Hated those who used it for evil even more. But whatever happened, he would make sure the poor dead boy got a hero's send off so he could sit in the hall of his gods and drink their ambrosia for eternity. That was his promise.

"Lord Hereward," the darrow said malevolently, pulling the surviving boy closer to them for protection as their human shield. The move wouldn't work. But the darrow didn't know that. "Your reputation is warranted, I see."

"Give me the boy, darrow," Hereward spat. "You've fucking lost."

"I don't think so. Make any move towards me, and this boy meets his maker."

But Hereward could see the desperation in the darrow's eyes. They were frightened and rightfully so.

Be careful; this one is nervous. They've already killed one of the boys— the other is close to death by their hands too. I can feel it.

Dorgan and Wallace approached. Dorgan was in human form now but wearing only his undergarments. He hadn't put on his clothing or armor before they'd left their tent. The sight amused Hereward, especially Dorgan's bulge, revealed through the thin material of his drawers.

Wallace said, "Let me kill the darrow, Papa. I'll make mincemeat o' 'em like they did to me Ma n' Da n' Sis."

Hereward said, "That's a good idea, son." He picked up a knife without taking his eyes off the darrow—the long dirk, sharp and looked after, that'd been thrown at him earlier. He handed it to Wallace, hilt first as was the correct and proper way; Hereward taught even when lessons weren't declared. "And don't forget to cut the fucking darrow up into small pieces. We don't want the crows choking on any big chunks, do we?"

"I will, Papa." Wallace's face hardened as he stepped closer.

The darrow looked shocked, their tattoos almost disappearing as their face flushed crimson. "You can't be serious? I will not die by a boy's hand."

Hereward snorted. "You can and you will, *darrow*, but not before we've fucked you up a bit so that my boy can have his revenge without the risk of your treachery."

"Ya, ya will an' all." Wallace tested the knife. He smiled.

The distraction of Wallace holding the knife, ready to use it, was all Dorgan needed, Hereward knew. With the speed of a lightning strike, Dorgan rushed at the darrow from the side. In a fluid motion, he yanked the captured boy out of the darrow's arms. The boy yelped but quietened as soon as he realized what was happening.

The darrow cursed.

When the boy was safe between Hereward and Dorgan so the darrow was left exposed, Wallace snarled like the dogs that would have savaged him because of the darrow's evil. The blade he wielded glinted as much as his eyes seeking revenge. Justified revenge.

"I don't even have a weapon," the darrow complained, even though arrogance flowed through their voice.

"You lie," Hereward spat, knowing the cunning of a darrow. "Dorgan, time to do your thing to even things up a bit here."

Dorgan, fast as lightning, transformed into a dragon and breathed his fiery breath upon the darrow, a quick blast. Not to kill, but to maim terribly. The stink of burning clothing and flesh filled the glen. When Dorgan ceased, smoke curling from his smiling mouth, the darrow was burnt over most of their body, a huddled, smoking mess upon the sand. He returned to human form.

"I am…defenseless," the darrow whined painfully.

Hereward was satisfied the darrow couldn't attack Wallace, the burns upon them too great for them to concentrate on the casting of magic.

"Me Ma n' Da n' Sis were as well," Wallace spat. "Least ya awake to face ya death. Me family didn't stand a chance. Ya got one. More'n ya deserve for what ya done." Wallace glanced at the dead boy, and sadness washed over him, but he quickly recovered as his attention returned to where it needed to be, facing the darrow.

Before Wallace could step forward, much to Hereward's horror, the darrow's eyes narrowed, and they began to glow with magic, a luminous blue against the dark of the forest and the few lanterns aflame around the arena. Hereward, realizing with dread what was going on, shot forwards to send the darrow to oblivion with his god. All too late. A magical bolt shot from the darrow's hands as soon as they'd quickly written their arcane but magical symbols in the air. Dorgan's breath hadn't disabled the darrow enough.

Fucking hell!

Thankfully, and to Hereward's profound relief because he should have run the darrow through, ended them, Wallace ducked out of its way, quick as a fox.

But the poor boy between Hereward and Dorgan wasn't so lucky. He was splattered to the four winds by the spell's impact and power, his blood and guts and fear staining Hereward's armor in thick, oozing clumps.

Dorgan gagged as the bloody splatter covered him as well.

The darrow's hand glowed again as they staggered to stand, still smoking from Dorgan's breath. "I may not have a weapon, boy, but as long as my heart beats, I do have magic!"

Wallace gasped and dropped the knife.

4
Oswin's Seen Future

OUTSIDE THE DREAD KEEP, the air was blistering hot and the sky dazzling blue without cloud. There wasn't even a breeze to offer any respite from the temperature, thick and cloying but dry. The great southern desert, the Hyruldon Expanse its proper name, was nothing but shocking yellow sand glistening beneath an unrelenting sun with biting flies and not much else stretching into forever.

Greysen gasped, trying to get oxygen into his lungs, unused to the outside world. The material of his clothing clung to his skin like the threads of it were made of suffocating boa constrictors. He itched, unbelievably so. He hated his clothing.

In contrast, Novane wore armor, metal tiles over thick leather. How was he not roasting? The lich also held a pole axe, his weapon of choice, and a scimitar was scabbarded at his belt. On his back, a bag was strapped to his shoulders. What the bag contained, Greysen didn't know. Did he really have to? Did he care?

"It's unbearable out here," Greysen mumbled.

Novane laughed, one like death's rattle. "Wimp *and* human filth. I can't see why our lord puts up with you. Oh yes, I know. Your holes still please him. Wait until they don't."

"You cannot goad me, lich." Greysen didn't want to speak Novane's name; the creature didn't deserve such respect.

Far to Greysen's left, the great undead army of Myrkul marched north towards the Kingdom of Thentathion, silent and deadly. A force of over two-hundred thousand skeleton troops. Amongst them were ghoul cavalry, lich generals, shadhavar, warg, and dire wolves. Undead bone dragons and wraiths circled above, staining the blue sky.

The sight was awe-inspiring and proof of the power of his lord.

Greysen had to complete his punishment as soon as he could. He missed Myrkul's touch like the desert around him missed the cold.

"You *will* fail," Novane blurted, bringing Greysen back to the moment in cruel disturbance, "and I will watch with satisfaction when our lord rips you to shreds while you plead for mercy. Oh, how I will be satisfied by that, human filth."

Greysen saw red. "Call me human filth one more time, and I'll—"

"You'll what?"

Greysen clenched his fists, turning the knuckles white. "I'll use one of the spells my magnificent lord Myrkul gifted to me to smite you, that's what I'll do."

"You rely too much on your trust of our lord. Demon magic is never without its cost. As all magic, really."

"Says a foul, lying lich hungry for power." Greysen took Novane's measure. The lich had backed away slightly. Good. "You only want to goad me. Get me to displease my lord so you can gain favor. I know your type. I won't ever do anything to displease Myrkul."

"You already have. Otherwise, you wouldn't be here, human filth."

Greysen punched Novane in the face.

The effect wasn't what he expected; the lich hardly moved. No blood either. Instead, Novane laughed. And laughed. He then turned towards the horizon and carried on with their journey as if nothing happened, using the pole axe like a walking stick.

But something had changed within his dark eyes. Greysen didn't know what, but it was something profound.

Without looking back, Novane called, "Perhaps there's hope for you yet, Greysen. Perhaps."

He didn't call Greysen human filth that time. He also wondered why. Greysen sucked in a breath and followed the lich—no choice, really—his temper cooling, unlike the desert air. His clothing itched. The flies stung. The heat suffocated.

Greysen was miserable.

After walking in silence for a couple of hours through the desolate, hot, uncomfortable sands with no end in sight, sweat staining Greysen's clothing in great wet patches under his armpits, Novane halted. The lich scanned the horizon, shimmering like an apparition from the heat haze.

Greysen didn't care about what the lich did, but now that he was no longer moving, he almost retched at the stench of himself, as smothering as the clothing he wore. Back at the Dread Keep, he was bathed in warm, fragrant rose water twice daily, his skin then rubbed in herbal oils after that. Until his lord used him as desired, all he had to do was wait amongst the pillows of his chamber in anticipation. Most times, he read from the extensive library Myrkul kept, books that recorded history since good and evil leaked out from the Void to create the known universe.

Myrkul took Greysen daily from off those pillows, sometimes twice.

Between those moments of carnal bliss, the agony and ecstasy of being fucked and needed and used, he was waited on hand and foot by many servants. Greysen missed his home so much. He yearned for it. Yearned for Myrkul, his lord and husband and god, even more. Why hadn't he listened? Why didn't he wait until the correct time to begin the advance as ordered?

No wonder he was punished in the cruelest way imaginable.

He'd been foolish.

But never again.

"Why are you just standing there? What's the matter?" he snapped at Novane finally, annoyed the lich wasn't getting Greysen out of the desert and to their goal faster—the good for nothing evil bastard.

A flash of a thought crossed his mind. He considered using one of Myrkul's spells to get him quicker to Invrawold where Oswin lived, but thought better of it, mostly because of Novane's warning. If the lich was telling the truth about demon magic. Greysen would wager he was lying. Still, he didn't want to waste the spells. He didn't know when he'd need them and what obstacles he'd face, though he was certain there would be many.

The lich produced a Seeing Crystal from a hidden pocket within his armour after spearing the pole axe's hilt into the sand to free both hands. "I felt a vibration. Something has happened to our target."

"What?"

"Patience, human filth." Novane stared into the crystal. "I'm about to find out if you give me a half a chance."

"You don't deserve anything from me."

"We shall see."

Greysen became even more annoyed again. "Just get on with it. And stop calling me human filth."

"Or you'll use the magic?" Novane rolled his eyes, sneering. "I've heard that one already. If you're going to threaten me, at least follow through. Use Myrkul's power. Smite me where I stand. See how far it'll get you."

Greysen harrumphed, and his mood darkened even more. "What's the crystal showing?"

"See for yourself." Novane threw the ball onto the sand at his feet, forcing Greysen to bend over and pick it up. "Oh, and while you're on your knees like the human filth you are, make yourself useful." To Greysen's shock and disgust, Novane freed his cock from his battle pants, an uncut but pallid little thing, sad really, but with a bulging dorsal vein that seemed to throb as his arousal increased. Novane's cock didn't stay little for long. He laughed maniacally with that death rattle of his.

Greysen shuddered in revulsion. His stomach turned. But the sight of Novane's cock, dripping with his lust and getting harder by the moment, stirred something within him. His yearning for his lord, no doubt. Not Novane. Never Novane. All the same, Greysen felt a painful pressure against his cage, agonizing and joyous at the same time.

He swallowed, picking up the Seeing Crystal as he forced the anguish of his yearning from his mind. It wasn't easy. He could still feel the remnants of Myrkul's love swirling deep inside him. Thank the lords of Nine Hells he was plugged, otherwise the demon seed would escape. He didn't want that to happen.

"How about you go pleasure yourself?" He turned away from the filthy lich to look at what secrets the Seeing Crystal had to reveal. He heard Novane stuff his cock back where it belonged, his laughter no less taunting.

From within the crystal, Greysen saw images form. It was like a fog was slowly being burnt away by the morning sun to reveal what lay beyond. He saw a man about thirty summers old, if not a year or two younger, stubbled chin, wide-eyed, and decidedly handsome with his hair as dark as crow's feathers and his smile as infectious as any. His skin was the beautiful color of burnished copper, and sweat shined from an exertion Greysen couldn't make out. There was no doubt the man was Oswin. Otherwise, why would the crystal reveal him?

More of the scene was revealed as Greysen stared. Sounds and noises became apparent too.

"Yeah, that's it," Oswin said, hissing through his perfect white teeth. The light from many candles around the bed he laid upon revealed his nakedness and his erection. The light also revealed two others with him—one a younger man than him and one a much older woman, but no less pretty.

To the woman, running his hand delicately through her long golden hair, Oswin said, "Pull back my foreskin nice and slow and careful. Yeah. Now suck on my knob. Yeah…oh yeah, just like that."

She worked studiously, reminding Greysen of himself when he serviced his lord. He yearned again and had to quickly chase away the thoughts from his mind before the cage caused him even more pain.

To the younger man, raising his legs so the woman had to move while attached to him, Oswin said hungrily, "And you, my liege. You can get your tongue deep into my arse. Fuck me with it. Fuck me good before you stick your fat cock into me."

The woman came off Oswin's cock with a pop, saliva glistening on her lips and blue eyes sparkling within the candlelight. "Gonna stick me like Carron's gonna stick you?"

"That's the plan, my dear."

"I want you to put a baby in me, just like Carron'll try and put one in you—even though he'll fail."

Oswin laughed. "Not for the lack of trying, isn't that right, Carron?"

Carron came up for air, a homely smile planted on his over freckled face. Now that Greysen saw him in more detail through the crystal, he realized the young man rimming Oswin wasn't as handsome as he first believed. His shock of red hair was not tousled nicely but in thick, ugly pigtails, and his eyes were beady even if blue, adding to his homeliness.

But the young man's name was familiar; Greysen couldn't place where he'd heard it before, though. Not yet.

Carron said, "I love you, Oswin. I love watching you make love to Lavinia while I do it to you. I think you should give Lavinia a baby. We could be a proper family then. Right?"

"Why don't you put one in her?" Oswin countered. "You know I withdraw before I blow so you can lick up my seed from my stomach."

"I like that, as well," Carron agreed, licking his freckled ruby lips.

"See? We can't decide." Oswin put his hand back onto Lavinia's head, pushing her back down to his cock. "You only fuck men, Carron, despite what your daddy, our King and protector, believes, and I'm a withdrawer."

Like a bolt from the blue above sizzling through the heated desert air, Greysen realized who the young man was. The King of Invrawold, Drake Marconi the fourteenth, had many, many daughters, but only one son. Carron Marconi. Based on what Greysen had already witnessed, the king wouldn't be getting another heir any time soon.

Oswin continued, "Sorry, Lavinia, just going to have to enjoy the moments we have together for what they are. Pure lust peppered with delicious debauchery."

Lavinia smiled while she licked Oswin's wet and hard cock. "Debauchery's right, seeing as Caron's the king's son and I'm one of the maids of his castle. What a mix we make, hey? It'd be a scandal if this got out, what we do here together."

Oswin said, "Funny you should say that. I only this—"

A banging door being opened forcefully silenced the words from Oswin's lips. Many men, soldiers of some description or well-paid mercenaries, burst into the chamber. Within a blink, and before Oswin could do anything other than look stunned, one of the soldiers pulled on Lavinia's long locks to expose her throat. His blade slashed across her neck and her blood poured all over Oswin and the bed.

Oswin screamed. Lavinia was cast aside, quickly dead.

At the same time, Carron was grabbed by four soldiers, punched into submission by one of them, and then dragged from the chamber without protest, his body as limp as Oswin's cock had gone.

Only Oswin remained.

From within the crowd of soldiers surrounding Oswin's bed, sneering at him, weapons at the ready, a short man stepped forwards. He was wearing the finest silks of the most expensive colors, purple and red, and his thick black hair was tied back to a ponytail. He oozed confidence and arrogance.

He said, "You have been wanting, haven't you, Mister Goodfellow?" with a voice cold and calm. The man was pure evil, Greysen knew. More than Novane.

Who was he?

The knife Oswin tried to reach was taken and thrown across the room to clatter away unused. Oswin was left defenseless, but he never, not once, did he let his sight wander away from the silk wearing man.

Oswin stuttered, "I'm n-not, Monk Wu, I swear it. I t-tried to…"

"Bring him to me." Monk Wu raised his hand. "Make sure he can't move a muscle. Restrain him if you have to."

"No!" Oswin cried. "Please, Monk Wu. I beg of you. I wasn't wanting. I just…I just got distracted, that's all."

Two soldiers grabbed him, roughly.

Monk Wu sighed, the sound cold and calculated. "I asked the

simplest thing of you, Mister Goodfellow, being an expert in herbs as you claimed. You were to poison the king's inadequate son. See to Carron's end as cleanly and discretely as possible. Leave no trace of your work. Instead, I find you in bed with him…" He gestured to Lavinia by his feet, all her blood staining the floorboards. "Along with a whore from the same castle."

Oswin's face drained of color. "What will you do to me?"

The two soldiers yanked Oswin off the bed. Seconds later, he was facing Monk Wu proper, the look of horror on his face frighteningly real. Oswin feared the silk wearing man beyond imagining, Greysen knew that much.

Now Monk Wu smiled, but it was an ugly scar. "You are an expert in poison, clumsy but effective, I admit. But I. I am an expert in the practice of lingchi."

"W-what's…what's that?"

Monk Wu produced a blade from his tunic's inside breast pocket, the finest weapon Greysen had ever seen. It wasn't a knife, far smaller. It was almost delicate in its simplicity. But he knew the steel edge of it would be sharp—no doubt sharp enough to cut the breath from an enemy if used correctly.

"Seeing as you're suitably attired for the occasion already, I will commence immediately."

"Commence what?" Oswin begged, lips trembling and eyes wide with fear.

The two soldiers held Oswin tighter. Another two joined them. But suddenly, Oswin no longer struggled, and his face slackened; no doubt, he must have realized his fate. Understood what lingchi was and the little knife involved in the practice of it upon Oswin.

With dignified resignation, something Greysen admired, Oswin explained, "I *was* going to poison him, Monk Wu. I swear it. I swear, I was. But…but I had to gain his trust first. I can't poison a man if I can't get close to him, can…can I?"

"Having Carron in your bed most nights for the past three months, I'd have thought his trust was gained long ago, wouldn't you? No, Oswin, you will die for your ineptitude. You will die slowly and painfully by lingchi…the death of a thousand cuts." And with those words, Monk Wu, delicately, carefully, methodically, sliced the little knife's blade across the underside of Oswin's left nipple, curling around it with precision and removing it. Blood oozed from the cut in a river, staining Oswin's stomach along with Lavinia's. Oswin screamed and screamed, deep from his lungs. The soldiers held him tighter. But he didn't struggle.

Greysen admired Oswin.

"That was the first cut," Monk Wu said calmly as he dispensed with Oswin's nipple, flicking it away as if it were a bothersome piece of lint plucked from his robe instead of from a person's body. "Nine hundred and ninety-nine to go—if you can live that long."

Greysen looked away from the Seeing Crystal in disbelief. He heaved a breath, feeling tightness in his chest. This time, not from the clothing chastity he wore. If Oswin died, Greysen's punishment couldn't be served. He'd never be with his lord again. He couldn't live with that thought. Ever.

"We must get to Oswin now."

Novane, as calmly as Monk Wu—which annoyed Greysen again—said, "This could be the future the crystal sees."

"What do you mean?"

"I mean what I said. The Seeing Crystal sees a possible future—although, from what unfolded, I'd say it's a certainty. This Oswin man you seek is getting himself into trouble if he thinks he can make a deal with Monk Wu to murder the king's son."

"We don't know everything, only what we saw."

Novane nodded. "This is true."

"And who's this Monk Wu character, anyway?" Greysen relaxed a little, comforted in knowing the vision was merely a possible future for Oswin not the definite reality. "Why does he want the king's son dead? Why doesn't he murder Carron himself? Why employ Oswin to do it?"

"Questions, no answers," the lich offered with a shrug.

Greysen's mind wheeled. He still had to ensure he got to Oswin as soon as possible. But how many days did he have left before the man would meet his fate with a thousand cuts from the little knife? Had Oswin only begun his mission to poison Carron or was it advanced by many weeks? Monk Wu said something about three months. Did Greysen have that much time?

As if to answer one of his questions, Novane said, "It will take us a month to get to Invrawold. We will then need a few days to locate Oswin. I would imagine the Seeing Crystal saw that far into the future to give us time."

Greysen was shocked. "I can't live that long without my lord!"

Novane didn't seemed concerned, offering his death's rattle laugh once more. Greyson was certain the lich knew how it annoyed him. "I offered you my cock to satisfy you while you're away from our lord's throne room."

"What do you take me for?"

"I take you for who you are," Novane snapped. "One who thinks he's needed and desired, and because of this, you offer yourself blindly, even if it debases you. Diminishes you. You believe you're worthy in the eyes of our lord, but you're not. You're worth nothing to him." Novane paused for a moment, and something struck his features, sadness perhaps, before he added, "Just like me."

The lich's words hit hard. But Greysen's thoughts soon turned to rage. What did Novane know about him? Nothing. Greysen fumed, and he clenched his fists. Yes, Novane *was* worthless. He was nothing but one lich lord of so many Myrkul had in abundance. But Greysen was unique...special. Worthy. His lord wouldn't have married him if he weren't.

He spat in reply, "Let me make this very clear so you'll understand without a shadow of any doubt, *lich*. I'll never, not even when the universe is nothing but dust and darkness, suck your cock. Never, not ever."

"We shall see."

5
Hereward's Dark Path

EREWARD, ALTHOUGH SURPRISED, DIDN'T worry when Wallace dropped his weapon—nay, when he threw it. In the few weeks since the boy had been with them, he'd taught Wallace many things.

One of them: sometimes cheating was a good thing.

Not cheating like in a shady game of chance played by cloaked rogues in dark alleyways with a ball and cups. No, Hereward would never teach such a thing. He taught the kind of cheating *needed* because it meant the difference between life and death. And right now, they faced a darrow spell-caster who was desperate, outnumbered, and full of potent, violent magic despite Dorgan's efforts to neutralize it.

No doubt the darrow was recharged and refreshed from the sacrifices they'd made within the fiery heart of their Yondàn, their Wicker god, which was why the poor boy standing between Hereward and Dorgan was blasted by the magical bolt into thousands of unrecognizable pieces and a splatter of coagulated blood all over the pristine sand. As such, the darrow was as dangerous as any beast, magical or otherwise. Again, Hereward cursed his stupidity.

Therefore, how could anyone call what Wallace did cheating when all of their lives depended on the outcome? Any sane person, be they a child or an ancient weary-boned warrior, would take any chance, *even cheat*, to cling to life's bosom for one more day.

Pride swelled as Wallace's intent became apparent. Hereward knew the move well even though he'd never done it himself. Wallace had thrown the knife as a distraction, and the ruse worked. Before the darrow could catch on to what had happened, Wallace charged.

A split second later, Wallace came upon the darrow, yelling his little war cry before punching them between their legs. A cracking thwack and an exasperated "oof" resulted as the darrow lost all the air in their lungs, and they hit the sand like a sack full of shit. When down, yowling in agony and clutching themselves, still smoking from Dorgan's breath, the darrow folded into the foetal position, eyes watering.

Wallace had hit them hard.

Fucking brilliant.

Hereward rushed over, yanking the darrow to their feet and rendering them unable to use their hands to make the arcane symbols needed to cast magic. Dorgan found a couple of dog leashes to use as binding. When the darrow was secured, tears still streaming down their tattooed face, Hereward felt better. A lot better.

"Fucking good move there, Wallace, my boy," he said, beaming at Wallace, his pride overflowing.

"Ta, Papa."

"Yes, it was." Dorgan chuckled. "I wonder who taught him that?" He shifted his gaze to Hereward.

Hereward shrugged, but smiled back.

Wallace, without delay, replied, "Papa, o' course." But he cradled his striking fist against himself, hissing through his teeth as he touched the reddened skin.

Dorgan immediately went to him, examining Wallace's hand. After a moment, he said, "Nothing looks broken, but you're going to have bruised knuckles for a while. Some swelling too."

"Worth it, it were." Wallace beamed a smile, revealing his teeth and the couple that were missing due to his age. "But I's 'fought for a moment I's were done for, 'cause 'fore I's hit 'em, I's didn't know if they's were a boy or a girl. Turned out good. 'Cause when I's punched 'em, I's found out real quick, didn't I's?"

"Found balls, did you?" Hereward asked, still holding onto his pride.

Wallace nodded. "I did, an' all."

But Dorgan's interest was now upon the darrow. "What have you got to say for yourself?" Venom was in the dragon's tone. Rightfully so.

The darrow spat at Dorgan in reply.

Wallace snarled.

Dorgan avoided the globule of saliva directed at him by a mere inch. He said, "Then I'm afraid we're going to have to turn you over to our Wallace. You have a debt that needs to be repaid in blood, darrow. One you will pay in full."

"Do what you want to me." Spittle dripped from the darrow's lips. The arrogance of before returned to their voice when they added, "It won't matter. The darkness and horror before this day will be nothing compared to what's coming." The darrow cackled a laugh, saliva still dripping. "Consider what I did to your family a favor, child. They won't get to witness the Purge of us all. You'll wish you'd been killed by those dogs, mark my—"

Hereward struck the darrow on the back of their head with his meaty fist, silencing them with unconsciousness. "Fucking darrow and their riddles."

Wallace said, "Me Da used to say ya ain't gonna git any good outta folks like them. Too secret they are. Don't trust 'em."

"Perhaps you're right." Hereward then pulled backwards on the darrow's arms so forcibly, terrible but satisfying sounds of two humerus bones being ripped from of their sockets—*pop crunch, pop crunch*—filled the glen.

The darrow awakened to yelp and blubber, tears streaming from their eyes as the vassals had done not long ago before they died.

Hereward wanted to kill the fucker. But no. That would give them what they wanted. Be the easy way out. And besides, Wallace had to get his vengeance; it was only right and proper. The blood debt had to be paid, something Hereward knew all too well.

Dorgan, obviously on the same page as Hereward, suggested, "Now that Hereward has disabled the darrow's ability to cast magic by breaking their arms, perhaps, Wallace, you could use them to practice your sword techniques on. That hessian dummy is looking a bit worse for wear. Time for a new one. What do you think?"

"Good idea, Pa." Wallace picked up the knife, testing the weight in his hand.

"But not now," Hereward interjected. "When we get back to camp, I'll string the fucking cunt from a branch. And for what they've done to your family, what they were going to do to you, you can stab them to your heart's content, Wallace."

Wallace nodded, brow furrowing as a darkness crossed his face when he looked at the darrow. "That I's will, Papa. That I's will."

As dawn broke, sending fingers of light throughout the forest and chasing away the swirling mists of night, Hereward packed up their camp. After that, and along with the packed-up tents, he secured everything they owned within the saddle bags hanging either side of

Missy the mare. He put out the campfire by pissing on it, leaving it a streaming pile of ash surrounded by wet rocks, drying quickly.

Not too far away, he could hear the cute shouts and growls Wallace made as he lunged, turned, parried, and practiced his footwork on his new dummy. Although, after a couple of hours practice, because the boy couldn't sleep after they'd returned, he'd made short work of the darrow; they now hung bloody, burnt, broken, and dead, hardly recognizable.

Good fucking riddance to them, Hereward mused.

The debt is paid—Wallace got his revenge, his sword god added to his thoughts.

"He sure fucking did," he replied out loud. When the darrow's remaining leg fell off with a dull, wet thud into the leaf litter, Hereward called, "Time to go, Wallace."

"Aw, Papa! I's were just gettin' started," he complained in reply, wiping his brow of sweat from his exertion. His short sword dripped with blood. "Can't we stay till Pa gits back?"

Dorgan had transformed into a dragon, scouting ahead. The edge of Fangmere forest wasn't too far to the north as Hereward understood, less than half a day's travel with all going well.

Beyond the trees, there was the great mouth of the delta, an expanse of water one couldn't fathom nor see the opposite bank of with the naked eye. It was fed by unnamed mountains ten thousand leagues from where they stood to the north east. Beyond the delta's water, the kingdom of Invrawold lay, the capital city not far from the northern bank. Oswin was there, according to last accounts.

That was what Abbot Hosho told him anyway. And who was Hereward to disbelieve a monk, and one he considered his father, no less?

"You'll get plenty of opportunity to use your sword soon enough, I promise." Hereward slipped the last of what they owned, Wallace's makeshift chamber pot, into the only remaining space within the last saddlebag.

Missy whinnied. Hereward swore the horse knew when her burden was filled to capacity. Although perhaps she was telling him to put Wallace upon her back. Most times, the boy rode her when they traveled. He got too tired too quickly if he had to walk all day.

Hereward retrieved fire-cooked bread he'd made earlier with his favorite damper recipe, the result salty and tangy and always filling. He offered a chunk to Wallace. "After you've cleaned your sword like how

I taught you, it's time you ate something. Won't grow up big and strong if you don't eat."

"Ya, Papa."

When Wallace had done what was asked of him, scabbarding his sword so Hereward could secure it to Missy along with everything else. He picked up the boy with ease, placing him carefully onto the horse's back. The most precious cargo Hereward had.

"Fucking hell, you're getting heavier, Wallace," he joked.

Wallace giggled. "'Ready growin' big n' strong thanks to ya n' Pa, ain't I's?"

"I'd say you are."

Hereward grabbed the mare's reins, pulling her gently along while he walked by her side, Wallace munching away contentedly on the heel of the bread. Soon, and with a smile on his lips and a warmth growing in his heart, he was walking northwards. Wallace had fallen asleep on the horse's back a while back. It had been an eventful night for him.

For all of them.

Hereward covered Wallace with his cloak to ward off any cold; the day was still young, after all. The heat of the sun wouldn't get to them in the depths of the forest until well after midday, if at all.

When he was certain the boy was both warm and secure, he whispered, "You're the fucking apple of my eye, you are, Wallace. There's a fact. Dorgan's too. And anyone who wants to take you from us ever again will get more than they bargained for. That's my oath."

Wallace didn't reply; he was deep in sleep.

Above and through gaps in the canopy, Hereward caught glimpses of Dorgan flying high, keeping watch on them both. He found comfort at the sight. He had his family with him. That was all that mattered.

Their journey led them along a winding trail. Hereward knew it well. He also knew who lived here as they came into a copse bathed in dappled sunlight. They were watching them. In fact, the creature had been spying on them for a while. Hereward smiled.

"Show yourself, you fucking bastard," he said but not too loudly to disturb Wallace's slumber.

"How did you—fine, I will!" was his resigned reply. "Lord Hereward," was added hastily afterwards.

"I knew because by the old gods and new, you stink so bad I could smell you a league back."

A plump, gray-haired, bearded, and furred satyr—devoid of clothing from the waist down but richly dressed above—stepped out from behind an ancient elm at the edge of the clearing. He was wearing a red crushed velvet jerkin adorned with jewels, emeralds mostly. Golden rings adorned the satyr's horns, his ears, lips, and nose. He was a sight. Fucking hell, Hereward had missed him.

The satyr said cheerfully, "Is that any way to greet and old friend, Lord Hereward?"

"In your case, it is." Hereward laughed, letting go of Missy's reins so he could embrace his friend. "How the fuck have you been, Gik?" he asked while slapping Gik's back heartily, the gesture returned.

But Hereward quickly pulled away once Gik's nature began to take over. The creature couldn't help it. Dogs did it to visitors; satyrs did it to friends. "And you can put that fucking little pink lipstick of yours away too. I'm not one of your bitches to mount, you dirty old goat." Hereward laughed even harder.

"Old goat? Old goat?" Gik laughed as well but didn't hide what was revealed because of his apparent excitement at seeing Hereward. "How rude."

"What? You aren't worried I called your fucking cock a little pink lipstick this time?" Hereward slapped his hand down onto Gik's shoulder. "Have you gone soft in your old age?"

Gik shrugged when Hereward lifted his hand. "Come to realize I've got what I've got. I can't help I was born a satyr and we've got the cocks of dirty dogs, can I? Although, thankfully, the lady satyrs don't mind; otherwise, there wouldn't be any of us left, would there?"

"You still trying to get your end wet inside any warm satyr cunt that'll have you, even after all these years?"

Gik sighed. "I have my days." His gaze slid over to Wallace asleep on Missy's back. "Say, who's the boy?"

"My son," Hereward stated matter-of-factly and as if it were the most natural thing in the world to say.

But Gik's thick gray eyebrows shot up his forehead. "Did you change your...*sexual preference* since the last time I saw you? I thought you only gobbled down on hunky men's cocks? Didn't think you were the type to stick a baby into a woman's belly to give you an heir."

"Relax." Hereward wiped his eyes of joyful tears. It really was good to see Gik again. "We adopted Wallace. Long story, but his family was killed so we took him in."

"Wish you'd adopt me."

Hereward laughed again. "You wouldn't know what to do with yourself if you were forced to wear pants *all* the time."

"True that. True." Gik sat down on a stump with a groan, rubbing his legs and wincing. "Besides, I'm getting too old for adventuring. And if you'd lived a hundred years without pants, you'd know why nothing's going to make me put any on now." At least Gik crossed his legs while he sat, Hereward's view no longer of the satyr's big furry balls and the little cock that came out for air every time the creature got a dirty thought. Which was often. The fucking dirty old goat. Hereward loved him.

He sat on a stump adjacent to Gik's, relieved for the rest. He'd been walking for hours. "So, what's news, old friend?"

"Oh no. You've got to tell me who this 'we' is you spoke of. Who did you adopt Wallace with, pray tell?"

"A dragon named Dorgan," Hereward revealed teasingly.

Gik blinked, even though the smile never left his face. "Oh, of course. A dragon and a knight adopt a boy instead of killing each other. Why isn't that in the stories they tell children?"

"Hey, that's a good one. I'll tell it to Wallace at his next bedtime. Been getting short on ideas with my stories."

"You tell stories?" Gik laughed again, one hearty and from his stomach to make it wobble. "Wonders will never cease. The great Lord Hereward, settling down and telling stories. What next? A castle on a hill to call your own?"

"Maybe."

"All right, I'll tell you what's new."

"About fucking time."

Gik's face turned somber. "There's a war coming."

Hereward snorted. "I know that already. Abbot Hosho has entrusted me and Dorgan to go find a man named Oswin who'll help our cause. It's all been whispered by the universe, so he tells me."

"No, no." Gik waved his jeweled hand. "I'm not talking about Myrkul's army even though that is a concern all mortals will have to deal with. No. I am talking about the Purge. The—"

"Wait, that was something a now dead darrow spoke of. What's it fucking mean?"

The satyr offered a bow of his head. "I'm not sure. But it involves demons at war with each other, all vying for supremacy. And when they battle, they will use the lands of the Eleven Kingdoms for their arena. And that can never be a good thing for any of us—mortals, creatures of magic, or immortals alike. Not even the gods, old or new. Not even you or your dragon mate."

Hereward considered Gik's words for a moment.

Just then, Wallace stirred. Missy had wandered close. So close, her hay breath found Hereward's nose, and Gik laughed when he recoiled from the stink. Horse's skin always smelt good, like barns and outdoors. Their breath, not so much.

Before Hereward could complain out loud, Wallace rubbed his eyes and yawned. With sleep still thick in the boy's voice, he mumbled, "The darrow told me somethin' 'bout a 'Al' someone or other…can't 'member his name." Wallace sat up, eyebrows raising with another yawn. He clicked his fingers. "Al-kwarm? Ya, dat's him. Anyways, him n' Murkool are fuedin' real bad, worse than the neighbors farmer used ta with his wife if dinner weren't on the table. The darrow told me so 'fore I stuck 'em through the heart. That's what they's meant by the Purge, I's reckon. A demon war's comin' ain't it, Papa?"

Hereward put the pieces together. "I think it is."

But he froze, realizing Wallace clearly meant the feathered demon Alquam, lord of agonizing darkness, wraith of malice, of eternal suffering, and master of misery. *Alquam.* The same demon who took the defeated Ealdræd into the Void to consume the fucking magician for eternity. Seemed if what Hereward was hearing was truth, eternity wasn't that long. Fuck!

Also seemed Alquam had an enemy. The demon god of the undead, of bones, of death, and the reaper himself. Myrkul.

Which then brought Hereward to a further thought. But before he could quantify it, his sword god said, *Ealdræd lives! Your revenge wasn't satisfied. Ealdræd lives, my love.* She sounded stressed, and he couldn't blame her.

"Are you sure the darrow spoke that, Wallace?" Hereward asked as a roiling dread stirred up inside him to make him feel nauseous.

"Sure as day, Papa, I's am."

"Fuck!" Hereward boomed. "You know what this means, don't you?"

At that moment, Dorgan returned from the heavens. He'd obviously heard the conversation from above—dragons had good ears. When he was in human form, he said, "What does it mean, lover?" He then held Hereward's hand, a stain of worry finding his face.

Hereward replied, "Means after we get Oswin, we're going to be making an alliance with the reaper, Myrkul. That's what it means."

"By the gods!" Dorgan said gasping.

Wallace's face drained. "Can't trust a demon, Papa."

"Perhaps not." Gik, however, was more philosophical with his next words. "But let's hope Myrkul sees things how you see them, Lord Hereward. Otherwise, your revenge will never be satisfied."

"And Alquam will consume the world, purge it of all living souls," Dorgan added with dread. "His anger will be great after I tricked him."

"I's scared, Papa—Pa." Wallace folded himself between Hereward and Dorgan; they held their son tightly.

Hereward admitted, "So am I, son. So am I."

6
Novane's Selfless Act

THE DESERT HEAT GOT even more stifling as the days and weeks wore on. Many times, the haze played tricks on Greysen's eyes; he kept believing he saw buildings to shelter within when there weren't any. He wasn't used to being so exposed. He found it difficult to breathe, and he swore he was cooking inside his own skin as the broiling sun beat down on his head and back relentlessly.

Greysen wasn't used to the exertion he had to endure either, and he trudged through the shifting sand over dune and valley alike. His pace was painfully slow, and each footfall seemed heavier than the last. What he wouldn't give to be back amongst his pillows reading his precious books, waiting with anticipation for his lord to use him. Have his way with Greysen's wanting body.

But that thought caused him to pause. Something the lich said earlier rang a bell at the back of his mind. Was he nothing more than Myrkul's whore disguised as his husband? But what else could he be? His fate was set. He would be Myrkul's until death. Perhaps even beyond the mortal coil if he had his way. If he served his punishment and pleased his lord.

Yes, that's what he would do. Serve his punishment, please his lord, then be his for eternity.

"We won't get to the oasis by evenfall if you don't stop dragging your feet, Greysen," Novane warned, bringing Greysen out of his reverie.

But was that concern disguised as disdain, he heard?

"I can't...go on," Greysen said with a rattling gasp as he collapsed into the sand, eating it seconds later.

He was done.

He'd failed his lord.

"It isn't far," Novane urged. "Less than a league over that dune."

"Leave without...me. That's what you want, isn't it, lich?" Greysen's mind clouded, and his vision became dark as if the blistering sun suddenly came to eclipse. Greysen knew he was done for. "To get Oswin...and claim the...*glory*...for yourself."

Without another word between them, Novane shrugged off his backpack, then picked up Greysen with ease. In one fluid motion, the lich slung him over one shoulder, Greysen's view of the lich's backside. Novane then picked up his backpack and continued towards the shimmering horizon, his pole axe used as his walking stick and helping to balance him.

Novane whistled a tune, fluent and melodic, as if Greysen were no burden upon him at all. Since when did lich's have an appreciation of music? Any sort of music. Did the undead even have a heart to be moved by such a thing?

Greysen couldn't ponder such things. He was too weak. As such, he let himself be carried without complaint before he blacked out completely.

When he woke, palm trees stark against the shocking blue of the sky came into view when his eyes focused. Greysen could taste cool mineral water on his lips. He licked them, desiring more. How long had he been lying here? The sun was still high. An hour or two perhaps? Unless it was the next day or even many days since the heat took him into darkness?

Standing over him, Novane stood guard unmoving, looking like a sentinel as he held his pole axe, his stern expression directed towards the horizon. He held a water container. Greysen took a moment to study the lich while he wasn't being watched.

In life, Greysen reluctantly admitted Novane would have been handsome. Even undead, the lich was striking. Most folks believed the undead were walking horrors, beings with flesh falling off them, mindless and hollow, but they weren't. Not at all. Sure, the skeletons, ghouls, and zombies were.

But not the liches.

Liches were men transformed into undead willingly to serve, the magic to do so leaving them as they looked in life. Sure, even though Novane's skin was the color of cold, white granite and the heart within no longer beating, the rest of him was beautiful. He was all dark wavy hair, aquiline nose, full lips, and a slim but muscular frame under his armor. He was tall, well beyond six feet in height. Taller than Greysen by a foot and a half at least.

Novane was imposing.

He was also a mystery, which annoyed Greysen. Why had Novane suddenly changed his tune from being an asshole to someone who seemed to care for him? He could have left him to die in the desert. But he didn't. What was his motive? Novane wouldn't do anything unless it benefited him. What was going on?

"Why didn't you leave me to die?" Greysen asked, sitting up on his elbows.

"You would never know the truths of things if I did," Novane replied enigmatically and without looking away from his study of the horizon beyond the oasis' palm circled waters. Water that glistened in the sunlight, cool and inviting.

Greysen wanted to bathe, but instead said, "What does that even mean?"

"You shall soon see."

He became irritated by the answer but decided the lich's words were unimportant. Besides, his own concerns far outweighed anything else. "I need to clean the sweat and sand off myself before we move on. I want to swim in the oasis, lich."

"Then go swim."

"I will need…" Greysen had to swallow his pride, bitter on the way down his throat. "I will need…you to remove my chastity so I can do so."

Now Novane looked at him, turning slowly. His eyes, ones Greysen always thought were cold like the rest of him, glistened with life like the water. They were even warm, matching the sun high above. Astonished, Greysen licked his lips, suddenly parched.

He said, "Gladly, Greysen."

Greysen's annoyance was soon replaced by something else. Something he couldn't quantify. He dismissed his emotions as a result of his own imagining after suffering from heat exhaustion. He stood, slipping off his jerkin, doublet, and unbuttoned his pants.

When without clothing, naked against the heat, relief washed over him. He breathed in deeply. He also felt arousal stir within him because of his freedom. Yet, like a splinter niggling but unable to be removed by his own hand, the golden metal of his cock cage shone brightly in the sunlight to remind him of his standing in life. Who he really was beyond the Dread Keep? A demon's obedient whore. But so what? What else was there for him?

The power and will of Myrkul was his destiny.

Novane was on his knees before him. With a touch like when he put the cock cage on, the lich was delicate and gentle, even when he removed the urethral insert attached to the device. Greysen moaned at the sting as it slid out of him. His relief was profound when he was freed of the metal. He shuddered with delight.

But his relief was also dangerous.

Greysen's cock stirred to life. More so when Novane went behind him and gently bent him over to remove the anal plug. Greysen shivered under Novane's delicate touch. But the moment of his elation was spoiled when he felt Myrkul's thick, plentiful seed ooze from him to run down the back of his balls and drip onto the sand in heavy drops between his legs. He was Myrkul's vessel. At the moment, he wasn't sure if he liked being so, even though the sensation of the demon's ejaculate being released made his arousal grow even more.

Or was it because of Novane's touch?

Greysen became embarrassed. Never before had he stirred in such a way outside of his lord's presence.

He became confused. More so when Novane said, "You shouldn't be put into chastity like you're owned, like you're nothing to our lord, Greysen."

"What do you know?" Greysen snapped, his mind a whirl. "When I have swum and done my business, you will put me back into my chastity and lock it with your magic. That's my lord's will, and I'll not disobey him. Do you understand me?" But he felt betrayed by his own words.

The hurt in Novane's warm dark eyes startled him.

"Yes…of course." Novane bowed, averting his gaze. "Forgive me. I didn't mean to suggest you would ever disobey our lord willingly."

Greysen became even more confused. Novane really had changed his tune. Had his near death brought things into perspective for the lich? If Greysen failed, so did he, after all.

But mostly, and with a good deal of guilt, he felt amazing since all his chastity had been removed and he'd become so joyfully aroused because of it. Was it wrong to want to remain as he was now? Remain free as Novane suggested? Would Myrkul even know if he didn't return to the shackles of chastity? Or that he had thoughts of himself and his own pleasure?

Novane added, "I will clean your cage and plug and prepare you a meal while you swim. Is there anything else you wish me to do?" The lich's voice was smooth and caring, gentle even.

Greysen was taken aback, a common thing lately. "I don't understand you."

Novane shrugged. "There's nothing to understand."

"I'm sure there is. One of the truths you spoke of earlier perhaps."

"Perhaps. But go bathe now."

Greysen agreed. The water was cool and refreshing against his bare skin and his newfound freedom. Being within the water was like being immersed inside a dream. A beautiful, dream. He felt so alive. His thoughts wandered as he laid on his back, floating, looking up.

With the endless sky above, beckoning him further into his thoughts and dreams, Greysen remembered his life before he came to the Dread Keep. The visions he saw pulsed as they coalesced into form. Often, these visions were too hard to grasp, but today, he could see. At the same time, they were like an agonizing spirit rising up inside him to consume all other thoughts. His mind took him to the time when he was taken in the dead of night by ghouls to the Dread Keep. To Myrkul. Greysen didn't scream. He'd wanted it. How could that be so? Why?

After his wanted abduction, he was presented to Myrkul like one would present meat at a feast. Even though his life before he gave himself to Myrkul was hazy, like memories lost within memories, Greyson believed he had a good life with his family. He had two brothers, three sisters as well, he remembered. They were always smiling, laughing, and carefree. They played folk songs long into the night by the open fireplace of their home while they danced. They were happy.

He was happy, he recalled.

Then, the ghouls razed his home village to the ground. The undead murdered his brothers, those who had brought him up along with his sisters, who were slaughtered too. He could hear their screams as their flesh was ripped from their bones and feasted upon. So much blood. His whole family was eaten. His beautiful sisters and brothers, no longer carefree and happy singing their songs of ages.

Only Greysen was spared.

The youngest of them all.

His marriage to Myrkul was one bathed in blood. He had no choice. He would be killed if he refused. The promise of eternal life was his wedding present—a present yet to be given still. Sadness swept over

Greyson. Had Myrkul lied to him? Was he never going to be anything but a mortal whore to a demon hungry for power over the living?

The remaining villagers were sacrificed as Greysen spoke his vows to his captor. Again, with no choice. He then gave himself willingly that night. He bled and hurt for days, unable to move after he was left on pillows, ravished and corrupted and alone in an opulent room that offered no comfort. He ached deep inside when he remembered the aftermath of what he'd agreed to. What he'd done to himself.

Guilt found Greysen.

He hadn't felt such a strange emotion for a long time. He gasped, pulling himself out of his memories. He had to get out of the water.

When at the shore, letting the air dry him, he relieved himself behind a palm tree's thick trunk. Novane approached. Strangely, Greysen didn't mind the lich watching him, even though he would never admit it.

While he pissed and pissed—his bladder had been full to bursting, he realized—his water splashing the wood of the palm, he said, "Why do you watch me, lich?"

"What else is there to do?"

Greysen ignored the reply. A weird sensation found him, making his stomach turn. "You don't have to return me to my chastity; I've decided I'll no longer wear my cage and plug."

He didn't know why he'd said those words. They shocked him even as they fell from his lips. He didn't deliberately want to disobey his lord, but something compelled him to do so. Then again, what punishment could be worse than what he endured right now? Even death's eternal embrace couldn't be any worse than suffering Novane's presence for a moment longer than he had to. He hated the lich. Hated him with a passion. But he hated himself and what he'd become even more, for he realized his life had the most important thing missing from it.

Love.

Was that one of Novane's truths?

He had love with his brothers and sisters in their rustic and simple home filled with song and laughter. Now, as a whore to Myrkul's whims, he had none. He had nothing. Greysen seethed. And his bubbling anger couldn't be let out on any other except the lich. How delicious.

Novane smiled. "Coming to your senses, are you?"

Greysen let his anger go, it was his only pleasure left to him. "You will not speak of any corruption against my lord. You will also not speak to me unless I ask you to. The sooner we get Oswin to our lord, the sooner I'll be rid of you."

Novane didn't reply, only bowed and backed away.

For the next few days, they remained unspeaking. No matter how far Greysen walked, the desert remained underfoot, the blazing sun above. How big was the Hyruldon Expanse? Were they at the edge of the sand or nowhere near it?

At least Greysen was becoming used to the walking, the heat, the exhaustion. Determination set his thoughts towards achieving his goal, and no obstacle was too large to stop him. When he got Oswin, and before he arrived back at the Dread Keep, he'd get Novane to put him back into his cock cage and return the anal plug.

Myrkul would never know.

Would he?

By the time he'd justified his actions in his own mind, the sky had purpled. Evenfall approached. Every night, Novane dug out a ditch in the sand with his pole axe on the leeward side of any dune large enough to protect Greysen from the winds; sand hid anything exposed when the weather was behind the grains. The winds always came at night. He'd suffocate if he weren't protected.

Novane always laid down a blanket taken from his backpack for Greysen to sleep upon. The blanket smelt of the lich—strangely, a manly musk with a hint of cinnamon and strong coffee. So unlike other undead, who reeked of dank and musty graves left open too long without an occupant. Greyson breathed in the blanket before his bone weariness dragged him into the abyss of sleep.

He slept serenely.

Novane always stood guard; the lich never slept. The undead didn't need to journey into the abyss at night-time; they lived it. They were the abyss.

Then again, Novane didn't seem that way at all. He was unlike any undead Greysen ever knew. How could it be so? Was it magic? Myrkul's will? Something else? What?

In the morning, the sun hot before it was fully above the horizon, Novane fixed Greysen's breakfast. A repast of desert hare infused with herbs and spices, exotic and tasty, cooked over a fire. Where the lich found the kindling, Greysen didn't know. He didn't even know where the fire was. Perhaps the lich used his magic to cook the meat and he only imagined a fire. Greysen didn't care about the details, because the hare tasted bloody good; its meat was prepared to mouth-watering, succulent perfection. He was satisfied beyond measure.

"Thank you," he offered as the lich watched him, as always.

The lich didn't reply.

Greysen said, "You can speak if you have something to say."

Novane offered Greysen a cloth to wipe his fingers dripping with tasty fat from the flesh and bone of the hare. "Would you like me to shave you?"

Greysen, surprised by the lich's question, felt his stubble. It rasped loudly under his touch. It had grown thick over the past few weeks, around his chin especially. "You just want to slice my throat open, don't you? Be done with me."

"If you want me to slaughter you like a farmer would a Spring lamb, I will." The lich smiled. "I would make it quick."

Greysen stood to face the lich, nose to nose. "You'd like that, wouldn't you? Then you could go back to our lord and revel in his glory while my body rots in the sand. You'd be a hero, winning our lord's admiration while my soul would be condemned forever. No, thank you."

"I can't go back. Not now, not ever."

"What?"

"You heard me."

There was something within the lich's ever watching eyes Greysen knew had always been there. He just hadn't noticed it before. Perhaps it was a warning, one revealed like a shroud lifted from a body to identify the victim underneath. No. Perhaps it was one of Novane's truths.

Yes, that was it.

But born from his thoughts, something terrible rose into his awareness. His stomach knotted, twisted. So much for the delicious hare. He now felt a terrible dread, one he should have seen coming earlier. He gasped.

He said slowly, "I can't go back either, can I?"

Sadness also found him, striking hard as if delivered with a hammer's blow. Greysen's insides turned uncomfortably, and he felt woozy.

"No. You can't," Novane confirmed.

Another realization struck Greysen. "The Seeing Crystal doesn't look into the future, does it?"

"No, it doesn't, Greysen."

"It only sees what's transpired. Oswin's dead, isn't he? Killed by the thousand cuts. Murdered by Monk Wu. Am I right?"

"Yes."

Greysen heaved a sigh of sorrow and regret as hot, stinging tears found his eyes. He became lost. More than he already was. What was he going to do?

But, lips trembling, he managed to say, "That's why you suggested I remove my chastity." Then another thought struck him. Another truth. "That's why you look at me like you do, isn't it? Your mind is always turning over as you wrestle with your conscience about what to do with me now that my failure has condemned you too. You want to punish me. You want to kill me. You just haven't done it because you haven't found a way to mollify your conscience. Have you poisoned the meat I just ate? Or are your methods far more subtle, lich? Am I forever lost within this desert thanks to your guidance?"

"That's not it." Novane came closer; their noses touched. Greysen felt a jolt of electricity shoot through him from the contact. He didn't dislike it. "And I can assure you, if I wanted to kill you, you'd be facing me and armed."

"Then...what is it?"

To Greysen's utter surprise and exasperation, Novane moved so he could press his lips against Greysen's. Greysen froze with his eyes wide in shock. Unbelievably, he also stirred, but unlike any way he'd ever done before. This time, his arousal was different. This time, he felt different.

He swayed where he stood, weak at his knees all of a sudden. What was that about? Novane caught him, holding him tightly. Before Greysen could contemplate the proper meaning of the kaleidoscope of emotions swirling within him, from confusion to doubt, to arousal and interest, Novane whispered, "It's because I have feelings for you, Greysen Nightbane."

Greysen took an eternity to process what had happened in the few passing moments since the sun's rising had broken free of the shimmering horizon line proper and the lich had kissed him under its glory.

When he'd gathered himself enough, warm within Novane's embrace, taking in the manly cinnamon and coffee scent he'd come to love because he slept on it every night, he said, "You deceived me. You made me believe I meant nothing to you."

Darkness then clouded over everything else. But most of all fear consumed him. Not fear of what Myrkul would do to him, but what he would do to himself.

Novane said, "Your mind was enslaved by Myrkul as much as your body. I just had to undo the knots, one by one. I am sorry I deceived you, but it was necessary."

"Didn't take long to release me, did it? Only a few weeks."

"The truth is the sharpest weapon when it comes to untying the lies that bind us."

Novane pressed his body closer to Greysen's, and Greysen let him, falling into Novane's arms. He couldn't help himself. He needed comfort, and it was a lich who offered it. He succumbed willingly. After all, that's what he did best.

A moment passed. Or was it an eternity? Greysen didn't care. He soon felt the lich's arousal. Although, to his surprise, it pressed against his own. Fear struck him. Fear of what would happen now that he'd been divorced from his lord in the cruelest way possible, the mental shackles broken.

As it had been planned without his knowledge, he was certain.

Yes, he'd failed his mission. But would he have ever succeeded? He doubted it. He understood Myrkul no longer wanted him. He meant nothing except as a warm place for the demon to stick his cock inside. Greysen felt sick to his soul. How could he have been so blind? The clues were all there. Why else would the demon have taken him twice before he sent him away? The lust they shared was Greysen's final moment as Myrkul's husband.

Sadness once again came to him, along with everything else roiling within. He never got his wedding present promised to him. He'd never even been told he was loved, either. Only that he was A Rúnsearc; a second prize, because it didn't declare love, only spoke of the shackles of lust between them.

And that hurt most of all.

Greysen began to cry, shoulders heaving.

Novane held Greysen's head against his chest with tender hands, comforting him. "I care about you, Greysen."

"You have a funny way of showing it," Greysen blubbered. "Remember when you flopped your cock out and wanted me to suck it? Is that how you behave when you care for someone?"

"I was angry because you couldn't see what I saw."

"As I'm angry now."

Novane held Greysen until his tears stopped flowing. The

hiccupping began. When they parted their embrace, his emotions left all over Novane's armor like an embarrassing stain, the lich grabbed his hands tenderly. They weren't cold; Greysen was surprised at that. Then again, he'd never been close enough to anyone undead to notice the temperature of their skin before. Not in the closeness of an embrace, anyway.

To his continuing astonishment, Greysen didn't pull out of the lich's grip. "I hate you more than I hate myself."

Novane kissed him again. Greysen, without hesitation, returned the affection as he became overwhelmed by the taste of the lich's lips, an exotic spice along with his own salty tears. He was full of regret for what he'd done to himself under Myrkul's influence. Embarrassed he'd been fooled with a promise of power he was never going to get.

But the promise was lost in the past.

He had a future to look forward to, as strange as it was going to be.

Novane said, "And I hate you, too." There was so much love in those words it made Greysen ache. "I always have, Greysen Nightbane."

"Fine. We hate each other." Greysen squeezed his hand, feeling his arousal build again. But again, the sensation was different, and he simply couldn't quantify how he felt properly. In a weird way, it was similar to how he felt about his brothers and sisters but annoyingly different to that as well. What was it he felt exactly?

Before he sent himself mad, he asked, "What's next, then?"

"We seek out Lord Hereward."

"Who's he?"

"The lord knight who also seeks Oswin because the Whispering Monks have quested him to do so. Oswin was a signpost in the turning of events that are to follow. He was important to the result of what's to come, because his life set in motion many things. Some terrible..." Novane smiled at Greysen with his mouth as well as with his beautiful onyx eyes, deep as eternity into the Void. "And some that are wonderful."

"But Oswin's dead."

By the Nine Hells, this day had been too much already. And it was only an hour or so after morning rise.

Novane shrugged, planting another kiss, welcome and warm, upon Greysen's lips. He also wiped away Greysen's tears with his free hand, a touch that was careful and tender. "Lord Hereward doesn't know that. Yet."

"And what's to come?"

"Something far, far worse than Myrkul's rage when he discovers I've failed my mission and you're alive."

Greysen gasped. "That's why Myrkul sent you with me; your job was to kill me, wasn't it?"

Novane nodded, confirming his words. Greysen's insides were a mess. As were his thoughts.

But he also found peace now that he knew the truths.

He continued, "But you couldn't do it. That's why you suddenly changed your tune after you saw what you did in the Seeing Crystal. Why you went from being an asshole to someone who cared. You came to realize, to your own detriment I might add, that you had feelings for me."

"Another truth you need to know is that my feelings for you have turned into such powerful magic within me, I'm more a man than I am a lich now. I have broken Myrkul's bonds upon me too. All because of you."

7
Dorgan's Difficult Decision

HEREWARD'S UNEASINESS DIDN'T LEAVE him. Not even when Gik clapped his hands and many satyrs emerged from the forest, carrying trays full of the forest's bounty and horns brimming with honeyed wine.

"Eat, drink, and be merry, everyone!" Gik announced.

The resulting feast was typical of anything the satyr could conjure from nothing and for no apparent reason. As Hereward drank and ate, becoming more satisfied his belly was being filled, and watched Wallace play with the younger satyrs—some game of hiding and searching—he put his arm tenderly around Dorgan's shoulders, pulling his lover closer. The honeyed wine, a strong concoction, made his head feel light as much has it warmed him.

"You've been quiet," Hereward said, realizing he'd been the same since hearing the news of Alquam's return.

Why couldn't fucking demons stay in the Void where they belonged?

Then again, a few more drinks would chase his worries away. Then he could get on with doing what he did best: drawing his god before his trembling enemies. Oh, and go find Oswin, of course.

"Just thinking, that's all," Dorgan said, placing his hand onto Hereward's leg and rubbing it.

Hereward appreciated his lover's touch, tender and warm, and he felt his cock stiffen. Obviously, wine didn't affect his libido. Thank the old gods.

"A copper for your thoughts."

Dorgan, his eyes distant even though his body was close, nodded. "It doesn't mean Ealdræd survived, you know. In fact, I would even go as far as to suggest the magician didn't provide as much of a feast as I'd promised the demon."

"So, what you're saying is he's dead. For good." Hereward snorted, then spat. "He'd fucking better be, or there'll be hell to pay."

And I would gladly help you create that hell, my love.

"He's dead," Dorgan confirmed, voice firm.

Hereward sipped from the horn, recently re-filled. "You sure?"

"Why else would Alquam return? The demon is hungry." Dorgan leant over and kissed Hereward's bearded cheek. "And the reason I've been quiet is because…it's because I've got something to tell you, Hereward."

Hereward felt his heart flutter with anxiety. "I don't think I can handle any more fucking bad news today." But his words weren't said with any emotion other than concern.

"Oh."

"Oh, what?" Hereward turned to look into Dorgan's eyes, blue and beautiful, beautiful like the rest of him. He suddenly feared the worse. His thoughts jumped to conclusions, the worst imaginable. Did Dorgan, his love and Wallace's Pa, want to leave him? Hereward, for the first time since Ayrdon died, felt loss stab at him like an enemy's blade had found his guts and twisted, twisted until he was done.

He fucking hated the feeling.

"Are you leaving me?"

"What?" Dorgan seemed genuinely shocked. "No, that's not it. I love you, Hereward. I love you with everything I am, right down to my dragon soul."

Hereward breathed in relief, then drained the horn of its contents, letting the sweet but tart liquid warm him further. He needed another drink.

"I fucking love you as well," he said, wiping his bearded chin with the back of his hand. His cock's increasing hardness made itself known even more when Dorgan moved his hand closer to Hereward's groin. "What's this about then?"

"I've got to try and stop Alquam somehow."

If Hereward had still been drinking, he would have choked on it. "You want to fucking do what?"

"I know the demon," Dorgan declared. "I've faced him before, remember."

"You've fucking got Abbot Hosho in your head, haven't you? Giving you grandiose fucking ideas!"

Dorgan spat a quick laugh. "No, I haven't. But I know in my bones it's something I've got to do. Please understand, Hereward. I don't wish to, but I must. If anyone can placate Alquam and prevent this so-called prophesied Purge, it's me."

Hereward found the conviction of Dorgan's word touching and honest. "What can I do to help?"

Dorgan smiled, one as warm as him. "After you make love to me, I need you to do as you said before. Find Oswin and seek out Myrkul to try and ally with him. The reaper's armies are marching north as we speak. The stage is being set; we just have to make sure act one never gets told, for all of our sakes."

Dorgan is right, my love.

I know, Hereward snapped back to his god in his head. *Doesn't make it any fucking easier, does it?*

Hereward snorted again. His heart ached and ached. He would miss Dorgan but understood his reasons. A person had to do what they had to do. That was the law of the wild. Hereward's law, as well.

He kissed Dorgan's cheek. "All right, but can we fuck for two weeks solid, so I get to have you in my arms for longer?"

"You're such a romantic." Dorgan brushed his fingers against Hereward's bulge. "And a big romantic at that."

"There's one other thing."

"Oh, what's that?"

"You tell Wallace where you're going and why. He deserves no less."

Dorgan's eyes returned to the distance; Hereward followed his stare with his own. Wallace was laughing and playing with two other satyrs, a game involving a ball being kicked between sticks at either end of a large circle bordered by stones. He looked so carefree, smiling and laughing while running, chasing the ball. Hereward loved seeing their son so happy, as a child his age should be.

Dorgan finally said, "I'll tell him after you've given me all of your love, Hereward. I need your strength and courage surrounding me right now more than anything. I also need you deep inside me to remind me what I'm about to do is something I'll miss so much, I won't be able to stand being away from you for too long."

Hereward threw away the horn, stood, and offered his hand to his lover with a knowing, loving grin. "Then let me give you all I can fucking give."

Dorgan accepted, coming to embrace Hereward. "We'd better tell Wallace we're leaving the clearing for a moment. Don't want him to worry."

"Good idea."

Hand in hand, they went to Wallace.

After explaining they needed to spend time together, something Wallace guessed the meaning of, he winked and said, "But don't go too far 'way from me, Papa—Pa." He then turned his attention back to the game, kicking the pig-skin ball into the goal and earning a cheer from the other satyrs.

Wallace also cheered, arms high and punching the air. He was pure happiness at the moment. The satyrs clapped Wallace's back in congratulations, and a quick hug or two were offered as well.

Hereward's heart warmed even more.

When Wallace came back to them, Dorgan said reassuringly, "We won't go far. And I'll need to speak with you when I return, Wallace."

"Ya, Pa." And with the affirmation, he returned to his game, the conversation over, back slaps aplenty came from his new friends.

"He'll be fine 'cause he's occupied," Hereward said. "Now it's only you I've got to fucking worry about."

Dorgan squeezed Hereward's hand, a gesture no doubt reflecting his intention. "Can you worry me with your cock more than anything else?"

"Fucking oath, I can."

Well beyond the clearing, far away from the festivities and games the satyrs reveled in, Hereward laid his cloak upon the leaf littered ground for his lover.

Dorgan slipped out of his clothing eagerly and with lust and love sparkling in his blue eyes. Sunlight dappled around him to make him even more beautiful to Hereward, skin glowing in moving patches. The sight was almost surreal. Dorgan was like an angel. But thankfully, an angel with a devilishly hard cock leaking his desires already.

Hereward fucking loved him.

He didn't waste any time, for their moments together were short for many reasons. He clambered out of his own clothing and embraced Dorgan, skin against skin, warmth against warmth, delightful and perfect.

Unlike before when they were intimate, Hereward felt different. Yes, lust was a part of what they had now under the shifting canopy. He lusted for Dorgan. Always would. But this time, this time other feelings swirled to make themselves known. Feelings Hereward hadn't felt for an age, not since the day he'd married Ayrdon all those years ago. He felt unadulterated love, visceral and perfect.

As he ran his hands all over Dorgan's wanting body, all muscles and musk, he felt even more overwhelmed. As they kissed, tongues connecting them like bridges, joining their souls, cocks pressed hard and bodies harder, feelings that this could be the last time he'd hold his man in his arms almost ended him.

Dorgan moaned.

Hereward did too.

They were soon upon the cloak, rolling wild, leaves crunching, dappling sunlight purifying them. Hereward's passion and the fever of his lust was pushed aside for something even more profound. Their raw need for one another beyond anything but just to be together. Hereward could feel it radiating off Dorgan too.

The connection he felt—body, mind, and soul—was so profound, growing like Spring flowers after a storm within him, that time and place held no meaning. Only Dorgan did.

The world could fall.

Armies of men and undead, delphin and darrow, could decimate what was left of the ruin.

Kings and queens could die.

Hereward wouldn't care.

Dorgan was his universe, and there was no whispering needed between them to reveal their intentions. Only the language of their entwined bodies. The realization made him shudder and gasp.

During the midst of their passion, sweat glistening within body hair over taut, heated muscles, Dorgan moved to take Hereward's cock into his mouth. Hereward grabbed Dorgan's head while his throbbing, aching hardness was prepared for what was to come. Bliss and belonging, along with everything else, roiled within him before they became completely one.

Then they were.

Again, with kissing and passion, love and lust, Hereward pushed his hardness ever deeply into the only man who mattered to him. The resulting tightness made him gasp. Dorgan cried out. The forest life fled. Then they settled into their own private rhythm, the heat and feelings of being one with Dorgan overwhelmed him further.

Hereward shuddered and kissed him more feverishly. In reply, Dorgan grappled, moaned, and writhed beneath him. They became a mass of hot trembling lips, quivering flesh, and writhing bodies.

Their dance of intimacy under the canopy continued. Hereward didn't care about anything else as his body moved in perfect harmony with Dorgan's. Hands, mouths, feet, legs, bodies, and cocks each other's. For all he cared, eternity could end and begin again. Demons could rise from the Void in its collapse and rebirth. Nothing could take away what he had with Dorgan. Nothing.

All too soon—or was it an age?—Hereward felt a different warmth between them. Dorgan was in the throes of ecstasy, gasping, trembling, breathless, as the warmth became known. He'd released himself. Dorgan's seed was now the glue that bound them even more, tight stomachs pressed in heated passion.

Hereward felt his own stirring rise. But even with his own release, he wasn't deflated nor satisfied. Neither was Dorgan. He needed more.

They both did.

Kissing and refired passion kept their cocks hard as they began their assent into wonder with each other again. Dorgan, soaked as he was, grew even more fervent with his need for Hereward.

Hereward obeyed Dorgan's need, for it reflected his own.

When both were spent of all within them, they laid together, still entwined, naked and raw, as their bodies cooled. The wind moved the canopy above, and with their calming, wildlife returned.

A big buck approached, curious, antlers like a velvet tree atop his proud head, ears turning as he sensed for danger. There was none. There was only love; Hereward's for Dorgan, and Dorgan's for Hereward. The animal nipped at the grass shoots peeking through the leaves, content.

As Hereward was.

"I've never felt about you as I do now," Dorgan said between kisses. "Your love for me then was…profound and so, so passionate."

Hereward admitted, "And I've never felt for you as I do now, either."

"I fear what my absence will do to you."

"You won't be absent forever." Hereward kissed Dorgan again, feeling himself stir again, their pungent musk surrounding him. He fucking loved it. He'd kissed off most of what Dorgan had released from his sweat laden skin, but he wanted more. So much more. "And when you return, what we just shared will be but a taste of what you should expect."

"I don't know what to say."

"Then let's fuck again."

"No." Dorgan came over Hereward. The dragon man's cock was as hard as his own once more. "Let's make love again."

"Now who's the fucking romantic?"

Hereward's heart sang; his pure love for Dorgan filled it to bursting. He was content, as much as he could be at any time in his life. But at the same time, concern found him. He realized with creeping dread that he didn't want Dorgan to leave him, even for a short while. He understood why Dorgan had to. Hereward wished he was going with him. But he also knew why he couldn't. He had someone else he loved as much as Dorgan to worry about.

Wallace.

Gik offered him more honeyed wine as soon as they emerged from the forest a few hours later, the day turning toward evenfall all too quickly. He accepted, but he didn't want to wash away the taste of Dorgan upon his lips. He wanted it to remain forever. He knew such a thing impossible, but the idea amused him.

He *was* fucking happy, after all.

A fire was lit. Large and crackling, sending lazy lit embers and curls of smoke up into the bruising sky. Many satyrs started playing lutes and pan pipes as the dancing began. And the clapping. And then the singing. Many more talked; they mostly told fables of long ago, when men slew dragons, not fucked them in the undergrowth with all of their love. The younger ones were a captive audience for such noble tales.

Wallace wasn't amongst them. He was with Dorgan. And whatever was said between them, it resulted in an embrace, one of father and son. Hereward joined them and held them both tightly as they held him. His heart sang even more.

Wallace's eyes were red and watery. "When do ya leave, Pa?"

"At morning rise," was Dorgan's short but honest answer.

"I'll miss ya so much, Pa."

"And I you, Wallace." Dorgan kissed the boy's forehead. Another embrace, long and loving, resulted. "And just so you know without any doubt in your heart, I love you as Hereward loves you. We both love you as any parents would love their son, even though we didn't make you."

"Family's family, be they's blood or not. Ain't dat right, Pa?"

"It is. You are a part of our family and you mean more to us than anything else, just so you know that."

"I's love's ya, Pa. Love's ya as well, Papa."

"I love you too, Wallace."

Hereward, choked up, his voice hoarse, said, "Fucking hell, I love you too, Wallace, my son."

I love you too, Wallace, his sword god said, even though the boy would never hear it. But Hereward would speak it, and he did.

Wallace wiped his eyes when they all parted, the silence between them punctuating the realization that there didn't need to be any more words spoken between them. Their love was wordless. Eternal. And above all, theirs.

After Wallace picked up his sword from the edge of the rock circle demarcating where he'd played his ball game, he declared, "Don't worry, Papa. I'll protect ya from the evil men who come in the night, I's will."

Hereward boomed a laugh. By the gods, his son was amazing. The boy filled him with pride as much as love. "Most who wish ill on others aren't fucking pathetic darrow tied up and hanging from a tree, you know."

Wallace swung his sword, the air sounding its protest as the thrumming rang out. Music to Hereward's ears. "But ya'll string 'em up for me, won't ya?"

"I sure will."

Dorgan said, "Then I'm leaving you in capable hands, Hereward, aren't I?"

At that—and halting Hereward's reply—Gik approached, bearing more honeyed wine and food on a tray for them to enjoy. Wallace's eyes lit up at the sight. After scabbarding his sword, the boy eagerly snatched up the pasties and sweetmeats offered and began devouring them hungrily, sitting on a nearby log.

Gik said, "I don't want to intrude—"

Hereward snorted a laugh. "But you fucking did, anyway." Dorgan offered a glance, then laughed as well.

Wallace was busy stuffing his face.

"Yes, well anyway," Gik continued. "I'm joining your adventure, Lord Hereward."

Hereward's humor left him. "Is that right?"

"Yes, it is." Gik offered a knowing wink. "You wouldn't know your left from your right when it comes to the lands north of Fangmere leading into Invrawold."

"I's knows me left from me right," Wallace mumbled with his

mouth full, grinning. "See?" He stuck out his left foot with the red-painted shoe upon it. "This here's me left."

"That's right," Dorgan congratulated, ruffling Wallace's hair affectionately.

Hereward's humor returned with a vengeance.

Gik also laughed. "Lord Hereward, you need me. And I," he gave a florid bow complete with a sweeping hand gesture, "am at your service, my Lord."

Hereward roared his arse off in laughter. When settled enough to speak, wiping his mouth and beard of spittle, he said, "You've got some big fucking balls on you because you think I don't know these lands better than you. Gik, you've just won me over with your sheer audacity. So fine, you can join us. We leave at morning rise, hangover or not."

Gik bowed deeper. "Thank you, my Lord."

"There's one condition."

"What's that?"

Hereward laughed again. "You wear fucking pants. The sight of your little pink lipstick when you get horny would wear thin after a while. Wallace doesn't need to see it, and I've seen it enough over the years, you fucking horny old goat."

"I'm sure I can find my traveling pair somewhere," Gik said enthusiastically. "Deal and done."

"Oh, but we're not done yet. There's one more thing."

"Go on," the satyr said more cautiously.

"No dry humping any of our legs or other parts, Wallace's especially. He's been through enough already. I don't want him scarred for life any more than he already is."

"What do you take me for?" Gik didn't sound offended. "But also done, and a deal."

"Good." Hereward clapped his hand onto Gik's shoulder, almost making him drop the tray of food and honeyed wine. "Otherwise, you'll find yourself cock-less from the neck down, my god ensuring your head is removed from you cleanly to make it so."

With pleasure, his sword god purred into his thoughts.

Gik's demeanor turned to one of nerves and he stuttered, "I...I-I u-understand and will d-do my b-best to guide you."

8

Greysen's Strange Emotion

THE HEAT OF THE wretched desert didn't bother Greysen any longer.

A different fire did.

Only Greysen didn't understand what the feeling was, not fully. Not yet. It wasn't the emotion he felt towards his brothers and sisters, vaguely remembered; it wasn't even how he felt about Myrkul before he was betrayed. The emotion he felt swirling within him, consuming him, was far different. He was a stranger within himself, walking the strange lands of his awakening conscience.

At least Novane walked by his side.

But again, that was...*different* and added to Greysen's turmoil. Before their kiss and Novane's declaration of his feelings, the lich had always led. Greysen knew by the simple gesture, they were now considered equals.

A strange notion to someone so long subordinate.

A few times, as they trudged through the sand, the lich reached out with his free hand to hold Greysen's. At first, he was startled, even though he accepted. What startled him wasn't the act itself but knowing that Novane didn't want anything from him after doing so. Holding his hand was just that, with nothing expected.

Greysen found a smile upon his lips. He hadn't smiled in an age.

Although, the expression was soon wiped from him when his thoughts darkened to what he'd become on a promise of power. Myrkul never held his hand for the sake of doing so. The demon never did anything unless it was for his own benefit. Greysen was never considered beyond how he could serve and be used.

He shuddered as he spiraled. How could he have been so blind? How could he have wanted to die for Myrkul's limited affection? He found he hated the demon as the poison of what he had been seeped more and more into his conscience. He realized he'd done more than supplicated to Myrkul's will. Greysen was responsible for the creation of his own worthlessness, the greatest crime of all.

The wounds of his past would take a long time to heal. Perhaps a lich who deceived his lord and master, condemning himself to eternal death, was the one Greysen needed to help him begin the process of his recovery. Time would tell.

"I will use the Seeing Crystal to locate Lord Hereward," Novane announced, disturbing Greysen's reverie.

The lich came to a halt, spearing his pole axe into the sand so he could retrieve the magical object from his tunic underneath his armor. He also let go of Greysen.

Greysen felt another foreign strangeness find him once Novane's hold became absent. His confusion became a miasma churning within him. The warmth of Novane's touch lingered as much as Greysen's awakening. As much as his regret and shame.

The magic the lich affected himself with because of his love for Greysen had made his skin warm, seemingly alive to the touch. Did Novane's heart beat as well? Did the once dead muscle, cold and dark within the lich's ribcage, add to his newfound life?

"What do you see?" Greysen asked, rubbing the palm of the hand Novane had held, then touching his lips where he was kissed; the strangeness within him got stranger.

"Lord Hereward is at the edge of Fangmere forest, about to cross the great delta into the Kingdom of Invrawold. He is with a satyr and a small boy. They are standing by a boat, discussing the best course to navigate. The satyr believes he knows the currents and eddies. Hereward disagrees." Novane lowered the crystal. "That is all the Seeing Crystal sees."

Greysen forgot his own concerns, if only for a moment. "He's going into Invrawold?"

"He is."

"Don't you think that's more than a coincidence?"

Novane nodded. "There is more taking place here than we are aware of. Perhaps Oswin's passing was the first portent of something unfolding even we cannot fathom."

"Maybe others will soon join the game of conquest Myrkul plays against the Eleven Kingdoms?" Greysen suggested.

"You're right." Novane returned the Seeing Crystal into his tunic.

"Myrkul's undead march north to wage war against the living, do they not? How many others will take advantage of such a distraction?"

"Knowing how Myrkul operates, with devastation his goal no matter the cost, I wouldn't be—"

Greysen's words were taken from his lips when a violent rumble and rivers of sand coming together, slithering like massive snakes just under the surface, dust flying, almost knocked him over.

Novane grabbed him, saving his fall.

From the sand, now risen and swirling violently before them, a creature emerged as if created by the earth itself. A canine-faced demon made of sand and attitude formed, snarling, the sound as bleak as the ages and the desert it was born from.

"Shayṭān!" Novane yelled, coming in front of Greysen to protect him, pole axe at the ready, fighting stance posed with swiftness and grace. "Anubian Shayṭān! What do you want with us? We are on a quest in our lord's name, the demon god of the undead, of bones, of death, and the reaper himself. Be gone from our path, Shayṭān."

As the demon formed proper, claws and muscles solidifying from the sands, large ears like a jackal its most prominent feature along with its elongated snout, it barked, "You cannot go beyond here, lich and *human*."

"Let us pass, Anubian Shayṭān," Novane commanded, brow furrowing and gaze intent. "We mean you no harm. Leave us the same, for our mission is of utmost importance to our lord."

The Anubian laughed a rasping cackle, like sand rubbing against sand within clasped hands. "Myrkul's will is far-reaching. As is his sight. You lie."

Greysen stepped forward but not beyond Novane's reach—he wasn't stupid. A demon, even a minor one like the Anubian, wasn't something to trifle with. Or provoke. "I'm Nightbane, husband of Myrkul," he said with as much conviction as he could muster, even though the words stung. Words he didn't want to speak again. "The lich speaks the truth. Now leave us be."

"I know exactly who you are, *human*." Again, the laughter came but now laced with disgust. "But you are husband to Myrkul no more. He is done with you, Nightbane." The sand beneath the demon pulsed with his power; the demon grew larger, blocking out the burning sun. "I have been commanded to serve you with your divorce and smite you into the darkness as the demon god of the undead, of bones, of death, and the reaper himself wishes it. Therefore, compelled as I am to serve him for eternity, it shall be done."

Greysen was shocked. Myrkul had planned his undoing all along, waiting for the right moment for him to slip up so he could enact his punishment. Had he done so since their marriage day? Greysen now knew it as so, right to his bones.

Myrkul was done with him.

The demon had sent his underling to finish him as proof. Greysen, therefore, was done with Myrkul. His stomach turned. Hate seethed within him. But his deceiving lord had made a mistake.

One Greysen would take advantage of.

Greysen spat, and said, "Even though I'm no longer Myrkul's whore, I still have power, Anubian." He called upon the magic, one of the three wishes gifted to him. He felt the power, black like tar, bubbling, oozing, crawling within him. It filled every cell of his body, revitalized him, even made him erect and aching with its potency. "You would be better served returning to the Void from whence you came. Myrkul's blessing is not one to live by. I should know."

The Anubian stepped back, no doubt sensing the surge of power within Greysen. With a cruel smile disforming his snout, the Anubian said, "I could serve you instead, Nightbane."

Novane laughed derisively.

Typical demon behavior, side with the one who presented the greatest threat, the most power. The Anubian was weak. But Greysen didn't want to deal with the inevitable betrayal if he agreed.

He didn't want to waste any more time, either.

With hands raised, black fire burst from Greysen's fingertips, cold as ice but smoldering and sizzling to rent the air. A devastating concussive blast slammed into the Anubian.

The demon howled an agonizing scream.

Novane had to step back from the force of the strike, arms raised to protect himself. Greysen's clothing ruffled violently, his hair more so. Using such dark magic was exhilarating and addictive, especially when he witnessed the result.

The ongoing roars and howls of anguish from the demon echoed over the dunes so loudly, even those within the lowest circle of Hell— the frozen wasteland where traitors rotted for eternity—could have heard.

Greysen felt invincible.

But the power, the feeling of greatness as Greysen controlled but a skerrick of Myrkul's evil, was also overwhelming.

And arousing as well—very arousing.

As the magical blast continued, the stink of thick oil and grease filled his nostrils as much has it stuck to his skin. His will to destroy every particle of the Anubian grew and grew. But Greysen soon felt himself drain as the magic drained. He shuddered as wave upon wave of ecstasy—a cruel effect of using Myrkul's magic—swept over him.

Greysen gasped and cried out. His body was no longer his to control even as the Anubian was sent to oblivion. He succumbed to his own physical failings fueled and heated by the promise of sexual relief. Myrkul gifted him magic, but the demon also gifted Greysen the reminder of what he was if he used it: a whore who was a slave to his own yearnings and shortsightedness. A mere human hungry for a promised immortality that would have never been granted.

To his surprise, Greysen ejaculated as the last remnants of power returned to the depths within him. The spell had been cast. It wasn't the end but the agonizing beginning. He collapsed. Overcome.

Novane had to hold him for an eternity as Greysen tried to claw back from within himself, swimming in the quagmire of his own arousal created by demon magic.

Sweat poured off Greysen. His breathing became hard and labored. Myrkul's magic was now dormant, two spells left, but the effect of it was far from over. He couldn't move as his cock stiffened to aching again. He moaned. He trembled and hissed from his teeth whenever he moved. His enslavement created by his own failing became even more overwhelming when he ejaculated again.

And again, he ejaculated.

He writhed and ached, completely vulnerable as pain shot through him to arrest his muscles, but he managed to stutter, "Myrkul's m-magic is c-cruel."

Greysen's erection wouldn't ease. It ached to touch himself anywhere, skin prickling. He was a stranger to his own physical self as much as he'd been to his own mind since he'd discovered the truths Novane spoke of.

He couldn't relax. Not for a long time. It was well past evenfall and only when billions of stars twinkled above in the cloudless sky, the moon in waning but still low on the horizon, when he came to be himself again.

When Greysen could finally stand, though weak, the lich laid

Greysen down upon the blanket from his backpack, but for the life of him, he couldn't know when Novane had dug out the shallow depression for him to sleep within. Greysen only realized he'd been in the throes of ecstasy for hours. His balls ached more than any other time in his life. He'd be sore for days, if not longer.

"I warned you demon magic wasn't without its consequences," Novane said gently as he helped Greysen sit.

Gingerly he did so, not letting go of Novane. "I should have listened to you."

The lich had found a thick tree branch for furniture, and a crackling fire also roared. He'd also cooked something. The food, whatever it was, smelt divine. Greysen's stomach growled.

"It wasn't your fault."

He harrumphed. "I hate you for what you've awakened within me, you know that, Novane. I hate your truths. They've destroyed me." Greysen laughed at himself, adding, *"You've destroyed me."*

Novane smiled and let go to offer Greysen a soup-like substance in a metallic bowl. Meat floated within a creamy broth that smelt of cloves, spice, and turmeric. Greysen ate hungrily, supping from a spoon with long slurps.

Novane said, "I could have defeated the Shayṭān without you using Myrkul's magic. I'm not without my own talents, you know."

"I don't want to ever use his magic again." Greysen flushed with embarrassment. "His magic had the cruelest effect on me it could, and…and I will need to change my…underwear before we can go on."

"Still hard, are you?"

"Painfully so."

Novane's eyes glistened, the deep pools of them reflecting the firelight. "Imagine if you were still caged. The pain would have crippled you for even longer than it did."

"Myrkul's intention while he sent his hunter for me, no doubt."

"I have a change of clothing and cloths to clean you in my backpack."

"Thought of everything, didn't you?"

Novane's face dropped. "I didn't think Myrkul would discover my failure so soon."

"That's why he sent the Anubian?"

"Yes. There will be others too. We must be on our guard at all times."

Greysen drained the soup bowl. "Then we've only got each other, haven't we?"

In the distance, Greysen heard a lion's roar, deep and guttural, so the noise could travel leagues to the members of his pride. Or to other prides in warning. He was surprised to hear anything after weeks of nothing but wind and the shifting sand. His puzzlement must have been written on his face.

Novane explained, "We are coming to the edge of the desert."

Greysen felt relief for the news. "Will the lions pose a problem?"

"They don't approach the undead."

"Fine for you, but what about me?"

Novane stood, going to his backpack. "I must clean you, otherwise your scent will attract them. A pride of lions will be easy to defeat, but I don't wish to do so if I don't have to."

Greysen became even more amazed by Novane. "You don't have to clean me. And I didn't know you cared about animals, being..."

"Being a lich?"

He flushed again. "Yes. Being a lich."

Novane leant down to kiss Greysen's forehead, his touch tender and again, wonderfully and surprisingly warm. "I care about a lot of things because of you and the feelings I have for you. I will do anything for you. If cleaning your seed from you because of Myrkul's magic is one such thing, then so be it. It is my pleasure."

"Myrkul never did anything but use me."

Novane kissed Greysen again, longer this time. "I will never use you."

"Nor take advantage of me?"

"Not even under pain of death would I ever do that."

Greysen felt his eyes sting with hot tears. "You don't know what you're saying. I'm not worth your affection."

"You are worth everything to me."

Greysen cried, and Novane held him. Held him tightly. He also did as he'd promised, helping Greysen change and clean himself. And even though his erection hadn't eased, aching unbelievably, Novane didn't take advantage of his weakened and aroused state. His touch always gentle. Caring. Wonderful.

"Your pubic hair is growing," Novane observed.

Greysen looked, pinching the hair to prove to himself it was there. "I want to let it grow. Shaving it off will remind me of..."

Novane looked up, his dark eyes deep pools of eternity and the bliss such a thing promised. "Of him," he finished.

"Of him."

When dressed, Greysen went back to the fire. Novane sat next to him, holding him. As flaccidity finally found him, *finally*, he settled. Sleep overtook him. While being held, caressed, hummed to with the tune Novane held on his lips from before, melodic and lulling, he began to fall into the beautiful darkness punctuated by dreams.

Before he did so, he said, "I still hate you, Novane."

Another kiss, that time on his cheek. Then upon his lips, tender and beautiful. Greysen let Novane deepen the contact. Their tongues touched and teased. He didn't become aroused, he'd experienced more than enough of that lately, but it did give him joy. Something to believe in too.

"And I hate you with all of my dead heart and black soul," Novane whispered in reply.

Greysen fell deeper into the lich's arms, warmth enveloping him. He was held even tighter. He returned it. He dreamt of Novane.

The dreams were disturbingly good.

9
Wallace's Own God

HEREWARD HATED THE FUCKING water. And after giving Dorgan a long, teary goodbye, feeling the loss of his absence in his heart already, the waters of the massive delta, the mouth of the Eleven Kingdoms, stretched forever before him.

The waters were quick moving, full of tidal rips, eddies, and bubbling but deceiving lulls. Hereward didn't like it. More so, because the red staining dawn reflected its crimson on the surface, dancing hypnotically and as plain as any omen could be.

Wallace's face was wet with tears as well. "Pa needs ta come back real soon." He wiped his eyes with the back of his hand, sucking in the air in uneven heaves.

Braver than Hereward, Wallace was. He could only nod in absolute agreement, unable to quantify his feelings but with his insides a complete mess.

I shall miss Dorgan too, my love.

Hand in hand, Hereward and Wallace watched Dorgan disappear into the distance, the great silver dragon off on his own quest as Hereward and Wallace were left to their own journey—one involving crossing a massive expanse of water. It was true what folks said: the other side wasn't visible. Hereward hated this expanse of water. Not only because armor and water didn't mix but for the fucking obvious fact he couldn't swim.

Gik came up to them, pulling on Missy's reins, puffing and panting as the satyr often did if required to do anything more physical than lifting a horn of ale or goblet of mead to their lips. They all stood by the shiny black pebbled shore, Gik smiling with an excitement only he understood. Hereward had a bad feeling.

"There's a boat over there," the satyr said. "Should be big enough for the four of us; Wallace and me are small enough to not worry it. But the horse and you, Lord Hereward, will have to stay in the center for balance."

Hereward let his attention be drawn to the boat in question, a vessel he'd ignored earlier because there was no fucking way in either Heaven or Hell or anywhere in between he'd get into the rickety old rotting death trap for anything. "Are you saying we're going to cross these choppy waters in that fucking thing?"

Gik nodded, oblivious.

Wallace, bless his fucking soul, said, "Should'a got Pa to carry us ova the water 'fore he left. Dat boat looks worse'n farma Erickson's shed after the woodlice were innit."

"It's a fucking death trap," Hereward agreed. "And yes, son, I would have got Dorgan to take us, but a certain fucking satyr promised us a boat with—and I quote—'no worries,' didn't he?" Hereward glared daggers at the satyr. "Well, Gik, that thing *is* a fucking worry. A big one. I'm not risking myself or Wallace in it. Find us another way to get across the delta."

Gik paled. "Y-yes of course, my Lord. Right away."

"Quicker than that, too."

Gik bowed. "There…there is a b-bridge…" After a thought, eyes brightening and with a supplicating smile, he added, "My dear friend, my Lord."

Hereward raised an eyebrow. "Why didn't you tell us that before?"

Wallace groaned.

"It's…not too far away but—"

"No buts, for fuck's sake," Hereward barked with a snort. "Anything will be better than trying to navigate the waters in *that*." He pointed to the rotted pile of wood struggling to look like a boat. "Now. Lead the way to the bridge, Gik."

Gik bowed lower. "Yes, my Lord."

"How far's the bridge 'way?" Wallace asked.

Gik tried to keep wearing his smile but failed miserably. If it were at all possible, the satyr paled even more. "Not far, Master Wallace." The words were spoken with a wheeze of panic if Hereward wasn't mistaken.

Hereward asked, "What's wrong, Gik?"

"Oh…nothing," Gik blinked, then looked at the water. "It's not far. And you did tell me not to mention any buts…so I won't."

"For fuck's sake, you're pissing me off, satyr…*my friend*."

"All right," Gik replied with a gulp. "All right. I'll tell you. The bridge is guarded by a river troll. A gargantuan and brutish beast as territorial as they come. We avoid her as best we can. Trolls eat satyr's for breakfast if they can get their claws into us."

Wallace gasped.

"A troll?" Hereward boomed a laugh. "Aside from being a bit cliché, a fucking troll's no bother for me or my god. Nor would it be a bother for Wallace's short sword either with all the practice he's had with his blade, come to that."

We will bathe the beast in its own blood, my love.

That we fucking will, Hereward replied with glee to his beautiful god. Defeating a troll to cross a bridge was a far better prospect than what the boat offered, for water held greater worries than shifting tides. Hereward shuddered at the thought of being dragged by tentacled arms into the dark depths. Helpless. Unable to breathe.

He fucking hated the water.

"If you say so." Gik bowed again.

Hereward touched the pommel of his sword god, hand itching already. "Then let's get to this bridge."

Wallace let go of Hereward to draw his short sword, the metal ringing as he did so. The blade's edge caught the light, sparking blood red down to its cross guards, reflecting the ominous dawn.

Was that a good or bad omen?

"Let's go, Papa!" Wallace let out one of his cute little battle cries, charging forwards across the pebbles crunching underfoot. "Gonna be ready for anythin', ain't I's? Even a' ugly ol' troll!"

"You sure are, son." Hereward felt pride well up inside him once more as he admired Wallace's tenacity, a nice change from the emptiness he felt in Dorgan's absence.

Gik looked worried.

To say the bridge was a proper bridge, made by many skilled hands under an engineer's oversight and worthy of being called so, was to say the boat Gik found them was seaworthy. Hereward liked the sight of the rope and plank bridge even less as an option to cross the delta's expanse the more he saw of it—and he certainly didn't fancy plummeting into the fucking deep to drown below.

Wallace's enthusiasm also waned as soon as the creaking bridge, covered in moss and lichen swaying like tendrils in the breeze, came into full view through mists that'd grown thicker by the delta's shore as they approached.

The air held an uncomfortable, almost unnatural chill.

"Fuck me!" Hereward shouted. "How the fucking hell are we supposed to get Missy across this excuse for a bridge? Fuck!"

Gik shied away. "It's the only other option, my friend."

"Now you're *really* pissing me off, Gik."

Wallace offered, "Maybe we's all swim? The shore's not too far 'way here, an' all."

"You can swim?" Hereward asked, surprised.

Wallace nodded. "Me Sis taught me 'cause she were all fancy for a creek boy," he explained. "Took me with her as a' excuse ta be with him…so I's got told how to swim."

Hereward snorted. "Perhaps I should have fancied a creek boy when I was younger. Fucking would have helped me now, if nothing else."

"Da used ta say creek boys were rough, an' all, only wantin' one thing from Sis."

"My kind of boy," Hereward said chuckling, remembering his youth and how he would chase any young man who so much as winked at him. After catching them, anything went…and usually did. Oswin, his first love, was one such boy, but a servant and not a free lad, like the creek boys of the farmlands.

"Were all well n' good till she were caught kissin' one o' dem creek boys. Then Pa tanned me hide as much as me Sis for helpin' her." Wallace giggled. "But I's knows how to swim, don't I's?"

"Unfortunately, there isn't the time to teach me." Hereward looked at the bridge with a good dose of dismay.

Perhaps it was sturdier than it looked.

As they approached the structure, the waters around the bridge's foundations, thick poles of timber felled from ancient redwood trees, now rotting, seethed and bubbled as if boiling. The mists swirled thickly, ethereal arms clawing at them, lulling them closer to the water's edge. The cold struck too.

But such a thing was only weather. The real concern would be what would come out of the water. River trolls were the largest of their species, and despite Hereward's bravado of earlier, one of them would present a problem. A problem of the muscled attitude with tooth and claw kind.

I don't sense any danger, Hereward's god stated.

Do you think it could be her? he asked, pondering the signs presenting before them.

Perhaps. A long way from where we last saw her, though. Hereward drew his sword in any event, automatic really, metal ringing. "Come face my god's justice, fucking troll. Then we can all get on with our business."

"*Hereward?*" a voice boomed through the mist, vibrating as a great war drum would the air, boom, boom, boom, making it pulse with its powerful registry.

He recognized the voice. "Garthana? Fuck me drunk, is that you?"

"It is I," she boomed from the mist, still hidden. Hereward looked forward to seeing her. Sure, she was as ugly as sin but also amazing beyond anything. The most magnificent creature of the Eleven Kingdoms, he'd put his right ball on it.

"Did you bring me a snack of satyr meat, Hereward?" she asked.

"Unfortunately, I didn't. Gik is a good friend," Hereward replied, not minding the river troll not addressing him as a lord. She was ancient beyond understanding, older than the roots of the mountains themselves; she deserved respect.

Gik, however, trembled in her voice's wake, scurrying behind him and Wallace.

"Pity," the voice in the mist replied. "My tummy rumbles now the stink of him has filled my nostrils."

"I'm sure you'll fucking live." But Hereward laughed. It was great to hear her voice again after such a long time. The 'Ancient Thing,' he sometimes called her. "The last time I saw you, you were swimming leagues north of here, causing the liosalfar grief."

"Their meat grew bitter on my lips and turned my tummy."

"More like the fuckers harassed you until you had no choice but to leave your ancestral home." Hereward only despised darrow more than he despised liosalfar, a race of ethereal beings who could shift through the planes of existence as easily as he breathed. Pompous arrogant arseholes. Evil too. Mostly.

"Who's the handsome young man with you, Hereward?"

Wallace hadn't left Hereward's side, even though he scabbarded his short sword with a click. He obviously didn't sense any danger. "His name is Wallace, and he's my beautiful son."

"Son?"

"Yes, me and Dorgan the Wise of Dragon Lake, adopted him after his family were left for dead."

"A darrow n' his men killed 'em." Wallace hocked and spat, the foaming globule falling short of covering his left red-painted shoe and landing on the black pebbles, oozing. "We's killed 'em back; the blood debt paid for, an' all."

"A terrible story." With those words, the mists thinned like magic, and a gargantuan hulking troll with the carapace of a great turtle, green with slime and weed, stones embedded into her thick scales, lumbered from the water. A behemoth. A monster. But one Hereward fucking liked beyond words.

One slow step, two slow steps. Three. Then four, agonizingly slower. Finally, when out of the water, dripping wet, limp black hair atop her large-jawed skull, two tusks protruding, she sat on the shore before them, crossed-legged. Her ancient bones creaked and popped as she did so. Her arthritic moans and groans echoed to reveal all too plainly her eternal age. She towered over the foundations of the bridge.

Gik ran.

The satyr didn't stop until he was cowering behind Missy. The horse didn't look bothered, obviously sensing Hereward and Wallace's ease despite what the satyr did. She nickered. Missy was trained well enough not to kick anyone behind her. Good thing for Gik. Instead, the mare was more concerned with trying to find grass amongst the pebbles. No luck. She nickered, this time in dismay. Hereward would give her a treat later, or if not, Wallace certainly would.

"For your story, Wallace, and to give you added protection when Hereward can't, I have a present for you here somewhere," Garthana the Ancient Thing announced. "But where is Dorgan, Hereward?"

"That's another story, one for a later time, my dear Ancient Thing." Hereward's sadness returned, stabbing at him like vipers in a disturbed nest. "But just know, he's on his own quest, and we'll leave it at that, shall we?"

Garthana nodded, a movement that would have changed the currents were she not above water. Everything about her was massive. Hereward couldn't help but admire the troll.

His god said, *She is magnificent, and it is good to see her again.*

She sure is…and it is, you're right.

But Wallace's eyes lit up. "What's the present ya gots me, troll lady?" he asked with the impatience of a child on a promise. As expected, really.

Garthana rumbled a laugh that shook the earth, making the pebbles around her vibrate and clink together. "Let me get it for you."

From within her clothing of river weed and detritus washed into the waters over the eons, she rummaged. Garthana produced a golden scabbard encrusted with rubies, emeralds, and diamonds; no doubt it once belonged to a king whose bones turned to dust centuries ago. The scabbard was for a large knife, but it would be a short sword for Wallace. She drew the blade after releasing a catch with a click.

The steel—dragon forged—glowed blue.

"'Tis a god!" Wallace's eyes widened. "Just like Papa's!" he exclaimed with a gasp.

"The blade itself turns red when danger is present," the troll explained. "Wear it close to your skin, Wallace, and you will feel the vibrations of its warning as well."

"Ah, so that's how you knew we weren't a threat?" Hereward interjected.

"Guilty as charged." Her laughter kept rumbling, shaking the earth and air alike. "And it is yours now, Wallace." She offered it to him. "Son of Hereward and Dorgan."

"Ta, an' all." Wallace accepted the gift humbly, bowing. "I'll cherish it more'n anythin' else."

Hereward ruffled Wallace's hair. "You'll need more lessons."

"I's can't wait."

Gik finally emerged from behind Missy, cautiously. "Are we getting on with the business of crossing this wretched delta or are we not?"

"Feisty for food, isn't he?" Garthana said.

"He is right though, as much as I want to reminisce about the good times with you, Ancient Thing, my lovely." He observed Wallace testing out the blade; it looked perfectly balanced for him. His stance had improved too, feet where they should be. Good boy. "But I don't trust that fucking bridge of yours to get us to the other shore."

Garthana came to stand, slowly, achingly. The mists returned. So did the cold, chilling Hereward to his bones as it bit at him, nipping like yapping lap dogs. "I shall carry you upon my back. All of you."

Hereward bowed. "We accept."

Gik almost swallowed his own tongue. "We do?"

"Yes, we fucking do," Hereward said, clapping his hand onto the satyr's back. "No arguments."

"None from me, Papa."

Gik sighed. "Humans…what can you do with them?"

"And if the Ancient Thing gets hungry on the journey, there'll be a ready snack for her. Am I right?" Hereward teased.

Gik curled the corner of his mouth nervously. "I can swim, my friend. Can you?"

Hereward then realized with dread what it meant to ride upon the troll's back. "Fuck!"

"Don't worry yerself, Papa, I'll hold ya hand." With that, Wallace clipped the scabbard onto the belt around his waist, attaching the lower part to his leg, doubly secure and close enough to feel its vibrations. He stowed his short sword in one of the saddle bags. He had a new god now.

Hereward once more felt pride as the boy beamed. "Thanks, son."

10
Greysen's Family Secrets

A T FIRST, GREYSEN'S DREAMS guided him peacefully to the next day, the dawn brilliant because it promised they'd soon be out of the awful desert. While snuggled into Novane, stirring to waking, letting the light slowly filter into his consciousness, he didn't hear the lich's heartbeat. Not even with his head closely pressed to Novane's chest.

He wouldn't either, not in a million years.

Novane was undead. Which again, was strange to him. Not in an unexpected way, because Greysen knew who Novane was. But strange in that the only person to show him true affection and not want something in return was a dead hearted monster.

A lich.

As he stirred, Novane still holding him tightly, more memory dreams punctuated his thoughts, dragging him under. Pulling at him. Begging their story to be told. These dreams weren't so peaceful, even though they'd started out as such.

Within them, he remembered more about his two brothers and three sisters and how they'd raised him. He was the youngest by far; his closest sibling, Brianna, was some ten summers older than him. Greysen was adored by them all, Tomas and Sara—the eldest—most of all.

Some would say Greysen was spoiled. Precious. A gift to the family. But he wasn't a brat because of the attention. He adored his brothers and sisters and the life they all had in that small, dusty house. Carefree and loving.

But...

As his memories came more and more to the fore, invading his dreams like knives held by murderers' hands, stabbing, stabbing, stabbing, he suddenly recalled how one of his sisters, Lily—the middle sister—was heavy with child.

He stirred but couldn't wake.

Greysen was shown when the ghouls came. When they cut the baby from Lily, mother and child screaming, blood everywhere. Everywhere. She gasped her final breath while Darrin, Greysen's other brother, tried to protect her and the baby, his pitchfork a helpless defense against the undead hoards. He was easily subdued, his throat slashed; the spatter of his blood, red ribbons of it, added to all the others.

So much blood everywhere.

Greysen remembered the unborn child was a girl. What shocked him was that the baby's body was twisted and deformed. Bright red skin, sore with welts, visible even underneath all the blood.

Another horror struck Greysen.

The baby was Lily and Darrin's, disfigured by their incestuous relationship. At that, he shuddered. He tried to pull away, but the dreams wouldn't let go of its grip upon him.

There was more to tell.

So much more.

Novane comforted him further but didn't rouse him to waking. Greysen's dream, now horrific, continued as he struggled between wanting to wake but at the same time wanting to keep dreaming for the secrets it would reveal.

And it revealed many more horrible truths.

He didn't think he liked his brothers and sisters any longer now that Myrkul's influence was dissipating from his unconsciousness and consciousness alike. Now he was no longer under the demon's spell of forgetfulness. Now Greysen knew another truth.

As more images swirled, new and even more terrifying, Greysen began to understand why he was so precious to the family. To Tomas and Sara most of all. He didn't recall anyone ever visiting the house. No one stayed. It was only his brothers and sisters. Always. Right up until he was taken by Myrkul's ghouls, eighteen summers old, not once did he see any of his siblings with any others other than themselves.

But some nights, there were noises from the bedrooms. Noises Greysen began to understand the meaning of as he came to maturity. Sounds of passion. The groans and moans as his brothers fucked his sisters.

Greysen squirmed away from what the dreams revealed, but still couldn't wake. Again, he was dragged into the memories, a new demon to curse him.

His brothers, big and strong and handsome, worked in the fields, their farm plentiful; his sisters, sweet and pretty and clever, did everything else, including helping their brothers when harvest came. They worked hard together. Played even harder together as well, it seemed.

Greysen was taken back in time to the night, well past evenfall and months before the ghouls came, when Brianna came into Greysen's snug, a small space dividing from the main room of the house where he slept. Standing over him, she showed herself to him. Her ripened sex. Greysen had recoiled. Rejected her. With hurt in her eyes, she left him, crying.

The others wanted to know what had happened. Greysen couldn't tell them, he was too distraught. He didn't like girls, and in *that* way, he liked his sisters even less. And even though he knew he was attracted to boys, the same went for his brothers. He didn't want them any more than he wanted his sisters.

Being with any of them was wrong.

With a start, sweat drenched, Novane holding him firmly and soothing him, Greysen went further back in time. Back to when it all began, his furthest memory. When the evil first germinated. Because living in a small house, far away from prying eyes, with so many, wasn't easy.

He recalled how he had to wash himself with Tomas and Darrin, as there was only one bath per day for the men of the house; otherwise, the water tank would drain too quickly before the next rains came. At first, all was well. Until Greysen got older and he grew hair in the places he didn't have hair before, around fourteen summers in age.

In that bathroom, door closed and locked, Tomas and Darrin began touching each other in front of him. They kissed as their cocks hardened, and their laughter grew just as virile. Their ejaculate, thick globules, spurted from them to swirl down the drain when the plug was pulled. Greysen began to cry himself to sleep most nights as a new fear came over him. The fear of what his brothers and sisters would do to him.

Tomas had called what he did with Darrin and Sara, Lily and Brianna, too, his 'deserved relief' from the day's toil. "Can't be all work, 'round here, can it, brother? Besides, we all love each other. What's the problem?" He liked to relieve himself often with all of them. Sara and Darrin most of all.

"But it's not right," Greysen complained when he'd plucked up enough courage to do so after Brianna showed herself to him again in the night.

"She only wants to love you as you deserve to be loved," Darrin said to dismiss Greysen's justified concerns and comfort him.

He wasn't comforted.

"I don't like girls," Greysen protested in reply, the only thing he could think of, even if the truth. A truth that wouldn't save him.

"Then I'll love you instead of her," Darrin offered, his perversion reflected in his eyes as he ran his hand under Greysen's pajamas, down to his groin, and to fondle him.

Greysen was paralyzed with fear.

When he could, when Darrin finally left him alone in his snug, he ran from the house and vomited into the hay beside the goats' pen. Yes, Brianna stopped showing herself. But in her place, Darrin began to take more of an interest in Greysen.

Now at night, his brother came into Greysen's snug, his arousal clear. He touched Greysen ever more inappropriately. Even more frequently too. Greysen hated himself, wanted to escape, especially after he had to wipe the stink of his brother's seed from off himself most nights.

Even when the others were around, laughing and singing, Darrin still touched him. Especially on his buttocks whenever he passed him by or served him his dinner. Greysen's role in the house was to cook for his perverse and evil family. He wanted to poison them all.

He didn't know how.

That's when he taught himself to read so he could learn the herbs needed to kill. He also learned of gods and demons, and how one in particular, Myrkul, demon god of the undead, of bones, of death, and the reaper himself, could give him some hope by killing quicker than any poison. If only he could figure out how he could summon such a savior.

Over the next year, Greysen became scared out of his mind. He cried himself to sleep more often than not, his tears his only comfort. His studies went nowhere. He wanted to kill himself but was too much of a coward to do so.

At fifteen summers, he desired nothing but the escape of death, to feel its cold, dark clutches envelope him with its eternity.

Darrin got bolder.

Even so, sometimes, and despite the guilt, Greysen even wanted his brother's attention, hating himself even more after they'd both gotten to their own relief.

But before the terrible memories - previously hidden from him but now starkly, horrifically, revealed - could let Greysen linger, he was propelled forwards in time. Taken to three years into the future. To a summer, bright and clear, birds chirping, harvested barley swirling in patterns from a warm breeze, dogs barking in the distance, when the biggest market day of the year arrived. Greysen had recently come of age; his present from his brothers and sisters was a day off from his chores.

There was no day off from Darrin.

Alone in the house, reading, thinking of how he could summon Myrkul to rid him of the nightmare he lived every day, Darrin came to him with lust in his wicked smile. But that time he had a different look about him. Deeper. More vicious.

With a wanting leer, he said, "Lily's heavy with the child I put in her, so she's not giving me any relief these days." The ominous warning in his voice was clear. "And I need more from you because of it."

Without giving Greysen a chance to respond, Darrin yanked him to his feet to come behind him, pressing him against the cupboards with rough hands. He pulled down Greysen's working pants as well as his own. Greysen, with a body-shaking gasp winding him, tears flowing, felt the painful all-consuming agony as Darrin pushed into him, hurting Greysen beyond belief.

In that horrendous moment, as he tried to disassociate himself from his own mind, disconnect to cope, eyes wet with tears, lips quivering, body in pain, so much pain, Greysen prayed to Myrkul.

He prayed, and he prayed.

Please, I beg of you, my lord, demon god of the undead, of bones, of death, and the reaper himself, save me from this living horror. Smite my family so I can be free of them. Please. Please, I beg of you. Take me too if you must. But please take them first so I can see them die in the knowledge their depravity and their singing and laughter has been silenced. Please, I beg of you. Kill them. Kill me.

That day, his prayers were finally answered. *Soon, I will do as you ask,* the baritone voice of the demon rumbled in his mind, rattling his skull to make him giddy while he was being raped by Darrin.

You will kill me as well? Greysen asked, pleadingly.

No.

Then what is for me after this horror?

Patience, my A Rúnsearc. Myrkul's voice slithered through him delightfully, making him shudder. His pain subsided. His prayers had been answered. Greysen was relieved beyond measure, even though he didn't understand what an A Rúnsearc was. What did it mean?

Myrkul continued, *My servants will come for you soon; they will slaughter any in the house but you. They will then bring you before me. From that moment, you will be mine as soon as I wipe away the memories you have of those who brought you up. Then, and only then, can your body, mind, and soul be given willingly to me without doubt. You will be my husband, my beloved, and my yearning, but you will also be the sheath of my cock. If you please me, I will give you immortality. If not, you will never have existed. Those are my conditions. Do you accept them?*

Without thought, "I accept," was whispered out loud as Darrin came to his relief.

Over the next few weeks, Greysen became more nervous with each passing day because of what was promised by Myrkul. Unfortunately, Darrin took Greysen whenever he could. Sometimes many times in one day. At night too. Sometimes, when his brother grunted behind him, he could hear the others clapping, singing, and laughing as if what was happening to him was normal to them. Which it was, he supposed, with a crawling dread in realization.

Greysen was sick to his soul. He couldn't rid his body of Darrin's filthy stain, his stench, no matter how many times he washed himself or induced himself to vomit, fingers jammed down his throat. How much of his stomach contents he splattered onto the straw of the goats' pen, bile and blood as well, he could never quantify.

Greysen hated them all.

He hated Darrin even more than himself.

But he had hope now.

"Thanks for the relief," Darrin always said, emulating Tomas, once he was spent inside Greysen. "You'll give it to me any time I want it, won't you, brother?"

Greysen couldn't speak, could only nod dumbly.

In that house, he lived in absolute fear.

What a nightmare he'd grown up in. He didn't remember all of it, even being away from Myrkul's influence now. Couldn't. Didn't want to, either. But just when he thought his dream couldn't get any worse, there was one last thing it had to tell him.

One last secret to reveal.

One more truth.

After the ghouls came, Myrkul erased Greysen's memories and clouded his mind as promised. He then become a slave to the demon's desires. There was no other word for it.

During the three years he'd spent in the demon's clutches, believing the pillows of his chamber were his sanctuary, Greysen was told many things. Many lies to ensure his servitude remained.

The biggest of them was how Abbot Hosho—the man he was led to believe was his father—sent him away a few years after his birth. Only two summers old. The monk gave Greysen to Tomas and Sara. He remembered being carried to the farmhouse and how Darrin and his sisters greeted him. Remembered the songs, music, and laughter too.

But those things were the veneer.

Scratch the surface and evil lurked.

Unspeakable evil.

For he now knew without a shred of doubt, Tomas and Sara journeyed to the monastery of the Whispering Monks to seek sanctuary and give birth before she showed too heavily. The monastery would have accepted them without question. Forgiven them their sins, as evil as they were, because that's what they did, those Whispering monks.

After a couple of years, Tomas and Sara returned to the farm with Greysen. No one outside the family was any the wiser as to who he really was; any story could have been made up. And it was. The story told as truth was that Greysen belonged to Abbot Hosho, and Tomas and Sara were to bring him up as a favor to the monastery.

As Myrkul told it, anyway.

Did Abbot Hosho know the lies spoken in his name by such a foul demon?

From the dreams, Greysen guessed how evil they all were. He also knew Darrin and Lily were about to travel to the monastery to give birth to their child. Again, a story would be made up about the child's appearance a few years later if she were to appear at all. Greysen doubted it from what he saw. She wouldn't have lived. Too deformed. The poor soul. The ghouls who sliced her prematurely from Lily's guts did her a favor.

But from all of what was revealed, one question remained: why wasn't Greysen deformed if he'd been the product of such evil? A creation of incest. For he knew with startling clarity, without doubt, that Tomas and Sara were his true parents despite what was covered up after they were butchered.

At that, Greysen woke up with a start, the dream finally letting him go, realizing its strangle hold. A cold sweat poured off him.

To Novane, trembling and sweating, he said, "You knew, didn't you?"

"I don't know what you're talking about," Novane said, untangling his arms from around Greysen.

They looked into each other's eyes, and Greysen saw truth there. The many truths Novane had spoken of earlier. "You knew what happened to me on that farm before I unwittingly summoned Myrkul to rescue me from the horror of it all, didn't you?"

Novane, without looking away, confirmed Greysen's words. "I did, yes."

"Does Abbot Hosho know?" Greysen seethed, anger flashing in his vision, Novane's face a blotchy mess of red and white patches before him. "I mean, there was that whole made up story of the monk being my father and Wymond being my brother, wasn't there?"

Novane didn't reply; he didn't have to.

"Why?" was all Greysen could ask without waiting.

"Because there's a greater power than even Myrkul at work here."

"What are you talking about?"

"Do you want hear the final truths?" Novane grabbed Greysen's hands; he accepted the touch, needing support right now. And the lich had been the only one who'd ever given it to him in all his terrible life, one only twenty-two summers old.

Greysen swallowed. "I do."

"Myrkul sent his ghouls to bring you to him, make you his, not *because* he heard your prayers, but because once he heard you, he realized who you were."

"And...and who am I?"

"Wymond *is* your true brother. Abbot Hosho and the universe herself are your *true* parents. You were born of magic, Greysen. Magic so profound, three came from the womb of heaven. Not one. Not two. But three." Novane paused, obviously to let his words sink in, before he continued, "Tomas and Sara's child, a boy, didn't live. He died in the womb, deformed beyond imagining. The sickening result of their sick relationship."

Greysen felt numb to his bones. "What are you saying?"

"I'm saying that from the three boys Abbot Hosho and the universe created from their magic, one was forgotten, never to be spoken of again until the time was right. Not even by Abbot Hosho, for he was hidden for his own protection. Justly so too. The other boy, Wymond, was chosen to remain in the monastery for whatever reason. And you…you, Greysen, were given to Tomas and Sara to be looked after."

Terror struck Greysen. "Abbot Hosho sent me to the wolves."

"But don't you see? Cruel as it was in hindsight, from the hell you lived through, a power far greater than what anyone has ever known has been forged. You will be a magician. The most powerful magician to have ever lived because of your suffering at the hands of your adopted family and Myrkul. The terrible emotions of your life's experiences have meant that you'll have an infinite pool of magic to draw from."

Greysen gasped. "My emotions made me powerful?"

Novane nodded. "Greysen, it is *you* Myrkul fears. That is why the demon answered your prayers. For he knew that one day, you'd smite him. Destroy him beyond imagining, as Abbot Hosho had foreseen it. What better way for Myrkul to watch you than to have you as his? But in the end, he was too scared of you. You had to go. You had to be killed. Myrkul couldn't do it…"

"Was that why he sent the Anubian to kill me? Because I will soon awaken?"

"Yes. The irony is that it was Myrkul himself who gave you the spark to ignite your innate powers."

"You mean the magic gifted to me will be the catalyst?"

"It has already begun," Novane stated seriously. "Look at how you reacted with just one spell cast. Once you get used to what you have inside you, once you understand the storm of your being, you will be unstoppable. And I am in awe of you."

Greysen's eyes widened as a realization struck him. He felt the rage subside to be quickly replaced by a different emotion. One that overwhelmed him to make him giddy. "If I am to be the deliverer of Myrkul's end, as foreseen, that's what I shall do. And it won't stop there. I will destroy Abbot Hosho as well for giving me to Tomas and Sara."

"Don't be too quick to condemn your father," Novane warned.

"Why not? I've been a pawn all my life because of his decision. I was abused and used beyond what anyone could endure because of him. Now it's time for me to get to the other side of the chess board and become a king. A king of destruction. And when I do, the world will turn red with my rage because of what's been done to me."

"There is one more truth left before you decide to destroy everything."

"What's that?" Greysen snapped impatiently.

"The third boy born from the womb of heaven, your eldest brother, is Oswin."

Greysen was taken aback. "What?"

"Abbot Hosho plays the long game of immortals, not those of mortals."

Novane kissed Greysen's forehead; he liked the touch. Gentle. Considerate. In response, he placed his arms around the lich more tightly. Feeling Novane's comfort radiate from him, one given without the expectation of something from him in return.

His mind cleared.

"But Oswin's dead. Isn't he? We saw him being killed by the thousand cuts. Didn't we?" Greysen wasn't so sure of anything any longer. His whole life, the lie as it was, had been turned upside down.

"I don't think Oswin's story is told yet, do you?" Novane gestured to himself. "And death isn't the end. Sometimes far from it. Last night, the Seeing Crystal revealed to me who he really was. Your brother. One of the three born from heaven. I saw him speaking with Abbot Hosho. They revealed the final truths."

"Then we've got to get to Oswin as soon as possible."

"We do—and we'll begin by meeting up with Lord Hereward in Invrawold. He will be there within the week's end."

"How long until we get there?"

"If we move quickly, we will arrive at the same time, give a day or two."

Greysen steeled his resolve when he stood, but he didn't let go of Novane's hand. He had become used to their hold. A hold that wouldn't lead to anything else if he didn't want it to. Perfect as far as he was concerned. Greysen would never be taken advantage of again. Not by anyone. Ever.

The horizon beyond the dunes beckoned.

With a pace far quicker than they accomplished through the shifting sands, lions no longer heard roaring for mates or the promise of prey, Greysen and Novane came onto green fields and bent windswept trees. They'd arrived in Invrawold. Only the great river to cross was left to them.

After not speaking for a while, the dreams he had still vivid, Greysen finally said, "Even though Myrkul clouded my mind to make me submissive to his will, he told many lies sprinkled with the truth."

Novane said, "And that's why Myrkul is dangerous; he knows there is nothing is more enslaving than lies weaved and turned from facts."

"Or liberating."

Novane nodded, offering his free hand to Greysen once more. Greysen accepted; he had come to appreciate the lich's hold. He even managed a smile, the expression strange but oddly comforting at the same time.

Soon, a stone bridge, well-built and wide enough for an army to march over without worrying their horses as they traveled side by side, loomed. The sprawling city, smog shrouded, dirty, busy with thousands upon thousands of folks going about their lives, lay beyond.

As the sight of people became common, Novane surprised Greysen. He held his hand more often. For no reason other than because he could. Greysen was impressed. And accepting.

At the city's main entrance, they came to an iron gateway, the structure reaching out with Gothic fingers of metal but also comfortable within a massive wall, like the stone was holding it in a lover's embrace. Greysen imagined it would take ten men to pull the chains to lift the portcullis of the gateway alone. He'd never seen such a thing; Myrkul didn't bother with heavy defenses for the Dread Keep. Demons were their own deterrent.

Two city guards came forwards to greet them; they were two disinterested souls, seemingly desperate for pay day so on their night off they could drink themselves stupid and piss away the evidence before they had to work again, beginning the whole cycle over.

Novane had their measure as well. "Night off soon, gentlemen?"

"Ai, too bloody right, an' all," the first guard said. He had greasy hair hanging in curtains underneath his steel helmet, a bulbous pock-marked nose, and beady eyes that didn't fit right on his face.

"Can't wait," the second guard chimed in. He was more handsome but not by much. He was thinner too. "Can we, Frenk?"

"Oh, no, Slen, we can'nee wait."

"Then have one for me," Novane said, coming closer to pat the ugly nosed guard named Frenk upon his shoulder.

Greysen could see the blood drain from both Frenk and Slen's faces as they must have realized who they were speaking to. Even though Novane looked more a man because of his own magic—the magic created because of his feelings for Greysen—he was still a lich. Still undead.

And there's nothing to disguise an undead from the living. Undead have a certain…foreboding presence about them. A presence which makes the living, even grown men too tough for their own good like city guards, quell in their own shadows and wish for their mother's protection.

"You…you m-may pass," Slen stuttered, gulping.

Novane walked away, disappearing into the darkness beyond the ominous iron monstrosity passing as a gate. Greysen imagined when the portcullis was down once evenfall fell, the people within would feel secure. He doubted it would do anything but provide an amusing obstacle from Myrkul's forces marching north towards them, but for now, those in the city believed they were safe.

They weren't. He almost felt sorry for them.

Greysen followed Novane, offering a knowing smile to Frenk and Slen as he passed. If he'd worn a hat, he would have tipped it. His smile would have to suffice for letting them pass without questions.

As he passed, Greysen could smell one of the guards had shat his pants. Novane certainly had an effect on people. He affected Greysen too, in a way Greysen couldn't quantify. Not yet. But unlike the guards, Novane's effects on him were pleasant.

The world inside the city was a completely different one to the outside of it. Greysen hadn't been in a large city before, only ever knowing a stuffy monastery, a rustic farmhouse, and two rooms within a demon's keep, one of them filled with the pillows representing his sexual slavery. And he didn't want to think about any of them. He wanted to take in what was around him at this moment. Amaze in it. Relish it.

Greysen had to admit, for the first time in his life he felt alive. And, amazingly, staggeringly, it took a lich, a lord of the undead, for him to experience such a thing. To enjoy what he saw now.

Greysen became overwhelmed by the realization.

He became even more overwhelmed, giddy even, by what was around him. Surrounding him, thousands upon thousands of people from all walks of life, bumped and jostled. The city was packed to the walls with activity of all and any descriptions.

Novane and Greysen walked straight into a huge market square bordered by the dark-bricked, gothic-inspired towering buildings.

People shouted from windows. Washing hung like the dead upon thin ropes stretched between balconies. Flags and pennants flapped. Greasy smoke swirled. Birds, pigeons mostly, flew in massive flocks to quickly settle on dark tiled rooftops only to take flight again from some unseen threat. Cats, no doubt. When he studied the buildings further, he saw a couple of the felines—feral or domestic, Greysen couldn't tell— slinking over crenelations, chimneys, and rooftop ridges with equal ease.

At street level, the sights and sounds, smells too, were both exotic and alluring, and assaulted his senses. Greysen didn't know where to look. People wore colors. Vibrant colors. Many shouted their wares at others who were shouting and gesticulating back. Everyone shouted.

Music played from a million instruments plucked, blown, and beaten by just as many street buskers peppered throughout the seething crowds around the stalls. The din was unbelievable, maddening, but astonishing at the same time. Greysen watched everything unfolding before him with his mouth open. He closed it. The taste of so many people so close—their sweat, perfume, hopes, and fears—was stuck on his tongue, bitter and sweet all at the same time.

Again, he was overwhelmed.

There were many races of people within the city, from humans to delphin to some Greysen didn't know. He did spy a high-born liosalfar within the heaving turbulence; they were a race not of one realm but many, their bodies a shifting kaleidoscopic curtain, both mesmerizing and beautiful. They couldn't be touched unless they wished it. A formidable enemy or valuable foe, Myrkul had once told him.

This liosalfar had guards. Monks. The monks, four of them, wore the same garments Monk Wu had. The same order, no doubt.

Greysen moved to Novane's side after weaving through many people. Again, and to his increasing delight, Novane slipped his hand into Greysen's. He felt a warmth of comfort, now achingly familiar, wash through him. He could get used to this.

"You keep holding my hand," Greysen said, well above his normal voice to break through the cacophony and closeness of the market square.

"Do you not like me doing so?" Novane asked immediately but didn't seem concerned.

"I'm not sure," Greysen lied. "Perhaps I like it. Perhaps I hate it."

"Then I will not do so until you decide."

Novane was about to pull his hand away, when Greysen increased his grip to prevent it. "Even if I do hate it, it gives me…comfort. As do your kisses. I don't think I want you to stop holding my hand or giving me your attention." And that was the truth.

"Very well." Novane smiled. "Did you notice the liosalfar over there with his friends?"

"I did."

"And did you also notice Lord Hereward?" Novane gestured with his pole axe to the right of where the liosalfar and their monk bodyguards stood. "He's over there by the fountain with the boy and the satyr."

Greysen was about to reply in affirmation when a market stall owner, a middle-aged woman with wild red hair and dressed like a jongleur, garish and flamboyant, shoved a plate of something steaming hot under his chin. It smelt pungent and spicy.

"Wanna try some, lovely?" she said, a friendly crooked smile accompanying her offer. "The first taste's free; any further bite is offered at a good price, guaranteed."

"What is it?" Greysen's stomach rumbled; he realized he was hungry. "It looks like some sort of meat."

On further study, the meat was sliced from some sort of large sausage, yet from no sausage Greysen had seen before. It wasn't made by any hand. It had a structure to it, three compartments. A part of an animal perhaps. Some sort of offal from the pale color of the flesh, the grainy texture, and the silvered skin sheathing it all.

"It *is* meat," she replied, still smiling. "A delicacy—the penis of a serpopard, it is. Right big bugger he was too. Took ten strong men to kill the creature for market. I marinated the meat myself. Only a copper for the plateful for you today, lovely."

Greysen didn't feel hungry anymore.

Novane's attention was drawn to the stall holder. The woman paled under his stare, obviously realizing what he was. She realized who he was as well, seeing as Novane was still holding Greysen's hand and her gaze slid down towards their connection. But she didn't seem frightened. She'd probably seen it all in the Great Market square.

Greysen said, "I don't think I'd like...eating dead cock, no matter how tasty you've prepared it with your fancy marinates and garnish."

The woman snorted a bitter laugh, her attitude changing dramatically to one of scorn and judgment. "Don't mind undead dick though, do you?" She pulled the plate away; her attention was soon on another customer who'd rudely nudged their way in front of Greysen.

Greysen was stunned. He slipped his hand out of Novane's, feeling embarrassed. Dirty. Ashamed. He didn't want people to get the impression Novane was his lover. He wasn't. Holding the lich's hand wasn't because of their relationship but the comfort Greysen needed after what he'd suffered. Why didn't people get that? Why did they have to judge so quickly? Why couldn't two men hold hands in friendship? Why did other meanings need to be read into the gesture?

Greysen said numbly, "I've decided I hate holding your hand. And I don't think you should kiss me anymore, either."

Novane didn't look happy; Greysen wasn't either.

"Very well," Novane said sadly. "But we must get to Lord Hereward before we lose him in this crowd."

11

Hereward's Lost Friend

THE WOODEN DOCKS OF the city of Invrawold, jutting structures supported by great stone pillars rooted deep into the riverbank, emerged from the mists Garthana created with her magic. Magic that hid her. Hid them.

Hereward could hear men shouting, confused and questioning. Dock guards wondering why the fucking weather had changed all of a sudden. He was amused by that.

When they disembarked from Garthana's shelled back, thanking her for the journey, one of the guards, a sickly-looking fellow made from pimples and grease, with a hooked nose and thick lips, emerged from the dissipating mists as Garthana swum away unnoticed.

Hereward almost barked a laugh at the poor man's face. The guard looked ridiculous in his armor too big for him. What's more, the helmet he was forced to wear—being in the regiment that guarded the docks—reminded Hereward of a cock's knob.

The guard, stunned, said, "Where'd the heck did you lot come from?" His gaze wandered over Hereward, Gik, Wallace, and Missy— no boat in sight.

Hereward simply replied, "See to my horse, won't you?" And he handed the reins to the guard. "Oh, and if anything happens to her, or if any of my equipment is stolen, I'll know who to come to, won't I?"

The guard seemed to shrink as recognition dawned. "Lord... Hereward?"

"That's me, the one and fucking only." With a sweeping gesture, he pointed out his companions. "And this here is Wallace and Gik."

Wallace and Gik nodded in turn.

The guard bowed to each. To Hereward, he said, "I'll see to it personally, Lord Hereward. Personally."

"Make sure you do. Now, what's your name and rank, guard?"

Hereward asked, thinking it would be best to know who he was entrusting Missy and all his worldly possessions to.

"Eddi, Lord Hereward." Eddi bowed again, sweat glistening on his brow. "Name's Eddi; I'm a private of the dock watch, day shift." After another bow, he added, "Lord Hereward."

Hereward liked the guard. Didn't know fucking why, but he liked him. "She likes oats with her hay. And the occasional carrot as well. See to it, won't you, Private Eddi? And give her a good scrub down too. She likes that as well."

"Yes, Lord Hereward."

When Eddi was out of earshot, the sound of Missy's hoofs clopping on the wood of the dock fading into the distance, Gik said facetiously, "He had a bit of a dick's head look about him, didn't he?"

Hereward, still amused but with his mind turning to more important matters, said, "Not his fault he has to wear that fucking phallic helmet. Poor boy."

Wallace wore his Wallace frown. "I's thought Eddie were nice."

"He is nice, Wallace." Hereward patted his son on his shoulder; Wallace's frown softened. "Gik was just trying to be funny, but he fucking failed miserably."

Gik pouted. "You were thinking the same, Lord Hereward. Don't deny it."

"Thinking something and saying something are two different things. One can keep others from believing you're a fool; the other will leave no fucking doubt."

"Wise words, an' all, Papa."

Abbot Hosho has been a good influence on you, my love.

"I fucking thought so," he said, answering both Wallace and his sword god.

All three left the docks. Gik still pouted but followed. Hereward knew the satyr would come around soon enough. Especially after they'd found the nearest tavern with rooms to stay in; a comfortable bed, plenty of flowing ale, and foods both exotic and familiar from all corners of the Eleven Kingdoms would see to his changed disposition quicker than anything.

It didn't take long to find such a place.

Hereward knew Invrawold City well; he'd been there plenty of times over the years. He preferred the wilds. The heat. The cold. The discomfort. His balls and arse crack sweating from walking all day, and the promise of sleeping under the stars with his lover.

He hated crowds.

Although, he had to admit, he enjoyed experiencing the wonder of the city through Wallace's excitement. He took it the boy's family never visited a city, any city. Hereward smiled every time his son pointed out something of interest—which was practically everything. Wallace's questions never ended, either.

"Why's dat lady walkin' on stilts?"

"Can we's git somethin' to eat?"

"How come dat man's jugglin' rats?"

"What's dat funny lookin' food taste like? Smells good, an' all."

"Oh…Oh! Can we go n' play dat game of cups n' ball? Dat cloaked man says I'll win if I's do. Got a copper, Papa?"

Gik quickly pulled Wallace away from the rogue.

Hereward took the boy's hand to ensure he didn't wander after that, thanking Gik before addressing Wallace. "That game of cups is called gambling, Wallace. Sensible folks don't fucking gamble if they know what's good for them."

"Why's not?" the Wallace frown appeared with the question. "Looks like fun, an' all."

"Because when the debt mounts and folks can't pay, they lose their hands, or, in the worst cases, their lives." Hereward spied three burly men with big double-handed swords in their muscled grips, hiding within the shadows of an alleyway behind the rogue, watching. Waiting.

Wallace's frown turned to shock. "They kill folks all 'cause o' a game?"

"Yes," Hereward said sharply to leave no doubt as to his meaning.

Wallace didn't ask any more questions, even though his eyes remained wide with wonder, mouth agape.

Soon, they approached the tavern Hereward was looking for, a place with a hanging, squeaking sign that read *Down the Goblin's Throat.* The establishment was one of his favorites in the whole of Invrawold City. A dive of a place with sticky floors and mushrooms sprouting from the heavy overhead beams and peeling wallpaper alike, but it served good ale, hearty home cooked food, and best of fucking all, had vermin free beds. Not like a lot of the other taverns within the dock quarter of the city.

As soon as he was beyond the threshold, the stench of stale beer, sweat, and last night's merriment splashed over the walls near the privy by those too drunk to open the door, swept over them. Hereward shouted, "Alistair, you old fucking dog! How the fuck are you?"

The tavern keep's expression brightened. He put down the pewter tankard he was cleaning, flicking the rag over his shoulder, to come around the bar and give Hereward a manly embrace of friendship, three slaps on each other's backs.

"Can't complain," Alistair replied. "No one really listens, anyway."

The keep was a dark-skinned, burly man, muscles bulging like potatoes in sacks, with a shiny bald head and rosy cheeks. He was tattooed. Not as much as Hereward, but his ink was impressive. Alistair was also covered in a sheen of sweat, even though it wasn't warm.

Hereward considered him a good friend. Better than most. Alistair had helped get him out of many scraps before he bought the tavern and settled down; he had a damn fucking good sword arm. Pity he only used it to pour ale now.

Alistair asked, "Staying the night...or many?"

"Don't know yet," Hereward admitted. "Got any spare rooms and some grub? I'm tired, thirsty, and hungry, and you know what I fucking get like when that happens."

"I do." Alistair glanced at Hereward's companions. "How many rooms are you after?"

"Two." Hereward gestured to Gik. "One for my good friend Gik here," then to Wallace by his side, "and one for me and Wallace." Alistair looked shocked all of a sudden; Hereward demanded, "What?"

"I don't mean to be disrespectful, Herry, but...but I don't want any undue attention here. The city's monks, a recent order who've gained the king's privileges, mind you, have become more...how shall we say? *Aggressive* in their ways lately to us normal folks." He leant in closer, eyes shifting as if he were looking for anyone listening. "There are even stories of folks disappearing only to turn up dead much later on with their skin, nipples, and genitals sliced off 'em. Terrible business it is. Terrible."

"Alistair," Hereward's confusion turned to annoyance. "I've got no fucking idea what you're talking about. I simply want a room for my friend Gik, and a room for me and my son, Wallace. My room with two beds, if you've got them."

"Oh." A great weight seemed to lift from Alistair's expression. "Thank the old gods." He motioned the cross over his chest. Since when had Alistair become fucking religious? "For a moment there..."

Then Hereward got it.

"Hang on. You thought Wallace here, a boy of only ten summers old, was my latest fucking lover? What the fuck, Alistair!" Hereward felt his insides turn in disgust. But once he considered it all further, he couldn't really blame his friend. He remembered—due to Alistair's familiarity and friendship—that he hadn't introduced Wallace as *his* son, just someone he wanted a room with. He most certainly wouldn't make that fucking mistake again. No way.

Gik gasped. Wallace's famous frown returned, but he didn't say anything.

Alistair apologized, "Rather ashamedly, I now admit, I did. Sorry." He then quivered a wonky smile in relief, softening his expression as his concerns obviously left him for good. He wiped his sweat drenched brow with the cleaning rag.

Hereward made a mental note not to drink from any newly cleaned tankards. But he was relieved he understood Alistair's mix up, even if he didn't appreciate the insinuation just because he didn't state the fucking obvious.

He shouldn't have to.

What had this city become since the last time he was here? Were these new monks responsible for Alistair's caution, as unjustified as it was in this case?

Hereward, as clearly as he could, and to leave no fucking doubt whatsoever, explained, "I fuck men, Alistair. Not boys. Just for future reference, even though you should have known that. Being gay doesn't mean I'm a fucking disgusting, perverted cunt, does it?" He felt heat rise up his neck and had to calm himself.

Easy, my love.

"Once more I apologize, Herry. The rooms are on the house, of course. So will tonight's meal be. A shepherd's pie fresh from the oven. Baked it only an hour ago."

"Not made from cat meat is it?" Hereward, mollified, suddenly laughed.

"Most certainly not." Alistair feigned offense, grabbing at his chest in emphasis. He also laughed. "Only the finest cuts of beef in my pies."

"I heard one vendor out there selling fucking serpopard cocks. Fuck me. What's going on in this city since I was last here?"

They laughed together with more back slapping. The tension had dissipated between them. Thank fuck.

"No cocks in my pies either—not unless you stick your own in it."

"Been there, done that." Hereward held his sides now, he was laughing so hard. Wallace and Gik joined in.

Alistair wiped his eyes of his laughter. "I remember when you were courting Ayrdon, and he bet you to do it. Remember? Oh, those were the days. What fun. What fun."

"I won the bet, didn't I?"

Hereward became saddened hearing his husband's name. Thankfully, he had Dorgan for a lover now. Had Wallace for a son too. Otherwise, he'd have gone mad, lost in the mires of his sorrow like some disconnected ghoul destined to walk alone for eternity.

We both miss Ayrdon, my love.

"You did," Alistair confirmed, knocking Hereward from his thoughts.

"But no, I'll pay for our stay." Hereward looked around; the place was in need of upkeep. The tables and chairs looked as though they'd been dredged from the river's delta. They were so old and worn. How many arses had sat on them and got drunk since they were new? How many times had the walls been spewed or pissed on? Far too many. "By the old gods, you need the coin. Two silvers a night still? And a copper for the food and an ale?"

"Aye."

Wallace, poking out his tongue in disgust, eyes squinting, said, "I'm glad we's ain't gonna eat any pie had willy's innit. Dat's gross."

Hereward felt his cheeks warm under his beard. He wasn't sure Wallace should learn about his past adventures, especially the ones where he got stonking drunk and did a lot of silly things with his pants down, flashing his bare arse and doing worse with his cock. Those were stories for later. Much later.

But the laughter returned, Hereward joining in along with Wallace.

"You won't, I can assure you." But Alistair bowed to the boy, offering his hand; Wallace accepted, now smiling. "And I'm pleased to meet you, son of Hereward, Lord of the Realm of Suvanwold, protector of the innocent, and upholder of the law of King Hurald."

Hereward interjected, "And 'holder of the Speaking Sword' as well."

Alistair's brows rose to crinkle his baldness in furrows. "Since when?"

"Long fucking story, but I'll only tell it once I've aired my balls, bathed, removed my armor, and got a few ales in me. We all need fucking freshening up, Gik most of all. He stinks like something's crawled up into his arse, died, and gone rotten."

"I do not stink!" Gik said. He sniffed himself, then dry retched while waving his hand to fan his opposite armpit. "All right...perhaps I do."

More laughter ensued.

Alistair said, "I look forward to the ale stories you'll all tell. Except for you, Wallace—you'll drink goat's milk. I look forward to your milk stories."

Wallace protested, "No fair. I wanna try a beer, an' all."

"When you've got hair on your chin, son, that's when you can drink ale. Not before," Hereward said in his best fatherly voice.

Gik said, "I've had hair on my chin all my life."

Hereward snorted. "You're a fucking satyr. You were born with hair on your chin, you old goat. You're all hair, in fact."

"Been drinking since then, too!" Gik said proudly. "Came out of the womb with a thirst on my lips and a tankard in my hands, I did. I turned out all right."

Hereward countered, "You hump anything that moves, with or without your traveling pants on."

Wallace gasped. "I don't wanna turn out like dat, Papa."

"You won't, son. Promise."

The laughter continued until they were shown their rooms.

The night was disturbed many times by Wallace's nightmares. Hereward calmed and comforted him each time, reassuring his son he was there for him and that he was safe. There wasn't much else he could do. It was a long night. But Hereward didn't complain; he wouldn't, not at all. Wallace was more important to him than anything, including his sword god.

He is important to me too, my love.

Hereward replied in his thoughts, *And to Dorgan as well—and I'm going to fucking marry the man the moment he gets back from his quest.*

Good.

Morning rise was announced when dirty streaks of light dared to pierce the even dirtier window panes of their room. Hereward yawned. Even though he felt like fucking shit, he had dawn joy, uncomfortably so, for he'd dreamt of Dorgan during the few moments when he'd gotten any rest.

Wallace was curled up in his bed, hair a nest, his frown there, finally sleeping. On Hereward's suggestion during one of his worst nightmares, Garthana's gifted knife was placed under his pillow. For added protection. Wallace also clutched his mother's shawl, for that gave him protection in a different way.

Hereward let Wallace sleep.

He crept out of the room, floorboards squeaking against their joints under his weight. The door complained when he opened it. He made his way towards the privy to do something about his morning state of being. Once relieved, bathed, and feeling fresher, he went down to the tavern's main room, descending creakier stairs. Alistair was already up. Gik was too.

"Sleep well?" Alistair asked; Hereward knew the man knew he hadn't. Folks in the adjacent buildings would have heard Wallace's nightmares.

Hereward didn't grace him with a reply.

Soon all were gathered, including Wallace. They ate a meal of bread, cheese, and leftovers from the night before…or many nights before. Hereward couldn't tell how old the food was since it all tasted the same—like tough old boots. The bread alone could have been used as a bludgeoning weapon. Still, it filled a hole inside him. What else was food for?

Gik ate with gusto, wanting seconds.

Wallace was cooked a special breakfast. Fresh crispy bacon, poached eggs, spicy sausages, and fried tomatoes—the traditional fry up of the tavern, Alistair claimed. The keep was spoiling the boy, to Hereward's delight.

Once fed, they were all ready to tackle the day. He noticed Wallace wore his knife in the proper way so he could feel its vibrations of warning before needing to see the drawn blade glowing red. Hereward's hand never wondered too far from the pommel of his god, either. It didn't itch. Not yet. But fuck, they day was only young. Trouble always had a way of finding him.

Within the crowded streets in the bustling market square, Hereward noticed two men looking in their direction, taking an interest most wouldn't. Didn't take long to get his itch, did it? He put his hand to his pommel, tapping it. One of the men studying them was undead, if Hereward wasn't mistaken. But not like any undead he'd seen before; he was more a man than anything. This could be interesting. The other man had a familiarity about him. Hereward couldn't put his finger on why, which annoyed him.

The undead and the familiar man approached. Hereward stepped closer to Wallace. Gik fell in behind Hereward. He then sensed something that made him feel uneasy. What or why, he didn't know. It didn't take long for his sword hand to grab the hilt, whole arm itching.

"Who the fuck are you two?" he asked without standing on ceremony.

The lich bowed. "Lord Hereward, I am Novane, lich lord of the Hyruldon Expanse, holder of the Seeing Crystal." He bowed again, lower, then gestured to the man by his side, a man who, on closer inspection, was handsome. Dark-haired, but darker deep in his eyes, like he'd been haunted by evil and now fought it. "And this is Greysen Nightbane, husb—"

"You forget, Novane," the man introduced as Greysen interrupted. "I'm no longer a whore to the demon god of the undead, of bones, of death, and the reaper himself. I'm just Greysen Nightbane, magician of the Hyruldon Expanse, for in the desert, that is where I had my awakening and my re-birth."

Novane's mouth fell open as something Hereward couldn't quantify came over the both of them. They certainly shared something between them.

After composing himself, the lich lord tilted his head. "Then we are both from the lost lands, Lord Hereward. And we are both pleased to meet you, finally."

"We are." Greysen tore his attention away from Hereward when he slipped his hand into Novane's; the lich looked surprised until Greysen, looking him in the eyes, added, "And I realized that I was wrong. I don't hate you giving me comfort, Novane."

"You just hate me," Novane replied quickly with no malice held in his voice.

Greysen offered a tiny, knowing smile. "With all of my damaged heart."

An acceptance then fell over them like a secret shroud, one profoundly and delicately woven. Hereward didn't fully understand, but he didn't care either. If they were lovers, they were lovers. If not, if their relationship was something different, something else. So fucking what?

What Hereward cared about was one thing only. After the introductions, it was clear he'd found Abbot Hosho's son, Wymond's brother. But Greysen was now an outcast instead of the one leading the undead army of Myrkul northwards, as he was told. It seemed events had turned again. What else had changed since he'd left the monastery within the Steps to Heaven mountains with Dorgan?

To answer his question, the lich named Novane said matter-of-factly, like only an undead could, "Oswin is dead, Lord Hereward—that is why we have sought you."

Hereward was taken aback. Fuck!

It took a long time for Hereward to process the news.

In the meantime, Wallace had introduced himself, as did Gik. Hereward had failed there again. But in fairness, all he could think about was how his first true love was dead. Lost forever. He'd never see him again. Never reminisce about the old times. He became saddened to his bones by that.

"How did Oswin die?" he asked bitterly.

Novane answered, "A monk ceremoniously sliced into his skin a thousand times, then cut off parts of him to complete his agony. That's how he died."

Hereward remembered Alistair speaking of the new monks in the city earlier and what they did to folks. Folks who disappeared. Hereward seethed, but he steeled his resolve. "Then we must find these fucking monks, because they sure have a lot to answer for."

"We will join you," Greysen announced.

"Fine by me," Hereward said. "But just know, any fucking deception, even a hint of it, and I'll get my son here to kill you with far less than a thousand cuts. That's my promise."

Wallace unsheathed his sword a little; the revealed metal glowed blue. Good enough for Hereward. For now. Good enough for Wallace too, and he grinned, revealing the gaps in his teeth where his adult ones hadn't erupted as of yet.

Novane bowed to both Hereward and Wallace in turn. "We understand."

Gik tugged on Hereward's pant leg. "Do you think these men over there are the monks we should be seeking?" he asked, pointing to four men guarding a highborn liosalfar.

"They are," Novane confirmed.

Hereward, having not let go of his hilt, his whole arm both aching and itching, moved towards the liosalfar. "Then let's go have a little fucking chat, shall we?"

Tread carefully, my love, his god warned. *These monks aren't Whispering ones but fighters, bodyguards. They have their own law here.*

I'll be my usual fucking delicate self.

That's what I'm afraid of.

Hereward led the group through the crowds, jostling and barging, to get to the highborn liosalfar. The monks wore purple and red robes with golden cords around their waists. Golden crosses hung from their necks too like gaudy souvenirs purchased from a temple's gift shoppe. To Hereward, they looked ridiculous. He was always wary of ridiculous looking men; they were usually proven to the most dangerous.

And from what he'd heard already, his assumptions were correct.

He moved so his bulk protected Wallace. Gik as well—not that the satyr had strayed too far away from Hereward's shadow anyway.

The liosalfar noticed their approach before the monks, dropping whatever trinket they examined from off one of the stalls, only to shimmer into translucence as the colors of their skin melted into another realm while they still remained in this one. Hereward didn't understand why they needed bodyguards. No living soul could touch a liosalfar if the touch was not wanted.

Then he remembered Novane was with him.

The liosalfar was wise to raise their defenses. Not that slipping into another realm, even partially, would help. Powerful undead—such as lich lords—could touch any being no matter where they fled, even those passed over into death.

Hereward was already beginning to see the benefit of having an undead as a companion. A magician would come in handy as well. As such, if Novane and Greysen proved their loyalty, they would always be welcome with him.

Hereward, anger rising, asked, "Which one of you fucking monks killed my dear friend, Oswin Goodfellow?"

The four monks, startled, then did something unusual. They ran. So much for their fucking bodyguard duties, the bastards. They left the liosalfar to experience the cold, undead clutches of Novane's hands around their neck.

Novane didn't disappoint. "Tell us where the monks went, and I'll let you live, liosalfar," he said sneering, eyes intense, lips curled.

"T-there! Over t-there!" With a shaking hand, fading in and out of reality, the liosalfar pointed down a busy street overhung with buildings and smog. Their neck shimmered bruising colors under Novane's hold, the colors of the liosalfar's skin above paling, no longer swirling.

Hereward could see a monastery at the end of the street through the curtain of pollution.

Greysen said, "Let's go!"
Hereward couldn't agree more.

12
Greysen's Awakening Realized

AS SOON AS NOVANE let go of the liosalfar, the being gasped. It spluttered at being choked by an undead who could touch them, clearly shocked. The liosalfar, colors returning, then shouted harsh threats about calling the authorities.

They were ignored.

Novane still held Greysen's hand. He was mistaken earlier to believe Novane's actions of affection didn't give him any comfort. It did. In more ways than he could fathom or count. Novane made him feel like he wasn't alone against the dark storm within him, churning up his dreadful past. The memories stabbed at him, tested him, taunted him, every time he closed his eyes. More so in his dreams. And besides, they only had each other, the two citizens of the Hyruldon Expanse. That had to count for something. Didn't it?

Greysen didn't care how many saw them holding hands. Wouldn't even mind if Novane kissed him. But the exploration of their shared comfort was for another time. Another place.

Now was for finding Oswin, dead or alive or otherwise.

Greysen didn't let go of Novane's hand even as they dashed through the crowded market square after the fleeing monks and up the street. Hereward, his son, and the satyr were already ahead. All had drawn their weapons, an act which cleared a path of gawking onlookers. As a result, Greysen and Novane ran unburdened and caught up easily.

Soon, the monastery loomed, a building more lavish in its architecture than most surrounding it. Greysen pulled the scimitar from the scabbard on Novane's waist with his free hand. He felt better armed. He couldn't fight with the weapon, but any defense was better than none. Better than relying on others. Better than using his magic again too soon.

His insides roiled as they ran into the monastery's main chamber, a massive expanse with a vaulted ceiling, and thick marble columns. It resembled more a lord's residence with its grand staircase, marble, and artwork adorning every available space than anything a religious order would occupy. These monks certainly had the king's favor.

Many monks greeted them. The monks looked prepared for a fight, standing in ready poses, some comical with their gestures.

His palms went sweaty, and a cold dread washed over him.

Greysen didn't get time to take in the scenery unbecoming of a religious order. Novane let go of Greysen's hand to get his pole axe ready. Hereward had already dispensed with two monks who dared get within his sword's reach, it's metal glowing blue beneath the dripping blood. The air smelt coppery sweet and tangy already. Greysen liked it.

The lord knight dared more monks to approach. "Who else wants to feel my god's fucking justice?"

One monk answered, waving their arms in some sort of fighting moves Greysen didn't recognize. The fool. Wallace moved quickly beside his father, stabbing at the knees of the monk brave enough to answer Hereward's challenge, his sword glowing red, Greysen noted. He assumed the change in color meant something but didn't know what. Whatever it was, it seemed to give Wallace confidence, and he fought expertly at his father's side. Not as much could be said for the satyr, who cowered behind Hereward's bulk, eyes screwed shut, trembling.

Greysen didn't understand why the monks didn't arm themselves. What use were bare hands and sandaled feet against cold, hard steel? Against Hereward and Wallace's magical swords?

The monk wounded by Wallace's blade, a knife really, staggered and clutched at the gash opened in his leg, blood oozing thickly from between his fingers.

Greysen moved closer to Novane.

Hereward pivoted easily as another monk rushed forward. With his sword, he not only decapitated the one confronting him but the wounded monk as well with one fluid motion. Both their heads thudded onto the marble with wet slaps and dead, wide-eyed expressions. Their final ones. Blood sprayed from veins, their hearts not yet given the news about their host's deaths. Their bodies then fell. One by one. Blood pooled and pooled.

"If you're going to fucking come at me one at a time," Hereward boomed, smile on his lips, "you're only delaying the inevitable. Come at me. All of you. I'm fucking ready!"

Many doors crashed open.

The monks came as asked, a swarm of red and purple, flowing, jumping, punching, kicking. Hereward was soon overwhelmed as more and more monks poured from the doorways around the cathedral-like foyer of the monastery, silent but deadly with their practiced moves. The art of their fighting.

Greysen gulped. He was unprepared for the approaching plague; there were so many of them. Like one of the warnings of the apocalypse, they crashed upon them all, and Greysen began to fully understand how hands and feet could be effective after all.

In numbers, anything could be deadly.

Novane defended Greysen, thankfully dispensing with monks as easily as Hereward and Wallace had. For someone more than half Greysen's age, the boy was tenacious, howling and growling as he injured the monks for Hereward to quickly send to the halls of their gods. Wallace would be a formidable and worthy knight one day.

But Greysen couldn't think about such things. He helped Novane, taking inspiration from Wallace even though not as practiced. He slashed the scimitar wildly, hoping it would hit more than the cloth edges of the enemy's robes.

As he thrust at one monk, another slapped the scimitar out of his hand. It skittered, twirling, across the shiny marble floor to land well out of reach. To get to it, Greysen would have to expose himself, go beyond Novane's pole axe's reach. He didn't want to do that.

But he had no choice. He couldn't be left without any defense, like the satyr. The poor creature was quickly overwhelmed, screaming for Hereward to save him. Hereward and Wallace were too busy. Again, blood flowed onto the marble. Not the blood of the enemy, though.

Greysen charged.

He had to help.

Three monks confronted him. He hadn't a chance. One kicked him in his stomach, folding him over, his breath taken from him. He clutched himself in agony. Novane screamed. Greysen couldn't get the precious air back into his lungs quick enough. He gasped and gasped again. The air still wouldn't come. He received more kicks. More punches.

Pain shot through him.

But as he fell to his knees, head down and holding himself, he realized pain was his old friend. His dark companion. And from within him, the ghosts of his past, specters with teeth and claws ripping at his insides, rose up to stain his every thought with their familiarity and friendship, their agony.

Their release inevitable.

Images of Myrkul flooded Greysen's thoughts. How, with great anguish, debasing himself unknowingly, he sheathed the demon's cock with his body willingly, blindly. Pain. So much pain. Greysen gasped again. The images were then replaced with those of his brother, Darrin, grunting behind him, pulling at his hips to get his hardness in more deeply. Pain surged once more. Hatred too.

Then, the hate changed.

What it turned into frightened Greysen beyond measure. He shuddered, let out a cry, and the monks stepped away from him, sensing something had changed. The air around Greysen vibrated like a rock had been thrown into a stilled pond. All too late for them. All too late.

Greysen seethed with his evil-born magic, now realized and revealed, his body glowing with blackfire, cold like ice and hot like fire, welcome and hated. Exactly how he felt about himself.

He righted himself and calmly, coldly, spat, "No pain you can serve to me can be any worse than what I've already suffered."

Greysen closed his eyes.

His power surged.

Then, a flash of white pierced his eyelids to make the darkness scintillate underneath his eyelids. He reveled in it. Breathed it in. Loved it.

There was no screaming.

Only silence and the fetid stink of blood coagulated by his magic followed.

When he opened his eyes, every monk lay upon the marbled floor, a mess of innards, viscera, blood, and gore. Shit and piss, too. Their brains, the white jelly meat of them, was splattered in thick, oozing chunks around their broken bodies. Greysen smiled evilly.

"You won't ever touch me again," he said to the dead monks. "Or my friends." He grabbed Novane's hand. "Or those who mean the most to me."

Hereward stood dumbfounded, his sword hanging loosely in his grip, dripping blood to add to the carnage before him. Wallace's mouth fell agape as the boy must have realized what had happened. His sword now glowed blue. Greysen understood the magic of the weapon; it no longer issued its warning. The enemy was defeated.

Wallace then shouted, "Gik!" He ran to the satyr, limp and cold eyed within the blood—Gik's own and that of the monks slaughtered like lambs by Greysen's magic. The boy fell beside his friend, tears flowing. Hereward joined him.

Greysen knew the satyr was dead.

He then became giddy. The erection caused by his power surge pushed against him, and a different ache soon overwhelmed. Within a rapid flutter of his calming heart, he staggered and lost his balance. Thankfully, he was caught by Novane. Otherwise, he would have hit the marble hard.

Novane soothed him as he began ejaculating over and over with all-consuming shudders, moans, and gasps. He was helpless. But the deed was done.

The evil within could rest again until called for.

"Are you all right?" Novane asked, concern weaved into his husky voice.

Greysen couldn't speak; the aftereffects of his magic still held potency. He hadn't called upon the second spell Myrkul gifted him, but the result was the same even though not as violent. Perhaps casting magic, his own magic, was like anything else, and it would take time to master.

He let Novane hold him.

An age passed.

When able, no longer releasing his seed, no longer quivering, he turned to see Hereward comforting his son through his blurred vision. They knelt by the lifeless satyr; Hereward was placing coins into his friend's mouth and beginning a hero's song of lament. Wallace joined him. Greysen was glad the boy had his father. Someone to look up to. To help him as he grew.

Novane comforted Greysen, running his hand over Greysen's sweat-drenched brow tenderly before applying gentle kisses to his clammy skin. Greysen was more than glad he had Novane. Beyond anything imaginable.

"Thank you...for being here for me, Novane...without asking anything of me in return," he finally managed. The last of the magic subsided, returning to the dark embers within him.

"I will never ask anything of you that you don't wish to give," Novane replied softly.

"I couldn't...I couldn't save the satyr, though."

Novane's deeply eternal black eyes reflected Greysen's sadness. "His death was unfortunate."

Before Greysen could stand under his own strength, he saw a monk come down the stairs. The way the monk carried himself—with an arrogance Greysen had witnessed before within the Seeing Crystal—he could only be one man. Monk Wu.

With him, Oswin walked. Greysen was stunned. Oswin, Abbot Hosho's eldest and first son and Greyson's brother, was shirtless. Barefoot too. Only pants—like those in a harem would wear—hung loosely around his waist.

But that wasn't the worst of it.

Oswin's golden brown skin was marred by a thousand white scars. His nipples had been cut from him too, scars only where they once were. Oswin's body was a ruin from his neck to below his pant line; Greysen imagined he'd probably had his genitals sliced off.

How Oswin survived the thousand cuts was beyond Greysen. Novane must have felt the same, because the lich gasped—the first time Greysen had heard him do so.

Hereward said, "Fuck me drunk! Is that you, Oswin? I thought you were fucking dead." His sword, his god as he called the blade, clattered onto the marble by his feet.

Wallace, eyes wide and wearing a frown like he owned it, took his father's hand. "What's happened ta him, Papa? He's…been mut'lated."

Oswin smiled coldly. "I'm not dead, am I?"

"No, you're not dead, Oswin," Novane said. "You're not even undead. You are walking death."

Part Two

Part Two

"As Alquam moves against Myrkul," Abbot Hosho began, "two boys with terrible pasts will help determine the outcome, whichever way it falls."

"You speak of Wallace and your son, Greysen?" the Circuitor asked thoughtfully, candlelight softening the lines of his age.

"I do. But, my dear friend, no matter their formidability because of their pasts, the stage is set, and the Purge is upon us." Abbot Hosho blew out a candle, smoke curling.

"Are you going with Kieron and Vash to Gateway?"

"I am." He blew out another candle, engulfing them in darkness except the moonlight creeping through the only window. "Dorgan needs us…but I fear it's too late already."

13
Wallace's New Adventure

WALLACE'S TEARS FOR GIK hadn't dried from his cheeks before the monk and the scarred man came down the stairs. Wallace stared at 'em. He stared and stared some more. He couldn't help it. The scarred man was someone Papa knew, but even so, Wallace felt fear crawl through him like weevils in the grain. Not 'cause of him, but 'cause of the other man. The monk. The monk scared him most of all.

He looked like a bad man.

Wallace held Papa's hand; in his other, his sword changed again to glow a warning red.

The monk wore the same clothing as those the magician named Greysen had killed with his magic when there were too many of 'em for Papa to handle. He'd never seen the likes of magic like that before. Greysen was a powerful magician; no wonder he collapsed.

Wallace couldn't help but notice how much blood and stuff folks had in 'em when he looked around. The floor was covered in it all. Red everywhere. Then again, Wallace was used to blood; the stain of his family's deaths would never leave him. And he had to admit, their murder had made him more determined to be the best he could be for 'em. For their memory. For Papa and Pa too.

The scarred man—someone named Oswin—said, "I'm not dead, am I?"

"No, you're not dead, Oswin," the lich lord who loved the magician said. Wallace wasn't sure that love was reciprocated. Not how Papa and Pa loved each other, anyway. The magician and the lich had a strange bonding. "You're not even undead. You are walking death."

Wallace felt Papa stiffen within his grip.

"And not just that, lich," the monk said, all smarmy and full of self-confidence. Wallace noticed Oswin didn't blink. Didn't look beyond the weird stare he gave to nowhere. The monk continued, "Because of Oswin's failure and vanity, his decadent lifestyle before coming to his living death, he has become a wight and my servant. He's bound to me and no other."

He's bound to me.

Wallace thought those words funny, and not in a laughing ha, ha kind of way, either. Before he could think on it any further, Greysen charged forwards, shouting something Wallace didn't understand. They were words shouted with rage, though.

The monk laughed.

Greysen suddenly staggered, uneasy on his feet. He reached out, desperate, and Novane quickly grabbed him again, holding the magician like he did after he'd cast his powerful magic against the monks and had collapsed. Novane kissed Greysen's forehead. Greysen looked drained. He shuddered a lot as well, lips trembling. What was that about?

The monk standing next to Oswin didn't seem to react, "I know you are still weak after casting your magic, Greysen Nightbane. I'm quite safe from you for the moment."

Papa let go of Wallace's hand, moving to protect Wallace. "You're not fucking safe from me though, are you, monk?"

The monk smiled. "I take it you don't know what a wight is, Lord Hereward." He then gestured something Wallace didn't get. Some sort of sign language. "Show him, won't you, Oswin? Show your first love what happens when you touch them."

Oswin came down the stairs. One step, two steps, slow and deliberate, still holding his haunting gaze. He extended his hands, reaching for Papa.

Papa was about to defend himself when Greysen shouted, "Don't hurt him! He's my brother."

"I'm not going to hurt him," Papa snapped back, veins in his forehead bulging. "But what the fuck do you want me to defend myself with, magician? A bad attitude and plenty of swearing?"

"Patience," Novane offered.

"What are we fucking being patient for?" Papa replied as Oswin swiped at him, still expressionless; thankfully, and with Wallace's heart in his throat, Papa dodged the attack easily.

But how long could such a dance go on before Oswin touched Papa and something terrible happened? Wallace had heard of wights in stories. Folks don't live long after they'd seen one, so he were told.

Oswin persisted. Coming forwards, always forwards. Slowly.

Puppet like. Controlled. The monk sure was enjoying himself as he watched Papa try and avoid Oswin's touch.

Papa kept dodging, diving, stepping over bodies to get away.

Oswin was relentless. And Wallace found he had no choice but to look at his sword and think of using it to protect Papa. The blade glowed red. Red as the blood everywhere. No surprise there. But what did surprise was that the color of the ghostly flames off the blade had shifted to a greenish hue. What did that mean? Garthana didn't tell Wallace about his sword turning green.

Before Wallace could consider this new turn of events, Novane stepped between Papa and Oswin, holding him back. Delaying the wight from touching Papa. Protecting Papa. Wallace imagined Novane was doing so to give Greysen time to recover. To get his powers back so he could strike at the monk, 'cause there was no way Greysen would use his magic against his brother. What brother would?

Which made Wallace think about what had been said before. *He's bound to me.*

What did that mean exactly?

Wallace was about to come behind Papa when he noticed his hand. Or, to be more correct, how he didn't notice his hand. He gasped. His sword was held by invisible hands. He was invisible!

He gasped again.

"You can't fucking control him forever, puppet master," Papa said, not to the monk, but to Wallace. Or where Wallace was standing all invisible, anyway. Did Papa know about this ability of his sword?

"I's understand, I's do," Wallace whispered.

Papa winked and whispered back, "You make me so proud, son."

"I's love's ya, Papa."

"I love you as well. Now go do your worst—and remember what I taught you."

Wallace nodded. Not that Papa would have seen the affirmation. Felt good to do it still.

So, with Novane holding back Oswin, Greysen lying on the bloody floor, still shuddering as the effects of his magic raged through his body, and Papa safe for the moment, Wallace made his move.

Sword in hand, he crept up the stairs.

Gotta kill the puppet master, he thought, hoping no one could see his sword floating in the air with no handler. No one did. They were too preoccupied. Which was just as well. Wallace had more than a tricksy mind as determination washed over him. He had a job to do.

Wallace crept and crept. Like a mouse, he moved. A mouse after the cat who guarded the cheese. Soon, he was behind the monk. As he raised his sword above his head, two hands holding the hilt, heart thumping, Papa's words during his lessons flooded his thoughts.

"Want a man to die quickly? Don't fucking stick him in his guts. Men with gut wounds linger, sometimes for weeks. A man can still swing a sword at you even with a gut wound. Remember that."

Wallace aimed for the monk's heart, remembering more advice: *"Standing in front of a man, yes, his fucking heart's a little to the left inside his chest, but that's the right to you. But standing behind him, aim left not right."* He remembered his left from right now—didn't even need to see his painted shoe for confirmation.

While the monk was enjoying the spectacle Oswin caused, unaware of his assassin, Wallace wasted no more time. He tucked away his papa's words. Now was the time to act.

With all his might, he plunged his sword into the monk's back, right where he should, at an angle to avoid spine bones but to stick the heart good and proper.

The monk didn't even gasp. Didn't even cry out or clutch at himself. Wallace would have liked to have seen the monk's face. The expression. The mix of horror and surprise at the last moment of life would have been priceless. Just like the darrow when Papa strung them from a tree's branch for Wallace to practice his sword skills on.

Skills he used on the monk.

After a long moment—standing upright only due to the fact the rest of his body hadn't realized he was dead—the monk slumped to the floor with a bloody slosh off Wallace's sword to then tumble down the stairs. The blade no longer glowed green, but safe blue. It was done. Wallace emerged like an apparition from his invisibility, something that took Novane and Greysen by surprise.

A moment of disbelief followed by the magician and the lich.

Wallace beamed the biggest grin he could manage—the look he gave when his ma used to catch him, all guilty, with his hands in the sweetmeat treats tin she'd freshly refilled. This time, he was glad he was the one caught. He was proud of himself.

Papa broke the silence. "You're fucking amazing, son!" He came up the stairs to hug Wallace, and Wallace held his papa tightly in return, feeling the warmth, the pride overcome him.

"Oswin?" Greysen said, almost a cry of desperation. Then fear. *"Brother?"*

That last word was said so desperately, Wallace pulled away from his papa to see what the matter was. Wallace took a moment to understand, for all he could see was Oswin standing there. The haunted look was gone, replaced by nothing. Nothing at all.

Then it dawned on Wallace.

When he'd killed the monk, the puppet master's strings cut, Oswin the puppet became lost, like flotsam floating down a river. The wight was no longer of any mind, not even his own, even though he was freed.

What had Wallace done?

Guilt found him, prickling at the back of his neck, the little hairs there standing to attention. But not 'cause he'd killed the monk, the man would have seen 'em all hurt; Wallace couldn't have that. Oswin, mindless before, was now just a shell. A shell of dead flesh for a dead brain to carry around forever. And it was Wallace's fault.

"He *is* in there; I can feel him," Novane announced.

Wallace shuddered a sigh of relief.

Greysen was trying to rouse anything from his brother. Holding him, letting him know he was there. Still nothing. "It's like he's down a deep well."

Papa said, "Then be there for him so he knows he can get out."

Wallace had a thought. "Ma always told us, the heart's the hearth of the soul, an' if ya curse the heart, ya curse the soul. Oswin's heart were cursed by dat monk, I know it. But if ya show Oswin he's loved by his family, that'll break the spell."

Greysen looked at him, blankly, almost with annoyance, until something dawned on him. "You're right! And…and a person's family is also a part of their soul, Wallace. And…and as such, I'm going to take Oswin to our other brother, Wymond, up into the mountains. All three of us will rebuilt our family's hearth as well as each other. We, all three of us, will no longer be broken."

"And I'm coming with you," Novane stated.

Greysen held the lich's hand in answer.

Papa said, "We have a different path to walk now, son."

"What's dat, Papa?"

"We've got to help Pa." He sheathed his sword, the rattle of metal against metal loud in the entrance foyer of the monastery with the dead all around. "We've got to go to that fucking demon Myrkul and end his days. I'll be damned if the land I love and uphold the law for will become a demon's playground."

Greysen and Novane shot a glance to Papa.

"Are you mad, Lord Hereward?" Novane questioned with a gasp.

Wallace asked, "I thought we's were gonna ask Myrkul for help against the other demon?"

"That's an even madder thought," Greysen chimed in. "Myrkul would never help you. He only helps himself."

"Exactly," Papa agreed. "That's why he's got to fucking die, because I know Dorgan will kill Alquam. Together we'll get rid of the demons who plague our lands. Come on, son, let's get started on our journey; the Dread Keep is a long way away. Best to begin it as soon as possible."

"But what about Pa?" Wallace asked with concern. "He'll need ta knows what we're doin' now we's changed things, won't he?"

Papa stood in thought for a moment, rubbing his beard. "I'll let Abbot Hosho know so he can tell Pa."

"You are in communication with the immortal monk?" Novane asked.

"I hope so." Papa snorted.

And for the longest time, he stood there still. Was he doing it now? Talking to the monk? Before Wallace could ask, Papa turned and heading for the door. Novane caught Papa's arm to stop him. A glance passed between them but then a relaxation of expression when Papa must have realized, as Wallace did, that the lich didn't mean any harm.

Novane said, "Take my Seeing Crystal as a gift for what you're about to undertake." The lich produced the object he was talking about. A round orb, clear but for a dark cloud churning in the middle of it, little sparks of lightning jabbing out of the ethereal mass to touch the inner walls in random bursts. "The Seeing Crystal will guide you to the oasis in the middle of the Hyruldon Expanse. You'll need it to rest before the last leg of your journey."

"How do I use its magic?" Papa asked, curiously, turning the accepted ball in his hand.

Novane replied, "Think of what you want to see, and it will be seen when you gaze into it."

Wallace wanted to look into the crystal, the urge coming over him stronger than anything. He fought it.

Papa nodded and pocketed the Seeing Crystal. "Thanks, Novane. Your generosity will not be forgotten."

Novane bowed. "You helped us today. Only fitting the favor is returned."

"Any other advice for us?" Papa asked.

"Seeing as you asked," Greysen replied, "don't let Myrkul cast any influence on you. Go in hard and go without regrets. Otherwise, you'll end up in his pillow chamber, a slave to his sexual needs until you're no longer desired—that goes for the both of you."

Wallace swallowed. Hard. He was beginning to feel the weight of Papa's decision. He didn't want to be a demon's plaything in any way. He didn't want to be anyone's plaything. A flash of the man's face, the bandit who'd raped him, found him with those thoughts. Wallace gasped, blinking away the image as if he'd looked into a bright light and could no longer see for a moment.

"Are you all right, son?" papa asked.

"Dunno." Wallace didn't lie...but it wasn't the truth either. He hated that.

Papa said, "I'm here for you now. You know that."

"I know."

Novane interjected, "I wish you both the best of luck."

Greysen shook Papa's hand, then Wallace's. "Any advice for us as we travel to the monastery of the Whispering Monks?"

Papa snorted. "Are you cut or uncut?" He was addressing them both.

"Uncut," Novane replied, both surprise and curiosity in his voice. "Why?"

"Then when the cold of the mountain gets unbearable, about halfway up it, piss into a bag that you've secured to yourself," Papa explained. "Don't take out your cock for anything. Not a good look, a frostbitten foreskin, that's for fucking sure. Seen plenty of men who had to get themselves cut after they've been touched by the cold. Some did it themselves. Damn mess it makes of everything too. The frostbite and the cure for it. Keep your mouth and nose covered best you can for the same reasons. The cold can mutilate and kill you just as quickly as any sword."

Novane winced, but Greysen took longer to answer. A pain came over him. Like the one Wallace had found flashing before his eyes earlier. "Before I got my pubic hair, a hair I grow proudly now after my divorce from Myrkul, my brothers..." He paused, and Novane held him. Greysen nodded. Wallace knew he wanted to say what he had to say. Get it out in the air. "My brothers, Tomas and Darrin, they held me down so they could cut my foreskin from off my cock. They said it was useless, and that only boys should remain uncut. Men should be cut. It was a rite of passage, they said. But after I became a man to them, that's when Darrin began…raping me."

Wallace was stunned and sad to the marrow of his bones. He wanted to cry. His eyes were watery, and he felt that heave in his stomach. That terrible heave. He came to hold Greysen's hand in comfort. "Ya do what ya gotta for yourself, as I do what I gotta for me."

Papa spat. "The fucking dirty cunts."

Tears began rolling down Greysen's cheeks; Wallace's too. "I got an infection. I was sick for weeks and weeks. I can now remember the searing pain of that cut made by a blade only sterilized by a candle's dim light. My sisters put herbs on my wound to try and heal it, but it took a long time. I endured my cruel circumcision, but not without great cost."

Wallace couldn't stand it. His world wobbled around him. Papa grabbed him to hold him. They all held him and Greysen. Except Oswin. He was still dead inside, the strings of control cut by Wallace's glowing blade, nothing left of him.

Novane said, "I will protect you with everything I am, Greysen."

"I know you will." Greysen sniffed back his tears. "And I believe I'm stronger because of what happened to me."

Wallace, wiping the tears away, blurted, "Same for me, an' all."

Something special came between Wallace and Greysen, stronger than the feeling friends shared, stronger than feelings of brotherhood as well. Wallace could feel it thick and vibrant, bathing them in its potency. They held each other with more intent, supporting each other to heal some of the damage of their pasts. Not all of it, nothing could do that. But as far as Wallace was concerned, their new bond helped. It was the bond of understanding.

Nothing was stronger.

After ages, long moments full of nothing but tears, they finally parted.

Wallace was reluctant to do so.

As they made their way to the door, Papa reached out to hold Wallace's hand. Another bond became apparent. A bond thicker than blood; one of found family. Safe within his papa's grip, Wallace got the wonderful feeling that he wouldn't ever let go. And even when his hand wasn't held, Papa's would always be there for him. Pa's too when he got back from this quest. He'd always be Hereward and Dorgan's loved and cherished son. Wallace couldn't ask for anything more.

He had a new family.

New friends.

A new life of adventure.

He wiped his face again, ready now to tackle what lay beyond.

14
Dorgan's Terrible Discovery

AFTER FLYING FOR A full moon's cycle plus a week, Dorgan didn't have any fortune when it came to finding the demon Alquam. The Iron Mountains were barren of any life. Only rocks, blackened and sharp like needles reaching to the heavens, greeted him. Nothing more. Not even lichen or mosses grew here any longer. No insects buzzed either. Had the demon come, decimated everything, then gone to ground?

Why Alquam would do so, Dorgan didn't know. Demons usually made homes of the places they destroyed and conquered.

Dorgan soon came to a plateau devoid of everything but rocks struggling over the eons to fight against the weather; aside from demons, water was the greatest conqueror of them all. Not even earth forged from the strongest stones could resist it given enough time. The rocks of the plateau were smooth, a sure sign of losing that battle.

He landed and, transforming into a man, he felt a cool breeze from the north, the land of permanent winter, caress his exposed skin. Goosebumps resulted, and he hugged himself to regain some semblance of warmth after being a dragon with fire in his belly for so long. His breath now visible, he realized he'd grown a beard during his travels; he ran his fingers down his chin, admiring his new whiskers.

He then looked up from whence he came. The clouds, massive water laden columns stretching from horizon to horizon, were in a strange, striated formation hanging from the heavens. That large, they looked as though they bent the mighty sky with their weight. Nature was majestic indeed.

But Dorgan had no time to admire the weather. He had a demon to hunt. Perhaps he'd find clues as to where Alquam had gone on the plateau itself. Perhaps not. He looked anyway. As he searched, the wind whistling through crack and gully alike created noises, and his imagination fired.

Some of the noises even sounded like a voice, one familiar perhaps. Dorgan turned on his heels, seeing if someone was behind him. No one was. Yet the voice continued, whispering. And if he wasn't mistaken, it was mocking and laughing too. A hungry voice. No wonder it was familiar. Probably the echo of the demon Alquam in this desolate place, Dorgan imagined.

He shook his head.

Ghosts of Alquam's narcissism, its taunting, didn't concern him. Finding the demon did. But where was the demon? Surely Alquam wouldn't hide. The demon loved confrontation—with Dorgan especially.

"Show yourself, Alquam; I'm here to parley!"

No answer but the whispering wind.

Dorgan had another idea. "I'm here to offer you a contest then. You love contests, don't you?"

Through the wind, gently, faintly, Dorgan swore he heard, *The first contest is to find me, dragon. Then we can discuss how your life will end for disturbing me.*

So Alquam was here.

"That's no contest. I will find you one way or the other. Why not make it interesting, demon? C'mon, you love challenges.

What do you have in mind?

"If I find you by day's end, I keep my life, and you return to the Void."

The wind laughed and laughed and laughed, hacking and full of hate and…something else. Admiration? Dorgan wasn't sure. *How I've missed you, dragon.*

"Your answer then?"

I have a better idea.

"Speak it. You know I'm worthy of whatever you offer."

This is true. But I have a secret. A great secret. I cannot return to the Void because of this secret.

Dorgan's interest piqued. "You want me to discover your secret?"

The wind whistled. *I do.*

"And if I do, what then, Alquam?"

By day's end, you will be free. If not, you will be devoured; dragon meat will satiate my hunger for a delicious moment. Now come. Find me and my secret. You don't have much time.

And Dorgan knew the words as truth, even if spoken by a demon. The sun was already close to the dead tree line, bruising the horizon with purples and yellows. What he didn't trust was Alquam. Demon's only told what they wanted others to hear for their own benefit.

"How do I know you're not leagues away? How do I know you're close enough to make this challenge fair?"

The wind laughed roaringly again, but no words accompanied it. Dorgan decided to keep searching. Alquam had to be close; otherwise, how could he devour him once the sun set and his failure was assured?

But he did add, "And if I discover your secret and find you before day's end, what will be my prize?"

Your life.

Dorgan swallowed down a good dose of worry. He'd forgotten that bargaining with demons was never a good idea. Such a thing always ended in misery. And no matter how much he searched the Iron Mountains, changing into dragon form to increase the area he could survey, he couldn't find Alquam or the demon's secret, whatever it could be.

The Iron Mountains were massive. A sprawling range, once the remnants of ancient volcanoes. Too many of them to count. To make it even worse, everything was the same tone, dark against darkness. It was like searching in the night for something with no light, searching for a shadow within a thick, ancient forest.

To make matters worse, evenfall would be upon him soon, and the mighty sky darkened further to remind him of that. Dorgan decided to land near one of the larger calderas he saw from above. He transformed into a man again.

Giving up so soon? the wind questioned along with its laughter.

Now Dorgan didn't reply.

I thought you valued your life, dragon?

"I do."

Then come find me.

"You are a black feathered demon within black rock. You could be hiding anywhere."

Are you going to be one of those sulking mortals who believes everything should be easy? Do you want for your mother's breast? Bah! If things were so easy, what would be the point of living?

Determination struck Dorgan. "I have time still."

Not much.

"Enough."

Dorgan walked down the granite crusted edge of the caldera, loose rock tumbling beneath his footfalls. He had to be careful. Many times, he almost lost his balance and had to pause to consider a more favorable path. There didn't seem to be one.

It seems to me, you need a little help, the wind whispered as it blew down the caldera's face, cold like Alquam's heart. But that time, the voice wasn't Alquam.

Who voice was it, then?

Dorgan froze for a moment in shock. Slowly, he turned, stones tumbling, only to be confronted by a familiar face. A beautifully familiar face. He couldn't help it; Dorgan laughed. "What are you doing here?" he asked.

Abbot Hosho's orange robe was vibrant and brilliant, even inspiring, against the purpling heavens and blackened landscape. His milky eyes shining, reflecting the remnants of the day perfectly, the monk replied, "I could ask you the same question."

Kieron came into the caldera, holding Vash's hand. "But Abbot Hosho won't ask you because he already knows the answer."

Vash giggled. "True."

By the gods, it was so good to see them all. Dorgan wanted to cry with joy, his heart pounding with gratitude that he was no longer alone. As such, Dorgan's embrace of his friends gave everything away as to how elated, relived, he was to see them.

They held each other for the longest while.

Dorgan's spirit sang, and his depression left him to make him feel at ease. He was glad he was no longer alone with only the wind and the voice of Alquam that'd been carried along with it. Seeing Abbot Hosho, Kieron, and Vash made one thing abundantly clear, though; he had to admit he missed Hereward and Wallace something terrible.

"You've grown a beard," Kieron observed.

Dorgan smiled coyly. "It doesn't suit me though, I'm sure."

"I think it does," Vash chimed in.

"And how is your son, Wallace?" Abbot Hosho asked once they parted, a knowing smile crawling over his old but ageless lips. Into Dorgan's mind, the monk said, *And Hereward loves you very much, but needs you to know he is going south to destroy Myrkul. The demons need to be exterminated from our lands.*

Dorgan didn't know what to say or do about the information, other than hope Hereward and Wallace would be all right. He hoped they would all be all right.

To Abbot Hosho, he nodded.

Besides, Kieron and Vash gave Dorgan a look that demanded an explanation. Of which he gave while they searched the caldera together, careful to hold each other for support in case of a terrible fall with the loose rock underfoot. He told the story of Wallace and how a wee boy of ten summers old came to be in his care along with Hereward and won their hearts.

"Hereward is his Papa, and I'm his Pa," Dorgan concluded. "Isn't that something?"

"It most certainly is," Abbot Hosho agreed. "But despite your good news, young dragon, I now have some bad."

Dorgan didn't like the sound of that. "Go on."

"I've made a terrible mistake. A mistake that could cost us all dearly if I don't do something about it very quickly."

"You?" Dorgan let his surprise show. "A mistake? I don't think so; you're infallible, aren't you?"

"Being immortal only means I've lived longer, nothing more. Perhaps time has given me some insight, let me see things many wouldn't, but all in all, I'm nothing but a fool fumbling their way through their life as best they can. Like all of us." Abbot Hosho offered the crook of his arm, and Dorgan accepted it, feeling better once he was closer to the monk. Kieron and Vash, still hand in hand, walked behind.

All of them walked together, many feet crunching over rocks, tumbling away from them into the hollow of the caldera below, a barren desert within a barren mountain. Usually, ancient sleeping volcanoes held a lake. Not this one. Dorgan imagined even water wouldn't want to visit for too long here, especially with a demon in residence.

Abbot Hosho continued, "I have caused all that will happen from these moments on."

"How?"

"If you let me explain, young dragon, I will tell you."

"Sorry." Dorgan felt his newly bearded cheek grow warmer. "Go on."

"No need to apologize." Abbot Hosho flashed a quick emotionless smile. "Years ago, to protect my three sons, I separated them. First Oswin, the eldest by ten years, then Greysen, from Wymond. I thought they would all be looked after. I believed they would all be safe. But I was wrong."

Worry prickled at Dorgan. "Wymond's all right, isn't he?"

"He is, even though his wounds affect him greatly, and he doesn't gain any more strength despite the passage of time. Again, a result of my doing. I didn't want him to love Beornræd. I feared the magician would take him from me, the only son I had left because I foolishly let go of the other two. A terrible and costly mistake, it seems. I should have kept them all together."

"You protected your sons by separating them—you said so yourself." Dorgan tried his best to comfort Abbot Hosho. He'd never seen the monk so upset, the expression on his ancient face furrowed and full of sadness. "You weren't to know how their lives would unfold without your guidance, surely?"

"I *should* have known." Abbot Hosho looked up at the wondrous sky. "But I became too self-centered. And that, my dear friend, is the biggest curse of being immortal, for when the end of life isn't a worry, life itself isn't either. My conceit flowed to those around me. To my sons. And for that, they have all suffered."

Dorgan had to accept what Abbot Hosho had told him. How could he not? "I don't understand what this has to do with what's happening now."

"Greysen, my middle son, through the abuse he suffered by the family I entrusted him to, became Myrkul's husband."

"I beg your pardon?" Dorgan's shock punctuated the question.

"The Purge that comes is my fault."

"What can *we* do?" Dorgan emphasized the *we* because if there was one thing he knew, it was that Abbot Hosho wasn't alone in the burden, even if he ignited the fire all those years ago. No one was alone. Not even Hereward.

"Things are being put into place at this very moment to get my three sons together."

"What will that do?"

"Hopefully prevent what is to happen," Abbot Hosho stated ominously, his expression darkening. Abbot Hosho paused, wiping his watery eyes with his free hand, his sadness radiating more intensely than approaching evenfall. "There is one more thing you must know."

Dorgan didn't like the sound of Abbot Hosho's tone and swallowed again. "What's that?"

"Alquam must be defeated."

"That I already knew."

Abbot Hosho smiled genuinely the first time since arriving. "And that's why I'm here with Kieron and Vash." He let go of Dorgan. "Come. There is a cave at the bottom of the caldera we need to visit."

The sun, now beneath the bending columns of clouds and sinking below the horizon, the day's last kiss of blessed light until next morning rise, marked their arrival at the cave Abbot Hosho spoke of. Dorgan swore he saw a dark figure take flight. He blinked. Perhaps the light played tricks on him. Perhaps not.

No matter.

What confronted him made him tremble in both shock and fear. He'd never seen such a thing. Never imagined it in his wildest nightmares. Kieron immediately transformed into a dragon, Vash climbing upon him, but Dorgan was stunned for a moment.

"There is the secret Alquam spoke of," Abbot Hosho said, gesturing before him.

"No wonder Alquam left the Void," he uttered, mouth agape as he took in the sight of eggs laid across the cave's floor. Thousands and thousands of eggs! "She had to lay her eggs, for she was the mother of demons!"

One egg, the closest to them, had hatched, the gore and stink of its cracking repulsing Dorgan. Even Abbot Hosho took a step back.

What came out of the egg, though? The dark thing that took flight? More importantly, where was it going? What was its goal?

Dorgan didn't get time to contemplate the questions buzzing in his mind like bees trapped in a jar, for Alquam, lord of agonizing darkness, wraith of malice and of eternal suffering, and the master of misery, emerged like a nightmarish apparition from the darkness.

With an ear-piercing screech, Alquam, sneering, yellow eyes glowing, said, "You've run out of time, dragon! I'm hungry after what I've done, and you and your friends are the first for my table."

Abbot Hosho calmly pointed at the broken egg. "And you have begun the Purge, I see."

"I have, immortal." Alquam screeched again, one of victory, Dorgan knew. "My alpha hatchling, my first love, will bring about the rout of humanity, of your civilization. I have gifted them with all of my knowledge to become a greater weapon against humanity. The Purge, as you call it, is upon you all. And I relish the destruction that will follow. Now, come closer…my hunger grows even more."

In defiance, Dorgan became a dragon.

15
Greysen's Dead Brother

THE POWER...

Novane struggled in Oswin's grip like a fly in amber, getting weaker all the time. Hands on neck. Tight. Throats squeezed. Tighter. And while they wrestled, Novane could only think about protecting Greysen, his broken and damaged man.

The man who he wanted—no needed—to unbreak, even though he knew Greysen's mind was like broken glass, never to be fully repaired. That was why his moods changed so much, hot to cold and back again; Greysen was constantly trawling through the shards of his past to try and pick a safer path, a way towards some sort of future unhindered by the demons that haunted him. Novane would try and provide the light to guide him. He would protect Greysen at all costs. It was his love for Greysen that had changed Novane. Made him a better man, even though he was broken as well. Broken beyond repair, he believed. Until Greysen stepped out of Myrkul's shadow.

Then things changed.

What better person to help Greysen, than him? Better than any other. But to ensure Greysen's safety, first Novane had to keep the wight from touching him, touching anyone. He had to prevent Oswin from doing so before the damage he wielded was irreparable and Greysen became truly lost to Novane. No easy ask for the power of the creature, a man once named Oswin, was infinite, endless, and seething, even though he was dead. It flowed through him like a plague over fertile crops to decimate. Destroy. Annihilate utterly.

Novane knew the link had to be cut; the power that came from the monk was like a bridge, bright and fierce, unwavering and relentless, fed exponentially. But how? The ugly and dark aura around Oswin wasn't his own but Monk Wu's. The man's hold over the wight. Relentless.

In contrast, Greysen's aura was beautiful, scintillating, especially around his crown, like a corona bursting from the sun during a solar storm. In further contrast, Wallace and Hereward's auras were alike—steady and full of their love for one another, halos of reds, blues, and greens. The colors of love a father has for his son, and a son has for his father, found or otherwise.

Novane realized he had little time left. Oswin's aura steadily became fiercer, dark sticky fingers reaching for him, closer and closer. Searching. Novane knew he couldn't hold back Oswin for long. He'd weakened. As a lich lord, Novane was powerful, but as a wight, his powers enhanced and controlled by Monk Wu, Oswin was more so. And Monk Wu was unrelenting, sending more of his energy to Oswin.

To no surprise then, the monk's aura was the most devastating of them all. The most violent, foul, and evil. It surged between monk and wight like twisting, turning ropes. Novane felt himself weaken further against Oswin's hold. Not long, and he would be done, unable to hold back the tide of the wight's power. Not long, and Oswin would be able to drain the living after Novane failed. Drain Greysen.

Novane couldn't let that happen.

But how could he stop it? His failure was inevitable against such power.

No one else could help him. He was alone, naked against the storm. Greysen was still weak from casting his magic; his aura told Novane as much. It flickered like candlelight in a breeze, the light colors dimming and brightening as the struggle within him continued. He would gain his strength. But too late.

Hereward's aura remained, but the lord knight couldn't touch the wight nor the monk. Both would drain every ounce of energy from him, leave him nothing but a dry husk. He'd be a dead husk—one even the gods he worshiped wouldn't accept into their halls, too strange, too unrecognizable, even for them.

Then Novane noticed something.

Where was Wallace?

Oswin tightened his grip, the transfer of power phenomenal through his dead muscles and sinews to his fingertips. Novane gasped, his eyes watering. Thank the Lords of Gluttony, Lust, and Greed, masters of the circles of Hell, he didn't need to breathe. But he could still be killed. Even undead like him could die. Remove the head, strangle it off the neck with enough force, and he'd be done for.

Where is Wallace?

Then, using his aura sight, he saw the boy. His annoyance,

frustration, and dread dissipated. Wallace, much to Novane's growing delight, had come behind the monk, dexterously sneaking, blade in hand and in the upraised position to deliver a killing blow. The monk was powerful but also mortal. Killable, especially with a blade plunged into his back. How Wallace had snuck behind him without being noticed, Novane didn't know. The sword Wallace held, magical by some ancient power, blazed green, as did the boy himself, overtaking his aura beautifully. Soon, they were the same color, boy and his weapon.

Novane then understood. The sword hid him, rendered Wallace invisible to all but Novane. The aura sight enabled him see the living, to tell the measure of a person, no matter how disguised, and had revealed the answer.

The sight had also told him Greysen was the one who'd saved him back in the Hyruldon Expanse—which they were now the lords of. The rest fell into place, including how Novane's heart, though remained un-beating, was for Greysen. Only for him. His broken love.

He would do anything for Greysen.

A split second later, the bridge of power was severed between the monk and the wight. Novane was flung onto the bloodied marble, slipping in the gore. Greysen came to him. Held him. He returned it.

The monk also fell.

The link had been severed. Oswin became nothing; without the monk's nourishment, he succumbed to the thousands cuts and the loss of blood. Yet, he didn't die. Not in the sense where many people once known to Oswin needed to stand around a freshly dug grave, speaking of walking through the valley of the shadow of death, interning his body into a wooden box to cover in dirt. Dead where he still walked, though mindless and a shell.

Dead beyond even the undead.

The worst dead of all, for there was no resting in peace for Oswin.

Confusion followed as Novane tried to recover all he had lost during the struggle with Oswin, insides roiling. He needed time. Some things were said; he'd said a few words himself. He didn't remember them all. Wallace was told how brave he was. How perfect the boy was because of what he'd done, his training serving him well. Novane agreed while Greysen held him, and he held Greysen. Hereward held them all, thanking them.

But Oswin stood motionless, his expression no longer haunting but blank.

Then the knight and his son headed for the door after a discussion about what path they must all follow. Novane declared his intentions again to Greysen, kissing his warm forehead over and over. They were to find their path to the Steps to Heaven mountains and seek Wymond. Novane was pleased with the decision. The closer to the mountains, the further away from the Hyruldon Expanse and the Dread Keep they'd be.

Soon, they stood alone amongst the carnage, the pools of blood darkening as it aged around the lifeless bodies of the deceased monks—the whole order of them, decimated. They were no more. There was nothing here. Nothing of worth, anyway.

Novane and Greysen left the monastery, Oswin following blindly when Novane cast a leash spell on the wight, simple but effective. The leash, unlike the bridge of power Monk Wu had created, wouldn't interfere. It would only ensure Oswin would never stray from them no matter how far they traveled. Good enough for now until they could find Oswin's spirit once more and bring him back from the worst death imaginable. And so, they went to the mountains. Only family could repair such damage.

Novane suspected Greysen's motives were also selfish, but not in a bad way. He needed repairing too. Novane could coax his love for Greysen along their new path, but to truly heal, Greysen had to know where he belonged.

And he belonged with his brothers.

Outside, in the light, in the fresh air, even if stained with the stink of humanity living in a crowded city, the aura around Greysen was almost repaired, the magic coming back to him in surging, pulsing, beautiful waves. His aura was dazzling. As was his love's magic. The well from which Greysen drew his new power went deep within him, no question. And yes, the reserve of it was infinite in the way it would be refilled given time, but not infinite as to the amount of power he could release in a single moment. A single spell cast. Killing all those monks had drained the well to the bottom.

Greysen had suffered because of the drain.

Novane never wanted him to suffer again. Not if he could help it. As such, and so he could no longer see anything else, he had given the lord knight his Seeing Crystal. Novane wouldn't need it any longer. He saw all he wanted to see in Greysen's eyes, those beautiful gray steely orbs they were. Endless. An indefatigable reflection of what was held within him.

Breathtaking, if Novane had breath to take.

Yes, Greysen had a broken past, a shattered present, but hopefully, with Novane by his side, a better future.

"What's the matter?" Greysen asked acidly, the gray of his eyes flickering something akin to annoyance. "You keep staring at me."

Novane shuddered. The merest look, the slightest glance, from Greysen made Novane lose his thoughts. He was consumed with a yearning he hadn't felt for a long time. But he would never do anything to hurt or hurry or hinder Greysen's recovery. It wasn't about him. It was about Greysen.

"Nothing."

Greysen's expression softened; another shift because of the broken shards he navigated within him. "What do you see when you look at me, Novane?"

"A lot."

"Do you see hate?"

"Yes." Novane paused, gathering his thoughts. "Amongst other things. Love, sadness, anger, regret. So many others too."

Greysen harrumphed, turning to ensure Oswin followed them. Novane's magical leash held. The humans of the city, thousands of them, gave the wight a wide berth. Some dropped their wares to get out of his way, fruit and vegetables scattered. Children were sheltered behind their parents' clothing to only then peer between legs, gawking. Most animals fled, tails tucked if they had them, but the cats stood their ground, looking on curiously as they peered over the gutters of overhanging rooftops. Novane liked cats. They could commune with the dead and undead alike. One large ginger tom, big balls and attitude, ears nicked from brawls after freshly spraying his territory, considered Oswin from above, green eyes piercing.

Thars the smallest hope for the lost wight, lord lich, he purred into Novane's mind as cats did without consideration of invasion or a care of it either.

Oswin needs the love of his brothers so he can emerge from the darkness, Novane threw back with just as much intention; cats didn't suffer fools. Being considerate wasn't in their vocabulary. They did as they did. Nothing more. Nothing less.

Perhaps. Perhaps not. The tom then flicked his tail and turned his attention to licking his fur before slumping to sun himself across the ridge capping, the conversation done.

Novane couldn't blame the tom for his observation. But even

though Oswin was a shell, worse than dead, his touch could still drain the life of any unfortunate enough to come in contact with him. For that he had to be careful. Greysen more so.

"And what does that mean?" Novane asked, coming back to the moment at hand.

"What does what mean?"

They were heading out of the city, the guards letting them pass without question. Good. Novane didn't want to stay a moment longer in the cesspit of humanity locked within bricks and stone surrounded by high walls.

Novane replied, "The noise you made. What did it mean?"

"I means I still hate you." Greysen reached out his hand to hold Novane's. "It also means I have other feelings for you."

"Such as love?" Novane replied hopefully.

Hope soon quashed. "I don't know what that is, so how can I feel it?"

"Feeling something, even feelings we don't understand, doesn't need to have meaning. It just is."

Greysen paused in consideration, his grey beautiful eyes shifting to something reflecting the darkness within him. "Everyone I've ever known has lusted after me. Used me. Abused me. How can I love when no one has loved me in return to teach me what it is?"

Novane didn't answer.

Out in the wilds, beyond the patchwork farmlands of various crops, cobbled roads, patches of forest hither and thither, and the hunting huts within, Novane felt a great weight lifted from him. He preferred the freedom of outdoors, especially after being confined within the granite of the Dread Keep for so long as Myrkul's slave, assassin, and whipping boy.

He kept hold of Greysen's hand, pole axe in the other; Oswin ambled behind, lurching to a quicker pace when the magical leash pulled. They had walked into Suvanwold proper, into one of the greater forests of the kingdom's north, Varwesh. Novane felt at peace. The animals of the thick woods of pine and ash with the occasional oak avoided them. Like those in the city, they sensed danger from the walking dead Oswin had become.

The sky glimpsed through the canopy, eternal and wondrous, blazed brilliant blue to give hope. Nothing better than a cloudless sky stretching above; no wonder the ancients worshiped it. Even Greysen's mood lightened.

But the shadows around them had grown deeper. Bright light no longer dappled as fiercely. They'd need to rest soon, Greysen especially. He looked weary. He hadn't spoken much either since they'd left Invrawold City and passed over the wide stone bridge. No doubt Greysen still treaded carefully through the shards of his broken mind, the journey almost an eternal one. Novane felt for him.

"I'll make us a shelter to sleep under," Novane announced when they came to a massive, moss-stained, twisted oak, boughs as thick as any he'd seen, thicker than a man could reach around.

"You don't need to sleep." Greysen slipped his hand out of Novane's hold, wiping the sweat from his palm down his jerkin's front.

Novane didn't sweat. He wished he did. To mingle their waters while holding each other would be something special, he imagined. "I will sleep with you to comfort you, as we did in the desert."

Greysen sighed. "If you want to."

Novane wasn't sure whether that was an invitation or something else. He shrugged and decided to get on with things. With a few hefty swings of his pole axe, leaf laden branches were cut from surrounding trees then draped over the oak's lowest bough to create a makeshift shelter, a bower. Not watertight, not pretty, but it would suffice.

By the time Novane laid his cloak upon the ground, the visible sky was bruising purples and reds, the day almost done. A gloom came over the forest; mists curled around trees, waiting for the temperature to drop enough so they would be free to roam.

Greysen crawled into the shelter after Novane prepared a meal of meat and vegetables he'd bought at the Great Invrawold Market. He didn't pay for cheap cuts, like offal or the cocks of serpopards, but more premium ones. Cost him a silver for two dozen packets, traveler's rations as they were known. For this meal, he'd cooked preserved chicken pieces, mostly the breast and thigh cuts because they kept better after being salted.

To his chagrin, he'd noticed the vendor had snuck in a few fatty Parson's Noses underneath the better meat. The bastard. A fortunate thing for the seller that Novane was no longer in the city. The man would have seen the glint of his scimitar's blade for cheating him out of the quality he'd paid for.

Novane also found root vegetables, potatoes, parsnips, and swedes growing wild, and made a stew over a fire. He added a few fresh herbs growing around in thick bunches as well. It smelt good. Tasted better. Well, Greysen ate it with gusto, anyway. Novane didn't need to eat, even though he enjoyed the experience, the textures and sensations on his tongue, especially when in the presence of such fine company. Greysen all the company he'd ever need.

All through this, Oswin stood not too far away, expression blank, looking at nothing. When the leash didn't pull, there was no reason to move. Dead didn't eat food, either, so Novane offered none.

Within their bower, Novane snuggled next to Greysen.

Greysen was asleep in moments, so Novane believed. After a moment, or perhaps a long time, he couldn't tell, the owls and other night animals began their activities. Some sort of foraging animal, a boar perhaps, snuffled through the leaf litter not too far away. Night settled. The animals still gave Oswin, who stood by a tree, as lifeless as ever, a wide berth.

Greysen began breathing heavier. At first, Novane was worried. He thought his love was having a nightmare. Sometimes he did. But this was different, the breathing different. Within the gloom, he was only able to see Greysen because of his aura sight. It burned brightly, touched by red, reflecting a sudden passion, and Novane realized Greysen was asleep, but this was no nightmare.

Heat radiated off him. His breathing got more intense, deeper. His stomach quivered, legs writhed. A moan. A profound shudder. Greysen moved a quick hand over himself, over what Novane could clearly see was his erection, faster and faster, and with increasing fervor and intent.

Novane, unable to help himself, watched as his love climbed the heights towards his self-reward. Why Greysen didn't ask Novane to help him with such a thing, he didn't know.

Until Greysen spoke, hissing through his teeth. "Yes…that's it, *Novane*. I want to see my seed drip from your hole and down the back of your balls. I want to lick it off. Arch your back. Do as I…say. Submit to me…yes. Novane, yes. You're so tight. Ahh. That's…that's it."

Novane was stunned.

Greysen's erotic dream was about him.

Him.

But was that how Greysen saw him? As Myrkul had seen Greysen? An object to ejaculate into. No love, only lust present. The only thing Greysen knew.

"Ahh," Greysen cried as he shuddered one final time, his ejaculate finding his trembling stomach in thick ribbons. It was then his aura had changed. Greysen had been awoken by his erotic dream.

Novane stayed still.

The aura of Greysen's seminal fluid glowed with life until it faded a few moments later; human seed didn't stay alive long if left to the air. He used his fingers to collect it, licking it off them one by one, swallowing it all down. He then turned away from Novane, back to him, as if nothing had happened. The heat from Greysen cooled, aura returning from the tainted crimson and golds it'd been before.

Novane was a little hurt.

But he also understood how broken Greysen was. Why he'd done such a thing without asking for assistance, said those things too. Tomorrow, he'd confront Greysen, clear the air. They couldn't go on if they didn't, Novane knew it.

The next morning, Novane prepared breakfast, his mind a storm of thoughts and feelings.

When he handed the repast of ration meat cooked in more of the forest's bounty, he said, "You want me, don't you, Greysen? And before you deny it, I heard you speak your inner thoughts last night. Your dream about me and what you want to do to me."

Greysen flushed red, high circles on his cheeks. He stuttered, then said, "Don't take stock in dreams, Novane. They are for fools and wishful thinkers. And you're not someone I lust over; you are my comfort. Nothing more. I thought we'd been through that already."

"I can be more than the man who gives you comfort in your waking hours if you wish it."

Greysen spat a lump of fat onto the ground, more cheap meat mixed in with the good. If Novane ever saw the trader who sold him those traveler's packs, he'd be dead. Deader than Oswin. He'd boil and render the man's meat and sell it to ghouls. Ghouls liked the taste of human meat no matter the quality.

"I will not submit to anyone ever again," Greysen stated emphatically. "Not even you."

"What if I don't want you to submit? A relationship can be built on something more than domination and submission."

"What?" Greysen looked up at Novane, the steel of his eyes glinting something he didn't understand. "Is that what we have? A relationship, lich?"

"I believe so."

"You're wrong. I hate you, remember."

"You lie." Novane could see darkness cloud Greysen's aura, a sure sign of what he observed was the truth; Greysen lied.

Greysen spat more food, that time the good meat. "So what if I do? Myrkul and my brother lied to me to get what they wanted from me. Perhaps I'm lying to you for the same reason."

"And what reason would that be?" Novane felt he was close, some of the shards within Greysen's mind almost stepped over. Not all of them, far from it, but a few. He hoped.

"I want to fuck you, nothing more."

"Then fuck me, if that will give you greater comfort."

Greysen looked shocked; aura blazing more red. "You would submit to me?"

Without hesitation, he answered, "I would." Novane grabbed Greysen's hand, held it tightly. "I would do whatever you wanted of me."

Greysen's aura darkened again. "Who do you think I am? Myrkul? Darrin? I'd never take someone in lust—even if they wanted it to please me." He then paused, aura flashing. "I...I *respect* you too much, Novane."

And there was the truth of it.

Novane bowed his head slightly. "And I respect you."

Greysen's eyes became watery. "What does this all mean, then?"

"It means we are...in love."

Greysen didn't reply at first. When his damaged man, a man of such beauty it killed Novane, did speak, his voice was unsure, his words wounded. "You are my comfort, Novane, and nothing more." More shards got in the way of the path.

"Can't we be more for each other?"

"I told you. I hate you," Greysen snapped, and with that, he got up. "I need to piss. Don't follow me."

Novane grabbed Greysen's arm, gently. "We need each other. I need you. I *love* you. Can't you see that? Together we can heal each other. I love you, Greysen Nightbane. *I love you.*"

Greysen's eyes widened. He didn't pull away. A tremble found his lips, and Novane could feel the tension of their love between them, greater than the bridge of power Monk Wu built to ensnare Oswin. Novane gasped at its intensity, his undead insides roiling wonderfully.

He'd never felt so alive. So vulnerable and consumed. His cock hardened, the discomfort of it another blessing.

But Greysen said, "You talk too much."

"Then let me kiss you so I can't speak any longer."

Greysen trembled, his expression softened as he fell into Novane's arms. Novane held him with all his might. All his love. Greysen held him back.

"Yes. Kiss me, *please*," Greysen whispered, quivering as their lips met.

16
Hereward's Greatest Lessons

WALLACE HELD HIS PAPA'S hand 'cause he didn't want to get lost in the crowd of so many people; more than six villages worth of folks in one street alone, he guessed. Together, they left the monastery after saying goodbye to Greysen, Novane, and Oswin. The terribly scarred man with no nipples scared Wallace. He had a dead look, like the Wicker Men the darrow worshiped. A distant look. Wallace didn't give him a hug in farewell.

The others didn't seem to mind.

"You're getting better with your sword, no fucking lie." Papa said proudly,

"Ta, Papa." Wallace knew he was getting better too.

They entered the Great Market square of Invrawold City. Everywhere, hawkers, beggars, traders, street performers, and buyers all screamed at him for something it seemed.

"Copper to tell your fortune, handsome boy."

"Spare a coin for an old man."

"Fresh caught this morning, for you, little lord, two coppers only. Fish that'll fill your belly, it will."

"How much is it worth to see me swallow fire?"

"Three cups one ball! Three cups one ball! Guess where it is to win silver! Lots o' silver! Three cups one ball. It's easy to win!"

Wallace wanted nothing but to hurry up out of the market square. He'd had enough of crowds. Folks only wanted coins from him. Not good folks they were.

"Goes 'way, will ya!" Wallace shouted at one woman who thought it best she stick her head close to his to scream her wares at him, some cheap tat with baubles and glittery things on it. Said it were for Festivus, whatever that was. Wallace didn't know and didn't care really if it involved buying junk for no reason other than to messy up a house and empty a purse.

"And now we've got to work on how you speak," Papa suggested when they were less restricted by pressing bodies and over eager sellers.

"What's wrong with how I's talk?"

"Nothing at all," papa replied. "But as a lord's son—and that you are, make no fucking mistake—sometimes common talk isn't desirable in certain situations. If you get my meaning."

Wallace was confused, and he felt a frown worry his brow. "I don't, Papa."

Papa huffed a breath. "To put it simply, you sound like you've come from the farms beyond civilization's arse crack. Not that there's anything wrong with it." Papa paused, scratching his beard, the *rasp, rasp, rasp* loud in Wallace's ears. "It's just fucking unfortunate that when some people hear you, they'll try and take advantage of you because they've judged you by your common tongue. That's all I'm saying."

"But I's has come from the farms back o' beyond, an all, ain't I, Papa?"

Papa chuckled. "And don't you forget it. But sometimes talking like you are gives people an impression of you that you might not want them to have," he explained again. It was the same way he'd explained it earlier, just with different words. Too many words.

Wallace blinked.

Papa then frowned as well. Wallace knew he was trying to tell him something. Trouble was, from the sound of it, neither of 'em knew what that was exactly. Which confused Wallace even more.

"Have I's done somethin' wrong?"

"By the gods, no." Papa's eyebrows rose up his forehead fast as can be. "Not at all. I'm just trying to teach you there're different ways to present yourself so you don't get judged, that's fucking all."

"Like how's you cuss all the time?"

"Yes, something like that. But don't take up swearing—bad habit that."

Wallace tried to understand, he really did. Unfortunately, whatever was being taught was lost on him without a better example. He shrugged. "I'd rather have me sword lessons, if I's bein' honest."

Papa sighed. "I tend to agree."

In front of 'em was a well-dressed man wearing all fancy finery, glistening jewels on thick fingers, buttons everywhere over a red velvet jacket. He had a round protruding tummy; the bulk of it probably prevented him from seeing his own willy whenever he peed, Wallace mused. The man raised a lace-cuffed arm and coughed, once, twice, into his hand, drawing Wallace's attention. Papa's too.

"What the fuck do you want, trader?" Papa questioned, unimpressed by the interruption, as Wallace was.

The man didn't seem worried, and with a voice as thick and sweet as treacle, he replied, "That's a fine-looking boy you've got there, sir. Fit and strong looking. Handsome too, I know it."

Papa snorted. "Thanks." He still didn't sound impressed.

Wallace wondered why. Someone giving him a compliment meant well, didn't they? *Didn't they?*

"How old are you, young man?" the richly dressed rotund man asked Wallace—who remembered his papa's words about impressions and the way he sounded giving away things he didn't want revealed. Something clicked. Or dawned on him, whichever neck of the woods you came from for whatever expression about coming to an understanding applied. Wallace liked the first one.

"I'm ten summers old, sir," was Wallace's simple reply, the words rounded out in his mouth as best he could manage so they came out as proper as he could achieve. He sounded strange to himself.

He saw papa grin at him. He'd done well.

The trader came closer, eyes shifting, before he whispered to Papa, "Would you consider selling him? Young, fresh-faced boys like him fetch a very good price these days with certain nobles and wealthy alike. Could be worth fifty gold to you or more. A princely sum for a princely boy."

Wallace was shocked, and he gasped. He felt his stomach turn something terrible, like he'd eaten an apple plucked too soon from the tree, all sour and flowery. He stepped closer to Papa. But he also knew his papa would feel the same way he did, and Wallace counted in his head the moments it took before something was said to reveal Papa's distaste.

To Wallace's delight, he didn't get past three moments counted before Papa said, "You've got some fucking big balls on you if you think you can come up to a lord and ask him to sell his son to you."

The trader shrunk, eyes fluttering. But a realization also came over him, overtaking everything else. Wallace didn't know what the expression was, didn't have the means to, but the man said, "I meant no disrespect."

While Papa eyed the man, his hand tapping the hilt of his sword god like always, *tap*, *tap*, *tap*, Wallace looked around to take in where they'd found themselves. They were in a long alleyway away from the rest of the Great Market. The dodgy part he reckoned; Wallace'd wager his best conker on it, the big shiny one he'd won off Jami Rojers last month in the final conker match before the seasonal harvest. What he saw around him filled him with dread.

Without worrying about forming proper words, Wallace said, "Are all dem boys n' girls in dem cages for sale, Mista?"

And there were a lot of children, ranging from those of about two summers old to barely older than Wallace, mostly girls of varying descriptions. A lot of 'em, both the boys and the girls, were crying, holding each other for comfort. Some looked stunned and defeated. Hauntingly silent like Oswin had been.

Wallace shivered. All the children wore only the barest cloth around 'em, enough to cover their private places and nothing more. Wallace got a bad feeling about where they'd found themselves. A slave trader's alleyway. A bad place.

As such, he moved even closer to his papa, also touching his sword. Wallace knew the blade glowed red as it vibrated its warning through him too. The trader was a bad man.

Wallace swallowed. Hard.

The trader said, "Why yes, they are. Many at bargain prices, my little lord. See for yourself. Have a good look. Perhaps one or two have taken your fancy already? I'll do a good price for you, and the more you buy, the cheaper they'll become for each one."

The man sure had changed his tune once he found out Papa was a lord and Wallace were his son all right. Just like old farmer Kennit used to get whenever he wanted to sell one of his ewes 'cause the fleece had gotten 'lumpy wool' and he didn't want to call the animal doctor to fix 'em.

Wallace felt heat rise up inside him. He didn't like the idea of children being bought and sold like farm stock, damaged or otherwise. Not one bit.

"You're a fucking low life bastard." Papa quickly grabbed the man by the scruff of his velvet and laced collar. "Tell me, what do you do with the ones who don't fucking sell, trader?"

"What I do is legal, and I don't appreciate this treatment, sir." The trader's eyes widened. A bead of sweat rolled down his temple. Hand trembling, he reached for a fancy handkerchief, the one sticking out of his jacket's top pocket. He dabbed it across his brow delicately.

"I'll be the fucking judge of that. Now tell me."

The trader wiped his brow again. "Some are given to the dog fighters. I get a silver for each one of those, better than nothing. But for better profit, most go to the butcher to be cut up for pet meat for the rich folks who can afford such luxury. I get a copper per pound for pet meat. A good trade, that is; I can get more than sixty coppers for each child that way. The bigger and older ones, a lot more."

Wallace felt his world spin around him. He wanted to throw up and couldn't help heaving a few times.

Papa didn't show his distaste as much as Wallace did, but Wallace knew it was there; he could see his papa's knuckles whiten on the trader's bunched up decorative collar. "You're supposed to feed and look after all slaves until they're sold by the fucking decree of King Marconi, you fucking little cunt."

"O-only within a m-moon's cycle. When the time's up, that's it. I can do with them as wish." The man nodded violently, trying to shake away Papa's grip to no result. "It's all b-business, you understand. All *legal* business. Nothing more."

Papa snarled. "And what happens to the children you sell?"

"They a-are…" The man gulped audibly; Wallace didn't like where this was going. "They are sold to the wealthy who will—"

"Who will either work them to fucking death within a season, cut them up to use their body parts for magic or the trade of it, or abuse them sexually until they get too old to please. Again, it's fucking illegal to sell to such trade. Am I fucking right?"

"Not illegal!" The man was livid scared. "Not illegal, s-sir, I tell you."

Wallace looked at the rows and rows of cages, stomach dropping. Those poor children. He'd heard of a few boys and girls a while ago in his village who'd been abducted from their homes when their parents were toiling in the fields. Rumor had it those wretches were used and abused in terrible ways, like what that bandit did to Wallace after he killed his family but worse.

Wallace began breathing hard.

He was sweating, cold and clammy all over.

Terror gripped his throat to almost make him choke as he remembered in stabbing, dreadful, debilitating flashes that god-awful night. Fleeting flashes, but so very potent. Wallace thought he'd blocked everything out of his mind when he was awake. But sometimes things got through, like the leering, ugly face of the man who'd touched his naked skin then did worse to him, whenever something triggered him—like now, as he gazed in horror at all those children in the cages.

Wallace shook his head, tears finding his eyes. But he pulled himself together. Had to. He wanted to be strong for Papa, even though he sometimes didn't feel strong. Papa needed him. And besides, he could cry later; Papa would let him as he held him tightly until the flashes were chased away once more.

Papa always let him cry.

Coming back to the moment, he realized Papa had his hand on his shoulder to reassure him—and Wallace felt a bit better for it. He also remembered he'd heard whispers, rumors, of young boys and girls going missing if they wandered too far into Warlock's Woods opposite Wooden Bridge Lane near his village, never to return. Perhaps they were captured and sold to the rich. But he'd never heard of their parts being used in spells. Not once.

The shock was palpable. His heart thumped hard. *Thump. Thump.* Harder still. He only thought it were eyes of newts and toes of frogs for a cauldron's brew, not livers of boys or spleens of girls.

He was equally saddened beyond words to hear of what happened to the children who didn't sell, to become food for dogs and cats. He was lucky Papa and Pa found him. Very lucky.

"You don't fucking ask your buyers what they'll do with their slaves, do you?" Papa seemed shocked. "Wonder what the authorities will have to say about your little operation here, trader."

The trader gulped again. "I don't ask; that's why business is good. No questions asked. And I...I..." But the man trailed off as worry found his face, the blood draining.

Wallace didn't know when, but Papa had released the man from his grip and drawn his sword, the point of it aimed right at the trader's groin. He still kept the other hand on Wallace, pulling him closer protectively. Wallace was once more grateful.

A nervous laugh leapt from the trader as Papa made him aware of what was going on too with a gentle shove of his blade. Wallace wanted the man dead and the children he'd captured released. Papa would want it, too.

To confirm his thoughts, Papa said, "People like you fucking make me sick to my back teeth, you fucking know that."

"I have a right to conduct business as much as any man," the trader said as defiantly as he could manage.

Papa scowled. "Not an illegal business, you fucking don't."

Then something changed.

The trader's frightened look turned to red splotchy anger. Through his teeth, tongue pressed just so between 'em, the trader whistled loud, short, and piercing, like a shepherd would to command his shepherding dog. At that, four burly men, all big rippling muscles, tattoos, scars—bullies, no doubt 'bout it—emerged like unwelcome apparitions from the darkness between the cages. They cracked their knuckles before they drew their swords.

Wallace drew his sword too, the steel a bright red fire.

The trader, now believing he was protected by his hired men, got bolder. "I do believe I'll take the boy from you, Lord whoever you are. He'll get me ninety coppers from the butcher's purse alone, all that muscle on him."

Papa smiled but not one of humor, revealing his teeth. Wallace recognized it as his best 'I'm going to kill you' look. "I'm Lord Hereward, and in case you don't fucking know, let me make it clear so you'll understand. If anyone so much as breathes on my son, they'll become feed for the crows beyond the city's gates quicker than they can blink. Got me?"

The trader's eyes widened again. "L-lord Hereward?"

"That's what I fucking said."

He stammered, sweat returning. "I-I didn't…I didn't k-know."

"Now you do." And with his other hand, the one resting tenderly on Wallace's shoulder, Papa squeezed.

Wallace understood the signal. With a mighty growl, a noise the gods in heaven would admire and tremble at the sound of, Wallace dashed forwards and slashed his sword across the trader's thighs just above the knees. Both of 'em cut open, and blood started trickling down the fancy material of the trader's pants before he realized it. He crumpled to the ground like a wet sack of spuds, screaming in agony.

That's when Papa charged at the four men.

Wallace came over the trader, sneering. He held the point of his blade at the trader's throat, the little notch in the neck Papa had taught him would hold a man down without too much strength 'cause even the slightest protest would slice his airways and veins open.

He grinned. "Make any move an' I finish ya." He pressed the flaming blade against the trader's skin a touch harder to reinforce his threat.

The trader gasped, unable to even kick Wallace's feet from under him as Wallace made sure he stood between the man's legs—as Papa had also taught him—to prevent the move. He also rested a foot, his painted red left boot, on the trader's groin. As Papa instructed, a man with his balls pressed against his pubic bone and a sword at his neck don't usually give any bother. *And if he does, you know what to do.*

Wallace certainly knew what to do.

But the trader stuttered, "I'll make sure I sell you to Rolland, you little shit."

"Who's he when's he home, den?"

"He'll make sure you suffer when he works up a sweat behind you, mark my words. Mark my words. Rolland don't even believe in spitting on his cock before he has his fun."

Wallace wasn't scared any more. No man could scare him when he had his sword in his hand and his papa by his side.

He said, "Been frew worse'n dat, Mista. Had a bad man make me watch me my family gets butchered like Spring lambs, an' after, he ripped off me clothes an' stuck me. More I screamed, harder he got till he were done. No. Nothin' scares me no more."

Wallace swallowed down bitter bile after admitting such a thing. That was the first time he'd spoken out loud to anyone other than Papa and Pa about that terrible night. He felt giddy. Sick. The pain of memory haunted him, but he would conquer it. He would.

With determination, he pressed his foot down; the trader winced, hissing through those teeth that'd whistled for his bodyguards. Wallace could feel his sword bite when the man moved. Satisfaction came over him at the sight of a trickle of blood running in a neat line down the trader's neck. He was a very bad man.

Wallace spat. "Papa were wrong 'bout ya. Don't feels to me like ya got any balls after all, do it now? Ya gutless too, I reckon."

The trader said nothing, but his eyes were murder.

Wallace knew the look too well.

It didn't scare him.

All of a sudden, Papa let out a cry. Wallace startled, his attention drawn for the barest moment, enough to see three men on the floor bleeding, one of 'em choking on their own blood, neck opened in a long red slice, but not enough time to realize his mistake. The trader knocked the sword from Wallace's grip, scrambling to his feet to stand behind his remaining bodyguard. He wiped his neck of the blood, his look even more murderous. With another piercing whistle, four more men came out of the shadows.

Wallace felt wounded because of his failure.

He'd let Papa down.

But Papa wasn't upset, far from it. "Oh look, more fun for my god!" he cheered, sword held ready, dripping blood onto the cobbles from the carnage he'd already caused. "Which one of you wants to feel her deadly fucking kiss first? I'll accept any volunteers before I start choosing."

Wallace stood ready by his papa's side, as he was taught. He sneered, and his blade a crimson flame. His anger was an even deeper color than that, for both himself and for the trader who dealt in the lives of children and wanted to make coin from Wallace's life too. He spat, a big, sticky, foaming globule that landed by the man's boots the trader cowered behind.

"No takers then?" Papa grinned. "Fucking fine with me!"

"Ya'll git yours," Wallace said disdainfully, swinging his sword to hear the deadly thrum it gave as it sliced the air, loving the sound.

But before Wallace could blink, Papa shot forwards, kindly removing the heads from two of the bodyguards' shoulders in quick succession, one, two, *plop*, *plop*. Blood gushed, staining the air. A coppery tang found Wallace's nostrils as the headless bodies fell. More blood, the crimson flow Wallace loved to see come out of bad men. The sharp smell too.

Papa grinned a sweaty smile. He roared, twirled, parried, lunged, and then thrust his blade into the third man silly enough to get closer than his sword god's reach, right in the groove where the man's thigh met his body. Wallace had been taught that was a good place to stick a sword; it severed a main artery and vein together, no recovery from it. The death was slow and painful, though. Papa's intention. That time there wasn't a spray of blood, just a thick black oozing between fingers as the man tried to stem the flow, failed, and then an agonizing scream before the man hit the ground, shuddering his final moments in absolute agony. Death's rattle. Wallace liked such noises from enemies too.

Papa moved onto the next man while another man came for Wallace. But Wallace knew one thing for certain.

Because of his youth, height, speed, and agility, he could outstay any attacker face to face, one on one. So as the burly bodyguard lunged with his sword, no doubt thinking he could dispense Wallace without undue effort, Wallace ducked and scrambled through his legs while the bodyguard tried to re-balance himself.

Wallace was taught wide fighting stances, which a lot of men used to help ground them while they swung a sword, particularly a heavy one. This presented an opportunity. One Papa had told him he should take advantage of. In this case, he did.

As Wallace righted himself behind the man, he swung his sword, cutting the man across his hamstrings. Not deeply, but enough to sting and cause hesitation from the enemy. Papa had also told him men don't wear armor or much protection at the back of their legs, inhibits movement. Good for Wallace. Very good.

The scream as the man dropped to the ground paled all others. Wallace's ears rang. But he came over the man, sword to the notch in his neck below his Adam's apple.

"Yield, do ya?" he said.

The man spat. "Go to fucking hell, brat."

Those were the last words the man spoke. Wallace applied pressure to the hilt, and the blade found the ground underneath the man's neck. One more pool of blood added to the others.

Wallace looked up.

Only the trader remained. The man had pissed himself, his fancy pants wet from his fear, urine dribbling down his leg to dilute the blood at his feet.

Papa asked, "Going to fucking whistle for more help, are you, trader? Please do."

The trader paled and trembled. "You...k-killed them all."

"*We* sure did." Papa was circling him, like a wolf would prey. "Now, you've got two fucking choices here," Papa continued. "You can release the children you're holding and give them to Sister Luci of the orphanage of which I'm a patron. Or, *I* release the children into her care anyway but I get to cut off your fucking hands so you'll have no choice but to live the rest of your days relying on someone else to wipe your arse and hold your cock when you piss."

"That's...that's n-no choice."

"You've got three seconds to decide."

Wallace's sword returned to its blue glow. All danger had passed. For him and Papa, anyway. The trader's fortune was less certain if he didn't make the right choice. As Papa had told him, if you give your enemy a choice, make sure you follow through. A reputation was just as important as the way a sword was handled. Seeing as the trader was unarmed, Wallace thought the choices Papa gave him fair.

No matter the outcome, the children would be freed.

And for Wallace and Papa, the outcome was good. The children were released, smiled for the first time in their lives, Wallace believed. Sister Luci was a lovely lady, all warmth and gratitude for what Papa had done. She promised she'd help the children with reading and other skills needed to get work when they were old enough. Gain a worthy life. Most would become farm hands, a few would become soldiers or maids or likewise, but all would be safe from something far worse than the butcher's block or the dog fighter's ring. Papa gave the orphanage lots of gold coin to help achieve all that too.

Wallace was happy.

Although seeing a man with no hands, enemy or otherwise, wasn't something Wallace wanted to witness too often. The trader's fancy cuffs didn't cover the gore too well.

The tavern was their next stop. It was later in the day, the warmth causing Wallace's brow to sweat. He wiped it with the back of his hand. Perhaps it was all the folks around who made things hotter. They sure talked a lot. All hot air, as Papa had said while they avoided one overenthusiastic merchant in the Great Market. What she was selling, Wallace didn't care.

He only wanted to get out of the city.

With Alistair's hospitality behind them, and a "You all come back soon," in their wake, Papa led Wallace to the stables. Missy would have missed them, he knew it, and he missed Missy.

Eddi, the private of the dock watch, greeted them. He'd been grooming the horses, brush in hand. He was covered in dirt from the stables but looked as happy as could be. Wallace was glad to see him again. Eddi was a good man.

"I think you found your calling," Papa said, patting Eddi on his shoulder appreciatively, a puff of dust flying.

"I have." Eddi beamed a smile. "Gave up the watch yesterday, 'cause Mister Brown the stable master said there was a job for me here if I wanted it. My tour was up, anyways. Plus, this job pays two more silvers a moon's cycle than when I was a guard. Better hours too."

Papa laughed. "And you don't have to wear that stupid fucking helmet, either."

"Darn, thing looked like a cock's knob an' all, didn't it?"

"Just a fucking little."

Both men laughed; Wallace giggled.

"Yeah, the only knob I want on me is the one I can stick into the whores after I get paid."

"Fucking good on you." Papa patted his shoulder again. "A man your age should get his cock wet as often as he can. Never know when darker days will come, now do you?"

The last part sounded ominous to Wallace. Perhaps it was; an army of undead were marching north as this very moment.

"Aye." Eddi contemplated something, his gaze distant for a moment, but he added, "Better get you your horse, then."

"Her name's Missy," Wallace chimed in.

"Aye, Missy then. I'll go get her. She was well behaved and—"

Before Eddi could finish his words, two young men with flourishing long blond hair flicked back and a sparkle of blue eyes came into the stables. They were kind of handsome but certainly comical in their looks, big noses and bigger lips, identical twins by the looks—or very close cousins. They were wearing motley coats, jingling bells an' all, tight tights, and pointed shoes, all patterned in garish stripes.

Wallace's eyes watered looking at 'em. They sure were funny but also interesting. One had a guitar on his back and a flute in hand; the other carried a big bag, no doubt full of tricks—metal rings, wands, ribbons, odd-shaped balls, and other things of wonder of their trade.

Traveling jongleurs, they were.

Wallace had heard about these kinds of folk. Most cost a pretty silver to see in shows of music, dance, jokes, tricks of the eye, and amazing acrobatics full of tumbles and balance. He was led to believe some ate fire and sometimes even swords, but he didn't know if that were true. He did know his family could never afford to go to a traveling jongleur show, not even at the back row.

Papa leant to Wallace, hand cupped to ear. "They may be alike in every way, these two clowns, but you can sure fucking tell which one of them got the lion's share of the family jewels." He gestured to the more confident of the two men, the one talking to Eddi, bargaining for the stable costs.

The man stood with his hips thrust just so, to let Eddi know he was a man of confidence, and his endowment would mean he should be respected. He waved his flute around like a wand, too. Pointing and jabbing it.

Wallace giggled. He felt himself flush and go warm. The talking jongleur's assets were obvious now that they were pointed out. "An' looks as though the other o' 'em only got the leftover family coins, eh."

Papa laughed. "Poor fucking bastard."

"But why does the one talkin' stand like dat, though?"

"Because if you ain't got a brain, best to have balls and let others know about it. Most common folks don't quarrel with someone who's got bravado and the balls to back them up."

Wallace found his frown. "What if'n ya got none o' 'em? Balls or brains?"

"Then you're fucked."

Wallace nodded his understanding.

To his surprise, the jongleurs owned a massive Clydesdale stallion, piebald and magnificent, probably worth more than all the coin in the world, he believed. The horse wore finery too in all sorts of colors, from flagged reins to a chequered saddle blanket, a matching flowing skirt, and a pretty bow in his tail.

The stallion nickered proudly, as if to say, *"Look at me, aren't I just the handsomest thing you ever did see?"*

And to Wallace, he was.

The stallion was magnificent beyond words.

The talking jongleur got first into the saddle, rearranging himself to get more comfortable against the saddle's pommel. Wallace giggled again, and Papa snorted derisively. With Eddi's help, the second climbed up to sit behind his brother, clinging tightly to him moments later.

But that wasn't the end of the surprise, especially when the talking jongleur said reprovingly behind him, "If you drop the juggling pins during today's performance, Horan, so help you, I'll lay you down like a woman and have my way with you, just like I did last night. You don't want *that* humiliation again, do you?"

The other, Horan, meekly replied, "No...of course not, Joran, I don't."

Wallace watched with growing repugnance as they left the stable, their horse's hooves clip clopping on the cobbles of the hay strewn floor, fading into the distance.

"Dey were brothers, weren't dey?" Wallace asked with a queasy swallow, frown still prevalent.

Eddi replied, "Jongleurs keep it in the family—their riches and those they bed."

"Oh." Wallace said, still shocked, tummy turning in disgust. "Why?"

"'Cause they're complete bloody inbred fuckers, that's why." At those words, Papa roared a laugh, adding, "At least Horan is getting his fucking fill by the looks of it. Could be worse."

Eddi laughed too. "Pity it's from his brother, though."

"And *that* was the fucking worse part."

Again, laughter from them both.

Wallace felt sicker, and he held his stomach for emphasis. "Ain't a law 'gainst family…ya know…gettin' in bed together?"

"There is," Papa replied. "But it doesn't apply to jongleurs." Wallace was confused, more than ever. Before he could ask, Papa explained, "They've got a powerful guild with kings and queens on their side as well as nobles. They can do no wrong. Professional entertainment is a valuable commodity, sometimes more than any other because it mollifies the masses. And so long as the guild gets their thirty percent cut to pass on half to the crown, no one's going to argue who jongleurs fuck."

Eddi added, "Coin makes the world go 'round."

"No 'mount of coins would make me git in bed with me Sis when she were alive," Wallace supplied.

"That's because you're not a jongleur," Eddi offered, "but decent and sensible."

Wallace was more than grateful for being brought up as a farm boy in a backwater village, then found by Papa and Pa instead of someone else. He dreaded to think if a slave trader found him. Or a traveling jongleur. He shivered all over at that thought.

Once Eddi got Missy for them, well looked after and happy she was, as promised, they were on their way. Wallace couldn't help but feel sorry for Horan as they passed the ridiculous iron gates of the city and were back in the great outdoors beyond the press of folks, pollution, and all the color and confusion of a big city.

Along the carriage wheel worn cobbled road out of Invrawold, tufts of grass either side Missy wanted to nip at but couldn't, heading towards the stone bridge, Wallace asked, "Why don't Horan do somethin' else if he's gittin' abused by his brother? Like how Eddi changed what he did 'cause he didn't like bein' a guard no more?"

Papa, holding Missy's reins as always when Wallace rode her—to keep her from wandering and nipping at those tufts of grass she so desired—replied, "Because the weight of Horan's purse helps him forget what he has to do to get it filled, that's why. Remember, Eddi gets more coin for what he's doing now. When coins jangle together, folks listen to its music."

Wallace screwed up his face. "Coin is evil, an' all."

"It's not the coin that's evil, son, but what people who want it do. Just look at the likes of the slave trader, the fucking cunt."

Wallace thought about his papa's words for a moment. "I'm happy with me sword helpin' me do right."

"Same here."

17
Alquam's Hatchling Born

FROM A CRACKED EGG, thick fluid oozed, clear and stinking of sulfur. Alquam looked on patiently, tired. Breathing hard. Guarding her brood had been exhausting, and there was no food in her belly. She couldn't hunt while she protected her eggs. Dared not leave them until they were all hatched—those that would.

She was elated one of her hatchlings would soon be free after so long. So long without the sweet, delicious flavor of meat. She was hungry, but soon she would feed. Soon her eggs would hatch. Soon.

A screech, then an arm emerged from the egg. Two arms. Another screech. Then a body, naked and steaming, red skinned but cooling as the foul ooze of birth sloughed away. The hatchling's teeth were already vicious in its slathering mouth, claws already sharp. The first to emerge was always of both sexes, both cock and cunt fertile. It also had all of Alquam's knowledge. The first was also always a shapeshifter. It had to be, to mimic their prey.

Alquam smiled and licked her beak with her forked tongue, pride filling her. Demon hatchlings needed to be ready straight from their emerging, and this one was terribly strong thanks to the feast Alquam consumed before she laid her eggs; Ealdræd had been good sustenance. Although, the feast wasn't quite enough. The dragon Dorgan had tricked her, but worse, the knight had wounded her prey, weakening him.

As such, many of her eggs would never hatch. She blamed Hereward for the consumption of Ealdræd ending far too soon.

The hatchling said, "What do you wish me to do?" Its mouth was stained with blood and dripping gore in ligamentous laces; it'd already devoured its egg mate to give it further strength before the next task. The next feed.

That was the way of things; two per egg, one survivor born.

Alquam replied, "Hunt Hereward. Devour anyone you need to find him but leave no trace of what you've done. Only Hereward will hear the message of my revenge. Only him. Then you can kill him too."

At that, the hatchling's cock hardened, leaking as much as its cunt. The smell of its birth and sex pleased Alquam. This one was determined to serve. To please.

The alpha of her brood was magnificent, intelligent beyond any hatchling Alquam had known. Devious, cruel, and cunning too; the victor of the first egg was always absolutely perfect.

The hatchling smiled evilly, deliciously, wonderfully. "My absolute pleasure, Mother." And with those obsequious words, the hatchling sprouted wings, black feathered like Alquam's, and took flight, leaving behind the ruined egg, the devoured gore of its hatchling mate, and the ejaculate it had spurted in joy.

When the hatchling was gone, ready to ruin Hereward and then the world to begin the Purge, Alquam found she was now ready for the dragon, the immortal, and their friends who approached the cavern that held her brood.

She was very hungry.

The hatchling came to a sprawling farm south of the Iron Mountains, patchwork fields stretching to the horizon. A man and his young son and daughter were tending to a field of barley that blew in flowing, shifting patterns from a southern wind.

The hatchling landed and approached them.

"By the old gods!" the farmer gasped, dropping his scythe, fear in his eyes as he drained white. The smell of his terror aroused the hatchling.

The son and daughter hid behind their father; the hatchling noted the son was ripe, recently so, but the daughter wasn't. No matter. They were inconsequential. The farmer was of more interest. For now.

"I am nothing of importance to you if you do as I ask," the hatching said.

"What is it…you w-want ta ask of me, demon?"

"Give me your clothing." The hatchling didn't make it a request, but a demand, one that had to be obeyed without hesitation.

A startled expression crossed his face, but there was ultimately supplication. "O-of course."

By now, the hatchling's cock was hard again, fluids dripping from both of its genitals. The farmer stared, never taking his eyes off the hatchling, as he disrobed. The son and daughter were crying, trembling with terror. The hatchling liked the sound of fear as much as the smell of it.

"What...w-what is yer name, demon?" the farmer asked as he handed the hatchling all his clothes, hands trembling. Humans were even weaker naked.

The clothing fit well.

"What's yer name?" the farmer repeated, as if it would make a difference to know.

"I have no name," the hatchling replied.

The farmer gulped. "I see."

The hatchling stepped closer; the farmer quaked even more, but bravely, stupidly, stood his ground. Sweat dripped down his paled brow. "I don't think you do. I'm hungry, and you will feed me now."

"I've got plenty o' goat in the meat larder, f-freshly slaughtered. Did it m-myself only a day or so ago. They'll taste good."

The hatchling smiled, revealing its multitude of sharp teeth. "I don't eat animals if I can help it, farmer. No. I want you to feed me your ripened son and virgin daughter. They'll satisfy my hunger better than any goat."

Flying with a full belly was much better.

The farmer wouldn't give up his son and daughter; the man wouldn't even cook them so that their fats would be tastily rendered within their own skins. Very inconsiderate.

Instead, the farmer thought picking up the scythe would make a difference to the hatchling's simple request. It didn't. The hatchling devoured them all, down to the marrow in all their bones, not even a stain on the barley left of them.

They tasted good, even though they had to be eaten raw, their blood sticky and cloying within warm viscera clinging to the hatchling's teeth. He would have preferred them cooked. Still, their screams were satisfying.

And arousing.

The hatchling came to Invrawold City, a smoky, stinking stain on the landscape that tainted the sky above it a dirty brown. Disgusting. The hatchling was repulsed. When the remaining eggs his mother laid were hatched, humanities end would follow. What glory that would be.

Coming back to the moment, the hatchling hoped someone within the city had seen Hereward or knew where he was headed.

The hatchling landed away from prying eyes behind a heaped pile of slate, the slag of an abandoned quarry. The pack of clothing it carried, both men's and women's attire he took from the farmer's home, pleased it. In its approach to the city, the hatchling decided to change into the clothing and body of a woman; it transformed into a nubile one, big breasted, but a commoner. That should get it into the human city without suspicion.

No one questioned a pretty, young fertile woman.

Two guards greeted it at a gate which looked secure but certainly wasn't. The structure was pathetic really. And to only have two guards on duty, even during the day? What arrogance humans possessed. What utter arrogance.

The hatchling approached the guards, lifting the skirt it wore to show a smooth bare leg to the guards. "Good mornin', gentlemen," it said. Its larynx shape had shifted as well to accommodate the sultry tones of a woman to startling realism.

"Holy gods, get an eyeful of that, Frenk," one of the guards said lustfully as he nudged the other.

"Dun'nee see the likes o' that every day, do you, Slen?"

"Aye, ya don't." To the hatchling Frenk said, "And what brings a pretty little thing to the big city all alone, lassy?"

This was where the hatchling had to be careful. "I'm lookin' for a place to stay while I try and find my good for nothing brother."

"What's his name?" Slen asked.

"Hereward," the hatchling said too quickly; the guards didn't seem to notice, too busy looking at the leg it'd exposed to dull their reason. Men full of the stink of their hormones were pathetic. "His name's Hereward."

Slen and Frenk shrugged in unison.

The hatchling wanted to rip their insides out of them, feast on the tasty bile within, until Frenk said, "Dun'nee know if he's here. Could be. But we ain't been on watch these last couple o' days—only seen a young man and a lich lord arrive which gave any interest, t'other day. Other than that, only the usual lot came, merchants and soldiers an' the like. No Hereward. Sorry."

"Try one of the taverns, lass," Slen suggested. "May be stayin' in one of them. Best bet is to try *Down the Goblin's Throat* first. Most travelers go there. Cheap and has cleaner beds'n most."

The hatchling smiled the best smile it could manage. "If I find Hereward quickly, then two lucky guards will get their cocks sucked until their balls are drained, I promise you both that."

Both Slen and Frenk's eyes lit up, mouths dropping open; the hatchling could sense their arousal, smelt it as well. They reeked of it. And the sudden wash of their sex hormones through them would create a delicious infusion throughout their meat, like a marinade. But such a feast was for another time. The hatchling had more important things to do.

Slen stuttered, unable to speak through his lust, and stood awkwardly and almost cross-legged, but Frenk managed, "Lassy, I sure hope you do find Hereward darn quick, an' all."

"I'm sure you do." The hatchling walked past them and into the city proper, already seeing, smelling, and experiencing the calamity of so many crammed within its stone walls, like caged food.

And the hatchling would give Frenk and Slen what they desired before devouring them. After all, human seed was tasty. A nice salty, bitter sauce—the perfect accompaniment to their meat and innards.

Down the Goblin's Throat wasn't difficult to find; most humans were more than happy to divulge any and all information to a woman who expressed certain desires in a way that suited them.

The hatchling despised them all.

A beggar, a disheveled looking man wearing nothing but stinking, sweat fouled rags hanging off him, was slumped in an alley behind the tavern the hatching walked through to get to its goal. Discarded waste surrounding him, hiding him. Almost.

The man hacked up phlegm, then coughed and coughed. "Nice pair o' tits ya got there, swee'heart." More coughing. "Can ya give man down on his luck a feel, eh? Me hands 'ave forgotten what they's like."

Those were the last words the beggar spoke. Unfortunately, he tasted foul, all stringy and dry. The hatchling wasn't satisfied by the meal, even though the beggar filled a hole within it.

"Soon you will feast on better meat," it said to itself as it came out of the alleyway and faced the tavern, a wattle and daub building. The tavern was also near the docks; the hatchling could hear the water lapping against wooden pylons not far away. But the foul stench of river rot, bird droppings, and refuse pumped into the water from the city's sewer almost overwhelmed it. It retched. Why humans needed to be surrounded by their own excrement was beyond reason.

Humans were worse than animals.

Good thing they tasted so lovely.

The hatchling entered *Down the Goblin's Throat*, glad to be off the street. A dark-skinned man, bald and succulent with plenty of fat around his muscles, tended a couple of disinterested patrons behind his bar. The tavern smelt of stale piss, staler sweat, and badly fermented ale; better than the stink outside of it, though.

The hatchling, voice as smooth as silk, sweet and innocent as it could manage, asked, "I'm looking for Hereward. Is he here by any chance?"

"And who's asking?" the barkeep said, a little too abruptly for the hatchling's liking.

The hatchling had no time for delay. "I'm his cousin, and I've not seen him in a while."

"Hereward hasn't got any cousins." The barkeep snorted a laugh. "And certainly not a pretty one like you, girl."

The hatchling became annoyed. "Is Hereward here all the same?"

"No." The barkeep turned his attention back to his patrons, but added, "I don't tell strangers where he is; that's his business, not yours."

The hatchling seethed at the barkeep's audacity, changing into its natural form, claws and teeth at the ready. Within a flash, it flew across the room, plunging its talons into the backs of the two men drinking at the bar, one hand into each, deep and deadly. The men didn't scream. They didn't even get a chance to shit or piss themselves with fear before they died. How disappointing. With little effort, the hatchling ripped their spines from out of their backs, blood dripping down its elbows to stain the pretty dress it wore.

"Now look at what you made me do." The hatchling threw away the spines as the two ruined bloodied bodies slumped off their stools to land on the slate with wet thuds.

The kills were unsatisfactory but necessary.

"Who…w-who are you?" the barkeep stuttered; now *he* was fearful and did indeed piss himself.

That was better.

The hatchling became excited, aroused; it felt its cunt moisten and its cock hardened achingly. This next kill wouldn't be a waste.

"I am no one." The hatchling licked its bloodied fingers, the salty and coppery taste divine. "But if you don't tell me where Hereward is, I'm going to feed you your own cock before I slaughter and eat you, relishing the look of horror and disgust on your petrified face as I do so. Do we understand each other?"

"A-and if I do tell y-you where Hereward is?"

"Then you'll just have a meal of your own cock."

"That's…that's n-n choice at all." The barkeep burst into a cold sweat, trembling and paling.

The hatchling came around the bar to confront the barkeep, claws at the man's throat, seconds later. He could feel the quickened pulse of the man, the life coursing through him. Not for much longer. The barkeep was backed against the wall. Nowhere to run. Nowhere to hide. Perfect.

"But it is your only choice, take it or leave it; you've been told the consequences. Choose quickly. Now."

With a swallow, more sweat, fear, and piss leaking from him, the barkeep said, "He…he went to the s-stables to collect his horse. That's a-all I know. I swear it. I swear it, so help me by the old gods."

The beautiful thing about when humans screamed in pain and terror was that their mouths were always so conveniently opened. Yanking a flaccid cock out by the roots and shoving it into a gaping mouth to stifle the screaming was even more satisfying than the hatchling would have believed. He even helped move the barkeep's jaw to ensure his cock, grisly and chewy from the sound of it, was masticated nicely before being swallowed. The hatchling thought that very considerate. As such, for dessert, the barkeep got to taste his own testicles—a delicacy according to goblins.

"The gods you pray to didn't help you today, did they? But you helped me, and for that I am thankful. That is why you still live. Have a good day, barkeep."

The hatchling left the barkeep a blubbering, cock-less mess on his tavern's dirty floor. The man was unable to move for the pain, clutching at his bloodied groin, tears streaming as much as his fear and sweat. Blood dribbled in bubbles down to his chin after the fill of his unexpected dinner; the man wouldn't be hungry for a while, for he had an ample cock for a human and big enough testicles too.

The barkeep kept moaning in agony, begging to be killed over and over. The hatchling, hearing it from the bustling street and remembering its mother's words about leaving no trace, returned to give him what he begged for. He tasted succulent and satisfying—the man stuffed with his own genitals.

The stables weren't difficult to find. Horses stunk too. Not as much as humans, and in a more helpful way; manure and hay a potent but unmistakable mixture.

A young man greeted the hatchling as soon as it stepped within the well-kept and tidy stables. Freshly swept it was as well. The hatchling had transformed into a man because the woman's clothing it wore before were too bloodied and piss stained; even after the barkeep's cock had been removed from him his piss still flowed, even when being slaughtered too. It went everywhere, even over the hatchling's pretty new dress. The outfit would need to be washed before the hatchling left the city so it could keep its promise to Frenk and Slen before devouring them as well.

Therefore, the hatchling now wore the farmer's son's clothing, the adolescent it'd devoured and enjoyed what seemed so long ago. It transformed into his likeness too, youthful and strong. But the hatchling was hungry again already.

The barkeep didn't satisfy.

"Hey there. What can I do for you, sir?" a young man holding onto a broom, sweeping fresh steaming manure into a pile, said politely. The poor unaware soul; he had no idea what confronted him.

"I'm seeking information," the hatchling said. "Have you been here long, stable hand?"

"I haven't—this is my new job. But I've been here every day and most nights too since I got the work. I love tending the horses. Found my calling, I have."

The hatchling didn't care what the young man liked; humans were so fickle with their interests. "What's your name, stable hand?" the hatchling asked politely. Politeness loosened tongues, after all.

"Name's Eddi, sir."

"Pleased to meet you, Eddi." The hatchling extended his hand; Eddi shook it. For a moment, the hatchling shuddered, it could feel the life pulse through the young man's touch. He so wanted to still it. But first answers.

"And you?" Eddi released his warm grip. "What's your name, sir?"

"John," the hatchling lied, but it was the only name it could think of—a common enough one for human men that wouldn't arouse any suspicion, the hatchling hoped.

"Well, John, what information are you after? I'd be happy to help if I can."

"I would like to know where Hereward went."

That's when Eddi's demeanor changed; his eyes narrowed. "Now why do you need to know a thing like that? Hereward's my friend, he is. And he didn't tell me of anyone looking for him."

The lies now flowed easily. "I want to be a knight, and learning the skills of the sword is important to be one. I'm tired of being a farmer—no glory in it, you see. My pa said Hereward taught young men such skills. Isn't that right?"

"Aye, he does."

"Then where has he gone, Eddi?"

At that moment a large stallion whinnied, stamping its hoof in distress. Eddi went to it, soothing his hand along its rump to try and placate the animal. "Easy there, boy. What's got you all nervous all of a sudden, eh?"

The hatchling knew the animal sensed what Eddi didn't: the imminent danger. That could be a problem if the young man caught on too. He'd flee. The hatchling couldn't let that happen, not without an answer to his question.

"Please, I am in a hurry," the hatchling said, keeping the impatience out of its voice as best it could. "My pa will tan my hide with his belt if I'm gone too long. Can you tell me where Hereward went?"

Eddi shrugged. "All I know is he went south with Wallace, his son. Told me he'd camp in Varwesh forest overnight first, then continue from there. Sorry I can't help you any more than that, sir."

"Oh, you *will* be sorry." Eddi's eyes widened as the hatchling transformed. "Seeing as you love your horses so much, Eddi, I think I have something special in mind for you after I kill you."

Eddi dropped his broom, stumbling back. "You're...evil...you're a—" He couldn't get the rest of the words past his trembling lips before the hatchling ripped him to shreds; innards, viscera, blood, and bone flew everywhere to stain the straw and the stallion's coat alike.

For something different, the horse screamed instead of the human as the hatchling dismembered the young man, eyes struck with terror, hooves stamping. When the hatchling had made mincemeat of Eddi, sliced him into small enough pieces for a sparrow's beak and nothing more with bloodied claws and deep satisfaction, the hatchling shoved all that was left of the young man into the horse's anal cavity.

No one would find the remains of Eddi for a while.

Not until the stallion took a shit, once the animal could relax enough to do so. The stallion was still frightened, even when the hatchling cleaned up the blood, washed its clothing in the water trough, dried it with its hot breath, and then slipped into the dress once again after transforming into a woman.

"Don't get too comfortable," the hatchling said to the horse, caressing it. The horse protested the touch, rearing up. "I can still come back for you to finish the job, you know. Horse meat isn't too bad to eat—only slightly worse than human."

The horse cowered in its stall, the sweat of fear covering his chestnut-colored coat.

With a final stroke across the horse's rump, clammy and cold, the hatchling added, "But first, I've got a couple of human cocks to suck before I can eat my fill again. A promise is a promise, is it not?" The stallion nickered in terror, baring his teeth. "See you some other time, then, friend. Frenk and Slen are eagerly awaiting their blissful death, and I don't want to disappoint them."

The hatchling left the stables, confident its goal was a little clearer; Mother would be pleased.

18
Oswin's Lost Mind

NOVANE BECAME LOST IN his damaged man's arms, the wonder of it was all he cared about. If he could be a part of Greysen, the healing part, he would. All he could do was support him, comfort him. Be there for him.

For eternity.

Their kissing, the dizzying wonder of being together because of their connection, the tender touches, hands clasped, then unclasped to hold each other, overwhelmed him. Novane was so stupidly, deeply, agonizingly, wonderfully in love; he couldn't help but weep because of the potency of his feelings.

Greysen wept with him.

Through the mists of his emotions, the clouds of his thoughts, he held Greysen tighter. As he did so, a strange sensation overcame him. At first, it startled Novane. No. Terrified him. Confused him. What could the feeling be? He had love. He had desire. He had Greysen in his arms, both of them pouring out their emotions for each other, hands trembling, embracing tight.

So what could it be?

Novane became even more scared as the sensation increased. It shot through him, pulsed and surged, loud in his ears like a rush of blood. Lub-dub, lub-dub. On and on it went. Lub-dub. Novane gasped, pulling away from Greysen.

"What's the matter?" Greysen questioned, aura changing to the curious but hurt colors of gold and magenta also reflected in his steely grays; Novane couldn't blame him.

Novane's lip quivered and his eyes widened as the sensation grew within his chest, lub-dub, lub-dub, lub-dub. He then knew what it was.

Impossible.

But it was there.

"I…my heart is b-beating…" He clutched his chest, feeling the thump through his ribs, something he hadn't felt for the longest time, the memory faded too far into the past to remember. "It's beating because of you…for you."

Greysen's expression relaxed; his aura returned to the brilliant corona it should be. "It's beating for me?" He pressed one hand against Novane's chest. "Yes, I can feel it. It does." With his other, he grabbed Novane's hand and pressed it to his own. "As mine beats for you. Can you feel it?"

Novane could, and it made him shiver.

For another eternity they felt each other's hearts beat out their love. They looked into each other's eyes, and Novane couldn't help but become lost within Greysen's, a gray ocean of delight, one he never wanted to be rescued from.

After the longest time, Greysen said, "Other parts of me have awoken, just as your heart has."

"May I touch you there?"

Greysen let go of Novane long enough to fumble with his pants and pull them down, underwear too. Novane gasped, delighted at the sight of his lover's cock springing up once it was freed, the knob of it firm and ripe and red, glistening with intention. Greysen was big. Beautifully so.

"You can kiss me there," Greysen whispered. "As well a touch me wherever you want."

Novane made the journey down towards Greysen's cock as pleasurable as he knew the destination would be. He relished it. He opened his lover's jerkin and lifted up the shirt underneath to expose his chest and stomach. From there, he started at Greysen's erect pink nipples, kissing them, sending delight through him and his lover. He then left warm trails down to the pubic hair Greysen had been growing since he'd left Myrkul. The hair, black and thick like a dense forest now, was full of the scents of his musk and alluring manliness. Novane loved how it was all grown; he loved burying his nose in it even more.

"Yes," Greysen moaned.

Greysen's flat stomach quivered as Novane, now on his knees, began kissing the erection that filled his every desire. He kissed the jagged circumcision scar first, tenderly, lovingly, as if his lips could heal it. He hoped they would.

More shivers from Greysen.

Novane took that as permission to continue, more so when

Greysen placed his hands upon his head. Not to force, but to encourage. And encouraged Novane was. Soon, he had as much of Greysen's cock as he could take in his mouth and was sucking deeply, using his tongue to massage along with the action.

Novane brought his hands up to cup Greysen's buttocks, firm and wondrous things they were. Beautiful. What made it more so was that Greysen didn't thrust but let Novane explore at his own pace. The salty tang of his lover's desire flooded his mouth. Many times, Novane came off Greysen's cock, slurping, saliva dripping, to send his tongue exploring around his fully engorged head.

More shivers punctuated with shudders from Greysen now.

Novane continued, taking Greysen deeper as he relaxed more, as he was trusted to do. His newly beating heart thumped louder. He was so alive. The most alive he'd ever been.

Another sensation also overwhelmed Novane as he worked his mouth, tongue, and lips along Greysen's hardness: the feeling of his own desire increasing. He was erect himself. The sensation of what he was doing encouraged even more from within himself. He too shuddered.

But he didn't stop.

Couldn't.

He wanted to satisfy Greysen more than anything else, prove to him love wasn't about taking without reward but giving because there didn't have to be one. Sometimes, even letting a lover come to their conclusion, selflessly, was a great gift to give. And Novane wanted to give that to Greysen.

With another shudder from Greysen, Novane feeling his cock harden even more in his mouth, almost to the back of his throat after warming up to what he was delightfully endowed with, more salt and tang found him. But the shuddering got more intense, Greysen's stomach rising and falling rapidly, body heated, cheeks flushed, eyes squeezed tight.

Then it happened.

Greysen let go of everything with a shout of relief, joy, ecstasy, wonder. A yell that sent the birds to flight. Novane was flooded with more of the taste of his lover, stronger, spicier, tangier, but even more delicious.

He let go himself as well.

Greysen collapsed as soon as Novane came off him for the last time with a satisfying popping sound, saliva and seed dribbling in thick ribbons over his chin and the ground alike.

Novane held Greysen with everything his new heart could give.

Greysen was crying again, his aura revealing all too clearly how much weight had been lifted off him, how now, finally, he'd realized love wasn't a selfish act. Novane cried too.

"How do you feel?" Novane asked as he gathered wood; Greysen was standing beside his dead brother. The man's look was still vacant, only the barest inkling of life within to prevent him from being permanently put into a grave.

"I…I don't know."

And Novane knew the words to be the truth. How could one quantify equality, respect, love, when it had never been given to them before?

"Are you all right?"

"I am." Greysen's gaze fell to Novane. "I want to do…something for you tonight."

"Only if you want to."

A cloud came over Greysen's aura. "I'm…I'm not sure." This was such new territory for him; for Novane, too.

"Then don't do anything. I'm happy to just make you happy."

"But it can't be like that forever, otherwise I'm no better than Myrkul. No better than Darrin, if I become selfish with what I want."

"You won't be selfish; I'll make sure of it."

"But don't you want something in return for what you've done?"

"What I did to you satisfied me."

Greysen's cloud dissipated. "You have to clean yourself up?"

"Yes."

"I'd like to help you."

Novane smiled and put down the sticks for kindling, coming to hold Greysen's hand. "I'd like that."

Greysen shifted his attention back to Oswin. "And besides, my brother needs cleaning as well; he's starting to stink like death."

"He *is* dead."

"No, he's not," Greysen retorted with conviction. "Oswin's in there somewhere. I know it. I just—*we* just have to try and help him find himself like how we both helped you find your heart."

The beating of Novane's heart was still strange to him, but he would get used to it, especially if it caused more passion for Greysen because it now worked.

"And we both helped you find your respect for yourself because you deserve it," Novane shot back, smiling.

"Exactly."

Novane kissed Greysen, lips against lips, warm and wonderful. "There's a pool not too far away fed by a brook with water fresh from the mountain snows. We'll all bathe there."

Greysen nodded, kissing Novane in return. "You will have to lead my brother to the water. I can't touch him, remember."

Novane did so. As he led Oswin by the hand, cold and clammy, he realized Greysen might be right. From the dead man's non-existent aura, a flicker of an aura emerged. Black and deep purple. Diminished. Weak. But an aura, nonetheless.

At the pool, surrounded by overhanging weeping willows, thick and plentiful, branches touching the water as if to drink from it, the golden sun dabbled all around them. The seeds of the forest danced in a breeze, mostly dandelion pods. Some landed in the water. Some would be fortunate enough to land at a place where they could germinate.

The place they'd found themselves was magical. Wondrous. Or was it Novane's new heart waxing lyrical about something mundane? Something as common as water surrounded by trees.

He no longer thought so.

No wonder painters used pigmented oils with linseed, setting up their easels in an attempt to capture the wonder of the natural world. This place was inspiring. The babbling brook. The shimmering waters. The tranquility of it all together unquantifiable. So beautiful.

But to Novane, what made it even more beautiful was Greysen being here with him. His lover now wore nothing, clothing discarded quickly, a picture of greater wonder. His slim but fit build, his manly hair in all the right places. Novane was helplessly in love. He wanted nothing than to give Greysen more of his love, taste him again.

Beside him, Oswin stood. The ghoulish reminder of why they were at the pool in the first place.

Novane undressed the dead man. Greysen was right. He needed washing. His clothes stank of a mausoleum, and that was being nice about it. The scars of Monk Wu's delicate blade covered every inch of Oswin's skin.

Novane became sickened by the sight of them all, far more than a thousand. Far more. But when he got to removing Oswin's undergarments, Novane discovered, to his surprise, that the monk's blade hadn't been so thorough.

Greysen must have seen it too, for he said, "Oswin still has his genitals intact." There was relief in those words.

Once again, Novane couldn't blame him. If there was life inside Oswin, life that could be awakened somehow, then at least, at the very least, he was whole in the way he would want to be. From what he'd seen in the Seeing Crystal before Monk Wu captured him, Oswin liked to use his cock a lot, and on both men and women, preferably together.

Perhaps there was something for him if he ever recovered. Then again, Novane had learned more than most that there was always hope.

Novane quipped, "I see the family's fruits didn't fall far from the tree."

Greysen laughed. "You like big cocks then, Novane?"

"Only yours."

"Good answer."

Novane disrobed and brought Oswin into the water. He washed the dead man and himself too, but as he did so, Oswin's aura grew in strength. Nothing like a living being's aura looked, far from it, but it was something. Not bright, but there. The deep purples were turning lighter.

When Novane was done, Greysen came closer. "At least he doesn't smell bad any longer."

"True."

And then it happened. From lips that hadn't spoken for a long time, parched and cracked and as dead as him, Oswin said, "Brother, help me." Those three words were spoken with a brief glimpse of recognition, of life, before the dead embers of his eyes returned, and his aura diminished to the black of before.

Greysen gasped.

Novane had to admit, surprise once more found him too.

"We must get Oswin to the monastery as soon as we can," Greysen urged. "I don't think we have much time."

"What makes you say that?" Novane asked, pulling Greysen closer, feeling his warmth underneath the cool water dripping from his skin.

"You heard him; he needs help to come back from the place where he's been hidden," Greysen explained, worry seeping through in his voice. "And I know we can't give that to him with just the two of us alone."

"He will need Wymond as well?"

"Yes."

"But why?"

"Because I believe I know why I was separated from Wymond and Oswin all those years ago. Why we were all separated from each other."

Novane didn't follow. "Why?" was all he could ask again, pathetically really.

"Because the universe from which we were created feared us, and Abbot Hosho was left no choice. He knew what we could do when we were together, Oswin, Wymond, and me. I'm already powerful, you know that; you've seen it. What potential has Oswin got when he awakens? He can already drain the life out of the living, even the undead; I saw how you were affected before Wallace severed Monk Wu's influence. That's why he was kept alive. The monk knew. Now we know. What potential does Oswin have? What potential do I have? And what about Wymond?"

Novane took his turn to gasp. "You...you could all be...gods."

"We already are." Greysen held Novane tightly. "We just have to realize it ourselves, and being together will ensure it. The power of three once realized is far greater than what we can do alone. Far greater."

"Then I am in love with a god, not a magician of the Hyruldon Expanse."

Greysen kissed Novane. "No matter what I am, the *damaged god* perhaps, all I know is that I'm in love with you." He then kissed Novane again but on the lips, slowly, tenderly, before letting go. "So, let's go; the monastery within the Steps to Heaven mountains awaits us."

"Our journey will not be too hasty, I hope," Novane said. "I would like there to be time to love each other; that journey has only just begun."

Greysen's aura intensified to a brilliance he'd never seen before, brighter than all the stars in the heavens together. His power was phenomenal, arousing, luring, intoxicating. "There will always be time for our love. Always."

He took Novane's hand and led him out of the water. Oswin followed, but perhaps not so blindly. Novane could see the dead man's aura intensifying, reflecting Greysen's but growing, blossoming, of its own accord as well. The emotion of Oswin's bond with Greysen, as brothers, was building the bridge even quicker.

Soon, Oswin, the lost god, *would* awaken.

And pity on those who had done Greysen, Oswin, and Wymond wrong when that happened. Pity on them all.

19
Wallace's Startling Discovery

HAVE YOU BEEN PRACTICING, son?"

"Ya, Papa, I's have been." Wallace couldn't help but feel greater pride; he'd been practicing his sword skills and the drills required for hours each day as they made their way south into the Kingdom of Suvanwold. Sometimes till his arms ached. Most times until he fell asleep atop Missy when it was time to move on, their belongings packed into saddlebags to help cushion his slumber.

After a week or so, Wallace wasn't quite sure of the time; days and nights melded into one because of the good times he was having with Papa. They found themselves within the great north-eastern forest of the kingdom. A big tree forest full of creaking boughs and whistling leaves. Papa said the forest was called Varwesh. Funny name. All in all, a nice enough place. Mostly 'cause it were full of birds, rabbits, and cute spotted deer Wallace wanted to pet, a few foxes and badgers he didn't, and beautiful migrating butterflies too. Rippling streams ran lazily between the great trees like silver ribbons. The canopy was open, as the trees didn't grow too close together. Plenty of air within Varwesh. It smelt kinda nice too, like fresh fallen leaves, pollen laden flowers, and medicinal bark all rolled into one but in a pleasant way.

"That's good to hear," Papa said. "Practice makes perfect, you know."

But Missy whinnied in protest, wanting to nip at the greener grass not too far from the dusty, winding path they traveled. Wallace was riding her, and Papa walked in front, pulling at her reins whenever she wandered. But for the moment, he let her munch. She nickered happily, the nipped grass broken down by her grinding teeth quickly. Wallace stroked her neck tenderly before he dismounted. He admired Missy, his faithful friend.

"You spoil that horse," Papa offered, but with no ill intention in his words.

"She's worth it, an' all." Wallace went into one of the saddle bags to retrieve a couple of carrots he'd been saving since they'd left the Great Market of Invrawold city. Missy took them gently from his hand, her hairy lips tickling him. He giggled.

Papa snorted. "'Suppose you're right." He looked around, rubbing his beard in thought like how he sometimes got. "What do you think about camping here tonight? I can set up your hessian dummy from that branch," he pointed to a large bough low enough near the largest tree, "to practice on."

Wallace nodded. "Sounds good, Papa."

Missy, having eaten the carrots, returned to the grass. It was then Wallace heard something new. He stilled, trying to listen with more intent.

Papa asked, "What?" But his hand touched the hilt of his sword god; he must have heard it too.

"Thought I's heard somethin', is all."

The sound came again, louder, echoing through the forest and scattering the wildlife. But Wallace breathed a sigh of relief. The noise was laughter, and it was coming from beyond the rise of trees not too far ahead of them. To him, it sounded like many folks laughing, having a good time.

And no wonder. When Wallace and Papa got there, a large clearing confronted them and Wallace sucked in a breath of surprise, shifting on his feet in excitement, eyes wide.

Almost cheering, he said, "It's Horan n' Joran, givin' a performance ta the woodcutters n' their families!"

"Well, fucking blow me down, you'd be right!" Papa got that look again, the one where he were about to make a decision. He winked at Wallace. "Best if we join the audience and have ourselves a good show, right?"

"Right, an' all, Papa." Wallace couldn't have been happier; never seen a jongleur's show before, he hadn't.

Without delay, Wallace and Papa joined the gathered folks, rough hard-working men and women of the forest, their children too, and watched Horan and Joran perform their tricks, strum and blow their instruments, and sing their jaunty songs. The onlookers joined in with the songs best they could, as did Wallace.

A life tis a life, and a life couldn't be better,
no siree, it couldn't be better so.
There's no fiddle dee dee and fiddle dee doe,
not when you live your life to the fullest.
Why be all down, don't wanna cut off yer nose to spite yer face?
Because I can tell ya all one thing, a nose is hard to replace.
A nose is hard to replace!

Then came the chorus, one that made Wallace laugh.

Noooo nose!
And if I could, yes siree, it'd tell ya a man looks mighty funny,
mighty funny without his nose.
A noooo nosed man.
Mister noooo nose!
What a sight, 'cause how would he ever pick it?

There were a few other verses, but that song was one of Wallace's favorites 'cause it also involved feet stamping and clapping in time with the music. He kept humming it even when the tune was done.

What fun!

While the juggling part was going on, Papa leant over to Wallace and whispered, "Let's hope Horan don't drop anything. Otherwise, he'll be fucked later."

"Ya're wicked, Papa." But Wallace, even though he felt sorry for Horan being stuck with a brother like Joran, couldn't help but laugh. More so because Horan didn't drop anything.

In fact, all told, Horan was really good.

So was Joran.

"I'm wicked like a fucking wildfire," Papa said cheekily, proudly even, as he dropped two silvers into a wooden collection bowl, *clank-clank*, held by a pleasantly smiling woodcutter's daughter with dirt on her cheeks and matted blonde hair but a clean smile who was moving through the crowd.

Wallace enjoyed the rest of the show.

He noticed Horan and Joran's Clydesdale, a magnificent horse for sure, was nipping at a large patch of grass, hay provided too. Missy had joined the stallion, happy.

There was also a round-topped wooden caravan, all fancy carved eaves and frames, not too far away and nestled between two ancient trees with twisted, knobbed bark. Wallace guessed the one the Clydesdale pulled holding all of the jongleurs' possessions.

The wood of the caravan was painted with even more gaudy colors than Horan and Joran's motley and tights. To Wallace, it looked as though someone had eaten all the terrible things he'd seen offered at the Great Market, and then thrown it all up over the outside of the caravan. *Joran & Horan, Jongleurs to the Famous* was scribbled over all that color like spidery veins in gaudy shades of gold and silver.

The show ended too soon.

To his surprise, the day had turned to evenfall, and Wallace, tired but still excited after the show, wanted to talk to Horan to thank him. He felt a kind of friendship towards the man. He couldn't explain it.

He approached the caravan and, stepping onto the wooden steps, Wallace heard voices. He paused, listening.

"Your performance was even more abysmal than usual, Horan," Joran scolded, voice full of arrogance and anger.

"But I didn't drop anything."

"No," there was a disdainful harrumph, "but your timing was off. And by the old gods, your bloody cock slipped again—the thing went near on down the middle of your thigh this time! What a complete bloody embarrassment!" There was silence for a bit but some sort of shuffling noise. But Joran's chastising wasn't over. "And a good thing we were only performing in front of the local bloody imbeciles where even a farting competition would have amused them, otherwise we'd have been laughed at. Laughed at! Me! The great Joran, laughed at. It will not do…"

Wallace giggled, quickly covering his mouth so he wouldn't be heard. He couldn't help but think about how farting *was* funny, and he was no imbe-whatever, as Joran had suggested. Neither were the other folks that word either, whatever it meant. Wallace had a feeling it wasn't a good thing to call someone.

Still chuckling to himself, he remembered how he would roar with laughter when Papa would wave his hand about, and say, "Eww! Who cut the fucking cheese?" when he farted, often blaming Missy. Oh, how he laughed.

But Wallace was brought back to the moment when, after more shuffling about and hesitation in the conversation, Horan said meekly, "I'm sorry, it won't happen again. I just couldn't—"

"I don't want bloody excuses."

"Sorry, Joran."

"And I most certainly I don't want weak apologies, either. Now bend over; it's time for your punishment. And no whimpering this time. Nothing worse, and I won't abide by it."

"Yes, Joran."

Wallace gasped.

The noises of Joran doing things to Horan were nothing like the noises Papa and Pa made when they were together. There was no love, no gentle moaning or kisses, no signs of affection. Wallace felt bile rise to the back of this throat, remembering the face of that bandit who had come into his home so long ago but still fresh in his mind. The hopelessness, paralyzed within the man's grip with absolute fear, begging for him to stop, crying, the look of pure evil in his eyes as he…

Then Joran and Horan's sex noises stopped.

Wallace ran to hide behind the back of the caravan, wiping his eyes of tears. Bitter, vile tears. He felt for Horan. No one should have to suffer such a thing for any reason. But what could Wallace do?

An opportunity came when he heard the caravan's door slam, and a dark shadowy figure—unmistakably Joran, leaving in a huff—headed towards the fire the woodcutters had set up. Papa was there, laughing and drinking with them.

Joran joined them, thunderclouds above him.

Papa said something, but Wallace didn't catch it. Joran was given a horn of ale by one of the woodcutters; he drank it all in one go and gestured for another—which was provided.

Wallace had more important things on his mind than Joran.

As he came back around to the steps leading to the caravan's door, he heard sobbing. He didn't knock before entering. The sight before him shocked him to his core, and it wasn't because Horan were slumped over a basin crying, shoulders heaving.

Upon a nearby round and polished table, Wallace saw what he could only describe as a man's willy and balls. Clearly, they weren't real. Probably made of tree sap or something similar, he thought. Fangmere forest had trees that made such a sap that could be used to make just about anything. It was then, when Horan turned to face him, he could see Horan didn't have a willy and balls of his own and must have used the ones on the table.

He gasped again, something which had become common lately, for sure.

"Who *are* you?" Horan plucked up the fake willy and balls and stuck them to the front of him before pulling up his tights with haste. Wallace was right. "And what are you doing in here uninvited?"

"Sorry." Wallace bowed respectfully to prevent Horan from staring. "I'm Wallace…an'…an' I's just came ta say I's enjoyed ya show. Didn't means anythin' by me…intrusion. Swears it."

Horan's expression softened. He sighed and then sat. Sighed again. "I suppose you want an explanation as to what you've just seen?"

Wallace shrugged. "Don't owe me nothin', does ya. None o' me business, is it? I's just liked ya show, like I's said."

Horan smiled, wiping his eyes. "I like you, Wallace." The jongleur gestured for him to sit.

Wallace did, smiling back. "I's like ya as well, Horan."

And somehow, much to Wallace's delight, there seemed to be a connection between them. An instant friendship. Wallace imagined it were mostly because Horan sensed he'd never tell his secret. And he wouldn't. It weren't up to him to tell.

Their conversation flowed.

"I've never wanted nor ever desired to be a woman, Wallace, even when I was a little girl," Horan explained. "I've always thought of myself as a boy—a man now. That's why I wear my *gentleman's bits* as I call them when I'm in my motley and tights, so no one gets a clue." Horan became even more reflective, Wallace hanging on his every word. "But I had to make them a lot smaller than Joran's real one. Otherwise, he would've got jealous and done far worse to me than stick me when I made any mistakes during our shows."

"Whys don't ya leave him if he treats ya so bad?"

"Because he's my brother," Horan retorted without hesitation. "And as arrogant and selfish as he is, I'm the only person he's got, that's why."

"Sorry, but I's don't git it. He's not treatin' ya right, is he, an' all. Why stay with him?"

Wallace knew being stuck in that way by anyone against their wishes was a terrible crime, and he simply couldn't imagine worse; only now, after months, had the nightmares finally eased enough from him to sleep most nights and still, he could still see that man's face leering at him if something triggered him.

"Not many people do." Horan settled deeper into the chair. "The truth is, Joran would be lost without me. You're not going to tell anyone about all this, are you, Wallace?"

Wallace shook his head, an act that not only showed he agreed with Horan but also helped dismiss the niggling doubts in his head. Again, none of this were his business. "No matter if I's don't git it, 'cause I don't, I's swears I's won't tell a soul."

"Not even your Papa?"

Wallace flushed. "I don't keeps nothin' from Papa. An' if he asks, I'll tells him. He's the only one though. Oh, an' me Pa, o' course…but he's not here." Wallace wasn't ready to tell Horan everything. Not yet.

"I understand." Horan brightened somewhat yet still held profound sadness, "But your Papa, who I recognized as Lord Hereward, won't tell anyone if he finds out, will he?"

"Not if I's swears for him not to. He's got a knight's honor, just likes me!"

Horan tilted his head. "That's good enough for me then, Lord Wallace."

Wallace laughed; he liked being called a lord. "Good fer me too." Wallace got up to put his hand onto Horan's shoulder, emulating the gesture Papa did when he liked someone. "Did ya want me ta stay for a bit? Keep ya company?"

"No. But I do think we should join the festivities at the campfire, don't you?"

Wallace agreed, "Sure. But I's gotta warn ya, Papa likes ta drink a bit, an' a lot o' times, I gotta put him ta bed. Snores like a demon too when he's drunk like dat."

Horan laughed. "I'm glad we're friends, Wallace. You've made me feel better."

Wallace extended his hand, and Horan took it. Together, they went to the campfire, a roaring, blazing monstrosity that would have warmed the whole forest. Many more people had gathered, which Wallace discovered was common when ale and wine were available. All that was missing were satyrs. At that thought, Wallace remembered Gik, and sadness found him.

Wallace drank fresh goat's milk, good too it were, and he felt better.

As expected, Papa drank too much ale from too many horns, and Wallace couldn't help but smile at him, knowing he'd have to set up the tents tonight. He was used to it.

After an hour or so, moon high through the gaping canopy lit by firelight, Joran stood, wobbled, then stated with a slur, "I need to bloody piss." The jongleur was already fumbling with his tights, freeing his willy; the man had no shame, even if he had a big one—so big, it were like a one-eyed snake.

Wallace blushed, looking away.

"Go piss, then." Papa laughed, clapping the jongleur on his back and making the man jump. "Don't make a fucking song and dance about it!"

Wallace giggled.

What else could a jongleur do but make a song and dance about everything?

20
Dorgan's Enemy Faced

ALQUAM HISSED AND SCREECHED at them, ear-piercing, her posture defensive, feathers ruffled. Dorgan realised she was unwilling to leave her eggs unprotected. Which meant two things: the demon would be protectively ferocious, but at the same time limited to within the surrounds of her nest, the confines of the cave.

Dorgan knew the information was valuable, but for the moment something else worried him. Concerned him greatly. The fetid smell inside the cave was unbelievable; sulfur, acid, copper, and other things all viler, mixed together to create a toxic potency adding to the already thick, humid air dripping from the walls and stalactites alike.

Everything seemed so close, dangerously so.

Dorgan's vision misted as he tried to blink away the foulness, something he could taste to the back of this throat, stinging, burning, making him cough. His scales glistened with toxic residue already, and if he were in human form, he was certain he'd be dying of suffocation and poisoning. The air within the cavernous hole at the bottom of the caldera certainly wasn't breathable.

As such, Vash—upon Kieron's back—suddenly became overcome, retching and coughing. The delphin collapsed, leaving their chunky spew that created a disgusting stain down Kieron's scales.

"By the gods, we can't stay in here, Dorgan!" Kieron cried.

Alquam screeched in satisfaction, Dorgan knew all the noises of pleasure, pain, and anger, the demon made. That screech was one of victory.

Kieron continued, "Vash won't last long! And neither will I!" Kieron spluttered a thick cough, turned, and then left the cave for the sweeter, cleaner air beyond the enveloping darkness.

Dorgan couldn't blame him; he was finding it difficult to breathe as well. He coughed too, chest suddenly tight. He wouldn't last long either. And from the corner of his eye, he could see Kieron, now returned to a man, had collapsed beside Vash; they were holding each other but both unconscious—that's how it looked to Dorgan. He wasn't too sure; his vision wasn't the best because of the atmosphere, cloying, noxious, and clouded. Kieron and Vash didn't look good at any rate.

Unfortunately, even though Dorgan's heart ached for his friends, he had to return his attention quickly to Alquam, not trusting the demon. When he was distracted, that's when she would strike.

Yet, for all the foul effects the air had upon them all, Abbot Hosho, his orange robe seemingly aglow within the gloom, didn't seem perturbed. Abbot Hosho stood beside Dorgan, serene, contemplative, staring. Didn't the immortal need to breathe? Perhaps Abbot Hosho was holding his breathe while he waited for the universe to tell him something, whisper its wisdom into his ear; if the universe's wisdom could reach into the nest of Hell they'd found themselves within, that was.

Without a chance to contemplate such things, Alquam screeched again. "You don't want to stay, Dorgan, *my old friend*? Pity. We could reminisce about old times, you and me."

"You know I can't, demon!"

"Yes, you can, Dorgan." Dorgan was shocked to see Abbot Hosho looking up at him, a twinkle in his milky, pupil-less, eyes. "You can stay and slay the demon. Destroy her eggs too."

Alquam screeched in annoyance.

"How?" was all Dorgan could utter before the toxicity of the air began to claw at his reason, choke him, and create confusion within his thoughts, images and memories swirling into a dizzying mess. He stumbled and coughed. He wanted nothing but to get out of the cave despite his desire to destroy Alquam.

The demon laughed, but Dorgan knew it was one of caution, of nerves. As Dorgan was just as curious about what Abbot Hosho had in mind as much as Alquam was.

Abbot Hosho raised a gentle hand, and Dorgan suddenly felt calm wash through him, stilling his muddled mind. He sucked in a cool, clean breath, lungs inflating fully, chest rising, and the joy of life renewed overwhelmed him. How? How was such a thing possible?

"I must tend to Kieron and Vash," Abbot Hosho said. "But for you, Dorgan, I have given you the gift of the outside air around you. It will stay with you long enough to do what you must do. It is all in your hands now. I'm needed elsewhere."

Abbot Hosho's words were true. Around Dorgan there was a bubble of air, faint but there, sometimes shimmering as it caught what little light there was within the cave. What magic had created it, he didn't know. Abbot Hosho's hand, as well as the universe's, worked in mysterious ways.

But Dorgan felt strong once again.

He breathed his fiery breath towards Alquam, signaling their fight had begun. A fight to the death. There could be no other way.

The blast of heat and fire from his mouth sizzled and cracked through the air, going beyond the bubble Abbot Hosho had created to become more potent within the toxic atmosphere beyond. It turned black. Like demonic blackfire! Another marvel!

Alquam screeched again and again, each louder than the last, but somehow the demon avoided the flames. Some of the eggs weren't so fortunate. The demon screeched. "I haven't eaten since you offered me the magician Ealdræd, Dorgan. You can imagine my hunger. I will enjoy feasting on you after what you've done."

"He should have satisfied you!" Dorgan yelled before Alquam flew at him, razor sharp claws slashing.

Dorgan dodged, but one of Alquam's claws, the longest, slashed across his scales below his neck. Blood flowed, and Dorgan yelled in pain, seeing red.

"Don't use up too much of your precious air screaming like prey, my friend. You're better than that."

"I'll show you who's prey!" Again, Dorgan let out his dragon's breath, his target always the eggs—and if Alquam got in the way, feathers singed off her, flesh burnt to render her useless, then so be it.

All the better for Dorgan.

But Alquam protected her eggs, as expected, taking the brunt of Dorgan's attack. Much to his chagrin, however, the demon didn't seem affected by his breath as much as he would have thought. As much as he would have liked. Damn it!

By the time Dorgan's breath was spent, mouth steaming, Alquam seemed unscathed. The only evidence of Dorgan's fire was the thick smoke, curling wafts of oily blackness, coming off of Alquam's singed feathers.

"You're going to have to do better than that," Alquam said, screeching again. This one was the screech of attack.

A moment passed. Nothing. And then the demon was upon Dorgan in a flash, tooth and claw, her foul breath upon him, worse than the air of the cavern.

Dorgan, with Alquam on the attack, defending her eggs and hungry, had no choice. He had to defend himself. And seeing as his fiery breath wasn't as effective as he'd hoped, their melee resorted to sharp claws and biting teeth.

Demon and dragon locked in combat.

By the old gods, Alquam was strong. Protective. Fierce. Just as Dorgan had feared. He slashed with his claws, missing Alquam as she twisted and dodged only to come at Dorgan quickly with her own reply, feathers flying. Screeching. Hissing at him, trying to goad him by feigning injury but not even touched.

Not yet.

Instead, it was Dorgan who felt the brunt of the demon's attack. Alquam's claws, sharp and pointed, dug into Dorgan's thigh, slicing down to the bone as easily as if through air. "You will be quite the feast," Alquam said devilishly, smugly, and all too confidently for Dorgan's liking.

"I don't think so," Dorgan replied struggling through the pain shooting through him, breathless but nowhere near affected, thankfully.

Again, Alquam was close. Dorgan lashed at her with his own claws but also prepared his breath once more. Not for her this time. He had another idea. When he breathed again, ready to let his fire release, the eggs beyond her reach were his target.

Many hundreds were consumed by the fire.

Alquam screeched and screeched, removing her claws from Dorgan's scaly flesh. Blood, thick and oozing, came from the wounds.

"You will pay for that, dragon!"

"What?" Dorgan retorted. "I'm not your friend any longer?"

"You were never my friend, only my prey. My food."

Dorgan steeled his resolve, thinking of Hereward and Wallace. "Sometimes prey can defeat the hunter, Alquam."

"Come and try!" Alquam screeched, one of hate but also with a touch of fear. Good. Dorgan knew he had the advantage here. "My hunger grows with each passing moment."

"You're on!"

Dorgan flew to the demon, sinking his teeth into the demon's neck and shoulder, tasting bitter foul ichor as it flowed from her. Bones crunched, and Alquam screeched in pain, agonizing, vibrating, ear-piercing pain. But Dorgan didn't let go. He pressed his jaws shut tighter, cutting through feathers, flesh, muscle, right to the innards of the demon.

The taste was foul.

Alquam thrashed underneath him. Her screeches became desperate screaming, but her claws scratched always, opening red ribbons across his scaled skin. Blood flowed. The air misted, and a red haze found his eyes. Dorgan became agonized to his soul, unable to breathe even the fresh air Abbot Hosho had provided for him. He was paralyzed by the demon's claws slashing, digging, searching desperately for purchase. Most found his flesh. Many, vital areas.

Dorgan wanted to scream, let out all his agony. But he didn't open his jaws. Alquam's ichor flowed down his throat, gagging him. He retched, but he still didn't let go. He couldn't. It was a battle to the death, and Dorgan knew without doubt that if he gave up his grip, the contest for his own life would be lost.

The contest for the rest of humanity as well.

Once Alquam's eggs hatched, the world would be overrun with evil. And then of course, all Dorgan could think about beyond the greater good was a better good. The love he had for Hereward and Wallace.

What would they do without him if he were defeated?

Once more, Dorgan's determination strengthened him. Alquam may have her eggs to protect, but they were unhatched, nameless, and didn't love her. Not like Dorgan. He had love. The love of his man. The love of his son. They were named. Important. And best of all, they loved him in return.

If that wasn't worth fighting for, then what was?

And that love was something a demon would never understand.

Dorgan clamped his jaws tighter, teeth meeting teeth, ripping Alquam's foul flesh. The demon's ichor dripped from his lips, sizzling on the ground upon which it fell like dripping hot tar used at the ship builder's yards to waterproof the wood of the seafaring vessels.

But Alquam wasn't defeated, though she screeched in pain. Dorgan was being cut to shreds, down to his bones, his own blood mingling with that of the demons, causing it to sizzle and steam below them both on the cave's floor.

Dorgan slipped on the carnage as he wrestled with Alquam, as the demon tried to break free. She couldn't. He'd not let go until the demon was done…or he was.

But the fresh air within the bubble became fouled with the stench of their injuries. Dorgan didn't know how much longer he could keep hold, keep his jaws locked tight. He began to feel giddy. Tightness found his chest, and a strange feeling overcame him accompanied by a heavy feeling throughout the rest of his body. The feeling of needing to sleep suddenly, limbs heavy and cumbersome.

With one final, determined, and painful move, knowing it would be his last if he didn't act quickly, Dorgan yanked his jaw so it not only tore Alquam's shoulder, ripped a gaping hole in her neck, but took off the demon's head as well. Thick spurts of ichor sprayed, sprayed, sprayed, until the body of the demon, covered in its own insides, and gore-soaked feathers, slumped to the ground.

The demon was dead.

Dorgan spat out the feathers, bones, blood, and sinewy muscle from his mouth, disgusted. The victory was but a fleeting moment of elation. The sleepy feeling that he had before increased in intensity, washing over him with even greater purpose. It was then, to his horror, that he noticed Alquam's claws, separated from her after her death, were lodged deeply into his chest. They were near his heart. Too near. He could feel it beat erratically, his breaths becoming short.

With a creeping dread, he knew his heart was beating his final moments.

But Dorgan wasn't done. Not defeated yet. He still held breath in his lungs, and that counted for something. His flames, again like blackfire, burned the eggs. All of them. He left nothing but a scorched, smoking ruin in the fire's wake.

When done, he collapsed into a limp mess of blood and fatal injuries upon the sticky ichor and blood-soaked ground. Darkness found him, tunneling his vision. But before the light within him went out completely, Abbot Hosho's face, serene and angelic really, came into his limited view. The monk was glowing, a bright corona of light surrounding him. His presence was beautiful. Like that of an angel.

Did mortals see the immortals as they truly were before they passed?

Abbot Hosho grabbed Dorgan's hand. It was then he realized he had returned to human form. He tried to squeeze the monk's hand back, let him know he was all right even though he was far from it. His heart fluttered. Then slowed.

Dorgan gasped a slow rattle.

Now, only numbness was Dorgan's friend. Before the darkness

overtook him completely, he whispered, "Tell…Hereward and Wallace I did this for them, and that…and that I…I love them."

21
The Hatchling's New Clothes

IT WATCHED.

The hatchling, crouching, waiting, wary of too many humans within the grove surrounded by ancient elm and ash, especially ones who had weapons, sharp and pointy, stayed hidden within the undergrowth. Weapons could hurt it during its infancy, slice its skin, make it bleed; it was defenseless against an experienced sword, a well wielded mace, or woodcutter's axe.

Lord Hereward frightened the hatchling most of all.

The hatchling could feel the lord knight's strength, his determination and protectiveness of not only what was right according to human laws but also of his son. His precious son. The hatchling decided the boy wasn't his target. To anger a father like Hereward wouldn't be wise. Swords stayed stuck when thrust into flesh, demon's or otherwise.

Yes, Hereward needed to be destroyed, not angered.

Mother wanted it so.

To do as she'd asked of him, the hatchling had other weapons. Better weapons than its claws and teeth. It had the desire to shapeshift, to deceive. The foulest weapon of all. After days and days of searching, it had finally found its goal, and now all it needed to do was find the right opportunity to strike. Patience. Patience. Patience. The deed would be done.

The hatchling smiled to itself, licked its sharp teeth.

As it watched, waited, and watched some more, one of the humans with Hereward, the showman, the joker, the one who fucked his brother, left the group by the roaring fire and approached. The fool. A lamb should never separate itself from the protection of its flock and its shepherd.

An opportunity had presented itself.

But the hatchling had to think quickly for the fool came, cock freed so he could relieve himself. He'd drunk too much. Stupid man. The hatchling considered what it should shapeshift into to entice the fool, muddy his mind, appeal to his carnal nature, lure him into the web of his own death. Trick him before devouring him.

Would the fool prefer the company of men or women in his final moments? Yes, the Joran fool fucked his kin. Stuck Horan in his arse instead of in his cunt. But that was done out of punishment, nothing amorous about it other than the satisfaction of humiliation. The feeling of power over another.

Humans often liked to spurt their seed into whomever they could to dominate them, reinforce their own false self-importance or compensate for their own failings. And the fool was the most useless of failures the hatchling had encountered so far. Pathetic, really. The fool wouldn't save his brother if it meant saving himself first. That much the hatchling knew.

At least the farmer protected his son and daughter before his end; the tavern owner didn't beg for mercy but for death; the stable hand named Eddi didn't scream; the guards Frenk and Slen died with a smile on their lips and their cocks still hard.

The same admiration couldn't be extended to the fool Joran. The hatchling knew the fool would cower, plead for his life, cry like a baby wanting for his mother's tit, and promise anything before his demise. But how delicious killing the fool would be.

How delicious.

As such, the hatchling, seeing as it was already wearing its pretty dress, shifted into a woman, buxom and beautiful. Curly red hair fell down to the shoulders. Green eyes. What stupid man could resist green eyes? Full red lips too. Lips most men would dream to have their hardened cocks inserted between.

The hatchling also shifted its body so only its cunt would be visible underneath the dress; it could feel itself getting warmer, wetter as its prey approached. It licked its teeth in anticipation, the pearly white teeth of the woman it had become to complete the deception.

Its most powerful weapon.

The fool Joran came into the undergrowth proper, holding his cock; he was well endowed, larger than all the men the hatchling had destroyed since emerging from its egg as Mother Alquam's alpha and pride.

The hatchling emerged from the bushes, revealing itself. "Want me to help you with that, handsome?" it said as pleasantly and alluringly as it could manage.

"Oh my!" The fool Joran was startled for a moment. "I didn't see you there, miss."

The hatchling noticed how the fool didn't stuff his cock back into his garishly striped tights or even offer to go somewhere else to do his business now that he'd realized he wasn't alone. By the Great Kraken of the Void, he was stupid. Too easy to snare, his death inevitable.

The hatchling would relish his passing.

It said, "Whether you saw me or not, do you desire my help?"

The fool Joran snorted a laugh. "I can't piss with you in front of me, can I?"

"Why not—shy, are you, handsome?"

"Not at all. I just don't want you to get your dress wet and ruin it—I tend to be a bit of a splasher." The fool never took his eyes of the hatchling's cleavage; it was correct in the form it chose. "I've drank a hell of a lot, you see. Now I'm paying for it, hey?"

The hatchling smiled and grabbed the fool's cock tightly, massaging its length. The fool gasped. A shudder ran through his lips, a tremble through his body, when the hatchling said, "Then piss into my mouth. I won't spill a drop, I promise."

The fool's eyes widened. "Ooh, you are a dirty girl, aren't you?"

"You like dirty girls, don't you?"

"Yes."

With its other hand, the hatchling lifted the dress, revealing its cunt to the fool, a shock of red pubes above the labia. "I can be dirtier. You'd like that, wouldn't you, handsome?"

More shuddering. "I...I don't feel the need to piss no more." And it was true; the hatchling could feel the fool's cock harden within its grip. "I much prefer to fuck you, now you've suggested it."

"A most excellent idea. Fuck me then. Fuck me like you want to, like I'm your dirty girl."

The fool clambered out of his tights and motley, shirt too, soon bare naked in front of the hatchling, his cock as hard as his sudden determination in his eyes.

This was too easy.

The hatchling laid down upon the crunching leaves, sticks poking into its back. It didn't care. It licked its reddened lips to wet them further, smiling to its green eyes. It was also wetter between its legs. So wet, the smell of its own sex was intoxicating even to itself.

"You are s-so very p-pretty," the fool stammered.

"As you are handsome," if forced itself to say. The hatchling then smiled as best it could manage and opened its legs to the fool further. His expression became one of delight. "Now come fuck me."

With one hand, the hatchling rubbed its clitoris—because most men, especially those like the fool, self-centered, wouldn't know where one was if it were painted with a bullseye on it. Men like the fool were only interested in sticking it in so they could huff and puff for a brief moment before they were spent.

So pathetic.

"You m-make me giddy with your b-beauty."

Now the hatchling was getting pissed off. The fool loved himself more than any other. No wonder even his brother hated him and only put up with him because together their act made them rich. "Are you going to fuck me or are you just going to stand there admiring your own erection?"

The fool nodded, coming out of himself while he stroked his cock to greater hardness. He came over the hatchling, grappling and fumbling. He stunk of testosterone, bitter and musky. Alcohol too. The hatchling hated the closeness of him, his sweaty skin against its own.

To make matters worse, the fool nibbled too hard on its ear, kissed its cheeks and lips while he pushed and pushed his cock into the wetness between the hatchling's legs. It shuddered with revulsion. It felt vile to have that part of a human inside it. Vile beyond words.

The hatchling had to force itself not to retch.

While the fool fucked blindly, gained a clumsy rhythm and moaning, he slipped his slimy tongue, thick and disgusting, saturated with saliva, into its mouth.

The hatchling became repulsed beyond imagining. How humans became a plentiful species if this was what they had to endure to procreate was beyond the hatchling's comprehension. The act of their sex was disgusting.

By the time the fool Joran ejaculated, thankfully quick, the hatchling had had more than enough. The time to kill was nigh.

Underneath him, and as the fool pulled out, his cock dripping with his seed and its own juices, the hatching shifted into a man.

A big, strong man.

The fool was startled while still blinded by his own ecstasy.

With strong arms, muscles rippling, the hatchling grabbed the fool and slammed him to the ground, winding him. "What…what are you?" he cried, still confused, still aroused but deflating.

"I'm going to take your clothing, kill you, then become you so I can kill my real target, fool."

"No…I beg of you." And there it was. The pleading. So pathetic it rankled the hatchling even more than when the man was inside it. "Please. Please, I'll do…anything. I don't want to die. Please." Ah, the bargaining already. The fool moved quickly through the stages of desperation, didn't he? "I'll do anything you want of me! Please spare me. I'm too handsome to die so young."

The fool's face was streaming with tears as he pleaded for his life, lips trembling, sweating, scared out of his mind. The hatchling laughed at him. Laughed in his frightened face.

But it decided to give the fool some of his own medicine before his end. The hatchling fucked him. Worse, the hatchling shifted so its cock grew and grew while it was inside the fool. The man convulsed with terror, pain in his eyes and all over his face. But he couldn't scream. The hatchling had covered his mouth to prevent him doing so.

More and more, the hatchling grew its cock, so large it ripped the fool apart from the inside. How delicious…and fitting. Blood spurted through the hatchling's fingers over the fool's mouth. More blood came, thick and oozing as the man convulsed, legs slapping the leaves, dying from the inside out.

"How do you like it, fool?" the hatchling spat, now feeling its cock fuck the fool's heart; the rapid, frightened, dying, beating of the organ against the knob of its cock strangely pleasant for a moment until the fool spluttered more blood, shuddered one last time, then dropped dead.

His eyes were frozen wide with his terror, his death mask.

The hatchling removed its hand. Thick black blood oozed from the fool's mouth in clumps. The copper tang of it exciting the hatchling more than anything. After pulling out its cock and returning it to a more appropriate size, the hatchling devoured the fool, flesh, muscle, gristle, and bone alike.

What remained wasn't much but was buried.

The hatchling then shifted into the likeness of the fool, ensuring every detail was perfect, including his ample endowment. After all, the man wore tights for his performances. Everyone knew what he had and could see it plainly. And deception, perfect deception as the hatchling prided itself on, was in the details. Right down to the mole on the fool's right buttocks.

When dressed into the fool's clothing, terribly gaudy and impractical, the hatchling stepped out beyond the undergrowth.

Hereward casually turned towards the hatchling as it approached the group of humans sitting by the fire. "Took your fucking time. What were you doing, getting in a wank as well as pissing behind the bushes?"

"A man's gotta do what a man's gotta do," the hatchling replied, its voice a perfect copy of the fools as well.

Wallace gave the hatchling disguised as Joran a strange look, brow furrowed. Did the boy suspect something? "Ya did drink o' lot, Joran."

Excellent. The boy didn't suspect a thing. At least it hoped he didn't.

"Yes, that's for sure. Got to be careful not to drink so much in the future, haven't I?"

"Ya, that's right."

But then, as the hatchling sat by the fire with the rest of them, planning how it was going to kill Lord Hereward now that it was close enough, a stab of pain found it. The hatchling gasped.

Horan asked, "What's wrong, Joran?"

The hatchling couldn't answer for a moment. Something terrible had happened. "Nothing," it lied quickly so as not to arouse suspicion. "And don't question me again...*brother.*"

Horan shrunk, and Wallace comforted him. Hereward snorted disgust. The deception was perfect. And the hatchling could take them one by one. But what had changed? The pain stabbed again.

Then the hatchling knew.

Mother had been killed. The hatchling could feel the hollow left because of her absence. Sadness overcame it for a moment. But also, something else. Because the hatchling, before the alpha, was now the prime.

As such, it had to name itself, for it was now the lord of the brood. The lord of the Purge that would soon decimate humanity.

It smiled, staring into the flames of the fire. *I will be Ugruthaan, Lord of the Great Purge, of blood and bone desired, and of pestilence realized. Yes, that will be my name. I am Ugruthaan.*

And with its new name, the plan had also changed. No longer was Ugruthaan compelled to obey Mother Alquam's wish. It now had its own agenda: finding allies. As such, following Hereward would be the best course of action as he traveled southwards with his son. The lord knight's death could wait, because once Ugruthaan allied with all those who opposed civilization, the Purge could begin in earnest. And it would be Hereward, unwillingly, who would help it do so. How delicious.

"What's up your arse, Joran?" Hereward asked. "You look down in the dumps all of a sudden."

"I need another bloody drink."

Hereward snorted. "More like you want to stick that big fucking fat cock of yours into someplace warm, hey?"

"Suppose you may be right about that, Lord Hereward." Ugruthaan slid its gaze to Horan; after all, that's what would have been expected going on the fool's past behavior. Deception was about the details. Always the details.

Ugruthaan stood, ensuring it sent blood to its cock to engorge it enough for all to see, including the boy. Wallace blushed red circles on his cheeks and looked away. Hereward continued as if nothing was wrong, sucking down another horn of ale in one go.

Horan stood too; Wallace grabbed him, but his hold was shrugged off. "I've got to go with my brother, Wallace."

"Ya don't have ta, Horan."

"You don't understand, Wallace. I do."

Together, Ugruthaan and Horan went to their caravan.

Yes, deception was all in the details. But now that Mother was gone, the brood destroyed, everything was upon Ugruthaan to continue the Purge. For demons, revenge was a dish best served piping hot and with plenty of blood!

Part Three

"Like false gods, there can be false demons," Hub said rather wisely—also quite, quite drunk as he sloshed ale in the direction of his mouth.

His drunk friend, Denny, replied, "Whatever, Hub. Humanity's fuckin' fucked, anyways."

"Why'd ya say that, Den?" Stern asked, equally as drunk as the other two.

Denny slurred, "'Cause false demons or real ones, Lord Hereward can only kill one o' 'em at a time and his son Wallace can only help him."

Hub, managing to take a draught from his tankard, said, "Let's hope Lord Hereward and his son have the speed o' the true gods, then."

"I'll drink to that," Denny said, rattling his now empty tankard against the bar.

"Aye, me too," Stern chimed in.

22
Myrkul's New Husband

THE VILLAGE WAS PITIFUL, as were the inhabitants defending it. It was no challenge at all to raze the place to the ground, return it to the mud, every pillar and post obliterated without effort, every citizen slaughtered—mostly farmers trying to scratch out a living with their families.

The only reason the village was given the merest consideration in the first place was that it was in the way. Simple. Myrkul's undead forces didn't divert their path for anyone or anything as they marched inexorably northwards. But the village was hardly worth destroying. Barely worth the time.

Myrkul, after his inevitable divorce to Greysen because the young man had become lax in his faith, had decided to lead his great undead army himself. The result of his decision had so far been underwhelming. One could even say…boring. Screaming farmers rushing to put out the fires burning their hovels was no entertainment, killing their families less so.

Myrkul settled back within in his throne of bones, sighing. Even though he'd left the Dread Keep, now residing within a grand and ornate marquee, his mobile command center where he was surrounded by ornate tapestries, exquisite furniture, and every other finery known to the civilizations he'd conquered throughout the eons, one thing was missing. He'd become lonely and needed—no, desired—a new partner. A new sexual mate.

A new husband, perhaps?

Myrkul believed being on the front line would pass time until he found another man, a mortal, who would sheath his cock, obey his every whim and desire without protest. So far, he had proven himself wrong. None worthy enough could be found.

The disappointment rankled like a festering sore. Why couldn't he find another man who would yearn to be owned by him? To be so would be an honor. Such a mortal would be powerful beyond their limited imagining. What human wouldn't want such a thing?

Hopefully his fortunes would soon change.

Maybe this latest village, nothing but a black smudge in the sky and a blacker smudge in the dirt left of it, had hidden bounty worthy of the effort. Perhaps it had a secret yet to be revealed.

Someone worthy amongst the survivors.

To Myrkul's continued annoyance, it always took an inordinate amount of time to find all of those who fled. Oh, how he longed for someone worthy enough to receive his seed. So far, the farm boys and their fathers he'd raped while he and his undead army conquered the greener lands to the north of the Hyruldon Expanse had provided nothing but momentary distractions.

There was one young man from a previous village, not yet of age, who showed promise. But he screamed too much, especially when Myrkul's cock ripped him no matter what hole he stuck it in. The stupid, useless boy didn't know how privileged he had been to be chosen for Myrkul's pillows. Now, like the rest of the villagers he'd conquered, his pathetic body joined the ranks of the undead.

At least Myrkul's army was growing. A consolation, he supposed. But he desired a man who he could take who wouldn't complain and had equal desire. Full of lustful yearning. Appreciative too. Was that too much to ask?

Myrkul sighed again.

A lich lord general, Myrkul didn't remember his name and didn't care, approached as the hordes of his undead army swept through the last buildings of the latest village, burning, killing, destroying, disturbed his thoughts. "What is it, General?" Myrkul snapped, shifting his weight upon his bone throne, annoyed even further at the intrusion.

"Your forgiveness, Great Master, my Lord, but I have found someone who may be of interest to you."

"I doubt whoever you bring me will interest me, going on recent experience."

The lich lord general turned and gestured to another. A moment passed; Myrkul's impatience grew as he waited. Grew too much. Then, before anger set in for an unwelcome stay, a young man was revealed.

With him came a horse, a chestnut stallion sixteen hands in height at the withers, held by reins in the young man's hands. The horse was handsome, muscular and fit. The man not so much with his insipid pallor, pimples, and hooked nose. What made him interesting though, somewhat attractive, was thick, curly, dark hair hanging over deep, brown, soulful eyes. He had full lips too. Lips Myrkul desired upon his cock. But he noted the young man's innocence had left him long ago; something unusual for someone so young. Alluring. He could smell the man's ripeness, the arousing aroma of his testosterone, musky and full. Good. Very good.

Therefore, to Myrkul's surprise, the lich lord general was right. He was intrigued. No longer bored, and his anger subsided too.

Myrkul sat up, hand caressing his chin as his thoughts turned wicked and carnal. "And who are exactly you, young man?" Myrkul felt arousal unlike any since Greysen had left, his cock hardening the more he studied the man who dared bring his horse with him into his grand marquee. Normally, such a thing was an affront, punishable by death. But somehow, Myrkul didn't mind. Not yet.

"Aye, I'm no one," the young man replied, his tone chipper but also holding darkness like the rest of him—terrible darkness.

Myrkul liked him already; the young man was a puzzle, enigmatic, and as such, Myrkul rubbed his groin. He knew he was leaking, could feel his pre-sex fluids oozing. This young man...what a delightful mortal he was. Delightful.

"Everyone is someone," Myrkul offered, enjoying the conversation already.

"Not I."

"Explain."

The young man cleared his throat. "I'm a nobody 'cause I was dismembered by a demon hatchling, and then I had me remains shoved into a horse's arse to hide the evidence. That's why I'm a nobody." The young man patted the horse he held tenderly, lovingly. "This is the horse I was put inside. I call him Vengeance."

"Do tell me..." Myrkul leant forwards, enthralled but not quite understanding. He was intrigued. How could he not be? "Tell me how you come to be then after such a death?"

"Well, you see," the young man continued, "Vengeance was owned by a magician. And that magician couldn't work out why his horse was so sick, so he cast healing magic on him over and over. Every day for weeks, he tried to heal him. Thing was, the horse wasn't sick at all; he had me in him. And it was the magician's magic that reformed me, repaired me, and brought life to me while I was inside Vengeance." The young man petted his horse again, his love evident with both his touch and his look. "When I was finally whole, a man again as it were, on one dark and stormy night, as it goes, Vengeance gave birth to me. Now, I'm forever loved by him, for I'm Vengeance's son, ain't I?"

Myrkul enjoyed the story. Without doubt it was true. The young man had magic in him. The same powerful magic of the stallion. They *were* one. "What happened to the magician whose magic resurrected you?"

"When I came out, I was naked, disorientated, and weak. Just like a newborn, I s'pose. Vengeance guarded me. But before I could stand on my own two feet, the magician tried to get to me, calling me a demon and shouting foul things in a furious rage. The magician wanted to kill me. Vengeance didn't want me hurt, so he kicked the magician's head in. He killed his master to protect me."

Myrkul's eyebrows beneath his great twisting horns rose. A rare thing for him to be surprised. "What is your name then, man born from a horse's arse who now thinks of you as its foal?"

"As I said, I was a nobody. But if you've gotta know, my name was Eddi, and I s'pose it was a blessing I became a stable hand after being a guard of the docks at Invrawold City for so long 'cause I was getting nowhere there." A moment of realization came over the young man. "I've got it." He beamed a smile, even if the darkness in his deep browns remained. "I'm no longer Eddi, but since I'm reborn, you can call me Khalaf, Master of Horses."

"Well, Khalaf, Master of Horses, seeing as you came to me, you can come and suck my cock as the reward for your tale. One I've enjoyed greatly."

"Why would I do that?"

Myrkul was taken aback. Another surprise. Two in as many moments. Unbelievable. He really did like Khalaf. "Because I will grant you immortality if you do, and afterwards, you can become my husband, the sheath of my cock, forever. What deserving mortal wouldn't want that?"

"I'm not mortal," Khalaf countered. "Vengeance and me are beyond mortality already, our fates tied. What else can you offer me?"

Again, and thrice now, Myrkul was both surprised and intrigued. "Explain, Khalaf, Master of Horses."

"Perhaps you misunderstand the reason for my visit." Khalaf came closer; Vengeance nickered, a dark twinkle in the horse's even darker eyes. "I'm the Master of Horses, speaker to horses, protector of horses, and I'm immortal as long as Vengeance lives, for I will forever protect them as they me."

"You are right; I don't understand."

"Are not the horses the backbone of civilization?"

"They are."

"And you want to break civilization? Have it at your feet to conquer and control?"

"I do." Myrkul felt his arousal again; Khalaf really was attractive, powerfully so. Myrkul was drawn to him as an insect would be to a Venus Fly Trap. Snap! He knew he would be enamored, pathetically and delightfully so, if Khalaf were to be his.

"Then with my help, you can do so."

Now it was Myrkul's moment to counter. "I have an army of undead. What more do I need?"

"You need me and my horses."

"Explain." Myrkul repeated, but for a different reason.

"I can command all of the horses of the world to rise up against humanity."

"An interesting talent. But that isn't what you want to do, is it?"

Khalaf faltered for a moment, Myrkul could see the tell, the quick flick of an eyebrow, the slight turn of a lip. "No."

"Then what do you want?"

"The hatchling's head who murdered me at my feet." To emphasize Khalaf's words, Vengeance scraped a hoof across the fine carpet, nickering angrily.

"Ah." Myrkul stood. "Now we're getting to the crux of it all. I can give you what you wish, if you give me what I desire in return. Simple, really."

"I'm not gonna be your whore."

"What makes you think you can resist me?" Myrkul laughed; by the Nine Circles of Hell, he was hard for Khalaf. "I will have you no matter what you believe." He undid the laces of his pants, freeing his erection, a pulsing veiny beauty, the knob of it already vibrant and full of blood, dripping his arousal. "Now come, suck my cock before my patience grows thin and you end up in a place far worse than inside a horse's arsehole."

"On one condition," Khalaf said defiantly.

"And that would be?"

"I become your husband but also your equal as we both help each other get what we want. No tricks, either. Or Vengeance will do to you what he did to that magician, without mercy, until you are pulverized into your fancy rugs here."

Oh, those words were like bliss. Myrkul stiffened even more, almost to bursting. His cock, thick and hard, pulsed in his grip. A long, sticky, clear ribbon of his pre-ejaculate dribbled onto the carpeted floor. His stomach turned with carnal agony. He relished, delighted, and yearned for Khalaf. He could also feel the horse's power. Even that aroused him beyond belief. "What is it you're saying?"

"I'm going to fuck you after I've sucked your cock to seal our marriage and deal, that's what I'm saying."

Myrkul once more was surprised. How many times was that now? Too many. But he was reeled in. He had to have Khalaf. "No one has ever fucked me. Not in a millennium. Not ever."

"Aye, there's always time to try new things. I should know." Khalaf patted Vengeance again; an approving whinny resulted. "Oh, and Vengeance will be our witness. My best man, as it were. He will also be my eternal guardian to ensure you keep your end of our arrangement and never deceive me."

"The horse?" But even though Myrkul questioned Khalaf, the power from the horse, from him, from the magically reborn, was undeniable. The air cracked with magic. Khalaf and Vengeance were powerful. And if there was one thing Myrkul loved beyond any other, it was power. Absolute power, absolutely.

"Yes."

Myrkul found himself intrigued beyond imagining. "Then, I accept."

Khalaf let go of Vengeance to come to Myrkul. With swiftness, and a dark but knowing look, he grabbed Myrkul's cock, squeezing it. Myrkul shuddered; the power of that touch alone shot through him like lightning born from thunder clouds before being released onto the deserving and undeserving alike below. He shuddered and hissed, licked his teeth.

Khalaf, Master of Horses said, "Myrkul, demon god of the undead, of bones, of death, and the reaper himself, will you be my husband?"

"I will, Khalaf, Master of Horses, my A Rúnsearc." And unbelievably, for the first time in memory, Myrkul realized he was speaking the truth, the yearning of his heart greater than the yearning of his flesh.

"And Myrkul, demon god of the undead, of bones, of death, and the reaper himself, will you also help me seek my revenge against the hatchling?"

"I will, Khalaf, Master of Horses, my A Rúnsearc." Myrkul hissed again with a strange pleasure far removed from lust. He then decided he didn't want to hurt his new interest, his latest fascination, his freshly gained husband. "But can you take me? Many promising suitors have failed before you. Only one could satisfy me recently, but he failed in other ways."

At that, Myrkul thought of Greysen, but only fleetingly.

Khalaf got onto his knees. "If I can take Vengeance, I can certainly take you, my husband."

23
Abbot Hosho's Costly Mistake

*Y*OU KNOW IT'S INEVITABLE, *my dear.*

Abbot Hosho didn't have time to contemplate the universe's words. How could he? Why was it that immortals could have eons pass without care, yet when it came to the moments that mattered, the seconds where a difference could be made, there was never enough time?

And during those precious seconds, that was when Abbot Hosho realized his mistake.

After giving Dorgan the gift of air, merely taking the molecules from one place and sealing them around the dragon so he could stay within the cave and defeat the demon Alquam, he rushed to Kieron and Vash's aid. Vash had been affected the most by the poisons within the nest, delphins were sensitive to such things, and Abbot Hosho wanted to make sure Vash was all right before anything else.

What happened because of his decision wasn't Abbot Hosho's fault. Not really. Yes, Vash—and even Kieron—needed him. Abbot Hosho believed Dorgan was able to easily take on Alquam. But in the moment of his decision, it turned out their needs weren't as great.

Abbot Hosho knelt beside Vash, touching them upon their cheek, praying they would recover without permanent damage, and using some of the power within him to speed the delphin's recovery. That's when the universe repeated her warning. A warning Abbot Hosho had at first misunderstood. There was no time to contemplate her words, anyway.

The inevitability of what is to be lost is assured.

Abbot Hosho looked up to the heavens. "Sometimes, just sometimes, I really wish you'd define the meaning of your thoughts to me a lot clearer."

The gray clouded sky was stained with smudges of ash from the caldera's edge. A mark on the world that went into his heart, the universe's too.

I'm eternal and endless, the universe replied, almost haughtily if Abbot Hosho wasn't mistaken, *and everything within me is a part of what I am, from the atoms to the mega clusters of galaxies and nebulae. Asking for me to give clarity would be like asking a human to listen to what a drop of their blood tells them. I can only speak of what I sense. And most times what I sense could be something that passed millennia ago or will come to be in some distant future when darkness begins to collapse in on itself.*

"Don't get all esoteric with me."

Never my intention, my dear.

Abbot Hosho knew her words as truth. He couldn't blame the universe, despite her maddening and enigmatic whispers—whispers which often needed contemplation, pondering, translating. Why else would there be a monastery full of monks for that very purpose up on the Steps to Heaven mountains?

It was his fault what had happened. He *was* warned, though. The inevitability of it clear now he'd thought about it. Abbot Hosho just didn't understand what *you know it's inevitable, my dear* meant when it was whispered to him as he went to Kieron and Vash's side.

Why had he been so...thoughtless?

Hereward would call him an oaf. He deserved it.

After a splutter, a noise that knocked him from his reverie, Vash did indeed recover. Kieron, now in human form, held them tighter, their world closing in around themselves, both smiling the joy of relief, kissing, whispering their love. But that was when, in the stark moment following, Abbot Hosho realised Vash would have come around with or without his help.

It wasn't the delphin's turn to perish here today.

The real inevitability was that he'd left Dorgan to the demon all alone. And something terrible, unthinkable, had happened. Abbot Hosho felt fear to his bones.

He should have stayed by Dorgan's side.

With a quickening of his heart, he got up, dusted off his robe, and he rushed back towards the cave's entrance. Before entering, he encircled himself with precious air.

What he saw took most of it away from him.

Alquam and her eggs were destroyed, but Dorgan had fallen.

The universe took in as much a breath as he did.

Dorgan was dead.

It was inevitable, my love, she repeated.

Abbot Hosho finally, maddeningly, understood. With Dorgan's passing, the final pieces had been set into place. One of the eggs had hatched, the only survivor. Alquam, though defeated at great cost, greater than imaginable when considered, had set upon the world her spawn. Her evil. Along with Myrkul, his undead army, and the new demon, humanity now desperately needed more than heroes. More than lord knights with magical swords and good folks with good intentions. Humanity needed allies. For the Purge would happen.

"I think it's time I accepted the terrible mistakes I made. Ask for forgiveness and try and make amends for what I've done," Abbot Hosho said sadly.

Which new god, which son, will you ask for forgiveness?

"Now *that* is the question."

But first, don't you think there are other matters to attend to?

Abbot Hosho sat by Dorgan's ruined body, profoundly sad, tears flowing, but with his responsibility for what had happened clear in his thoughts. He'd done this. He'd killed Dorgan. He crossed his legs, closed his eyes.

"Yes," he replied as he began the process and cast the magic to project himself, body and mind, to where he needed to be, "Hereward and Wallace will be told."

24
Horan's Surprising Skills

WALLACE HAD ONLY JUST finished pissing in his chamber pot, having enjoyed the drumming sound it made when his water hit the pewter, before Horan appeared from around the big tree to startle him.

"Gods, Horan, ya scared the crap outta me!" Wallace made sure he didn't double knot the laces of his pants; when he were desperate to go next time, that's when those kinds of knots stayed knotted. And he sure didn't fancy peeing himself 'cause he couldn't get 'em undone in time. Papa would roar with laughter; he s'posed after the embarrassment, he would too.

Wallace smiled at the thought.

"Morning, Wallace," Horan said without so much as a blink, as if sneaking up on someone answering nature's call were normal for 'em. But then his friend's look went dark, darker than the night had been before the insipid dawn of this morning. Even now, it seemed the day struggled to get started, nothing but a bleak gray within grayer clouds. At least it wasn't a red dawn. Papa would have cursed then. Cursed about omens. Bad ones.

Wallace picked up the filled pot and tipped the contents, still steaming and warm, over the tree's roots. "What's a matter?"

"Joran's been acting really strange these past couple of days."

"What? Joran actin' strange?" Wallace snorted a laugh. "There's somethin'."

"Stranger than usual, then," Horan clarified. "We haven't done a show since the one you watched the other day, and he says there's no rush to do one either. He's not even practicing. He always practices the routine."

Wallace shrugged. "Could be he wants a break from doin' all dat jugglin' an' singin' stuff?"

Horan shifted his weight. "I don't think so." He leant in even closer. "He hasn't even…you know…had me lately, either."

Wallace's eyebrows shot up his forehead to join his hairline, he were sure of it. "Ya want him ta do dat? Ya like him stickin' ya?"

Horan's cheeks reddened. "I don't dislike it if that's what you're asking. My brother and I have a special bond. He needs me as much as I need him, and that's one of the ways we express our need and love for each other."

Wallace became confused; he knew his latest frown left Horan little doubt as to what his thoughts were. "I don't git it."

Horan folded his arms. "I'm not asking you to get it, I'm just telling you my brother is acting strangely lately. He's not his normal self, and I'm worried about him."

"What ya want me ta do 'bout it?"

And Wallace didn't mean for his words to sound harsh, far from it. But if Horan was concerned, perhaps it was Horan who should see Joran. Wallace certainly didn't want to. The man gave him the creeps. Worse heebie-jeebies than the slave trader back at the Great Market in Invrawold City. That's why when Joran were around, he answered nature's call behind trees.

Normally he wouldn't care about such things. He'd use his pot wherever. And what's more, when he didn't use his pot, he'd piss on the campfire to put it out after morning rise if Papa didn't. But not while Joran were watching. Nope.

"Will you come with me when I do?"

Wallace swallowed. "S'pose so." And as soon as the words fell from his mouth, he regretted it.

Together, they approached the caravan; Missy and the piebald Clydesdale stallion named Mista Kokoschka, nickered; Wallace thought they were nervous. He couldn't blame the horses. Even though the wooden built caravan was painted in garish and clashing colors, it held a certain doom over it. Like stormy clouds over the county farmer's market when even Missus Crabtree's tasty home baked apple and cinnamon scrolls and other fancies couldn't brighten things up—not even with creamed butter lathered inside 'em.

Wallace's stomach growled at him for the thought. He missed sweets. Out in the wild, it was all meat and meat and perhaps some veggies if they could be found. Most of which all tasted like the dirt they'd been pulled from no matter what went with 'em. The wild potatoes were the worst. Papa called 'em goblin's balls. They usually had thick, leathery skin and were as hard as rocks inside, even if they were boiled for ages. Papa would say, "How about tonight, we have stewed rabbit without its fucking goblin's balls?" He'd then roar with laughter.

Wallace was thankful whatever they were going to eat was minus the potatoes—'cause most of the time they ended up throwing the things at each other in jest. Wallace would then laugh as he chucked 'em while dodging those thrown by Papa. He laughed even more, would almost split his sides, when he got papa 'tween the eyes with a goblin's ball! So funny.

But such good times were quickly forgotten when Wallace and Horan confronted Joran inside the caravan. The curtains were all drawn, the inside gloomier than the outside. And no lie, the place stunk like someone farted after eating eggs and cabbage.

Even Horan looked stunned.

Wallace grimaced while he tried to hold his breath and failed.

"What do you want?" Joran snapped, voice huskier than a woodcutter's the next morning after too many ales.

"I'm worried about you, that's all," Horan said meekly, kneeling beside his brother.

Wallace stayed at the door. Papa always told him, "Being near the door, son, is the best way to get out of a place fucking quick smart!" He couldn't agree with the lesson any more right now. He pressed his back to the wood of it, in fact.

"Why?" Joran spat.

"I'm worried," Horan began, "because you don't want us to perform, you don't want to practice, and you've been doing nothing but sitting here in the dark for days now. It's not like you, Joran."

"You're just getting pissy because I haven't fucked you up the arse lately." He laughed maniacally; Joran's face somehow seemed to change when he did so, like his skin slipped from his bones for a moment.

Wallace wasn't sure what had happened, but it scared the spit outta him. Joran was more than creepy. He was also as mad as the old alchemist who'd visited the village one day claiming he could turn straw into gold, which of course never happened.

"Leave me alone," the jongleur acidly added, unblinking. "Unless you've got something worth telling me other than your own pathetic insecurities."

Wallace couldn't believe his ears, the wood of the door pressed harder against his back as he thought about making his dash. He felt for the handle, the cold metal of it a pleasure to touch.

"*This* is what I'm talking about!" Horan said. "How you've been behaving lately. It's not like you at all."

Joran's mood suddenly changed; his features softened, and a quiver of a smile overcame him. Wallace couldn't believe the turnaround. Talk about a shift in personality. Worse'n spring weather Joran were, an' all.

Joran said, sickly sweet, "How about you tell me where Lord Hereward is headed, and then perhaps we can...return to our shows."

Wallace blurted, "What'dya wanna know dat for? None o' ya business where me Papa n' me are goin', is it?"

"Wallace is right. What do you want to know that for?" Horan asked.

"To plan the shows. If I know where we're going, then I will know where our best audience will be, won't I?"

Horan looked confused, as much as Wallace felt, no doubt. "Remind me why we're traveling with Lord Hereward now?"

"The road is a dangerous place. What better protection than a lord knight of the realm?"

"That's a weak reason, and you know it." Horan shook his head. "We've traveled plenty of times. No one wants to harm jongleurs; we bring joy to the folks. Or have you forgotten that, Joran?"

Before Wallace's eyes, Joran's face shifted again, rippling; it were like the man had a demon inside him, he was that scary. "You will do as I say, Horan. Now tell me where Lord Hereward is headed, or we're done. We're over. The act is over. The fame over. The fortune gone. Everything will be finished. It's over!"

"You're not acting yourse—"

Before Horan could say the rest of his words, Joran flew up from the chair he was sitting in and grabbed him around the throat. Horan gagged, face getting redder and redder by the second. "You will tell me what I want to know, or I'll fucking kill you, bitch."

Wallace had two choices: run or help.

He chose the latter, 'cause his friend needed him right now. And if friends couldn't help each other, what good were they?

He rushed to Horan's aid, grabbing Joran's arm. Gods, the man were strong. Wallace couldn't even budge them an inch, even when hanging off them. Horan's face was turning into a terrible shade of purple, he was gasping in spluttering choking coughs.

"Leave him 'lone!" Wallace screamed. "Let Horan go, ya demon! Let him go!" But not matter how much he pulled, yanked, kicked, twisted, or even bit Joran's arm hard as he could, Joran's hold on Horan remained steadfast. He was a demon of a man—one with the strength of one, at least.

Horan eyes began to roll into the back of his head, and he didn't look good, veins bulging on his temples and becoming as purple as the rest of him.

"P-please...*please*...Joran..." Horan gasped.

Joran, without blinking, which was still weird to see, said, "Tell me where you father is heading, Wallace, or Horan here dies. It's up to you."

"I ain't tellin' ya nothin'. Nothin'."

"So be it." And with that Joran threw Horan to the floor without care. *Thud!* the caravan shook! The sound of it was sickening, like wood splintering it was so forceful. Joran came over his brother, pressing his foot onto Horan's throat and using all his body weight behind him to do so. Once more, Wallace couldn't make Joran budge. He got scared. For Horan and himself.

Joran, calm as can be, asked, "You'll tell me what I want to know, won't you, *brother*?"

Horan was gasping, spluttering spittle, eyes bulging. Once more, his face was turning terrible shades. "He's...he's heading...into t-the Hyruldon Expanse."

Joran took away his foot; Horan coughed and coughed, grabbing his throat. Wallace went to him. What he could do, he didn't know. But he was there for Horan.

"Ah, he's going to the Dread Keep, is he?" Joran smiled knowingly, wickedly. "Why would Hereward willingly visit Myrkul?"

"I...I don't...k-know," Horan spluttered, still hacking coughs.

"No matter." And with that, Joran barged past Wallace, sending him into the cupboard with a crash and clatter of crockery, before leaving the caravan.

Wallace weren't hurt. But the burst of light coming with the open door was as stark as what Joran did to Horan. After composing himself, Wallace went to the caravan's sink to fetch Horan a tankard. He filled it with water and got one for himself as well.

When he offered one of the tankards to Horan, hands shaking 'cause of what had happened, he said, "I don't think dat were ya brother. Somethin' real funny 'bout him, and I's ain't talkin' the laughin' kind o' funny, either."

Horan took small sips, his breathing becoming more regular. "I do believe you're right." With more sips, the color was returning to his face.

Wallace breathed a sigh of relief Horan were safe.

That afternoon up until evenfall, they searched for Joran. There were no hide nor hair of him, even when they backtracked where they'd been over the past few day's journey.

Wallace was thankful for not seeing him, despite feeling bad for Horan.

But what confirmed Wallace's suspicions that Joran wasn't Horan's brother, but some sort of doppelganger or worse was the discovery of a lot of blood within the woods not far from the first campfire. The blood didn't belong to any animal; fur or teeth and claws, bones too, were always found with butchered animals, especially trapped ones like what was common in the woods.

The only thing Wallace and Papa could find was a black painted fingernail within the blood and leaves, a fancy diamante thing glued to it. A fingernail painted as Joran's had been the first night Wallace seen him perform with Horan for the woodcutters and their families. After that night, Joran's fingernails weren't painted at all, now Wallace thought 'bout it. Seemed doppelgangers didn't account for vanity or even showmanship.

It became clearer Joran was dead.

"Probably a fucking demon, I'd say. They can do that, demons," Papa explained. "They can shift their form. Disguise themselves to get information out of folks."

Wallace said, "An' we told dat demon what it wanted ta know."

"Wasn't your fault." Papa spat into the dirt, then snorted. "From what I heard, you had a choice, son. And you chose to help your friend. I'm proud of you. Damn fucking proud." Papa ruffled Wallace's hair affectionately.

"Ta, Papa." Wallace beamed a smile before a thought came over him, wiping it away. "Wish I's had me sword on me. Could'a made a difference. Could'a helped Horan better."

"Let that be a lesson, son."

Wallace nodded, agreeing.

Horan took the news of Joran's death hard.

The days melded into weeks without so much as a blink. The weather turned warmer and warmer the further south they traveled. The sun grew more brilliant, 'specially by midday. There was a different smell to the air too. Like freshly harvested hay and blooming field daisies. Bees and other insects buzzed everywhere. Mosquitoes became more common too. Wallace didn't like the bites he got; he seemed to attract the bugs. They never went near Papa while Wallace itched and itched wherever he wasn't covered up at night-time.

He and Papa stayed in the caravan with Horan while they continued their journey. Missy and Mista Kokoschka got on well. Then again, being from a farm, Wallace knew horses. When Missy came into heat, as the season approached, then things would get interesting. Nothing stopped a determined stallion.

"Fucking hell!" Papa said after the first morning they'd slept in the caravan's beds, stretching, yawning wide, looking refreshed and happy. "It's mighty fancy sleeping in here!"

Wallace couldn't help but giggle. "Didn't make no difference on how much ya farted frew the night though, Papa, did it?"

Papa shrugged. "Don't want me guts to explode if I kept it all in, do you, son?"

"Nope, Papa." Wallace roared a laugh. "Don't want dat at all."

"Enough said, then."

They both laughed.

Horan wasn't inside the caravan when they woke most mornings. The jongleur seemed to be an early riser—even earlier than Papa who always rose with dawn's sun. Wallace preferred staying in bed, 'specially in a real fancy one with a comfortable goose feather duvet and more than a thin blanket between his skin and the dirt of the ground like how he usually slept inside his tent when he couldn't be bothered setting up the portable cot.

This morning rise, Horan didn't come into the caravan at all. To Wallace, that was strange. Horan always came into the caravan after doing what he needed to do and tended to Mista Kokoschka, now Missy too.

Wallace thought it a good idea to mention it to Papa.

"Probably misplaced his cock somewhere after taking a piss this morning. I bet he's out there in the woods looking for it."

"Ya know 'bout dat?" Wallace said with surprise.

"I sure fucking do." Papa then became contemplative before adding, "My brother Beornræd's got a cunt," was all he offered in the way of explanation.

Wallace decided to let things be. Horan was liked by Papa, and that's all that mattered as far as he were concerned. "Gonna git somethin' ta eat. Starvin' I's am."

"I'll join you." Papa grabbed his sword god, strapping the scabbard of it to his belt with practiced ease. "I could go for some left-over rabbit stew without its goblin's balls for breakfast, right now."

"We's don't have any goblin's balls left anyways, only carrots n' dem parsnip things. Maybe a couple o' dem baby cabbages if I's look hard enough."

"Fucking good thing too." Papa slid Wallace a knowing glance, smiling wide. "Goblin's balls have been tasting even worse the further fucking south we've been going. Imagine what the fucking things'll taste like by the time we get to the Hyruldon Expanse."

Wallace shuddered at the thought, hoping the potatoes didn't grow that far south.

As papa went to the caravan's door, opening it, letting in the new day, Wallace remembered to get his sword from under his pillow. He rushed to fetch it, not wanting to get caught without his weapon again. Lesson learned.

As Wallace and Papa left the caravan, coming down the creaking wooden steps, they were confronted by half a dozen men with scarred and dirty faces, sneering, brandishing rusted weapons and worse attitudes. One of them were bald, but the rest had hair cut to their skin. Easier to keep away lice without hair if sleeping wherever they could on the run. Bandits they were.

Wallace gasped, his thoughts flashing immediately back to the terrible night he'd lost his family. The face of the man who'd attacked him filled his mind once more. His mocking laugh, his joy at Wallace's pain, it all came flooding back all too soon. His heart skipped beats and, his skin crawled, 'specially where that evil man had touched him. Wallace moved closer to his papa, cold sweat forming on his worried brow.

He were scared.

But Papa, without hesitation, drew his sword god, the metal of it hissing beautifully as it slid out of its scabbard. "Looks like there's some fucking folks here who want to taste blood for breakfast, son, instead of rabbit stew!"

"G-git 'em…Papa!" Wallace managed with a whispering squeak. But somehow, and he didn't know how considering he was frozen with the fears of his memories, he'd drawn his sword too. The steel glowed a fiery crimson.

These men were trouble.

The biggest bruiser of the lot of 'em, demanded, "Give us all yer coin, and no one'll git hurt." The man held a woodcutter's axe, tapping it into the palm of his opposite hand threateningly.

He weren't no woodcutter. The man's whole body were all muscle on muscle in lumps, including his thick neck, looking like sacks of freshly picked goblin's balls. Woodcutters mostly had thick arms from cutting down all 'em trees and a lot of fat on 'em 'round their bellies from eating and drinking too much. These bandits were lean muscle all over from doing their dirty evil business, preying on innocent folks. For what? A few pieces of silver?

Wallace hated them.

Papa snorted. "Fucking come get what you want, then. My god's ready to give you plenty of metal to fill your pockets and fill the fucking rest of you all with it too."

The thick-necked man sneered. "Think yer tough, don't ya, knight?"

Papa, shrugging, spat, "Come fucking find out."

"We will, won't we boys?"

And with that promise the bandits charged, their weapons at the ready.

The wonderful thing about Papa, Wallace thought, was that no matter who he faced, be they demons, fighting monks, darrow, or folks foolishly wanting for a fight, he didn't seem to blink, quick as lightning to do what had to be done.

Before Wallace could raise his own sword, the blade now glowing green, Papa had relieved two men of their heads. Quick and neat. Funny thing, seeing a headless man's body flap about for a split second before slumping to the ground in a dead thud, blood oozing. Never get used to that. But to see an enemy that way was all good.

'Specially bandits.

Papa was onto the third man, slashing left and right, quick, quick, sword god thrumming and hacking in half the feeble weapon the bandit wielded—to the man's shock—before Wallace realized, he was invisible, knowing so because he was unable to see his hand holding his magical sword. Seemed his sword protected him once it sensed his fear. So that's how it worked.

And Wallace, thanks to Garthana's gift of protection, wasn't as scared. In fact, he steeled his resolve, and as he pushed his haunting and terrible past into the back of his mind, putting away the images of that evil man as best he could, he came around the bandit Papa was fighting.

The bandit was good with his weapon, a match for Papa. That were until Wallace sunk his sword into the bandit's side and pushed it in as far as it would go—and seeing as the green glowing blade could be seen out the other end of him, was far indeed.

Wallace withdrew his sword and moved onto the next closest bandit, the one approaching Papa with a sneer and a, "Ya pissin' me off, and I'll git ya fer killin' me mates, ya fucker."

The man Wallace had previously stabbed, let out a weird, choking "errrgh" sound before his eyes rolled back, clutching at where he were punctured, and then kindly dropped dead.

Good riddance ta bad rubbish, Wallace thought.

Papa kicked the dead man aside without so much as a glance. To the approaching bandit, he goadingly said, "I'm going to fucking kill you and the rest of your so-called mates to really piss you off. How about that?"

"Ya son-of-a—" And that's when his head went flying, thudding onto the ground near the horses.

They whinnied in protest; Wallace couldn't blame them.

Which left two bandits standing, their confidence draining from them.

One of them Wallace could take on, seeing as he were still invisible, but the other bandit, to his surprise, was already being dealt with. And not by Papa. Horan had acrobatically suspended himself upside down from a branch of an overhanging tree, holding on to the bough with his feet turned just so to slip a garrote wire around the bandit's throat. Silent and deadly.

So that was where Horan had got to, hiding himself until the moment was right. Clever. The garrote Horan used with expert hands, hands used to playing instruments, juggling things, and, it seemed clear now, strangling folks with a lute's wire. The garroted bandit's body added to the rest of 'em, piled up like wood for the fire. Or more than likely, feed for the crows and worms. Papa wouldn't give these men a proper send off. They would never sit at the halls of their gods, drinking ambrosia and laughing for eternity. They didn't deserve it.

Now one bandit stood alone, sweat trickling down his brow. Wisely, he hesitated, fumbling with his rusted axe like it were suddenly too hot to handle. His eye quivered. He were scared. Good.

Papa, ever with a quick summation of any given situation,

announced, "Looks like you've got no mates left. Do you want to fucking join them, or are you considering a different career now?"

The man paled. "I...I..."

But before Wallace could hear Papa's answer proper, he felt a rush of wind against him, ruffling his hair and his clothing, and sending a chill through him. The forest became silenced, insects and birds included. The quiet was deafening. Even the trees, with their swaying canopy and creaking boughs, no longer made any sounds.

What were happening?

Nothing moved. Not the bandit. Not Horan. Not even Missy and Mista Kokoschka. Wallace's sword's blade also changed its glow, turning to the wonderful color of safe blue. He became visible.

Which meant whatever was happening wasn't a danger.

But again, what was it?

Papa must have been clued in. "Well, fucking well. If it isn't Abbot Hosho; what brings you to me at a time like this, old man?" Papa then held out his hand. It seemed only he and Wallace could move. No one else could; they were frozen, but not 'cause of any cold weather. All except the strange old bald man, milky eyed, and wearing an orange robe who accepted Papa's gesture of greeting. "Wait. Let me guess. You've got something to show me. Right?"

The man named Abbot Hosho, a monk of some sort, nodded slowly. In a whispered voice, he replied, "I've haven't got anything to show you or Wallace, but I've got something to tell you both."

Wallace didn't know how the monk knew his name. And even though it was strange, Wallace felt comfortable within Abbot Hosho's presence. Being near him was like being near a warm, crackling fire when outside it hailed and the winds blew the window's shutters from their ties, it were so fierce.

"Then...*tell* us," Papa said hesitantly.

Wallace quickly realized the appearance of the monk wasn't something to take lightly. His presence was for an important reason. Something profound had happened. Wallace's stomach turned.

He didn't like when his insides did such things.

Never good.

Wallace was found correct when, with great sadness weighted upon his head, Abbot Hosho said, "I am so sorry, my dear friends, so sorry, but I have to tell you that Dorgan is...dead. He was..."

Wallace's didn't hear the rest of what was said as his world collapsed in around him. Weakness found all his bones, and he fell into a heap upon the leaf litter that didn't make a crunching sound because of the monk's magic. He'd dropped his sword. Didn't know when. Without further thought, and upon the cold ground, he began to cry. It poured outta him. Papa cried too, but he picked up Wallace to hold him; Wallace held him back with everything he had within him.

Within the strange bubble of suspended time Abbot Hosho had created, gods knows how 'cause it were more than by magic, Wallace cried and cried while being held by Papa as he held him back just as tightly, because that's all they could do.

Hold each other and cry.

25

Novane's New Friends

NOVANE DECIDED, DUE TO somewhat selfish reasons, to take the longer path to the Steps to Heaven mountains. His love for Greysen demanded it. Was that selfish really then?

Let the Great Kraken of the Void judge him if it were.

As such, the path he chose wasn't across the stone bridge going directly into the kingdom of Suvanwold but along the great delta's northern bank. From there, they'd come to the tussocky hills of Invrawold, patches of forest within them daring to defy the sweeping winds over the open lands, the trees bent. One thing Invrawold was never short of was wind. Once they crossed the delta, they'd then come to Fangmere forest, the red ravines where the ruined Silver Tower once stood, and then the mountains themselves.

A journey of weeks and weeks.

Novane looked forward to the time with Greysen. More to what they would discover, the exploration and consummation of their love. He'd noted how Greysen's affection had grown. Not only did they hold hands as often as possible, but plenty of kisses, most passionate, also became the norm.

Many times, Greysen's kisses left Novane gasping, lips tingling. They also left him hard. Very hard. He ached, no yearned, for more physical love with his damaged god, but he would never be the instigator. Their progress was up to Greysen, for Novane would never do anything to hurt him—even through his affection.

Oswin, always following them like an obedient dog, halted when they came to a copse of twisted, bent over trees, ancient and weathered, between two large hills. Novane noted the vulnerability of their position.

Greysen must have as well; he let go of Novane. "What's wrong, Oswin?"

"Danger," the lost god said, the word was gasped from his deadened lips as if a crypt had been opened and the stale, foul air escaped.

Novane shuddered, and not many things made him do so, being undead. Pole axe in hand, he stood ready, scanning his surrounds.

The wind blew.

For a moment, nothing was seen. Nothing heard but the whistling wind. Always the wind, whipping at clothing, cloak, and hair alike. Not until Novane looked into the copse where it was darkest did he see movement. Then, the movement came into the dull light of the grey clouded day. What was revealed surprised him.

Children stood before them.

There were six of them of varying ages, but most were prepubescent. One girl, five boys; the eldest, the girl. All were dirty, looking as though they clung onto the last threads of life, physical representations of the tattered clothing hanging from their emaciated skin and protruding bones. Three boys had the unmistakable paunches of malnutrition. No doubt they were all starved and destitute. But the worst of all, they all had some form of deformity, from a missing eye, fingers, or hands, to others more severe.

One child, the youngest boy, had a grossly misshapen skull, beady eyes, and the rest of his face was lopsided. He didn't stand straight.

None of them did.

Novane didn't believe the children were the danger, as Oswin wasn't looking at them. His attention was on the hills beyond the copse. So who, or what, was the danger Oswin spoke of, then?

"Who are ya, comin' into our territory?" the girl demanded, standing firm, the hard look of a hard life upon her grotty, scar-riddled face. The scars on her skull clumped her dirty golden locks.

Greysen stepped forwards, bowing slightly. "I'm Greysen, magician of the Hyruldon Expanse. This is my partner, Novane, also of the Expanse." Greysen turned to Oswin. "And that man behind us is my brother, the lost god. His name is Oswin."

At the word 'god,' the children gasped, looking at each other in wide-eyed wonder.

The eldest boy, fifteen or so, one-eyed but brilliant sparkling blue, said, "Will ya help us, magician with a god as a brother n' the undead for his boyfriend?"

Novane pushed the danger Oswin spoke of to the back of his mind as he thought about the boy's words. He *was* Greysen's boyfriend. How strange to hear it spoken by a stranger. He felt...elated.

Yet another thing he'd never felt before.

"Who are you then," Greysen asked, "if you wish us to help you?"

"And help you with what?" Novane chimed in.

The eldest girl stated, "We are the Forgotten." With growing sadness, she explained, "And this is all that's left o' us."

"Forgotten by whom?" Greysen questioned, both surprise and hurt in his expression. Novane wondered why. They were only children, probably runaways. Children were always running away.

The one-eyed boy, face screwed in anger, replied, "We're the ones the slave traders can't even sell fer dog bait. Not even good enough fer pet meat, either, we ain't. No quality to our bodies or bones, see? Folks are scared we'll give their animals the curses and poxes we have." He paused to catch his breath, face red. "We aren't cursed or diseased. But not even the orphanage wants us 'cause of the fear. Sister Luci don't want no children who folks reckon are cursed. She only wants the handsome n' pretty ones who'll get homes and good work one day. We'll never get homes. That's why we're the Forgotten."

Novane was curious how such wretches had survived the wilds of Invrawold. Although, from the state of them, their survival was on a knife's edge. One of the boys looked as though death's touch was tapping on his shoulder already, his aura weak. They all desperately needed food and fresh water.

Greysen must have thought the same. He was already searching inside Novane's backpack, handing out their ration packs to each child. He smiled as he did so, his movements careful and tender. Again, Novane wondered why.

"Thanks," the girl said accepting the food; all the others were tearing into the packs with their teeth, supping on the contents hungrily. "It's the Salt Devils who want us for their mines. It's them who want to work us to death. But two moons ago, we escaped 'em, just as we escaped the slave traders o' the city three 'fore that. Good at escaping, we are."

The children all nodded. "Good at escaping," they repeated.

Novane realized that, by their count of moons, the children had been in the wilds for almost one-hundred and fifty days. Too long. Novane imagined they were near the last days they could cope with. A good thing they were found. If captured again by the Salt Devils, it would have been the end of them; devils don't abide their slaves deserting them, the punishment death.

Greysen was comforting the youngest now. "Salt Devils?"

Novane knew who they were. Evil bastards. Crusty skinned demons who mined for salt and other consumable minerals; they were the merchants of the demonic world. They didn't care who they enslaved to work their mines. Human suffering especially wasn't something that concerned them. A policy which extended to children, obviously. The poor things.

One-eyed boy said, "They hunt us all the time—that's why there's only six o' us left. Used to be thirty."

"Help the Forgotten," Oswin's parched voice whispered, again like the wind across graves.

Without hesitation, Greysen said, "Yes, we'll help you. But take us to where these Salt Devils are. We'll make sure they never hunt you again. You'll never be slaves again, I promise."

Novane added, "And tell us your names."

The girl nodded. "I'm Scar, 'cause o' me scars," she explained, shrugging but now munching on her ration pack, a satisfied look upon her.

One-eyed boy said, "I'm Cyclops." Novane didn't need to be told why that was his name.

Then it went down the line.

There was Handy, because he had no hand; Twist, because of his hunchback and other physical deformities; and Club, for he had no toes and only four fingers and one thumb between both of his hands.

The last boy, the youngest and the most deformed, said weakly, "Name's Precious."

"And that you are," Greysen said to him, hugging him. Precious smiled a crooked smile, but one filled of hope. "All of you are." And Novane could see tears roll from Greysen's eyes.

That was when Novane understood.

These children, these lost souls, these Forgotten, must have reminded him of his own terrible past. How he'd been treated. How he'd been forgotten, only useful to others when it served a purpose. Like how these children were only useful as slaves in the mines of the Salt Devils, nothing else left for them.

Novane wanted to comfort Greysen as Greysen comforted the children. But there was no time.

Oswin began to shuffle towards the largest hill, despite the leash spell still in effect. Perhaps the spell never worked in the first place and it was only Oswin's will which kept him following them.

"Danger," he repeated. No doubt the mines weren't far away. The hills of Invrawold were famous for the riches they held, from salt to talc to gold.

Trust devils to exploit others to get to them.

Scar and Cyclops led the party towards the salt mines beyond the nearest hills. The wind seemed to cut to the bone here. One hill had a huge dead tree clinging atop it, the skeleton of branches twisted bent after surviving a lifetime of endless weather. The tree was burnt by a lightning strike or a dragon for fun. Either way, it was the only other landmark for leagues in either direction aside from hills and the copse of trees the Forgotten had emerged from.

Greysen and Oswin followed Scar and Cyclops, the rest of the children behind them. Novane, however, scouted ahead. He used his aura sight to see if he could spy upon the devils before they saw him.

Salt Devils were cunning, tough, and cruel, but they weren't able to see very well beyond the darkness of their mines. Novane believed he had the advantage.

He believed wrong.

A cry, warbling and piercing, blew with the wind towards him. The unmistakable sound of warning a Salt Devil made from a sack within its throat, an adaptation which helped them breathe in the thin air underground, rang across the windswept hills.

Novane froze.

He couldn't see the devil, not even its aura. Where was it? Novane, unsure, stood ready though. The motion had become something he didn't need to think about. A good thing too. From seemingly out of the ether, out of nowhere, perhaps springing from the ground itself, a Salt Devil came upon him, growling, its sword swinging; the metal of it thrummed too close to Novane's ear.

A swing he managed to block with his pole axe in the nick of time.

"You'll have to do better than that, devil," Novane barked and then spat, once more at the ready. But now the advantage of surprise had been lost, and he wouldn't be caught so vulnerable next time.

The Salt Devil's aura glowed blistering red with dark splotches cascading through it, as expected for creatures of evil. "Why are you here, lich?" The devil stood firm as well.

Novane didn't answer; he could see in the aura, now flashing purple—the color of disinterest. Whatever he said wouldn't be listened to, anyway. Instead, they both stared at each other. And stared. Novane realized almost too late that the Salt Devil was delaying. He cursed himself. He turned just in time, managing to dodge another attack from a Salt Devil who'd been sneaking up behind him, their weapon parried with ease. But that time he was lucky.

He should have known better. Devils meant deception.

"Two against one isn't fair," Novane said, mockery in his voice; he knew he could take on ten devils without breaking a sweat now that he was aware of their tactics. He just hoped Greysen, Oswin, and the children didn't get too close while he did what he had to. He didn't want to see any of them hurt.

"Why are you here?" the first Salt Devil repeated, voice as crusty as it's skin.

They weren't great conversationalists, Salt Devils. "Why are *you* here?" Novane asked cheekily but aware of the movements around him.

There was no reply.

And yes, Novane could take on ten Salt Devils. No problem. But when he suddenly witnessed the auras of more than one-hundred of them glowing, red and black and angry, approaching fast from the leeward side of an opposite hill, he decided he'd attempt to do the same thing the devils had done to him earlier. Delay.

As such, he said, "I'm here to offer my assistance, devil. Nothing more."

"What assistance can you offer us?" the second snapped acidy.

The other Salt Devils were getting closer, warbles from their throats as war cries. Unfortunately, Greysen, seemingly oblivious, also approached. Novane had to do something fast. The last thing he wanted was Greysen to use his dark magic to then become incapacitated just as more and more Salt Devils arrived to overwhelm them. Magic had its uses, no doubt. But Novane didn't believe it would be useful here. They'd be overrun, overwhelmed by Salt Devils too quickly. Yes, Greysen's powerful blackfire would destroy a lot of them. But not all.

They'd all be captured for slaves for the salt mines.

Time to show his mettle and his usefulness.

Novane's thinking was simple. Salt Devils were like cockroaches. Kill six, twenty more were hidden. There could be thousands upon thousands of them under the surface right now. Never mind the hundred he saw above ground, coming fast.

Now was not the time for being showy or too confident. Now was the time for being clever and cautious. Now was the time to put into place a plan that would exterminate the vermin that infested the windswept hills of Invrawold once and for all.

The children Greysen had already grown attached to depended on him and him alone to act in the best way possible to gain the best outcome. Besides, even though Novane's heart now beat, he was undead. Salt Devils weren't.

Undead could fight forever.

Could devils?

He was also a lich lord, and he had a trick or two up his sleeve that devils didn't. The time to act was upon him.

Without further delay, Novane gave a quick thrust of his pole axe into the guts of the first Salt Devil, piercing its crusted skin and killing it instantly. "I changed my mind; I'm not here to help you, but kill you all." He swung around, slicing the second Salt Devil into two.

Devils, like demons, bled dark, sticky ichor. He knew the tussocky hills would soon turn black with devil blood.

He mentally counted the moments before the swarm of devils came within the reach of his pole axe. He didn't need to count for long. Good. If Novane was going to do anything, he was going to fight for his love of Greysen. Nothing gave him more power. Heaven help the devils who dared face him, for they'd need more than the old god's graces to survive Novane's fury.

It may be written in ancient books that Hell hath no fury like a woman scorned. They were wrong about that. To Novane, Hell hath no fury like an undead reborn because of his newfound love. An undead who loved was the most powerful force on Earth. The universe. Why? Because it'd never happened before.

Novane was the first.

The auras of the Salt Devils grew more crimson with their anger. Even better. Angry devils were devils who made mistakes. Novane couldn't help but smile, annoying them further.

"Come, devils!" Novane hissed, dispensing with the first two easily; they screeched and gargled ichor from their throats before they fell by his feet, twitching, then dead. "Come and see what happens to those who dare face me."

Novane was soon surrounded.

He absolutely loved it.

But he knew with crawling dread, even though he could fight for an age, that Greysen would soon arrive. Novane hadn't scouted too far ahead. When Greysen did, he'd join in the fight. Greysen was Greysen. His love. But then the children would be left exposed and vulnerable. Oswin too.

Novane moved with the quickness of lightning. He drew his scimitar. With both weapons, he sliced, thrust, and stabbed at every devil he could, twirling, dodging, and feinting at the same time. His movements flowed, his thoughts of nothing but the strength Greysen's love gave him and his love for Greysen. He was powerful because of it.

Black ichor, stinking like sulfur, filled the air. Novane, if human, would have coughed, become overcome. But he wasn't. He didn't care about devils bleeding to death. The more of them that did so, the better.

He smiled even more when the ichor splattered to the ground off the blades of his weapons in thick, clotted ribbons, the dried grasses covered by the foulness and beginning to smolder. Then fire, the smoke of it blacker than the ichor itself.

Again, he would have been overwhelmed if human. But he had to be careful of the flames. He could still burn. He turned and ran down the hill, letting the devils chase him for a moment.

A ruse.

He soon set to them again with his scimitar and pole axe. Slash, slash, slash. Ten devils were sliced open in vital areas, clutching at their wounds in disbelief and desperation, before joining the stinking filth on the smoking ground. Why was it that no matter who it was—human, beast, creature, or whatever—at the moment of death, they were always surprised? Novane wondered if he would be when his end came.

But he didn't have time for contemplation.

For most other species, seeing twenty or thirty of their kin so easily and expertly killed, would have seen the rest turn and run. Not so with Salt Devils. They became more determined. And angrier. More and more came. They swarmed over the hills like ants from a nest before a mighty storm.

"Shit!" Novane spat.

Time to use a different tactic.

He sheathed his scimitar, the hilt clicking into place, but still held his pole axe in a way which meant business to any devils coming too close. For a moment, it seemed to work. The devils had become more cautious, obviously realizing Novane was a threat they needed to consider more wisely. Although, the devils wouldn't remain so. When more of their kin arrived, their confidence, naturally, would grow.

Novane closed his eyes for the briefest moment. He knew where his enemy were in his mind's eye. They offered no immediate threat. With his aura sight, he reached out, seeing the crimson and black swirling around the Salt Devils. Lich's didn't have much magic, but what they did possess could be just as effective as the strongest mage when used in a timely manner. Like now.

Sure, he didn't want Greysen to use his magic; that would incapacitate him for too long. But Novane wasn't burdened by such restrictions. He opened his eyes, concentrating on the auras seething before him, angry and wanting blood.

His blood.

With the subtlest move of that hand that once held his scimitar, an arcane gesture to help him focus, and a powerful thought directed outwards, he touched the auras of the Salt Devils surrounding him with his own.

The result was instantaneous.

When infected by the invasion of another aura, those affected became confused. Some would stand, doing nothing. Others could go mad, for their inner self had become foreign to their outer self. The mind's will didn't command their bodies any longer. It wasn't as simple as that, but in effect, by changing an aura, manipulating it, Novane fought the devils with his mind as well as his weapons.

The battleground had changed to *his* battleground.

Yes, he needed to concentrate. Keep his hold upon his enemies. Keep his aura within theirs to continue staining it, manipulating them to his will or at least incapacitating them. But he would do so while he sliced at devil flesh with his pole axe. Because if fighting a voracious but simple-minded opponent while they were in control of their faculties wasn't strenuous for Novane, then fighting them when they were incapacitated by their own inner selves was dead easy. Too easy, really.

Novane was enjoying himself.

Unfortunately, his joy didn't last long. More and more Salt Devils came out of their nests within their underground mines. Too many for Novane to influence with his aura magic at once. Sure, he'd undermined hundreds around him, but he couldn't make them do anything they wouldn't normally do. Aura magic didn't work like that. It couldn't make someone fight a friend or ally. Nor could it make them kill themselves. Pity.

Novane swung his pole axe with more fervor.

He concentrated, keeping his aura magic around him as far as it could reach. At least the devils who wandered too close would become stilled or mad before they met their fate on the black, ichor-soaked ground. Smoke and the acrid stench of sulfur grew thicker and thicker as Novane dispensed with as many devils as he could.

He knew he had limits though, especially when he both fought and used his magic. Concentrating was tiring, even if physical exertion wasn't. He felt his aura, the dome he'd sent forth to surrounded himself with, faltering. He couldn't help it. Maintaining it was never infinite. Aura magic, like normal magic, had limitations. Consequences. One being that when the devils had their own auras back, they'd be pissed worse than before.

Perhaps then they'd make for more formidable opponents.

Novane would soon find out, for his aura projection collapsed as he dispensed with six Salt Devils coming back to themselves. The others surrounding him, hundreds upon hundreds, let out their warbling war cry, throats inflated like frogs croaking.

Quickly, Novane had to begin fighting for his life; he drew his scimitar once more. As he slashed, sliced, and thrust with both blades, devils screaming, attacking with tooth and claw as well as their weapons, he realized he couldn't hold back the hoard much longer.

More Salt Devils came. The hills were infested with them. Salt Devils weren't like cockroaches at all. Not even ants. They were like a plague.

Novane slashed and slashed. Ichor flowed. He was struck a few times, the air tainted with his own coppery tang as well as the sulfur stink of the enemy.

As more Salt Devils came, their weapons wielded high, Novane stumbled. Too many dead around him. Too much ichor. Too much smoke. He couldn't fight when he had to worry about his surroundings.

"Giving up?" Novane shouted, not for anything but to see what the reaction would be.

It wasn't good.

The Salt Devils were tenacious, ferocious, and above all, they all had one goal. To get Novane.

Again, Novane stumbled. But that time not over a dead body, but a devil that had feigned death so it could grab him around his ankle. Hold him.

Novane gasped as the Salt Devils gained more confidence. He swung his pole axe in great sweeping arcs. The devil that held him remained firm. Novane couldn't break free.

"You've lost, lich," one of the closest devils said, laughing.

Another said, "You will make an excellent—"

Blackfire silenced the Salt Devil; their body, all of them, from bones to sinew, blood and ligaments, were scattered to the unending winds.

Novane turned.

Greysen's hands were extended, his magic, powerful and deadly, far deadlier than anything Novane could conjure in a thousand lifetimes, flowed from him. Twisting, sizzling, crackling, like it was alive. Salt Devils exploded all around, black ichor in fountains. The hills were soon ablaze where the devils fell, greasy smoke staining the gray skies.

The children stood behind Greysen, eyes wide with awe. Scar and Cyclops also had a relieved look upon them. Precious cried with joy as Handy held him, comforting him. All the children comforted each other as Greysen continued to cast his dark magic.

Despite the outcome of Greysen's aid, the fight wasn't over, even as Novane dismembered plenty of the devils alongside the blackfire. The Salt Devils didn't turn and run from Greysen. His magic, the blackfire which decimated them like Death's scythe shearing through fields of mortals close to the end, could only affect those close enough to him—as Novane knew.

The other thing Novane knew: Greysen would collapse soon. Overwhelmed by his own magic. He was already starting to weaken. And Novane was in no position to rush to his side. Too many devils between them, for no matter how many they laid waste to, two more came. Then two more. Their numbers increased exponentially. And with Novane's aura magic spent, his pole axe only able to do so much, he held little hope for victory.

Greysen then collapsed.

Novane gasped in horror.

The children, equally horrified, went to him and tried to work out what was wrong. Novane could only watch helplessly as Greysen shuddered, the look of pain and ecstasy equal upon his twisted, handsome face.

The Salt Devils sensed the victory Novane felt slipping away. Many came around Greysen. Cautiously as they didn't know of his failings. Novane did.

"Greysen!" he cried, the agony of his love being vulnerable enough to still his newly beating heart.

Then, as the Salt Devils gathered in numbers like wolves around freshly felled prey, their auras changed. No longer were they stained with anger. Now, they flashed with green between the blackness spoiling their inner selves.

Novane wondered why, until he saw Oswin.

The lost god, not alive, not undead, not anything explainable, touched each devil as he came to them. The devils, having made contact with Oswin, immediately dropped dead, like puppets with their strings cut. No sound came from the fallen except the soft thud as they found the ground. No ichor flowed either.

Oswin killed silently.

Efficient.

Horrific.

Effective.

Novane could do nothing for the fight but watch in awe as the children had done earlier. One thing he could do was go to Greysen. Without hesitation, he did. When by his side, he held his love, cradling him. "I told you not to use your magic unless you had to."

With shudders of climax still coursing through him, Greysen stammered, "I-it was n-needed."

The children tried to comfort him too.

Cyclops asked, "What wrong with Greysen?"

Scar thumped him. "Magic isn't for free, silly. Greysen has paid a price for the magic he cast."

Novane noted how attentive she was. "That's right."

Precious, tugging on Novane's tunic, pointed at Oswin. "But what 'bout the lost god?"

"Oswin is different," was all Novane could say in reply. It was like explaining why the sky was blue; it just was. There was no explaining it.

"Magic," Club said, shrugging.

"Magic isn't for free," Scar repeated. She turned to Novane, who was brushing his hand gently over Greysen's cheeks, trying to help him settle. Greysen kept shuddering. Scar added, "But what's the price a god has ta pay, Mista lich?"

"Oswin's already paid it ten times over."

The children nodded, seemingly understanding. They were better than Novane, that was for sure, for he didn't understand the depths Oswin swam within. Didn't understand Greysen's or his own, either.

The Salt Devils, those who survived Oswin's deadly touch, scattered across the hills, yelping in retreat. A good sight to witness.

Novane looked up, breathing a sigh of relief and thanking the gods or the universe or whoever the hell was watching for the turn of events.

Greysen, his love, his life, was unharmed.

Novane's heart beat happily. Until, everything seemed to freeze, like time itself had decided to take a moment's pause after what Novane had endured. Even the clouds in the sky stopped scudding. The wind halted. That was the strangest thing of all. Like suddenly an old and dear friend was no longer present but there was no reason for their absence. Even the smoke and fire off the tussocky hills, blackened with burning ichor, had become frozen in time. The curls of oily smoke didn't move. They no longer continued to stain the sky.

Novane turned to look upon Greysen. He shuddered once more. At least he wasn't caught in whatever web had been cast around them.

Oswin approached. "Father comes."

And before Novane could even begin to fathom his words, an orange-robed man, bald-headed and with pupil-less eyes, came from the hill beyond, smiling but nervously if Novane wasn't mistaken. The children gasped.

Cyclops said, "'Nother god's come!"

Scar explained, "No. Not a god. A monk!"

Club and Handy held Precious, fear striking them, their tears flowing for a different reason, but Twist said, "Not a normal monk. A Whisperin' one, he is! Heard o' 'em 'fore in fairy tales, I have."

Greysen pulled himself out of Novane's hold, quivering and sweating. "Even if it disables me for the rest of my life," he sat up, wobbly and unsure, still straining, eyes full of the agony of his bliss even as blackfire began to crackle from his fingertips, "I'm going to kill my father for what he's done to me."

26
Khalaf's Power Realized

MYRKUL HAD NEVER BEEN entered. Never had his horns held, head pulled back, throat exposed, while another grunted behind him. He liked it. Not for the physical aspect. That didn't please him. He hardly felt it—a minor discomfort if anything; Khalaf wasn't exactly well endowed, not for a demon's satisfaction, anyway.

No. He enjoyed what Khalaf did because Myrkul felt all too delightfully the power tingling through him, coming from Khalaf to then go into every fiber of his being. Real power. Magic. Dark magic born from a dark and twisted birth.

Myrkul growled and snarled his joy, his cock hard, pre-ejaculate dripping onto the silk of the bedclothes, staining it, as he worked himself up. All the while, Khalaf's body slapped against his buttocks, slap, slap, slap mechanically; the man even grunted in time with each thrust, as if achieving the movement were a victory. Myrkul wondered if Khalaf had ever had another before he came out of Vengeance. Probably not. Before he was powerful, before he was Khalaf, Eddi would have been a nobody. Who wanted a nobody?

If it weren't for the magic within Khalaf, the raw power Myrkul knew he could control given time, as he would control Khalaf, he would have been killed the moment he dared bring his horse into the grand marquee. His horse slaughtered too, fit for nothing but food for dogs.

As Khalaf thrust and grunted and thrust, Myrkul wished his new husband were a few inches more. Many inches more, truthfully. Enough so Khalaf's cock could at least touch Myrkul's' prostate. But alas, no. Khalaf had the failing of his species. Big minded but not much else. No wonder humans were so easy to conquer; play to their aspirations, desires, wants, and they were putty in his hands. As Khalaf would be.

The horse would be a problem, though…

"Yes," Myrkul hissed through his pointed teeth, "that's the spot, my husband. You're so good. You're sooo good," he lied—something that'd become more than a skill since he'd hatched from his egg and devoured his egg mate for sustenance.

"You love being my bitch, don't you, husband?"

The words surprised Myrkul for a moment. "Yes," was again the lie he replied.

Myrkul could feel Khalaf work himself up to a faster, harder rhythm, but only because of the increased noises and speed of thrusts. Nothing else was felt.

Another surprise came from Khalaf. "Come for me before I come."

Myrkul wasn't even close. Far from it. All right, he was hard, but that was only due to the magical intensity he felt from Khalaf being so close, being inside him. He had to be careful here. If he didn't submit enough, Khalaf would suspect he was being used.

Then again, perhaps Khalaf already knew and was taking advantage. Myrkul shook his head to rid himself of the thought. No human was that clever. He touched himself, masturbating his hardness to get himself worked up. It didn't take long; Myrkul knew how to please himself. Yes, he would have preferred to fuck Khalaf and seen his expression as he was fed a cock that would split him, make him bleed, sore for days. But for now, Myrkul did as he was asked.

He shuddered.

"That's it, bitch!"

Myrkul let his seed spurt onto the silk. He became aroused even more as he smelt himself. Until Khalaf grabbed his horns tighter, pulled him back, and gave a final yell and thrust. Seemed his husband had come to his ending quickly. Thank the Great Kraken of the Void.

At that, Myrkul shuddered again.

That time was no lie because he could feel a sudden intensity of power, the raw, unhindered energy of Khalaf's seed swirling inside him. Now *that* he liked. "That was so good." And that time, again, there was no lie. A part of Khalaf's magic had become a part of him. Enhancing his own. Making him more powerful.

Perhaps being the submissive had its merits. He wouldn't do so for long, though; Myrkul only submitted when it suited him, while he gained power, while he used the opportunity presented to begin controlling Khalaf completely.

Khalaf pulled out of Myrkul.

To once again astound him, his husband went and sat on his throne, opening his legs, offering Myrkul the sight of his pink virgin anus. An alluring view.

Khalaf was tasty.

Myrkul felt a thirst rising.

Khalaf then commanded, "Come tongue my arse while I think of what our plans together will be." The lust and want in his eyes were still evident even though his petite uncut cock had softened.

"Yes, my husband." And Myrkul knelt before Khalaf.

While he worked his forked tongue across the puckered skin of Khalaf's anus, saliva dripping, making it wet, so wet, Khalaf's eyes were screwed tight from his obvious delight, stomach quivering, legs shaking. Myrkul relished both the reaction of what he did, and the sensation of the act itself. Khalaf was smooth-skinned, hairless where it mattered, and delicious in body and form. Just how he liked his men.

Myrkul's thirst grew as he rasped his tongue, over and over, across the delicate parts of Khalaf, including his perineum and balls, wetting them all equally. He even licked the taste of himself off his husband's foreskin and cock. That was different. Myrkul liked it.

He then wanted, no yearned, to fuck Khalaf. He would be so delightfully tight. Oh, to hear him scream and scream while he was entered would be music to Myrkul's ears. Nothing better than a virgin's scream of want. Nothing. But for now, he would let his husband believe he had the power, that he was in control.

For now…

As Myrkul worked his tongue, thought about his plans, the power he'd gain, he became hard again himself. He touched his own erection once more.

Khalaf must have noticed. "If you wish, I'll suck you again to help you with your little problem there."

"Little?" But Myrkul wasn't affronted, far from it; he considered how he enjoyed being Khalaf's bitch, but only because it served a purpose.

As Khalaf's seed continued to release its dark magic within him, make him shudder from the potency of it, Myrkul knew his husband was powerful beyond even himself. He had to tread carefully. He realized he could be a moth to the proverbial flame because of his need for Khalaf's magic. He would soon desire nothing else. Myrkul couldn't get burnt.

"Compared with Vengeance, you are."

"Yes, Khalaf, my A Rúnsearc," Myrkul replied between long licks of his tongue across Khalaf's quivering, sensitive flesh.

But something then changed. Khalaf sat up, looking affronted, brow furrowed. "I'm not your beloved." He pushed Myrkul away, closing his legs and no longer exposing his anus. "Beloved aren't born from outta horse's arses. Don't call me that again. Hear me?"

Myrkul trembled from the power of the touch upon his forehead. He tried not to show it, but knew he'd failed. Khalaf smiled when he replied, "As you wish, of course."

"Then stand up so I can suck on you. We will discuss other matters when you're spent."

Myrkul did so, presenting his erection to Khalaf, offering himself. While his husband took him, sucked and deep throated wonderfully, the seed within Myrkul continued to infuse its power into every cell of his body, enhancing his own magic, evolving it. Myrkul would do anything to have more of Khalaf's magic.

Anything.

Once Khalaf had drained Myrkul of what he could give, taking every drop, the relief, the agony, the bliss of it overwhelming to have such power so close, they both dressed.

Usually, Myrkul demanded his previous husbands remained naked and to wait for him within the pillows until called for. The horse master was the first he didn't make such a demand of.

There was a good reason for that.

As soon as they were done, Khalaf gave a kiss on Myrkul's cheek and then went to Vengeance, petting him tenderly, lovingly, whispering words into the horse's ear. Words Myrkul didn't hear. But he understood. The one thing Myrkul had learnt from their short time spent together: the horse Vengeance was never far away. Always watching.

Now Myrkul knew why.

The stallion was like a conduit of power. The air almost sizzled with the connection. Therefore, without the horse, there was no magic for Khalaf. And if Myrkul slaughtered Vengeance, destroyed the horse utterly, he would be able to dominate Khalaf like he'd dominated his past husbands. Force himself upon Khalaf, bend him to his will. Valuable information. Myrkul smiled. Valuable indeed.

"And what plans did you think of while my tongue pleasured your anus, my husband?"

"Ugruthaan is devious, but I know the demon stalks Hereward."

"Then we must find Hereward."

"We won't have to."

"I don't understand."

"Perhaps I need to fuck you again so you'll have some more sense pounded into you, Myrkul. You forget, Hereward stalks you because Greysen and Novane failed you—as you stupidly planned all along."

Myrkul was surprised, and not for the first time today; more so when Vengeance nickered, answering Khalaf's whispers. "How do you know these things?"

"You stupid demon," Khalaf snapped. "I know because Hereward's mare Missy told Vengeance, and Vengeance told me."

Myrkul bowed. "You *are* the master of horses, and I apologize for my lack of understanding, husband."

Khalaf smiled cruelly as did Vengeance with a snort. "Don't let it happen again."

"I won't. Of course, I won't."

Khalaf extended his hand. Myrkul took it for a brief, tantalizing moment before he had to withdraw. He gasped, rubbing his hand as if he'd been burnt. He had been, really. His skin was marked, blackened. The spark of magic, the power supreme and overwhelming, surged almost out of control when they made contact. It was too potent for Myrkul to take. He knew why. Khalaf was touching Vengeance at the time.

Myrkul smiled, knowingly. He realized, and didn't know why he hadn't before, that Vengeance and Khalaf were one and the same. Two parts of a whole. There was no bridge. No conduit of magic between them. They were one.

It all made sense now.

Imagine then, if Vengeance also fucked him, gave Myrkul his seed as Khalaf had given his. He would have the whole of what they possessed, all their magic together. Myrkul shuddered delightfully at such a thought.

But could he take Vengeance as he took Khalaf? Khalaf's seed still released its potency within him. No. He knew he couldn't. Not yet. He would have to find a way in which he could do so. Had to.

He couldn't help being the moth to the flame.

"I didn't realize how handsome Vengeance was. He is a mighty stallion, there is no doubt of it."

Khalaf snorted. "You only say that because you've only just discovered that if you submit completely and take us together, you'll gain even more power. So predictable. Vengeance told me you'd try your sweet talk with your forked tongue."

"A tongue you enjoyed, might I add."

Khalaf offered a grin. "As Vengeance will enjoy it."

Myrkul stood silent for a moment, contemplating his next words carefully. It seemed the human was cleverer than he gave him credit for.

Vengeance nickered.

Before Myrkul could offer any words, sweet or otherwise, Khalaf added, "I take your silence to mean that you will submit to Vengeance as you've submitted to me because you crave the full potency of our magic?"

"Yes." And Myrkul bowed again.

Khalaf ran his hand over Vengeance's withers. "You were right," he said to his horse.

Vengeance nickered again, flicking his mane with his head's movements this time. The horse then whinnied. A lot to say to Khalaf, obviously.

"What did he say?" Myrkul asked.

"He said to gather the generals," Khalaf said victoriously. "Tell them we must march to Thentathion Prime, as that will be our staging ground once we've conquered the city. Make the arrangements as soon as possible. That is where we need to be. Vengeance has foreseen it."

"What then, husband?"

"Once we've conquer Thentathion Prime, we need to make sure we're prepared for Hereward, and ultimately, Ugruthaan's arrival."

"We will be prepared," Myrkul said confidently.

"Good." Khalaf gave a look to Vengeance Myrkul didn't understand. Curiosity washed through him. Before he could ask what their silent communication meant, Khalaf continued with his instructions, his voice more languid and alluring. "Once you have done this, Vengeance and me will show you the true power of our magic as you beg for more underneath us. You will be even more powerful. But only once you have done as we've asked."

Myrkul shuddered, afraid and enraptured at the same time. He felt his cock harden. He licked his lips, then bowed, hoping he wouldn't become a slave to what was offered. "I will not fail you."

"I'm sure you won't."

Vengeance nickered; Myrkul believed it laughter.

Thentathion Prime glistened like a jewel amongst the scree it was built from within the southern shadow of the Steps to Heaven mountains. Towering buildings painted with golden rooftops dominated the cityscape. A white wall, crenelated and decorative, surrounded the inner city; another guarded the outer part where houses were nestled. The city was well protected. Trebuchet and other siege engines were seen. An army too. The leaders of Thentathion Prime had prepared for their arrival, it seemed.

But no matter what they had at their disposal, their defenses were no match for the undead horde Myrkul commanded. Tens of thousands against a few thousand. No match at all. As expected, the undead army swept through the city as though the structure were made of paper, not stone. The wraiths and undead dragons attacked from above while skeletons, ghouls, and the lich generals conquered below.

Upon the sweeping plain, broken shale and rock its dominant feature, Myrkul stood watching the carnage, listening to the screams of the vanquished, relishing the moment when he would get his reward for doing as Khalaf asked most of all.

Atop Vengeance, Khalaf commanded, "Kill all the nobles and royal family. The city's army too. Every man to the last. But leave the citizens and the city guard alive—we will need them later." The lich lord generals bowed and turned to do their duty, riding swiftly upon shadhavar to relay their orders quickly.

Myrkul said nothing.

Khalaf was striking, even if not handsome. His beauty came from the power he radiated along with Vengeance, like the fires of purgatory Myrkul wished to burn within. Myrkul was enamored. The most he'd ever been in all the eons he'd lived.

Oh, how he craved for the power he'd receive; his cock hadn't softened since they'd left for Thentathion Prime two days ago. He would burst soon. But he had to have patience. Had to wait.

It would be worth it.

With a smile, Khalaf looked down to Myrkul as if Myrkul meant nothing to him. Which he didn't. Myrkul, even though a demon, was nothing but an ant in comparison to Khalaf and what he commanded. Myrkul became even more aroused by those thoughts. It was certainly different to be the submissive. His cock ached. He wanted to be taken by his husband again. Fucked. Used. Abused. He then wanted to be taken by Vengeance. Perhaps have the both of them together, as promised.

Yes. How he yearned for such agony of bliss. For such power to be given to him through their seeds.

Khalaf, sneering, but obviously misinterpreting Myrkul's thoughts, said, "Don't worry. I'll make sure you have plenty of boys and men to rape or have your way with. Think of them as my gift to you."

"I am blessed for whatever gifts you give me." Myrkul bowed—but that's not what he wanted at all. "But you know I want you and Vengeance more than anything."

"Patience."

"I am trying."

"Have your fun first. Rape as many as you wish. I will give you what you deserve soon enough. We both will."

Vengeance nickered.

The city of Thentathion Prime was ravished, the royal family slaughtered from the children to the eldest as well as all the nobles, their sons and daughters too. The citizens were spared, as instructed, but their hell was only just beginning.

Myrkul knew how they felt.

It was delicious.

With the smoke of battle settling, Khalaf and Vengeance rode through the cobbled streets, heading for the palace. Myrkul followed obediently, like a dog wanting reward. For that's what he was. Waiting for his master to reward him.

When they entered the palace, Khalaf dismounted. He looked around the massive throne room, airy, marble, gold, and finery everywhere, smiling with satisfaction. "This palace will be a good home for us, won't it, Vengeance?"

The horse whinnied, Myrkul knowing it to be the sound of satisfaction from the animal. Myrkul also noted how his husband didn't include him in his words. He ached for attention from Khalaf. Yearned for more power as the seed within him had been spent. Myrkul felt weak now he that no longer felt its magical potency.

He missed it so.

To the left of the throne, gilt and jewel encrusted, the lich lords had prisoners on their knees. All of them young men from twenty summers in age to a lot younger. One or two of them but boys. They were workers of the city—blacksmiths, farriers, carpenters, stonemasons, and builders. They were all fit. Handsome too.

Khalaf went to the throne and sat upon the velvet cushion, shifting his weight to get comfortable. "These men and boys you see before you have volunteered."

"For what?" Myrkul asked.

Khalaf draped a hand lazily over the throne's arm, looking nonchalant. Vengeance came to him, nickering. He was patted, the connection between them clear. There was nothing but love. There was also power. So much power it cracked the very air.

Vengeance nickered again; more horse laughter, Myrkul imagined. "You have had an erection for two days now, I've seen."

Myrkul swallowed. "I have."

"These volunteers," Khalaf swept a gesture to his left, "will be the ones to help you with that. The one who pleases you the most, will keep his life. The rest will be slaughtered."

Myrkul looked at the men and boys offered to him. They were suddenly a sorry looking bunch. Miserable. Pitiful. They wouldn't please him. "You might as well kill them all now and be done with it."

"I want to watch them at least try and please you, husband."

Myrkul looked up to Khalaf. "I don't want them."

Khalaf shifted his weight again. "Oh, I know what you want."

"I am only yours," Myrkul whispered.

"Then as mine, you will do as I say, or you won't ever get the power you crave from either me or Vengeance. Do I make myself clear?"

Myrkul nodded. "You do."

"Good." Khalaf offered his usual grin as Vengeance nickered. "Now free your cock and choose the first to try to please you. This will be fun to watch."

Vengeance whinnied.

Myrkul felt debased. He also felt cheated. He was told once Thentathion Prime was conquered, and it was done so easily, he would have his reward. He didn't get it. Anger boiled within him as he undid his pants.

Yet, despite his thoughts, he was still hard. Being so close to power did that to him, he realized. In reply, and after he saw one of the volunteers stand to accept his fate, he mumbled, "I choose that one." He pointed to the curly, blond-haired young man, handsome and dressed in finery, like he was someone of importance, but trembling with fear, sweat dribbling down his brow. He was young, perhaps twenty-five summers old. For the first time in forever, Myrkul felt sorry for a human he was about to conquer.

A lich lord jabbed the blond with his sword.

"What's your name, volunteer?" Khalaf asked the young man as he got to his feet and was forced back onto his knees in front of Myrkul.

"My…n-name is…Aron…my Lord," Aron replied, as he took hold of Myrkul's cock, hand quivering to reflect his terror. Myrkul sighed. Aron was going to die.

Khalaf sat forward. "Well, Aron, if you please my husband, you can walk out of here a free man. If you don't, the lich behind you will remove your head, and your body will become feed for the crows."

Aron was wide-eyed and clearly scared out of his mind. "What w-will please you, Myrkul, demon god of the undead, of bones, of death, and the reaper himself? What can I do for you to keep my life, as worthless as it is to you? I have…experience in such things." And Aron squeezed Myrkul's cock more tightly; it felt good.

At that moment, Myrkul felt a connection to Aron. One of sympathy for sure, but also because the man really did want to please. How refreshing. He could see that in his eyes as well as the fear. "There is nothing you can do."

"I beg you. I will do anything," Aron said, tears welling in his eyes. He began kissing Myrkul's cock with his plump, ruby lips, as ripe as he was. He also licked in long lashes, then teased the corona of Myrkul's knob with his tongue made harder to give a different sensation.

Myrkul had to admit, Aron's technique and determination aroused him further. He *was* experienced. Perhaps he was a young lover to an older man? Perhaps a lover to many men? Aron was intriguing, and that, in the end, excited Myrkul more than anything else. He came to his full erection, aching, balls tightening. Aron's eyes brightened, and he took as much as he could of Myrkul into his mouth, gulping, slurping, worshiping; the throne room filled with the sounds of Aron's efforts as he sucked a demon's cock for his life.

Myrkul smiled.

Aron would have made a good husband if he'd known of him before he'd met Khalaf and Vengeance.

"It seems to me that Aron pleases you after all, husband," Khalaf said, derisively, disturbing Myrkul from his thoughts and the sensations Aron gave him; the young man's chin wet with his own saliva as he kept sucking, licking, and kissing as if all he saw was Myrkul's cock and nothing else. Again, refreshing. He liked the feeling of being dominant.

Then a thought struck Myrkul. Was more power really worth being submissive for? He began to doubt it. Began to question himself.

While Aron brought him to climax, rather expertly, Myrkul decided to be who he was supposed to be; his approach to orgasm giving him a newfound clarity. He was, as Aron had said earlier, the demon god of the undead, of bones, of death, and the reaper himself, after all. Such a demon god shouldn't submit to anyone. Not even the master of horses.

Not even for the promise of more power.

Myrkul let out a roar as he blew his load down Aron's eager throat, shuddering, relishing the feeling of being satisfied by someone who he could certainly conquer in all ways. As it should be.

The young man moaned his thanks for what was given and how his life had ultimately been spared. Aron came off Myrkul's cock with a popping sound, smiling. Myrkul couldn't help realizing how beautiful it was to see the result of what he'd done glistening on Aron's lips and chin as he looked up at Myrkul, pleased he'd pleased.

That was power.

All the power he needed.

Myrkul turned his attention to Khalaf, and said, "I think it's time I woke up from the fantasy I've been caught in, like a fly caught in a spider's web."

"What are you talking about?" Khalaf said, concern drawing on his brow.

"I need to be who I am supposed to be—a demon who conquers humanity not bows to it, no matter what promises are made."

"And you will get what you've been promised." Khalaf stood, his worry increased.

"But at a cost."

"Everything has a cost."

"Not for me."

He touched Aron upon his head, letting the young man know he would want more. There was a nod. Myrkul was pleased. It was then he saw he was flaccid for the first time since they'd left for Thentathion Prime. A true indicator that Myrkul didn't need Khalaf to give him any more power; he had enough of his own. He was satisfied. And it was Aron who did it. Not Khalaf.

He was Myrkul, not some mortal's bitch.

With blackfire tingling on his fingertips, feeling his own power surge, Myrkul turned to address his lich lord generals standing behind the rest of the volunteers. "Take my ex-husband and his horse and lock them up in the dungeons of the city. I will deal with them later."

Khalaf gasped. "What do you think you're doing?"

Myrkul ignored him. To Aron, he said, "Remove your clothing, for once the filth in here has been cleaned away and the stench of horse cleared, you will become my new husband. Powerful beyond your imagining. Do you accept?"

"I accept." Aron smiled, causing Myrkul's ejaculate to dribble from his lips, down his chin, and onto the marble. "And thank you, my Lord. I'll serve you always, willingly and obediently." And he then disrobed without delay.

Myrkul liked what he saw.

Yes, the young man was handsome. No doubt. A good cocksucker too. More than likely he would be great to fuck. Myrkul also noted that Aron was better equipped than Khalaf by far. Perhaps he'd let Aron fuck him from time to time. That thought aroused him, until he was brought back to the moment by Vengeance approaching, hooves clip-clopping starkly upon the stark white marble.

It seemed Aron's beauty had distracted him.

A fatal mistake.

Before he could defend himself, release the blackfire and smite Vengeance and then Khalaf, the stallion's hooves, alight with power and terrible magic, came down on him.

Myrkul was trodden into darkness.

Myrkul remembered how devastatingly dark and ceaselessly cold, cold to absolute zero, the Void was. Lonely, freezing darkness. His last thoughts before the Void froze him into the clutches of oblivion, clawing at him with the icy tentacles of the Great Kraken, were, *I'm sorry I betrayed you, Greysen…and I really wanted you as my new husband, Aron. You would have served me far better than Khalaf ever could,*" before his eternal end came…

27
Hereward's Terrible Loss

HEREWARD FELL TO HIS knees.

Overwhelmed.

Devastated and grief-stricken, hollow at the same time.

He held Wallace, held him like he was the last precious thing left to him, and he was. He cried great ugly blubbering tears that wet his beard, tasted bitter on his lips. Bitter to his soul.

Wallace cried even more.

What made it worse, when Wallace kept saying, over and over, "Why, Papa? Why did Pa have ta die, Papa? Why?" Hereward couldn't give him an answer. And not only could he not do so, he could see the pain he had in himself within Wallace's teary, bloodshot eyes, the expression on his face reflected back. And that hurt the most of all.

Even more, when after an age, Wallace said, "Don't ya dare git killed, Papa. I need ya like I's need the air. I'd die without ya. I'd die…"

Hereward, thinking his tears spent, nothing left in him to fuel them, cried again, holding Wallace once more. He had no answer for his son. How could he? The journey to the halls of one's god was never something predicted. When the time came to sip ambrosia, laugh with lost loves and family, then the time came.

Nothing anyone could fucking do about it.

Nothing could prevent it, either.

"It w-was his…time," was all Hereward could splutter, tears and snot and grief all over him in equal measure.

He wiped his face many times, but whenever he fucking did, more emotions flowed. More grief. More deep loss and emptiness. Emptiness to the point of feeling eaten from the inside out.

Thank his sword god he had Wallace, the only spark of life left in him now. His heart, swollen with sadness, only had enough love left for his son, no other. Ever. It was only him and Wallace from now on.

Only fucking him and Wallace.

And I will always be with you, my love, his sword god chimed in.

Hereward thought in reply, *You're a part of me, so you'll never be forgotten.*

I am. And Wallace needs you more than ever now.

I know. But the fucking thing is, I need him more than ever too.

Silence.

If there was one thing left in the world to fight for, to remain alive for, it was Wallace. He wouldn't let him down, and it would take all the demons within all Nine Circles of Hell to stop him from giving Wallace everything he had. Probably even more than that.

And with that thought, Hereward steeled his resolve, wiped his face, and straightened—not letting go of his precious son. Wallace still heaved his emotions, tears rolling down his plump cheeks, face red.

Another age passed.

Within the bubble of suspended time, Hereward didn't notice Abbot Hosho crouching next to him, coming to prayer beside him. Beyond the creaking boughs of the trees—which no longer creaked, of course—they faced the sun. It's rays, frozen beams of light, no longer dappled as the universe paused, held her breath for Hereward and Wallace. For their mourning.

Hereward couldn't think of anything more appropriate to do than look up at the wonder they'd found themselves within. The moment in time and isolation Abbot Hosho had blessed them with.

Abbot Hosho whispered, "Kieron and Vash have set up a pyre for Dorgan and will send him into the halls of his gods soon in the proper way."

"I wish I could be there," Hereward replied, once more eyes misting, tears falling soon after. "For him."

Wallace had settled but was hiccupping, as the young tended to do when overcome with emotions. Hereward couldn't blame him, the pain still growing within him.

"Use the Seeing Crystal Novane gifted you."

Hereward had forgotten about it. Without another word, because talking was painful, he retrieved the orb from his tunic's inside pocket. He thought about Dorgan.

Holding it so Wallace could see too, the crystal revealed what he wanted to see after a swirling of the clouded ether within its glass construct. There, like magic, there was Kieron and his lover Vash, placing the coins upon Dorgan's tongue respectfully.

At that moment, Hereward had to stifle back more tears. Wallace cried again, moaning his grief as they both watched. Hereward realized he'd needed the finality of witnessing his love pass, a hero's passing. That would at least give him something. A small fucking something.

Better than nothing.

"Goodbye, my beautiful dragon, my heart. My great hero. Goodbye," he managed to whisper, the words barely passing his salted with his tears lips. "May your journey to the halls of your gods be swift and your afterlife filled with love. I will see you when my time is done. I will. I promise."

"G-good…bye, P-Pa," Wallace stammered, sinking into Hereward's arms deeper, his body shuddering, but managing to keep his tear-filled eyes upon the crystal's vision as Kieron transformed into a dragon and breathed his fiery breath onto the pyre of wood and sticks they'd made for Dorgan.

Kieron and Vash both sung the song of a hero's passing when Keiron returned to human form, watching the flames and smoke carry Dorgan away. They both held each other, weeping.

Hereward wanted to reach out and touch Dorgan as he burned, as the smoke swirled, sending his soul to his god. He was aching with the love he'd lost, unable to say goodbye in the proper way. Hereward yearned to be with Dorgan, hold him one last time, lament his passing.

Wallace cried and cried.

Hereward, unable to believe it, let himself go even more; his feelings, sadness, love, memories, and grief, all poured out of him for what seemed another eternity. He didn't fucking care.

When the fire was spent, Dorgan truly gone, Hereward pocketed the Seeing Crystal and held Wallace, wrapping both his thick tattooed arms around him tighter. He never wanted to let his son go. Never. Not so long as he fucking breathed the sweet air of life, anyway. And Hereward would make sure he would keep doing so for as long as he could. For Wallace.

Abbot Hosho had finished his prayer. When, Hereward didn't know, but the monk then touched them upon their foreheads.

Wallace settled, only sniveling and hiccupping now.

Hereward felt a calm wash over him with the touch, repairing a little of his emptiness. He took in a deep breath.

To Abbot Hosho, he said, "Who do I have to fucking kill to avenge Dorgan, monk?"

"Alquam's only surviving child—now in the guise of Joran," was all the monk whispered before he faded from view and time returned almost cruelly. A wispy ghost of a voice added, "Go to Thentathion Prime. An answer to a piece of the puzzle about why this has all happened will be there."

After that, birds chirped, deer played and fornicated in the undergrowth, and the sun's warm rays livened as the canopy swayed and creaked once more.

Life, as it were, returned to normality.

Hereward and Wallace's life, however, was changed forever.

"What answer, monk?" Hereward said to the air where Abbot Hosho used to be.

Of course, there was no answer.

The remaining bandit dropped his rusted weapon and ran back into the woods. Hereward let him go. He didn't have the strength to fight anyone. He only wanted to hold Wallace.

As the day darkened, the sun's warmth gone and a chill finding them with the arriving mists swirling around the trees, Hereward stood. He brushed off the forest floor from himself as a newfound determination settling upon him.

Wallace, having gathered firewood, still red-eyed, trails of his tears staining his cheeks, said, "What now, Papa?"

"We hunt a fucking murdering cunt of a demon, that's what we do now."

Wallace nodded, agreeing. "Where do we go ta find it?"

"We keep on the path," he stated. "The demon we need to kill is the same one who murdered the clown Joran."

Wallace seemed shocked. "He is?"

"He fucking well is."

Horan, also having gathered sticks, approached. "I don't think Joran...I mean, the demon will go into the Hyruldon Expanse."

"No. He won't, you're right," Hereward said.

Horan continued, encouraged, "I think he'll want to gain allies— or at least dispense with any opposition."

Horan is a smart one, isn't he? his sword god said.

Hereward thought for a moment. "We're now going to Thentathion Prime."

Wallace, frown striking him, "Where's dat?"

Hereward replied, "Thentathion Prime is the jewel within the shadow of the Steps to Heaven mountains and within the Kingdom of

Thentathion itself. But I must warn you, Wallace, and you too, Horan, the customs the folks have who live there are a bit fucking different."

Horan and Wallace looked at each other.

"Different how?" Horan asked before Wallace obviously could.

"Just stick with me. I'll make sure they keep themselves to themselves. All right?"

"Ya, Papa."

Horan agreed too. But after a moment, Horan said, "Something happened didn't it?" Hereward knew the clown wouldn't have known about Abbot Hosho's arrival. Time had been stopped for Wallace and him, after all. Horan wasn't a part of that.

Hereward, without going into details and without dredging up his emotions that'd only just settled, simply said, "Not only was your brother killed by that demon, my love Dorgan was killed by its mother as well."

There was a moment of confusion, before Horan replied, "Then I will join you with your cause."

"Fucking fine with me."

Wallace, put his arm around Horan. "Dat would be mighty good o' ya, Horan. Ta."

28
Khalaf's Merciful Gift

ARON GULPED. THE TANGY, bitter, and salty taste of Myrkul's seed was still fresh in his mouth, but what he witnessed was even more bitter. He'd never seen anyone, let alone a demon, get pulverized underneath a stallion's hooves before. Hooves aflame with magic. It was shocking beyond words. So much blood. Enough to make Aron's stomach turn. And it jolly well wasn't his fault he pissed in fear, his fluid splashing onto the marble to dilute the demon's blood in puddles by his feet.

The unpleasant man named Khalaf, pimpled and pock-faced with a hawkish nose and thick lips, the city's new leader and the master of the magical horse, casually sat back down onto the throne, the one he'd stolen from a good king.

Khalaf said dismissively, "Lich lords, kill the volunteers. They serve me no further purpose." And with the command, swords began slashing and stabbing. More blood was added to the demon's as young boys and men were murdered without thought.

Only a few got a chance to even scream, they were dispensed with so quickly.

Before Aron could blink a tear of grief for their passing, he was seized with rough, undead hands. For the second time in as many moments, he feared for his life.

He also considered his life's choices.

Seemed sucking cock didn't always get you what you wanted, no matter how good it was done, did it? If he'd had known sooner, he wouldn't have learnt how to do it through hours and hours of practice on any man needing a blowjob but not wanting to pay for it from a Mentula Guild member. Aron'd even got his gag reflex under control for the most part by the time he'd come of age so he could then join the Guild and get paid for what he did. Finally. To tell the truth, now twenty-five summers old, he'd lost count of the number of cocks he'd had in his mouth over the years.

Then again, he hadn't become the chancellor's son's favorite cocksucker for nothing. Aron could suck on noble-born cock better than he could any other, including a demon's. He'd made Myrkul ejaculate fast enough, despite the size and shape of it which had proved a challenge.

Fat lot of good it all did him. He was going to be killed, all because he'd volunteered to be here in the throne room when the city was taken over. Although, he knew he had to if he was going to have any chance of helping those who survived the attack. Conquerors needed their sexual gratification as much as any other, and when they got that, they tended to be less...murder-y. And Aron, being a Mentula Guild member, was now in a position of honor and responsibility.

It simply would have been expected of him to volunteer. He accepted that fate willingly, if only to save the others. Besides, he also had his status to uphold. A proud status, one where tradition and duty were his considerations; the men of the Mentula Guild were almost like the currency of the city. Sometimes more valuable. And with his blessing of stunningly handsome looks, fresh and innocent, a fit body, and most importantly in his job, a big enough cock that every man paying for his services loved to admire, Aron was always going to be a member of the Guild.

What other job was there for him?

As such, he was never out of work and rich beyond imagining. He could honestly say that kneeling for a living, being showered with coins, gifts, and attention, was all he'd ever wanted to do. And no baker, stonemason, blacksmith, or farmer could say the same as Aron. They led hard lives; Aron led a life where he only needed to get his clients hard. Big difference.

He was jolly well valued.

Mentula Guild members were considered above all others in status within the kingdom; except for the nobles and royal family, of course. No one was above them...before they were all murdered in cold blood during the conquest of the city. Which was why it was left up to Aron to do what had to be done; he was the highest official left. He didn't even know if any other Guild members survived.

That's why he *had* to volunteer when Khalaf asked for men to do so. Pity the others who did were killed, despite Aron standing to try and save them. Such a waste. All of it.

What he'd done was for nothing.

He felt himself release his bladder again as the fear of his death clung to him worse than the reaper's final touch ever could. He yelped as he was pushed.

But before he felt the cold kiss of death from the point of a blade at his back, Khalaf interjected, "Except him. Bring Aron to me. I have a task for him. One he won't be able to refuse."

Aron knew he wouldn't, no matter what it was. And so, as a proud Mentula Guild member, a valued citizen of a once proud city, he was taken to his new lord and master. Perhaps sucking cock wasn't a waste after all. His career choice a jolly good one. Thank the Guild!

When Aron was presented to his new lord, close enough to smell the stink of horse upon him, Khalaf said, "Don't be afraid; I've given you the gift of your life."

"I'm...n-not, my Lord."

The horrible, evil man upon the throne smiled, a smile that was even uglier than the cratered scars upon his face. "Tell me about yourself before I give you your task."

So, Aron did. He told the master of horses everything including how he had always wanted to become a cocksucker for the status it gave, practicing on his friends and strangers alike before applying proper to the Mentula Guild. The day he was accepted into it the happiest day of his life.

He'd jolly well cried with joy for hours.

"And this here is Hamish," the Guild Master had said with a gesture after handing Aron his certification, the paper confirming his new standing, and a medallion of the purest gold stamped with the Guild's coat-of-arms—one which had a stylized cock within the motif, of course. He'd have his wrist tattooed with the same crest later that day to complete the initiation. "He will teach you ways to pleasure a man you would have never considered."

"I shall do my best to learn," Aron had replied.

Aron then described Hamish to Khalaf. He told how his trainer was a bulk of a man, like all those from the south-eastern kingdoms really, rugged but with hearts of gold. All muscles too. Hamish had dark, beautiful skin, darker than ebony, and towered above all others.

He also described his trainer's cock, because why wouldn't he? That organ, beautiful in every way, including its eye-watering size, had been an important part of Aron's life. And besides, it was certainly something to talk about...Aron could go on and on.

He said, "By the glory of the Guild, Hamish's cock swung between his legs like it had a life of its own it was that bloody big, my Lord," he described. "Had an end on it as large as a new season's apple, as well."

Khalaf didn't seem impressed, though.

But Aron remembered how much he'd enjoyed sucking on Hamish's blessing while he was taught better techniques, how to breathe properly, use his tongue, lips, and hot breath with gentle hands and a gentler voice.

And from there, he told of how Hamish trained him. Khalaf interrupted at that point. "Show me what you were taught by this expert in your art," he said as he freed his cock from his pants, presenting it for Aron to service.

Aron was used to the sight. He was jolly well in his element, after all. "I shall show you the seven secret touches. They were what I used on Myrkul to make him ejaculate quickly...before he was...you know."

Khalaf offered another ugly smile.

But Aron's confidence grew with each moment. More so, as he saw the effect his words had had; the man on the stolen throne had pulled back his foreskin to reveal a dew drop of pre-ejaculate glistening from his hardening, reddening swollen end. Khalaf wasn't a big man in that way, no more than four or five inches erect. But Aron knew, no matter the size of the equipment, the way to pleasure it didn't change— nor did the pleasure it gave change either.

Khalaf's eyebrows rose, and the horse beside him nickered. "I'm intrigued."

Aron could see how intrigued he was. "Then I will get on with it, my Lord."

"Yes," was hissed between teeth.

The first touch was always a kiss to the sensitive part underneath the swollen end, where the foreskin was joined to it by a bridge of skin: the frenulum. From there, the touches became progressively deeper until Aron felt the familiar warm, sticky fluid being shot in spurts down his throat as the reward for his skills. The horse master tasted sweeter than the demon had been. But the taste didn't matter. Only the fact it was tasted.

An indication he'd done his job well.

When he came off the Horse Master's cock, licking his lips and smiling his wet post-blowjob smile, he said, "Did you enjoy the seven touches, my Lord?" already knowing the answer; it was swirling around in his stomach.

"I did." Khalaf stuffed his wet cock back into his pants and tied them up hastily. "Now for your task."

"Yes, anything."

"I want you to go with Vengeance and seek out Lord Hereward. I can't wait until he gets here. I have plans and revenge to get on with."

Aron became confused for a moment. "You don't want me to keep pleasuring you, my Lord? It's what I'm good at, after all."

"No." Khalaf patted the horse upon his neck; the animal nickered almost lovingly. They then brought their heads together, touching. Words were whispered. Words of love. Aron had heard of people who loved and slept with horses.

Thank the Guild, the Horse Master continued before Aron could picture them together any further. "I want you to seduce Lord Hereward. I then want you to convince him to join me and my army of undead so that together, we can defeat the demon Ugruthaan."

"Even if I could seduce him, would Hereward join you?" Aron asked, not disrespectfully—he loved his life being in the world of the living—but out of curiosity.

"He will when you tell him that I'm his old friend Eddi, now Khalaf, Master of horses, and that I have defeated Myrkul for him."

"I see." Aron felt doubt for the first time.

"Don't worry, Vengeance will protect you if needed until the task is done. And besides, I've heard Lord Hereward can't resist attractive men like you. You'll have no trouble completing what I've asked of you if you're as good as you say you are."

"You just experienced how good I am," Aron replied, almost wounded and forgetting everything else.

"I'm not a good gauge of such things."

Aron knew what Khalaf meant; the man preferred a horse's company, Vengeance's in particular, despite coming quickly after Aron pleasured him. Then again, perhaps seeing Myrkul being killed by his love aroused him so much that no matter what Aron did, he would have succeeded. What a waste of the seven touches. He could have just sucked on Khalaf's cock any old how, probably could have just licked the end of it to achieve the same result.

Indeed, what a jolly well waste of his talents it had been.

But for the second time in a day, he questioned his life's choices.

Aron, riding atop Vengeance, left the city's palace within the hour to get on with his task. He questioned himself again, sad to see his home overrun with undead. The citizens, despite what he'd tried to do, were all now slaves.

Again, he had no time to mourn.

The stallion was huge, and Aron could feel the horse's strength underneath him. Feel the taut muscles of the animal's back tighten and loosen as he trotted through the city, people scrambling out of the way. He could also feel something else. Something that seemed to crackle in the air all around him.

He understood it to be magic.

Vengeance was powerful in all ways. No wonder Myrkul didn't stand a chance. In a strange way, Aron pitied Ugruthaan. He only hoped he didn't have to service the horse as a part of his task before he got to Hereward.

You won't have to do that, I can assure you, were words whinnied into Aron's mind, a strange intrusion into his thoughts. *You don't please me in the slightest, Aron. To me, you're insignificant. Only Khalaf pleases me, as we are one and the same.*

It took a moment for Aron to process Vengeance's words. And how it had happened. More magic, dark and evil. After the shock, he stammered, "I...I didn't mean any d-disrespect, my Lord." Aron thought it wise to call Vengeance his lord as well.

Just do as you are told, and you will continue to lead the rich life you've become accustomed to. Khalaf will pay you handsomely if you succeed.

"Thank you," Aron said graciously, the stench of magical ozone finding his nostrils and making him reel.

He had to steady himself, especially as he rode upon Vengeance bareback, the horse not accepting the restraints and humiliation of saddle, bridle, and reins.

And what's more, when you're done, you will no longer need to service any other, for you can live your life on your back in Lord Hereward's bed if you so wish.

"You misunderstand me," Aron said as delicately as he could muster. "Money is jolly lovely to have, no question, but when I've seduced Lord Hereward and done as you've asked, I'll continue to service others as I desire. It's what I do, after all. I'm a proud Mentula Guild member. And besides, there's nothing better than swallowing a paying man's ejaculate, now is there?"

Vengeance snorted loudly, mockingly. *Whatever pleases you.*

"So long as I do as I'm told and I jolly well succeed in my task."

You're a fast learner.

"You jolly well have no idea."

The outer wall of Thentathion Prime was damaged near the golden gates, the pristine white walls blackened. Men and women were already repairing it, toiling under the hot sun, watched by their undead masters. A wise decision to spare most of the citizens of the city, Aron thought.

Wise indeed, Vengeance chimed in to interrupt his thoughts. *And my idea—everyone needs their beasts of burden; sparing the citizens of the city gave us ours.*

"I don't know if I like you reading my mind, my Lord."

Too bad.

Aron had a feeling that would be his answer.

They didn't ride far from the city's limits when Vengeance came to a halt, sniffing the air, mane whipping about in a sudden breeze kicked up by dirty storm clouds on the horizon. The wind blew from the northwest which wasn't unusual for this time of year; winds were strengthened by the great delta's mouth, so the Kingdoms of Delta, Invrawold, and Tower Keep were windy places. Far windier than Thentathion or Suvanwold.

"Which way?" Aron asked, not really caring about the answer. He only wanted to take his mind off the darn wind. It bit worse than swarms of insects.

Aron hugged himself, realizing only then that he wore his best finery, hastily slipped on after Myrkul was killed and he'd sucked Khalaf's cock. He tugged at his waist coat. How he wished he wasn't in silk and brocade and plumes of lace where it mattered to enhance his lines and make him more attractive to potential paying clients. How he wished he'd at least worn his overcoat.

You'll freeze to death out here at night. Vengeance nickered, which sounded too much like laughter, again mocking as if Aron's discomfort pleased the animal—which it probably did.

"Then we'd better find Hereward before evenfall, so I can warm my bones by a fire, hadn't we?"

He's not far.

"How do you know?"

His horse told me.

Aron couldn't help but ask the next obvious question. "How far?"

Vengeance lifted his head once more, sniffing and whinnying. On the horizon, to the west of the Steps to Heaven mountains where

Thentathion Prime lay like a jewel gifted by a handsome suitor, a dark forest loomed to stain an otherwise beautiful sight. Like a flaw in a diamond.

Aron had heard the woods of it were haunted. Ammanroth was its name, ancient and full of more stories than any man had told him before he'd had his ejaculate swallowed. Then again, he'd heard a lot of things from his clients. Nothing loosened a man's tongue more than when his blood engorged his cock and the promise of sexual release was offered.

Aron smiled at that thought. Oh, the state secrets, the politics, betrayals planned, alliances forged, enemies made he'd been trusted with while sucking cock was criminal, really.

By the Guild, he loved his job—his life.

Up until now, of course.

He certainly wasn't sure how Hereward would take his sudden arrival. The knight would sooner stab him with his sword, he'd heard. Again, from the most reliable sources: a talkative noble enjoying being serviced.

He is within the woods of Ammanroth as we speak, Vengeance replied.

Not far then, perhaps a few leagues. "Jolly good."

Vengeance then burst into a gallop, the ground beneath his hooves a blur and the forest looming far quicker than Aron would have imagined. He'd never known a horse to move so fast; it was as if the very earth itself gave up to Vengeance, letting the horse travel across it without burden or the consideration of distance.

The horse was made of pure magic.

They were within the dark woods before the sun could climb across the sky towards its slumber. Then a campfire was seen, bright within the gloom. A jongleur's caravan was there, painted in gaudy colors but no doubt livable. Two horses nipped casually at fresh grass within the clearing.

But most important of all, especially for Aron, he saw Lord Hereward, the man unmistakable. He was as big as Hamish, more muscular if it could be believed. By the Guild, he was attractive. A thick beard graced him. Men with beards did something for Aron. Did a lot for him, to tell the truth.

Next to Lord Hereward stood a boy, kindling in his arms for the fire, no more than ten summers old at a guess. There was also a jongleur helping gather wood. A man. Although, Aron got a strange feeling from him. Which was odd. He usually got the measure of most men straight away. Had to in his job.

They approached the campfire, and Vengeance nickered, drawing their attention.

Lord Hereward immediately turned to them. "What the fuck do we have here? Who are you?"

The knight's eyes roved up and down Aron's frame. He felt a tingle from the study. A pleasant feeling. Seducing the knight was going to be a doddle. Jolly good. Jolly good indeed.

Aron dismounted, bowed with a flourish of his hand, and introduced himself. "I'm Aron, Mentula Guild member of Thentathion Prime, and I have word for you, Lord Hereward, if you'll hear it."

The boy dropped the pile he carried next to the stones surrounding the campfire with a clatter, the sticks scattering. "What canna fancy man like him tell us?"

"I'm sure we'll find out, son." But Lord Hereward's gaze fell upon Vengeance; his face then clouded over, going dark, as if storm clouds brewed in his mind. Aron then knew he suspected what Vengeance really was.

But he couldn't think of such things. Didn't want Vengeance knowing anything he shouldn't. It was hard to not do so, but thankfully, the jongleur, puzzlement on his brow, but the bulge within his tights not quite sitting right, in the wrong place if Aron wasn't mistaken, provided a distraction when he questioned, "What's a Mentula Guild member?"

Lord Hereward laughed, then spat, "He means to say he's a professional cocksucker."

The boy gasped. "Gods, who'd wanna put willies in their mouth for a livin'? Dat's not right, is it? Should only do dat for those ya love, right Papa?"

"Right, son."

The jongleur seemed uncomfortable and didn't add any further to the conversation. He was a curiosity. But Aron had other things, more important matters to attend to. His life, and keeping it, being the top of the list.

Aron simply smiled. "Could we perhaps talk in private, Lord Hereward?"

Lord Hereward shrugged. "If we've fucking got to, then I suppose we can. But what's said to me can be said in front of Wallace, just so you know."

The boy named Wallace, Lord Hereward's son, Aron now knew, neatened the pile of sticks by the fire, his gaze shifting to one of distrust quicker than Aron could blink. When done, he then went close to his father's side, eyes narrowing to slits of suspicion. Aron swallowed, his confidence draining. Perhaps seducing Lord Hereward wasn't going to be so easy after all. In his experience, the disapproval of a young son, especially one not of age, always hindered what had to be done.

And this time, Aron had a lot at stake if he failed.

Determination found him. He jolly well wouldn't get himself killed under Vengeance's hooves just because some boy didn't like or understand why he was a Mentula Guild member, an important part of his cultural heritage, a person of importance, and that his father's cock was next on his list to service.

And service it he would. It helped the knight was damn attractive.

Damn bloody attractive.

Lord Hereward and Wallace sat on a log by the campfire. Aron joined them after being asked to do so. The fire was warm and welcome. A tankard of beer was offered by the jongleur before he disappeared into the sanctity of the caravan. Aron sipped on the drink, so small he only got the barest taste. The brew wasn't pleasant. Too full of yeast. He normally didn't drink, but in this instance, he thought it best he'd at least pretend.

"Well then, fucking spit it out," Lord Hereward demanded impatiently. "Tell me the news you need to tell." Again, the knight's gaze wandered to Vengeance before returning to Aron.

Don't fail now, Aron, Vengeance said, reminding him of the terror which faced him if he failed. *Or I will kill you and everyone here before you can scream for mercy.*

Lord Hereward must have noticed he was staring at the horse, terror-stricken, even feeling his own cheeks drain. Vengeance radiated power. Magic too. Worse than before.

Aron stuttered, but nothing coherent came out of his mouth.

Wallace looked confused, a heavy line creasing his brow.

"Giving you fucking trouble, is it?" Lord Hereward asked. "Your horse, I mean," he clarified, again glancing at Vengeance.

The knight knew.

"He is," Aron whispered, shrinking and wishing he could just get into Lord Hereward's pants and be done with the rest of the nightmare. Sucking on the knight's cock right now would ease him. Put his mind at rest. "Perhaps w-we should...talk inside the c-caravan?"

But Vengeance heard him. *If you think you can deceive me, think again. My patience is growing thin. Do as you've been—*

Aron didn't get to hear the rest of the threat, thank the Guild. Before he could return his attention to Lord Hereward, try and get on with what had to be done, a meaty fist smashed him in the side of his head at the temple. Pain shot through him. Terrible pain. He wobbled and dropped the tankard, the ale within spilling over him and ruining his finery. He felt himself go giddy; the campfire spun before he lost sight altogether.

Then there was nothing but darkness…

29
Novane's Infinite Love

NOVANE KNEW IN THAT terrible moment there was nothing he could do to stop Greysen. If he did, Greysen would never forgive him; their relationship over before it had begun in earnest.

Yes, Novane worried about Greysen, was scared for him. How could he not be? He knew the magic Greysen would call forth from all the hate leaching through the broken pieces within the darkest recesses of him could destroy him. The darkness, once manifested in full, would surely change Greysen forever.

But Novane would have to accept such a thing. For if he couldn't let Greysen heal his past in his own way, mend all the terrible threads of his life and the broken shards in his mind left in its wake, then what was he worth as someone who loved him? He would be nothing.

Greysen came to a wobbly stand. "You dare confront me...*Father*?" he spat, blackfire twisting like macabre wire around his hands. Crackling. Darkening Greysen's expression further the more it grew and grew.

Novane smelt ozone, powerful and pungent.

"I am here to talk to you, Greysen, my son," Abbot Hosho said, raising his hands in a sign of surrender and of submission too, Novane believed.

"Too late for that."

Abbot Hosho walked quietly closer, taking small steps; it was strange to see the robe not fluttering in the wind as there was none for the first time upon these hills in an eon. That was the power of the immortal. The power of the universe with him.

Novane began to worry even more, the Forgotten moving behind him; Precious was still crying, the rest trying to comfort him. They failed.

A thought struck him as he looked between the children and Greysen, blackfire almost at the stage of release. "Perhaps we should—" But Novane was interrupted without consideration by Abbot Hosho, the monk's focus only on Greysen.

"It's never too late to talk," Abbot Hosho said.

Greysen shouted, "It is for me!" And with those words, spat in anger, frustration, and lots of other emotions Novane could only guess at, Greysen released his blackfire magic, dark and terrible, upon Abbot Hosho.

At first, there was silence.

Then, a wave of energy hit Novane, making him step back. It felt as if the very air, the molecules within it, had been ripped apart. The sound that struck Novane deafened him, then made his ears ring, his newly beating heart skip.

The children screamed in fear and horror.

As did Greysen while he directed the blackfire towards Abbot Hosho. All of it. Everything within him, Novane didn't doubt. The blackfire was like a behemoth sprouting from darkness, emerging to destroy everything in its wake, Abbot Hosho included.

And it would. Novane feared that most of all.

The ground in front of Greysen rumbled and rippled as if a massive earthquake shook it. The tussocky clumps of grasses were uprooted, rocks cracked, and soil became displaced. But that wasn't the end of it. No. Only the birth. The shock wave created by the massive, twisting streams of blackfire, searing and cutting through the air, went into the ground as well.

The ground shook worse. Novane had to steady himself with his pole axe. The salt mines around them, once hidden, collapsed one by one, killing the remaining Salt Devils trapped below. Killing their slaves. The dirt, sod, and rocks became their freshly made tombs.

Novane felt tears roll down his cheeks as he witnessed the destruction. Hills that'd been standing windblown for centuries were no more. The earth nothing but ugly scars as the shock wave expanded like a bubble, destroying everything in its wake. Boulders the size of houses, the bent trees, everything, was blasted out of the way as the blackfire flowed from Greysen.

What made Novane gasp in even more horror, made the children scream and cower even more, was when the blackfire struck Abbot Hosho. Novane didn't know why, but the monk hadn't moved an inch even knowing full well the magic was heading for him. Why? Novane couldn't even begin to guess.

But when the blackfire struck Abbot Hosho, even the heavens went dark. The sun hid, eclipsed by the release of energy. Birds fell from the sky, disintegrating before hitting the ruined ground. The massive explosion, dark as the magic, bloomed and bloomed, overtaking everything within Novane's sight.

He cried at the sheer power of it all.

Cried and cried.

From the wake of the strike, thick, powerful tendrils of blackfire along with oily smoke, even blacker if possible, shot forth in all directions. Novane believed those sitting within the halls of their gods or deep within one of the Circles of Hell would have felt Greysen's magic and been frightened by it as Novane was. The magic shook the world with its terror, a terror filled with sadness, anger, hatred, abandonment, lies, and everything else Greysen had been before the moment of its release.

The blackfire shook the world, letting everyone know of Greysen's pain. Novane collapsed to his knees, unable to bear the emotions that came with the blackfire magic. He wept his heart out.

The universe wept too.

Then, silence.

Deafening.

Until Novane heard himself shuddering his tears. He felt a touch upon his forehead and looked up. Abbot Hosho's pupil-less eyes seemed to smile at him even though his mouth didn't, remaining firm.

"H-how?" was all Novane could splutter.

He tried to look beyond the orange robe of the monk but couldn't see anything. Nothing but blackness, like he was in the Void and not standing on ruined earth. All he needed to see was the tentacles of the Great Kraken, and he'd know this was his end.

He couldn't see where Greysen was.

Panic stabbed at him as much as fear, as much as regret. He should have tried to stop Greysen. Why didn't he?

Slowly, very slowly, the edges of the blackness began to weaken. Novane could see sky. Ground. He could hear the children crying. It was like he was entering the world again, born into it anew. He also found he had a newfound determination. If Greysen had survived, he would do everything, anything, including sacrificing himself, to make sure nothing like this happened again.

As if reading his mind, which he probably was, Abbot Hosho said, "Greysen will recover from what he did here today...but it will take a long time."

"Those words don't fill me with confidence."

"Which ones?" Abbot Hosho didn't release his hand. Novane felt at ease as more and more of the darkness retreated. "The ones I said that spoke of Greysen recovering, or the fact that when an immortal says something will take a long time?"

Novane, stunned, uttered, "Both."

Then the darkness retreated completely. Greysen was unconscious, the children around him crying, trying to comfort him as much as they tried to comfort themselves.

Novane blinked.

Everything changed.

The day seemed towards its end, orange and lilac already coloring the sky. How much time had passed during that blink? Hours? Days? A week? Scar and Cyclops had fetched a wooden wheelbarrow that Novane only just realized Oswin had been holding all this time, the kind they would have been forced to use within the salt mines. Novane didn't need to guess what the barrow was for; the children were already lifting Greysen into it. They weren't crying anymore. They seemed more determined.

"What...what happened?"

"Time isn't linear when the universe moves her hand, Novane."

"That's not an answer."

Abbot Hosho lifted his hand from Novane's brow. He missed the gentle touch. It had seemed to fill him with a kind of reverence, an angelic light now gone. "It is the answer you have."

But Novane had moved on, no longer caring about the inconsistencies of immortal magic. "What will happen to Greysen?"

"The better question would have been, what will Greysen do without your love?"

Novane played the monk's game. "Greysen will always have my love. Tell me, what will happen to him? To me? To us?"

Abbot Hosho smiled for the first time. "And the love the children will give you three, now that you've found each other."

Novane looked at Oswin, standing silent as always. He then saw Cyclops, Scar, Twist, Handy, Club, and Precious. He held a newborn admiration for them as they lovingly tended to Greysen. He felt tears again. But tears of love and hope this time.

The monk was right. In a strange, unbelievable way, they had become family. He also knew, in that moment, that Greysen would be all right, even if it would take a long time for him to recover.

His heart sang, beating faster. "What happens now?"

Abbot Hosho replied, "I have already spoken to Oswin and the children, and now I will tell you. You must all go to the kingdoms of Arbour Keep and Dyathian to help gather allies against the evil approaching."

"The Purge?"

"It has begun," Abbot Hosho confirmed. "I have Kieron and Vash returning to Elemeria to ensure the delphin are with us once more. I have Undar doing the same, as we will need the Ardunàym Clan and many others, as many darrow to join us as we can get."

"The whole of the Eleven Kingdoms," Novane clarified.

"Even more than that, perhaps." A weight seemed to come upon Abbot Hosho's brow, his shoulders slumping from it.

"You're trying to make up for your past sins, aren't you? By helping us now. Humanity and its many races, I mean."

Abbot Hosho nodded. "We all have sins, but mine are the worst of all. Just because I'm immortal doesn't mean I'm infallible. What I did when Greysen and Oswin were born was unforgivable, even though I did so for the balance of the universe." Sadness washed over him. "Decisions made are decisions made. I cannot change what I did. Greysen and Oswin know this."

"Will they ever forgive you?"

"I don't know."

Novane swallowed. "Then what will happen between you?"

"Whatever happens is whatever happens." And with that, the monk faded away, the wind returning. But before the orange robes disappeared completely, he added, "By the time you get to the Kingdom of Arbour Keep, Greysen will awaken. Until then, take heed of my words, and look after each other…"

He was gone.

Novane began to believe he was never present in the first place. How else could the blackfire not have affected him?

Scar ran up to him, grabbing his hand. "Come. We've gotta long journey ahead o' us."

Novane saw that Oswin had picked up the barrow's handles, pushing it and Greysen. He would do so endlessly, without rest. Oswin would protect his brother. Perhaps that was a part of his healing and another machination of the universe's hand.

No matter. Novane had a new purpose. If the Purge was upon them, then when Greysen woke, there needed to be a world for them to love each other within. He would do his part as had been tasked to him. Novane loved Greysen. He would move heaven and earth to keep them together.

"Yes, we have a long journey ahead of us, Scar."

"Best get started on it, then, eh?"

"Best we do."

With Scar holding his hand, Novane went to Greysen. Cyclops, Handy, Club, Twist, and Precious greeted him with a group embrace, one he returned. He smiled, feeling complete even though Greysen wasn't able to hold him. Oswin, always silent, began to walk, pushing the barrow over the ruined and blackened earth.

When the children let Novane go—or had he let go of the children?—he came to look upon his love within the barrow. Greysen looked asleep, not unconscious. But it was the first time Novane had seen a softened face upon his love, one not marred by any other emotions or his inner darkness. Had he been healed now that the darkness had been drawn from him? Novane didn't know. Wouldn't know until Greysen woke.

Novane leant down and kissed Greysen tenderly on the lips. They were warm. A good sign, even though the journey would be long.

For all of them.

30
Aron's New Skill

FUCKING GREAT," HEREWARD SPAT, standing over Aron's still unconscious body after having dragged his sorry arse inside the caravan. "Now we've got a dandy," he poked the side of the man in the ribs with his foot, "and a clown for company, Wallace!" He glared at Horan when he'd said *clown*; Horan wisely kept quiet. Quiet as a fucking church mouse. Smart of him, considering the mood Hereward was in.

"Why'd ya hit him 'fore, Papa?"

Hereward, knowing all too well the influence of magic, especially on those with weaker minds or dispositions, shifted his gaze from Wallace to Horan and back again. "To break the link between him and that fucking horse he rode here on. That horse is evil. Magic fucker, I reckon."

Horan said, "The magical stallion has now bolted as far as I know; Mista Kokoschka took offense to him being here and drove him off, I reckon. Never heard such a commotion."

"Missy's in heat," Wallace offered, shrugging. "In me 'sperience, no magic'll stop a stallion like Mista Kokoschka from gettin' to his mare. Dat magic horse prolly knew what were good fer him an' scarpered."

Hereward snorted. "Probably thought there was no use hanging around once he saw me hit Aron. Their cover was blown, as it were. But I'd say he wouldn't have gone far." He poked Aron again; that time the man groaned, seemingly coming to. "But hopefully fucking far enough so we can talk without being heard."

"You think the horse can do that?" Horan asked.

"Never trusted fucking magic," Hereward replied. "Now get up, cocksucker; I know you're awake. Time to tell us your story—and if you lie, or I don't like what you tell, you'll find yourself stabbed with my sword god many, many times. Do you fucking understand me?"

I've never spilled the blood of a Mentula Guild dandy before, Hereward's god said excitedly.

Aron lifted his hand to his forehead, moaning. He sat up. Horan offered him a glass of water from the caravan's sink. He sipped carefully from it, hand shaking the contents to make it ripple like many stones had been thrown into a pond.

Before Aron could speak, still gathering his wits, Hereward imagined, and likely gathering the excuses he would try and make sound plausible to avoid death, Wallace asked, "Aron's not evil, is he? He seems ta be alright ta me."

Without delay, Hereward replied, "He's not evil, no. He's telling the truth so far as I can tell. See that tattoo on his right wrist?" Both Wallace and Horan looked; the wrist in question was exposed because of the glass Aron held, as was the tattoo.

"I see it, an' all," Wallace said.

Horan nodded.

Hereward continued, "It's his guild mark, tattooed with special gold-infused ink and a complicated design to prevent forgers from imitating it. And from the phallic look of it, it's true what he said when he told us he was a member of Thentathion Prime's Mentula Guild. Those fucking tattoos don't get put on just anyone."

Wallace looked confused. "Dunno what fallic means, but ta me looks like he got a fancy lookin' willy inked on'ta him."

Hereward laughed. "You got it, son. You got it."

Wallace's mouth formed a perfect 'O' and he even said, "Oh," to emphasize it. "Ya mean he...he really does suck on willies fer a livin'?" The distaste on his expression was obvious. "I's fought you were jestin'."

Hereward couldn't blame him. But his mood lightened. Wallace always did that, bless him to pieces. What Hereward would do without him, he wouldn't know. There'd be nothing left to live for.

Nothing.

But he thought he'd best explain southern culture as best he could, seeing as that's where they were heading. "Being a Guild endorsed cocksucker is an honor and privilege. Like the mayor of a town Aron would be to them, to explain it in a way you'd understand, Wallace."

"Would he be rich like one, an' all?"

Hereward nodded. "Aron would even be privy to every fucking secret mentioned in the royal court and beyond. He would basically have as much power as the king, if not more."

Horan slapped his hands onto his thighs in both disgust and

disbelief. "Now I've heard it all."

From that, Hereward knew Horan hadn't traveled into the kingdom of Thentathion before, nor been to one of its cities or towns and experienced its unique culture. "They do things differently down south," Hereward explained, finding the whole thing suddenly amusing. "I did warn you."

"How can Aron be more'n what a king is?" Wallace asked, looking confused again.

"Hard to explain, especially for someone of your age, but just know, Wallace, it's their culture. Men join the Mentula Guild, have done for eons, to become an integral part of their society. Aron here is respected and admired where he comes from, and that's all there fucking is to it."

Wallace was staring at Aron but still frowning his famous frown.

Horan had folded his arms, unimpressed. "I suppose women can't join that guild? The southerners are famous for being elitist and sexist, after all."

"They aren't like that." Hereward didn't know what the clown was going on about. Horan hadn't seen things with his own eyes; Hereward had. He'd been to Thentathion Prime itself and knowing a culture was understanding it. Abbot Hosho would be proud of him if he heard him now, that's for sure. "Men and women can be members, but the men are more desired there, just as women are more desired in other cultures."

"If you say so," Horan replied.

Wallace said, "I wanna know more 'bout Aron an' his culture."

Hereward obliged, telling what he knew without getting too detailed for Wallace's ears and innocence. When he was old enough, able to understand that having your cock sucked was something amazing and intimate, a special experience, especially from someone loved, Wallace would be told more. But not until then.

He did mention, "There was this one cocksucker...Hamish was his name. He was so fucking famous, he's said to have prevented a war between three kingdoms with his skills."

He then remembered how much he'd enjoyed his time within the white walls of Thentathion Prime in his younger days before he met Ayrdon and married him. In fact, he recalled how his cock was never dry, he'd gotten that much action being loose of purse and horny as fuck. Bad combination in a place like Thentathion Prime.

He hadn't been back since.

"I really don't understand," Horan said, looking dark all of a sudden. "And Aron had better not think he can get any secrets out of me. I'll kick him where the sun doesn't shine if he thinks he can."

Wallace shot a surprised look at Horan. Hereward knew why. Horan's cock was fake, and a professional like Aron would have already suspected something amiss with the traveling clown. Hereward had after a time. Didn't see why Aron wouldn't, either. Nor any one with eyes, really; Horan's cock slipped down his inside leg more times in a day than Hereward could count.

Why didn't Horan tie the thing in place or secure it within better underwear, like how Beornræd did for his?

Aron cleared his throat, knocking Hereward form his reverie. "The great and honorable Hamish not only prevented a war," Aron explained, fully coherent and putting down the glass, "he also invented the seven touches. It was that which saved the day, so to speak."

"What's dat? The seven touches?" Wallace asked, confused and curious, that famous furrow of his well planted upon his brow once more.

"Never mind," Hereward replied, putting his hand onto Wallace's shoulder, but only doing so to direct him to the caravan's door. "How about you and Horan go tend to the horses? I want to have a nice little chat here with Aron alone." And with that, Hereward then touched the cold, hard hilt of his god.

I love when you ready me.

Aron seemed to drain of color again as his gaze wandered to Hereward's sword. "What did you want me to tell you?"

"Everything." Hereward came close until they were almost nose to nose. "Fucking everything."

And so, Aron told all, from the moment Myrkul, Khalaf, Vengeance, and the undead army arrived to conquer Thentathion Prime to the moment he woke up and was offered a glass of water by the jongleur.

"Horan is an odd one, isn't he?"

"What do you mean?" Hereward replied.

"He has the strangest looking bulge I've ever seen on any man. And yes, I know men change sides with how they dress down there, but Horan's seems to move of its own accord and in all directions too. And as you jolly well know, I've seen plenty of them to know a fake when I see one."

Hereward couldn't help but be impressed. Aron had worked it out and knew the truth even though he'd only seen Horan for a very short amount of time. No more than an hour all up, not including the time he was out cold, of course. Not that it made a difference. What Horan had or didn't have was his business, not Aron's or even his.

"I don't care about that. What I care about is who this Khalaf character is, you've mentioned. Are you fucking sure he said he was once Eddi? Eddi the stable hand?"

"As sure as I know the seven touches."

"Fuck!"

Aron looked surprised. "What's the problem?"

"Nothing worse than having to kill an old friend."

"I take it that means I'm returning to Thentathion Prime with you?"

"It does." Hereward took his hand off his god, using it to then scratch his beard, rasp, rasp, rasping, while he thought. "And it also means you're going to have to learn a new trade, cocksucker." For the first time he used the word 'cocksucker' with the respect the title deserved, as Aron deserved, being a Mentula Guild member of Thentathion Prime.

Surprise and sheer terror-driven shock crossed Aron's face. "What do you have in mind? I don't know anything else but how to—"

"I know what you *can* do." Hereward relaxed a little. But only a little. "Now I want to know how well you can handle a sword."

"You want me to…fight?"

"No."

Relief passed over him before he asked, "Then why do I need a sword?"

Hereward gave Aron a humorless stare. "Because I can't be fucking everywhere at once, and if you want to live long enough to keep your illustrious career, I suggest you learn how to defend yourself."

Aron audibly swallowed. Hard. "I'm simply no good with a weapon."

"It's easy," Hereward said. "Stick the pointy end into your enemy. Can't go fucking wrong."

"I'm sure there's a lot more to it than that." Aron cleared his throat.

Hereward snorted a quick laugh, still humorless. "Like how sucking cock is more than sticking it in your mouth?"

"Exactly." Aron didn't seem to get the sarcasm. Hereward shrugged; such things were subjective, after all.

"All right then…" Hereward knew teaching Aron anything was

going to be a challenge; the man was soft. He wasn't being disrespectful but observing a fact. Soft men were fucking attractive. He only meant that Aron seemed to be in touch with himself, had no walls around him. Hereward admired that too. It also meant Aron would have never had to defend himself with a weapon. Others would have done that for him, being in the position he was back in his home. "To put it so you'll understand, the seven methods of the sword are stance, lunge, parry, riposte—or counterattack after a parry—high thrust, low thrust, and swish."

Aron's eyebrows rose slightly. "That, I could learn, now that you've put it in those terms. The seven secrets of the sword! Wonderful! Who will teach me these secrets?"

"Wallace will."

Aron then seemed hurt. "Why not you?"

"Because, and I'm talking honest here, I don't fucking trust you."

"Oh?" Aron frowned. "Are you suggesting that I'll try and seduce you after all? As I was instructed to do by Khalaf and not because I would jolly well desire it? You are a devastatingly handsome man, Lord Hereward. I would gladly get on my knees for you without any thought of reward. None at all."

Hereward considered his next words very carefully. "I can't disrespect Dorgan's memory so soon after his passing."

Aron stood, a disbelieving crinkle formed on the corner of his lips. "Are you saying you're attracted to me as much as I am you?"

Now Hereward swallowed. How could he not be attracted to the man? Those curls, golden blond and falling against the fresh face of his youth. Ruby lips. Bluest blue eyes with bright hazel flecks like flakes of gold to match his hair within them. His body, fit and fine, slim but not overly so. Tall too. Fuck, how could he not fall for him?

Hereward gathered himself but shifted his weight uncomfortably to make the floorboards creak. "I'm saying that love hurts more than any sword wound ever could. And each time someone I love goes to the halls of their gods, I lose a piece of myself with them. A piece I can never fucking replace." Hereward felt his eyes sting. He thought of Ayrdon, Dorgan, even Camdyn. Sadness found him. Profound. Bitter. Enveloping. "And I can't love again. I only have enough left of me for Wallace."

Silence fell between them.

Hereward hoped it was the silence of understanding. Aron gently broke it when he said, "I think I'll just go see where Wallace has got to. Perhaps start my lessons now." Aron turned towards the door.

"To answer your question…"

He turned back, facing Hereward, those blue, gold flecked eyes dazzling and something to get lost within. Very lost.

"You give me a fucking hard-on that could gag a magical horse. Just so you know, cocksucker."

"Good to know." A smile. "And just so *you* know, I would have gone against the Mentula Guild's edicts and bent over for you, something we're never to do. We're only to kneel. But I would have done anything you desired as I find I desire it myself. Just so you know."

Hereward smiled back until he felt his emotions suddenly choke him. The smile left his lips, and he had to clear his throat. "Perhaps if I'd met you in another lifetime, Aron, we could have made something of it together. But not now. Now I'm too hollow and bitter, and you deserve better than me."

"I…understand." Those two words said with as much sadness washed through them as Hereward felt.

Quietly, Aron left, the door closed carefully to darken the previously bright interior of the caravan; Aron's absence was profound.

Hereward was alone.

Just as well. He wanted to kill something all of a sudden. His anger for a husband, lovers, and friends he'd lost all too soon, and all the other emotions because of it, swirled within him, churning, making him feel giddy. And seeing as there was now no one around to stick his sword into, a vase or three smashed against the wooden painted walls would have to suffice.

I miss Dorgan too, my love.

"Everything hurts so fucking much."

I know. But Aron is willing to help you heal. Even I can see that. Perhaps he's just what you need.

"I don't want to be a number, another cock added to his list. I want to be loved. I *need* to be…loved." Hereward's tears began to fall. He didn't wipe them away.

I believe he does too. I sense he wants to change.

"We shall fucking see."

After days and nights, each getting warmer, they traveled into the kingdom of Thentathion without incident, heading for the capital city.

Hereward had been right about one thing. The fucking goblin's balls got worse the further south they went. They no longer picked them.

They hadn't seen hide nor hair of Vengeance either.

When they were within the southern shadow of the Steps to Heaven mountains, they came to a snowmelt stream sheltered all around by high ground and thick bushes and a few ancient trees.

"We camp here for the night," Hereward declared, knowing the horses would need watering after traveling all day, sweat on them in a sheen.

He also wanted Aron to get as much practice with the sword as he could before they arrived at Thentathion Prime proper. The more he got used to the weapon, the better chance he'd have when things got too close for comfort with the enemy. And this time, they were dealing with undead. Nasty fuckers they were; they had no mercy for humans, or any living soul, really.

Wallace said, "I'll go git the wood with Horan, Papa."

"No." Hereward put his hand upon Wallace's shoulder. "I want you to hang your hessian practice dummy and teach Aron how to perform a proper high thrust. He bends his fucking wrist too much, I've noticed."

"That'll git his arm broken, inna fight," Wallace suggested.

"See? You're a good teacher already. You've got a keen eye and understand how to use and respect a sword better than anyone else I know."

"Ta, Papa." Wallace then ran his foot across the dirt in a circle, hanging his head low; something was wrong. Hereward didn't have to wait long to discover what it was. "But do I have ta teach him today? He…Aron, I mean…I'm not sure 'bout him. Don't really like him if I'm tellin' ya the truth."

"You don't like Aron or you don't like what he does because of the position he has within his own culture?" Now Hereward could hear Abbot Hosho in his words, like when he'd judged the darrows unfairly who fought with him against Ealdræd to defeat him—without whom, he'd be dead.

"He told me other day dat families of boys comin' o' age paid him to suck out the first of their sons'…seed," Wallace explained hesitantly, going red in the cheeks. "In Aron's culture it sees 'em as a part o' their society after it's done, an' all. Told me dat's how important he is, to be givin' such a thing to do."

Hereward felt the urge to go punch some more sense into Aron. "That sort of fucking thing isn't for you to hear."

Wallace swallowed, his eyes pained. "How can Aron do the things he does for men he don't love? For strangers? Ya wouldn't do that. Ya'd only do it for Dorgan, 'cause ya loved him like he loved ya back. In me way o' thinkin', Aron ain't no better than a bandit, doin' what he does ta git coin. Kind o' makes me feel uncomfortable when I'm near him, being honest."

"I can't answer that, Wallace. I fucking can't." Hereward respected Wallace above any other and understood how he saw Aron, a strange man from a strange land with an even stranger culture. A culture which had customs Wallace couldn't fathom because of where he grew up and his experiences so far. And for that, Hereward couldn't blame him. "But I can say I will never ask you to do anything you're uncomfortable with, even if it's being near a person who makes you uncomfortable. You go gather wood. I'll give Aron his lesson today."

Wallace breathed a deep sigh of relief. "Ta, Papa." And with that, he ran to Horan who'd already begun gathering sticks. At least Wallace understood the traveling clown. Made friends with him too.

"I didn't mean any offense when I told Wallace about myself. Honest as I stand here, Lord Hereward. Honest as I jolly well stand here," Aron said, approaching after tending to Missy and Mista Kokoschka.

Hereward shot him a glance. "Wallace has been through a lot in his short life. Things you couldn't imagine. Thing a lot of folks can't fucking imagine. I don't want to see him hurt any more and that includes you keeping your stories to yourself from now on. Fucking get me?"

Aron bowed respectfully, minus the flourish of hand this time. "I deeply and humbly apologize, Lord Hereward."

"Apologize to Wallace, not me."

"I most certainly will."

Hereward could see the effort the man was trying to make, the honesty of his words. Seemed no one really understood others, not until they got to know each other better. Still, he shouldn't have been talking like that to someone as young as Wallace, and not to a boy who hadn't been brought up within the kingdom of Thentathion, having no idea about their ways.

Hereward told Aron as much.

With your usual finesse, I might add, his sword god chuckled.

Hereward ignored her, but to Aron, he said, "I'm having doubts about taking my son into Thentathion Prime. I'm not sure I want to go there myself." But he remembered Abbot Hosho's specific instructions. Surely, the old monk wouldn't lead them astray. Surely not.

Abbot Hosho wouldn't do that. I know it.

Aron's expression hardened. "I will protect Wallace with my life, as you protect him, Lord Hereward. That is my promise to you, my duty. By the Guild, that's my duty."

Hereward snorted a laugh. "You can't even hold a sword properly. How will you protect anyone, even yourself?"

Aron didn't flinch. "You forget what you just chastised me for. The city may be conquered, but I have many who will fight for me to their dying breath because of who I am. Many of whom I helped initiate into our society when they were old enough, most times for no cost because I believe in paying it forward. These men are strong and true, and they will join our cause, Lord Hereward."

"Sucked that many cocks, hey?"

"You may mock me, Wallace may hate me for what I do, and Horan may avoid me because he doesn't want me to know his secret, but I am an honest man. I can't change who I am, I can't shy away from my responsibilities or shirk my duty to my people and my Guild. When I tell you I have many friends, many men who will lay down their lives for me, that is the truth."

Hereward was stunned. "Wallace doesn't hate you."

"But you mock me, for I am nothing to you."

"You don't fucking know me very well, Aron."

Aron looked surprised now. "You didn't call me a cocksucker that time."

"And you can just call me Hereward. Drop the 'lord' crap from now on."

"I take it we've reached a milestone."

Hereward shrugged. "We've reached an understanding. Now let's see how you hold a sword. And don't drop your wrist this time or I'll kick you in the balls and then you'll have no choice but to kneel."

"I take it you won't get your cock out if I do kneel, even if done so in pain."

Hereward laughed. "No fucking chance."

But he found he was feeling a connection to Aron, a connection of attraction that went beyond the superficial, like how he felt for Dorgan, may he rest in peace. Sadness struck him, deep and unrelenting. Hereward didn't want to get hurt again, and if he got into a relationship with Aron, he knew he would be.

Besides, he didn't like how he told Wallace what he did. He should have known better. Yes, Aron's culture was different, but respect of such worked both ways. Wallace isn't Thentathion, far too young to know anything about it, either. Hereward made a decision. If Wallace was uncomfortable, he'd not make matters worse. His son was everything to him.

"Also, I reckon you should go apologize to Wallace right now while I set up the practice dummy."

"As you wish...Hereward." A smile.

Hereward smiled in return, unable to help himself. He could get lost in Aron's smile.

31
Alquam's Final Legacy

UGRUTHAAN HOCKED AND SPAT, the foaming globule of fluid and mucus sizzling on the hardened sand before desiccating into an ugly greenish stain. He smiled. That's what he thought of humanity. Something to chew on then spit out. And where he was headed, he would begin doing so as soon as he could.

He would begin the rout of humanity. Then he'd purge them from the many lands until the whole world was rid of them, leaving only enough to keep for his larder. How many would he need? A few hundred breeding pairs?

That should suffice.

He'd kept the form of the jongleur Joran for his journey southwards. He liked it. Sure, the man's body was all sinew and skin, taut muscles from the constant acrobatics he'd done during his life, but there was one part of him that was perfect. His cock. The ample appendage had already proven useful with those Ugruthaan had encountered along the way. All of them screamed until they were hoarse while they were raped, dismembered, and then eaten. Men, women, children, it didn't matter.

They didn't matter.

In the end, they were only food.

Ugruthaan didn't care a passing thought about their pathetic lives or what they meant. To themselves or each other. To him, they were nothing but lambs to slaughter. Less than that. He actually began relishing the destruction he'd caused and the acts which achieved it, all thanks to Joran's form.

He looked up. The relentless sun above didn't bother him, even though sweat trickled down his back. He needed shelter. He also needed food. He then saw the dark tower of his goal in the distance, shimmering in the heat haze.

He'd found the Dread Keep.

Ugruthaan, surprised, sensed the uncountable dead under his feet as he approached the tower. Some had been buried eons ago, others more recently. He knew, as he trod towards his new home, sand crunching underfoot, that the dead underneath him, once resurrected, would become his army to conquer the Eleven Kingdoms.

He knew that, yes, humans could be killed, but they could also become undead to fight against him again. Then again, undead could also be killed, but that was far more difficult and would take up more resources. He wanted that.

He had to act quickly. The dead underneath him were *already* dead, had been for eons, and they would be perfect for his needs. Simply perfect. What could kill them once they were reanimated? They would be mindless undead—better than the recently turned, as Myrkul's forces had been, for they'd held some semblance of their previous humanity. Not the dead beneath him now, though. They were too lost and could be commanded without fear of insubordination.

He knew his army of dead would be invincible and limitless once he resurrected them. After all, there were far more dead in the ground than those standing alive after generations upon generation of humans had lived and passed.

Ugruthaan smiled again as he entered the Dread Keep after pushing on the iron door, which gave easily. The interior was all dark granite and iron; it created a chilling coolness when compared to outside. It was also empty. Excellent. He knew Myrkul had gone north to Thentathion Prime, but that was all he knew. The demon could be dead for all he cared. He certainly wouldn't be able to have his keep back.

It belonged to Ugruthaan now.

And there would be no alliances. He would conquer alone with his dead army. He needed nothing else, other than the memory of Mother Alquam to inspire him to keep him ever hungry for victory and the food humanity would provide—those he spared, at least.

He approached the place where a throne would have sat, now empty except for the multi-stepped dais. He would need to make a new one. Perhaps out of bones. That would fit here.

A door opened at the far end of the cavernous throne room, and the sound of it shutting again echoed. For a moment, Ugruthaan was startled. Until he saw a ghoul enter. The creature didn't look surprised to see him here.

"What do you want?" was all it asked, not really caring for an answer, Ugruthaan observed, because the undead kept plodding along until it passed him. It held a cloth. No doubt it was the cleaner or butler of the Dread Keep.

Myrkul, if anything, had a sense of humor.

"I want nothing but your obedience. For I'm your new master," Ugruthaan supplied, his voice as commanding as he could muster without being too domineering. The ghoul wasn't his enemy. Not even food.

"As you say, Master."

"I do say." Ugruthaan sat on the dais, thinking again. Before the ghoul disappeared to perform his eternal chores, he said, "Fetch me Myrkul's grimoire. I know he kept one; he was the demon god of the undead, and he would have needed to convert the living to supply his army."

"Yes, Master."

Ugruthaan clicked his fingers. "Oh, and also get me the tools, fragrances, and incense needed to cast the spells to accomplish many, many resurrections. I'll begin summoning the dead beneath the desert around us first. We will go from there."

The ghoul dropped the cloth, as if doing anything out of routine was an inconvenience, and turned towards the door from whence it came. "As you wish, Master."

Ugruthaan snapped. "I do wish. Now get to it. I have kingdoms to destroy and humanity to purge from their lands. And I don't want to wait a moment longer."

The ghoul gave a dusty sigh. "I've heard it all before. You demons are all the same...Master."

"Do you dare defy me?"

"I don't dare anything, Master." The ghoul hacked a rattling noise; was it laughter? "I'm three-thousand years old. I've seen kings, queens, demons, and gods rise and fall. I've seen immortals come and go from the pages of history also. Now is your time, perhaps. But I know one thing..."

"What's that?"

"I'll be here long after you've become nothing but a whispered name spoken to frighten children at bedtime."

Ugruthaan smiled even though the ghoul annoyed him. Good thing for it that he needed an assistant. For now. "Then I will make sure there is no one left to whisper about me from now until the end of eternity."

"I've heard that before also."

"Just do as you're told. And don't come back until you have everything I need. Be quick about it."

"Yes, Master." The ghoul shuffled away, anything but urgent.

Ugruthaan, however, realized it would take a lot of time, too much perhaps, to resurrect enough dead to create a sizable army for his needs. Then again, in that time, the Purge would have well and truly started, as was his destiny to see to completion. Mother would have wanted it. Then, no human or enemy could stand in his way.

But first a little patience. Time was what Ugruthaan needed. The more time that passed, the more dead he could resurrect, and the greater his strength would become. The more effective the Purge.

He wouldn't tell the ghoul such information, though.

32
Vengeance's Last Stand

AFTER ANOTHER TWO DAYS journey, the massive city of Thentathion Prime loomed, its structures almost touching the sky, largest in the whole entire world, Wallace thought. Beautiful too. By the gods, the city were all clean and white against the rock-strewn plain and the mountains behind it. The city's building even had golden rooftops.

Wallace was in awe at the sight.

Thentathion Prime sure weren't like Invrawold City, the only other city Wallace had been to. The other city were a cesspool in comparison to what towered before them now, all majestic, with its many colorful flags snapping in a light, warm breeze and eagles soaring above, riding the thermals.

Aron, chest puffed out and tears of pride welling in his eyes, said, "Welcome to my wonderful home, gentlemen. Welcome to Thentathion Prime."

Horan looked as impressed as Wallace felt.

Papa, always observant for other things replied, "Pity the city now fucking stinks of the undead."

That brought Aron back to the reality of it all, Wallace reckoned. For he said, "Yes, quite right you are, Hereward. And to avoid our unwelcome guests, I know a secret entrance into the city."

Papa snorted. "That what you calling those who murdered your royal family, the nobles, and anyone else who happened to be in the wrong place at the wrong time to conquer you, *unwelcome guests*? Fuck, I would have called them far worse than that."

Wallace didn't need to imagine the words Papa would call 'em.

Aron didn't say anything further. Better he didn't.

Wallace couldn't concentrate his gaze on any one thing 'cause there was so much to see. Thentathion Prime were huge. Huge!

After settling Missy and Mista Kokoschka within a safe place hidden away from sight of the city's outer wall, leaving them in a sort of alcove, cool from shade, and providing plenty of feed and water for 'em too, Aron led them to his secret entrance.

They followed quietly, including Papa.

When they got there, Wallace couldn't believe it were a secret at all. How could it be? Only a farmer after drinking too much homebrew after harvest would have missed it, and that would be 'cause he had collapsed into unconsciousness after the first bottle. The 'secret' entrance were a massive iron and wooden double doorway not far from the main entrance—no more than spittin' distance, as Wallace's da used to say—guarded by a single city guard, all fancy golden armor, no less.

Aron didn't seem worried. Perhaps the undead army only entered through the main entrance, knowing they had an easy victory. But surely, the conquerors would patrol their conquered city? See a not-so-secret door?

There were so much Wallace didn't understand. As such, he couldn't help but feel nervous. He also felt his sword vibrating its warning through him while scabbarded to his side. Which was not unexpected; the enemy was within the city, too close, patrolling it or not.

Horan whispered, "I don't like this."

And Wallace tended to agree. "Feels somethin' like we're da mice comin' ta a trap baited with cheese, don't it?"

As they approached the guard, Wallace noted how Horan no longer wore his motley tights. Seemed either Papa or Aron had told him to get a better fitting willy or wear different clothing. Horan chose the latter. Wallace was relieved.

As Aron approached the guard, there was surprise followed by recognition from the man, halberd readied then relaxed in his grip. Wallace knew it were a halberd and not a pole axe because of the style of the blades, broader on one side, smaller on the other, and the pointed metal end of it; Novane's pole axe only had one blade on one side and no metal point.

During his thinking, which Wallace found common lately, he missed some of what Aron said to the guard. "…so glad you're alive, Aron! So glad!" What he didn't miss was the way the two men hugged and then kissed on the lips, almost intimate except for it being so quick.

A strange greeting, for sure.

The guard, a big man with a bigger mustache, then hugged Horan and kissed him; the jongleur were too startled to speak, but blushed bright red. The guard, Wallace didn't hear his name, then went to Papa.

Papa accepted the hug but put his hand up to prevent the kiss. "I only let the men I fuck kiss me," and the guard nodded acceptance.

He came to Wallace. "What's your name, young man?"

"Wallace, sir, an' all." But before the guard leant down to either hug or kiss in greeting, traditional for him or not, Wallace quickly, but not disrespectfully, said, "Sorry, but I's don't want no stranger touchin' me like how ya did ta the others there."

A look to Papa from the guard, a knowing nod from Papa, and then he said, "No need to apologize, Wallace. My name's Clem, not sir, and yes, I can see how our ways can be strange to outsiders. I understand why you're cautious." He smiled through his thick mustache. "But just so you can gain some understanding, Aron was kind enough to bring me into our society when my family didn't have two coins to rub together. I owe him so much, as I now hold a place of importance here, being captain of the guard. A far better life than what would have waited for me otherwise."

Wallace knew what all that meant. "I's understand."

"And just so you understand further," Clem went on, "within the Kingdom of Thentathion, those not yet of age can either get a kiss upon their forehead or a handshake in greeting."

Only Papa kissed Wallace on his forehead, and only after telling him his bedtime story and he'd tucked him in for the night. As such, Wallace stuck out his hand. Clem smiled again, full and wide, and shook it, two quick pumps of the hand, a quick release.

Clem then stood tall. "I'm going to protect you while you're in the city, Wallace, for that's Aron's wish as much as it is mine. Please, come with me." He turned to Papa and Horan. "All of you."

Wallace wasn't so sure how anyone could protect him from an army of undead, except for Papa perhaps. But he nodded, anyway. To be polite.

Papa didn't seem to look worried, unlike Horan, who was sweating fear. Wallace went to him. "Ya okay?"

He swallowed. "I'm kind of scared about all this; I'm not a fighter like you and your father but a musician. Simply a musician."

"Clem reckons he's gonna protect us."

Horan quivered a nervous smile. "I sure hope so. But to tell the truth, I have more faith in your father protecting us than anyone else."

"Same." Wallace watched Aron and Clem lead them into the city, banter and backslapping aplenty. "But ya'd think the city weren't taken over by the way they're actin'."

Horan sighed. "I miss Joran so much." The words were spoken more to himself than anyone else. "If he hadn't got so stonking drunk, which I warned him about, he wouldn't have gotten eaten by that terrible demon, and I wouldn't even be here." He sighed again.

Wallace let him be. What could he say? Horan spoke the truth, even though Wallace found Joran creepy before the demon took his body as a disguise.

Papa was uncharacteristically silent, which worried Wallace more than anything.

No sooner had they entered the glistening city proper, Clem explained, "It seems our conquerors have been rather lax, Aron, Lord Hereward." He swept a gesture over the streets before him, neat and clean, folks of all walks of life going about their business and greeting each other with hugs and kisses as if nothing were the matter. "After vanquishing our army, they only took over the royal quarters and the noble houses, leaving the rest of us alone. The enemy haven't moved from there since."

"The undead army numbered in the tens of thousands," Aron said, surprised. "I saw them before I volunteered to go to the palace to try and placate Khalaf, prevent further bloodshed."

Papa, breaking his silence, interjected, "So where the fuck are they all?" He grabbed the hilt of his sword god, the blade hissing as he drew it, metal flaming blue as Wallace's flamed red. "The undead army wouldn't have all fucking fit inside the palace and noble's houses, now would they?"

Clem's mustache twitched. "I can't say. All I know is that our new leader, the Horse Master, Khalaf, likes to celebrate a lot. He even invites families to join in with the decadence he so enjoys."

"What's a deck dance?" Wallace asked, knowing what a harvest dance were, but had never heard of the thing Clem had mentioned.

Papa answered, "Means our *friend* Eddi has turned into a selfish prick drunk on power. That's what it means."

"Ah." Wallace couldn't understand why Clem didn't say so in the first place, instead of using fancy words. Fancy word tellin' men were usually snake-oil salesmen in Wallace's experience.

From there, they were led through the beautiful streets, ever higher, some so steep they needed to get a breather halfway up before going on. Along the way, Aron hugged and kissed plenty of others, guards and ordinary folks alike. All were thrilled to see him. He really were a loved and respected person here.

By the time they'd reached the inner wall, the buildings even more wondrous, more golden roofed, with brickwork painted whiter, if at all possible, and stained-glass windows too, Wallace allowed folks—mostly guards—to peck him on his forehead in greeting. He were tired of sticking out his hand after they'd met so many. And seeing as it seemed to be the normal thing to do, feeling more comfortable about it 'cause it were all done respectfully, he kind of got used to it. But he always, always made sure it was clear he gave any of 'em permission to do so *before* they kissed him on his forehead in greeting.

"I'm so proud of you," Papa said, patting Wallace upon his shoulder with the hand which didn't hold his sword. "You're learning to set your own boundaries."

"I'm tryin'."

"You can't do any more than that. And if anyone, no matter who they fucking are, makes you feel uncomfortable, you let me know."

"'Fore or afta I kick 'em in the balls?"

"Your choice."

On the other hand, Horan seemed to enjoy himself, and kissed plenty of folks back on their lips after the hugging. He'd relaxed a lot. Papa remained stoic and only allowed hugging.

Every time they met someone new, they told the same story about Aron. How he'd helped them become who they are today because of what he'd done for 'em. Wallace, though he'd never admit it and couldn't have expected it, was beginning to like Aron, despite him being a bit...*weird*. And that were the only word Wallace could think of but it didn't really do what he felt justice. Not at all.

As they walked on, he soon realized Papa liked Aron too; they were doing that whole knowing glance thing between each other, like how he'd seen him do with Pa when he were alive.

Wallace knew that look and what it meant.

But for the moment, another curiosity sprung to his attention. He went to Aron, who'd just finished greeting another guard, complete with laughter and genuine respect shared. It was nice to see city folks being nice to each other. Really. Thentathion Prime sure were a strange place; again, far different from Invrawold City. Everyone seemed to shout at the top of their lungs there. Not here. Here they all liked hugging and kissing.

After Wallace gave the newest guard permission to greet him too, he said to Aron, "What happens ta the folks who don't git their initiation when's dey are old enough?"

"A good question, Wallace." Aron clapped another guard upon his back warmly in passing. "And the answer is the only blight on our otherwise fine city." There was a pause, the color draining from his otherwise rosy cheeks. "The men whose family…cannot afford a Mentula Guild member to ensure they're recognized, initiated if you like, become indentured servants. They're given menial tasks which they must do until they can afford a Guild member to bring them into society."

Papa said, "Which never fucking happens does it, Aron?"

"Alas, no. After all the rent, food, and keepings are taken into account, there's nothing left to save. Which is why I try and help as many as I can, you see. The people of this city, the people I love, should have every opportunity in life, no matter their social standing. That's what I believe."

Horan said, "A good belief."

Papa nodded. "You're a good man, Aron."

There was that look again between them, Wallace noticed. He couldn't help but smile. Papa smiled, too—and it were good to see such a thing splitting his beard. First time it had happened since Pa passed, Wallace knew.

But Wallace had to ask, "What 'bout the women, then?" He then thought of Horan. "Or dose who might be…ya know, different." Again, the word didn't sum up what Wallace were trying to say. Horan were far from different to him. He were a friend. A good one. And he were who he were too. But once more, he couldn't think of a better word, which frustrated him.

"Girls…" Aron shifted his gaze quickly to Horan before returning his attention back to Wallace. "And those who are *different*, as you say, Wallace, are automatically recognized and respected when they come of age. It is only the men who must become accepted into society by someone like me. That is the way of things." Aron shrugged. "Always has been."

One guard interjected, "And by the Guild, we're grateful for the likes of Aron and what he does for us ordinary men. My uncle, rest his soul, spent his life in a coal mine, indentured until he gasped his last breath. Never got the coin together; worked to death, he was, the poor man."

Wallace wanted to talk more, still curious, but Horan screamed to end any chance of it, "Look!" There was the look of fright struck on his face. Terrible fright. "Up there!"

And that was when Wallace saw a blur rush past him. He realized it were Papa, yelling his war cry along with plenty of cussing, sword god raised high, sprinting towards what Horan had pointed to: three skeleton soldiers coming down the hill brandishing swords that glinted to tell him they were sharp.

Clem said admiringly, "Looks like the Horse Master will soon be dismounted from our throne, now that Lord Hereward is here to lead us to victory."

"Hereward *is* a wonder," Aron agreed with even more admiration. "And the leadership we so jolly well and desperately need without the royal family and nobles to guide us."

Wallace wondered why they hadn't resisted before now; the enemy wasn't exactly overrunning the city. Then again, he realized that what he'd seen so far had given him the answer. The Thentathions were passive folks. More about caring and love than fighting and war. He'd also bet their army, so easily defeated, weren't even an army like any other city would have. They probably couldn't even hold their swords properly, more interested in kissing and hugging everyone in sight than facing their enemies.

He were also surprised the city had guards at all. Perhaps with all the golden metal they wore, sparkling, unscratched, polished to perfection, it were only for show, like pretty ponies at a harvest festival. Wallace smiled at that thought, for it fit well. And there were nothing wrong with it, either—except when an enemy broke down the gates and defenses had to be coordinated. Then the guards, the army, and the whole of Thentathions Prime, as Papa would say, were fucked!

He raised his blade, blazing crimson, and ran too. He was by Papa's side by the time they got to the skeletons. There were only one left.

"Leave this one for me, Papa!" Wallace yelled along with his own distinctive war cry.

"Be my fucking guest!"

The skeleton, silent with its scream 'cause it were only made of bones, tried to lunge at Wallace. Bad mistake. Leaning too much into a lunge took one off balance. The skeleton soldier was smashed in two, its bones clinking on the pretty cobblestones before it probably realized what were going on. If it realized anything at all.

"Here they come!" Clem shouted as he joined them with Aron and a handful of guards. Aron was armed, but Wallace could tell the man had no idea how to handle the sword in a pinch; he kinda held it like its metal hilt were too hot or something, tentative and with a pained expression.

Papa came to stand next to him. "I'll protect you. Nothing fucking sexier than a man who holds a weapon to help folks even if he isn't used to swinging steel about."

Aron gulped and smiled. "T-thank you…Hereward."

But the moment between them was short-lived. Wallace were sad for it, until a whole hoard of skeleton warriors appeared, charging right at 'em. He suddenly had other things to think about.

Papa shouted with glee, "Bring it on, fuckers," as he swung his sword, his god thrumming beautifully. "Come taste the blade's edge of my god! It's so good it'll send you all into oblivion!"

And a blink of an eye later, Wallace, Papa, Horan, Aron, Clem, and all the others were in the midst of battle, bones going everywhere. The only sounds were that of snapping, sliced, or mangled bones which then littered the cobbled road like macabre confetti, clink, clink, clinging.

Wallace were working up a sweat, but had to admit he enjoyed himself. Skeleton soldiers were good practice. Better than hessian dummies, anyway. He even kept his smile from before as his sword blazed red while he hacked his path up the street towards the palace.

"Come taste me steel," Wallace shouted, emulating his papa.

Papa laughed. "Don't get too fucking cocky, son. Pace yourself. There'll be plenty of opportunities ahead, mark my words."

"Ya, Papa." And Wallace took the skull off the vertebrae of his closest enemy with one quick swish of his sword.

Clunk! It hit the cobbles to then roll down the street.

Aron and Horan were doing fine for men who'd not had much practice with a sword other than a few lessons. To be honest, and to Wallace's continuing amazement—and not in a good way—Clem and the other guards were no better with their weapons than 'em. Yep, the guards of this city were show ponies, all right. Nothing wrong with that except when the undead flowed out of their hidey-holes like rats within the grain scared by big tom cats let loose on 'em.

Papa dispensed with four skeletons, slash, crash, smash, with sword, fist, and forehead alike, enjoying himself.

Wallace got rid of two at the same time.

At least the skeletons who fell didn't get up, become reanimated or something equally worrisome, the pile of bones mounting behind them. That were something. And for their efforts, they soon came to the palace gates, gilt and wondrous with the love of the artisans who'd made 'em. The building itself were of the finest and fanciest Wallace'd ever seen, all covered in gold, dazzling bright, doorway to rooftop. Statues, crenelations, and beautiful stonework adorned it. It loomed majestically over all others.

"To the palace," Clem shouted, flailing his halberd around as though he were whacking weeds in a maize field. Crude, but as far as the skeletons went, for they were no challenge except for their numbers, effective against them.

Lucky for Clem and his guards, really.

Papa kicked open the gates. They rattled. Wallace went through them, joining Papa inside the palace's foyer, grand and opulent and gaudy, moments later.

When Aron joined them, he said, "What's that?" pointing with his sword at their newest enemy—no longer skeletons but something which struck the very fear of any god, old or new, into Wallace.

"Wraiths!" Papa said, taking a step back as two of 'em glided, their haunting and silent scream far more terrifying than any the skeletons did.

"How do we fight ghosts?" Horan asked.

Papa said, "Have any of you got any Holy Water?"

"Not on me, no, Lord Hereward," Clem replied, patting his tunic. "Fresh out, I'm afraid."

Wallace weren't sure if the man were poking fun or not, 'cause who would carry Holy Water on 'em, anyway? Then again, the Thentathions were different. Anything were possible when it came to 'em. Telling the truth, he couldn't work 'em out. And above all, he couldn't help but think that when he came of age, he didn't want to be anywhere near this city. Didn't want any stranger touching his willy for any reason, initiation or whatever it were called, or not. Not even for all the coin in the world. No way.

He shuddered at the thought.

Wallace would only ever want someone he loved doing anything like that with him—maybe not even then. Wallace saw how much the love of another hurt Papa. He didn't want to be hurt by anyone. That's why Papa had to live.

And that's why Wallace had to protect him at all costs.

Papa interrupted his spiraling. "Then you'd better start kissing your arse goodbye, Clem, 'cause without any, there's no way of affecting a wraith. Cold, hard steel doesn't work on them, no matter how expertly its wielded."

Aron piped up, "There's a palace vestry not too far from the foyer. I can go look. Perhaps there'd be some in there."

Papa nodded. Aron, with a nervous smile that time, ran to his goal, disappearing down a hallway to the left.

Wallace liked Aron more'n more; he'd proven to be a man of tough resolve and action, despite what he did as a Mentula Guild member for goodwill or coin or otherwise. Again, Wallace shuddered.

"An' what'da we do in the meantime, Papa?" Wallace asked, sheathing his sword, still burning with crimson fire, and regretting he had to. He wasn't scared, though. Not yet. And he knew why.

It were 'cause of what Papa said in answer. After looking at him, then the approaching wraiths, Papa said matter-of-factly, "We fucking run!" And he grabbed Wallace by the hand and charged down the corridor opposite to the one Aron ran down.

Horan, Clem, and the other guards didn't need to be told twice. They ran. At full pelt too, like stuck pigs, their fancy armor clattering and clinking, also huffing and puffing from the sudden exertion, red faced and sweating.

Wallace turned back to see where the wraiths had gotten.

To his dismay, the undead had followed 'em. Without mercy, it seemed. Unrelenting. One poor guard, the young man who told of how lucky he'd been not ending up like his uncle thanks to Aron, was surrounded, falling into the undead's wispy, terrible, long-fingered grasps to then be clutched in death's embrace. To Wallace's growing horror, as soon as the young man were touched, his skin began to shrivel like an apple left on the tree to rot. He also screamed the most horrible, dry, hoarse scream Wallace had ever heard before he were silenced. Nothing was left of him but a pile of bone and fancy armor on the pretty tiling.

The wraiths turned their attention to the rest of 'em.

Wallace ran with more intent, as did Papa and Clem and the surviving guards along with Horan. Aron still hadn't joined them. Perhaps the vestry didn't have any Holy Water. A thought that made Wallace become anxious and finally afraid for the first time since encountering the enemy. He didn't know when, too worried about other things, but he'd become invisible.

Papa must have noticed. "Stay that way if you can. There's another way to deal with wraiths."

Before Wallace could answer, Clem said, "What's that, Lord Hereward?"

"We cut off the head of the one controlling them." And upon speaking his answer, Papa barged through a set of massive double doors, causing them to clatter on their hinges.

The throne room, massive columns of marble, gold everywhere, came into view.

Wallace snuck around the group as they entered, splitting off from them. Best way to plan a sneak attack while Papa distracted Eddi, the man who now called himself the Horse Master. Whatever that meant.

He didn't need to wait long to find out.

Within the throne room, along with ghoul and lich lord guards, a familiar horse stood next to Eddi. Eddi sat on the throne, looking pleased with himself, dressed in royal robes of the deepest purple and more gold finery, buttons and embroidery along with lace bunched everywhere. He looked worse'n a pompous, trumped-up popinjay, as his da would have said. Wallace knew Papa would have agreed with the assessment.

"Lord Hereward!" Eddi said without delight in his voice. "So glad you could come."

Papa didn't look at the man. "Ah, so that's where the horse got to," Papa said, putting on his best 'I'm going to kill you, your horse too' voice with plenty of snarls thrown in.

He stood ready with his sword god.

Wallace had to stifle his amusement at Papa's bravado to keep from being found out.

"Yes, you've met Vengeance, haven't you?" Eddi said.

Papa snorted. "A monk told me you fell out of its arse to become the fucking cunt you are now. Shame. I liked you before that happened, Eddi."

"My name is Khalaf, Master of Horses! Not Eddi!" The man stood, affronted, face purpling as much as the finery he wore. "Eddi is no more. He was murdered by a demon. I'm what's left of him."

"The good parts got left inside the fucking horse then, eh?"

At that moment, the two wraiths entered the throne room. Eddi...or Khalaf waved his hand. They halted their advance, hanging motionless like ghostly kites on a non-existent breeze. "I will forgive your indiscretions towards me, Lord Hereward, and spare your life and those of your friends."

"At what price?" Papa demanded.

Horan, Clem, and the other guards huddled together, weapons nervously at the ready and keeping as far away from the wraiths as they could get, even if in the same room as 'em. Wallace had an idea. One he hoped would work.

"We both have the same demon to hunt, I hear. The one who not only murdered me but also your beloved," he shifted his attention to Horan for the briefest moment, "and the jongleur's brother. Am I right, Lord Hereward?"

"Who fucking told you that?"

"Same interferin' monk, I reckon."

Papa snorted again. "Pity he couldn't talk any fucking sense into you."

Confusion crossed Khalaf's face. "What do you mean?"

"If you'd fucking listened, you would have got your sorry arse off that throne and left the city, let the good folks here be, and used your undead army to hunt and destroy the demon before he could gain any allies or an army of his own."

Khalaf laughed. "Oh, that. No, I disbanded the undead army; I only kept those I needed to ensure my safety. The rest are now scattered across the southern kingdoms."

Vengeance nickered.

"You did *fucking what?*" Papa's mouth fell open, as did Wallace's and everyone else's. "Why the fuck did you do that, you useless fucking limp cock?"

Khalaf sat, unoffended by Papa's insult, resting his arm over the throne's nonchalantly. "I kinda like this city and the comforts it offers. Never had it 'fore. Always been a servant, never a master, you know. And now I *am* a master, I not only enjoy the food and wine and the night-long parties, I also enjoy having my cock sucked whenever I so wish it. I can assure you, Lord Hereward, it's not limp when there's someone on their knees and eager to please me." He paused in thought for a moment, smiling ugly, before adding, "You know, there's plenty of men here who keep offering, too; I can't keep up. Something to do with a certain guild they're a part of, or whatever."

"Careful," Clem spat. "You disrespect the honored with your vileness, Horse Master." The other guards grunted agreement. "You're not welcome here, you murderer. Do us all a favor and be gone."

Khalaf laughed. "No, my friend, I think I shall stay. And I'll continue to enjoy the city's comforts for as long as I see fit. Isn't that right, Vengeance?"

Vengeance whinnied in reply.

It were like the man spoke to the animal. *Prolly does, an' all*, Wallace thought. *Prolly does more with it than talk too*. Even from where Wallace hid, he could see the love between 'em—love no keeper should have of his animals. Folks who slept with animals were usually run out of the village.

Wallace shuddered at the thought. What Aron did for a living seemed mild and almost normal when compared with what Khalaf did. Who Khalaf was. An evil man who only cared for himself and his own comforts.

No ruler, that's for sure.

Papa stepped forward, testing the weight of his sword god. "Not only will you not have my loyalty, I'm going to stick my sword into your guts, cut you up into small enough pieces to shove back into your horse, and then cut it up, making sure neither of you never fucking ever come back again."

"I don't think so," Khalaf said, gesturing to his undead guards and Vengeance.

At that moment, Aron came into the throne room, throwing Holy Water all over the two wraiths. To Wallace's amazement, they sizzled and hissed and then disappeared. Pity the trick didn't work for the other undead. They charged for Horan, Clem, and the city guards.

Vengeance did as well.

But the horse's goal were Papa. Wallace gasped. Khalaf must have heard him, for he said, "There's another in the throne room. Find him! Find him and kill him!"

Then, as Wallace had heard the elders of his village once say, it became a real shit fight in the town square. And it did, even if it were in a throne room. Swords, halberds, and other weapons, maces—and axes, and clubs included—were soon tangled in deadly melee.

Papa hacked off an arm of a lich lord, no blood, before Vengeance were atop him. The horse's hooves glowed with fire, brighter than Wallace's sword glowed green.

Wallace's heart found his throat, making him gasp, as Vengeance reared then came down on Papa with a thud.

"Fuck!" Papa screamed as he dodged the hooves in the nick of time. The marble beneath him cracked deeply with an almighty thump.

But Papa didn't get time to rest. Vengeance were upon him again. Papa slashed with his sword god. It only swished the air, the horse able to somehow dodge the attack, moving quicker than the eye could track.

Wallace didn't know how.

Magic, no doubt.

What's more, the others were occupied with the lich lords and ghouls, the fighting not going well for 'em. They were outclassed and outnumbered. Two more guards, good men, were already dead. Three were badly wounded. Clem even had a gash across his arm that didn't look too good, dark blood flowing. It were his sword arm too. Aron stood by Clem, defending him best he could—which, despite his efforts, weren't much. His wrist was too limp; he hadn't learnt to hold a sword properly yet. He wouldn't last long.

Wallace swallowed hard.

He had to do something.

Come Hell or High Water, he had to put his plan into place, no matter how much it scared the spit outta him. He had to. Papa needed him.

With all the resolve he could muster, he made his way toward the rearing horse, knowing full well it were the animal which held all the power. If all folks could hear what horses said, not one would act the way Khalaf acted, like the horse were the master, even if loved.

Papa dodged another attack, hooves aflame even brighter. One got him on the shoulder. He screamed. Wallace's heart stopped before staying lodged in his throat. Papa were all right. But there were blood. He swung his sword god again and again, desperately, some finding their mark.

Which only made Vengeance madder.

Quick like lightning, the horse reared and thumped, reared and thumped, over and over, cracking marble when not striking flesh and bone. Papa's flesh and bone. Beaten and bloody, Papa slowed, exhausted, heaving heavy breaths, staggering. He looked a sight. Even his beard were bloody.

Wallace was scared outta his mind.

"Fucking dirty beast," Papa spat, globules of congealed blood spattering upon the cracks by his feet from his cracked and bloody lips. "Come taste the steel of my sword god again. I can see you're just as badly hurt as I am."

Even though Vengeance was slashed open in many places, flesh hanging, streaked with gore to his fetlocks, that was when the horse calmed. The animal was breathing hard too. Muscles twitched. Although, it no doubt it sensed victory.

Vengeance whinnied, then snorted.

Before the horse could rear again, attack papa perhaps for the final time, Wallace jumped onto its back. All too late for Vengeance to realize what was going on. Even though at the last moment he was sensed, Vengeance turning, bucking, trying to dismount him and then stomp on him, Wallace held onto his mane for all his life, thrusting his sword into the back of the animal's head when he got the chance, deeper and deeper with all of his might. He screamed his war cry, his anguish, his victory.

To Wallace's surprise, Vengeance didn't fall but stood fast.

Yes, blood flowed from the horse's mouth and nostrils, bled out the other side of its head, glowing green, but it didn't seem to affect the animal. Wallace were shocked. More so, as blood poured in gushes all over the marble, Vengeance didn't seem affected.

After another anxious moment followed where Wallace was puzzled by what he could do to kill the animal. He withdrew his sword, only to stick it back into the horse in a different place, again with all his might and pushing as deeply as the metal would go.

Now Vengeance staggered. But like a tranquilized horse before succumbing, Vengeance also became stubborn, determined not to fall. For a downed horse were a dead horse, in Wallace's experience. And Vengeance clearly wanted to hold onto his life of magic and dominance.

Too bad Papa had other ideas for him.

"Didn't think to look for my son, did you, fucker? Even though you knew he was here. Your folly, not mine." And with those words, spat with blood and anger, Papa plunged his sword god into Vengeance's chest, right into the horse's heart.

Vengeance fell.

Wallace jumped off in time.

Then Khalaf, no longer supplied with the flow of magic to keep him alive after his strange rebirth, screamed in agony, his body twisting and writhing on the throne. Which confirmed in Wallace's mind that it were the horse who held all the power all along.

It were strange to see a man fall to pieces. Bit by bit, parts of Khalaf fell off of him as the magic dissipated. Wallace winced at the horrific sight, and Papa staggered to him to hold him. Wallace held him back, even though there was a hiss of pain as he did so.

"You were amazing, son." Papa kissed Wallace on the forehead before collapsing to the floor. Worry found Wallace, and he went to hold his Papa as tightly as he could.

"Don't you dare leave me, Papa."

"Not planning to. But I think I need an ale—a fucking big one."

Soon, all that were left of Khalaf's body was a pile of gore at the foot of the throne. The man was dead…again. This time for good.

Papa groaned, bleeding badly. Wallace didn't know what to do. He searched the room, seeing if there were any help. Thankfully, when Vengeance and Khalaf were defeated, the remaining undead fled the city. Aron and Clem came to Papa and Wallace.

Aron quickly removed his shirt, tearing the silken finery of it into strips. "Take off Hereward's armour. Quick as you can and carefully too," he said to Clem.

The captain of the guard did so without delay. Wallace helped. With Papa's wounds revealed, terrible wounds already bruising where there weren't cuts and blood flowed, Aron began bandaging them.

Horan came over, offering to help by giving his jacket to be used as bandages and helping apply them. They all helped. All the surviving guards too. Papa was the savior of their city, after all.

When bandaged as best could be for now, Wallace couldn't help but admire Aron even more. He also realized, in the moments of care, careful and lovingly done, Aron had feelings for Papa.

As it were clear Papa had feelings for Aron.

And before Wallace could offer his thanks, the doors to the throne room opened. More city guards entered, but there were others with them. They wore finery, just like Aron's.

An escorting guard, one who'd helped in the fight earlier, announced, "Clem, we've found two surviving members of the nobility; they were being held in the dungeon. Could only get to them when the undead turned tail."

Aron stood and bowed, as did the others. Except Horan; they weren't his nobles, after all. "I'm honored you survived, Lady Chancellor."

"As am I and my son, Roderick," the lady replied, offering her bow to Aron.

The noble named Roderick, the chancellor's son, approached Aron, eyes watery and red rimmed. Wallace knew how the man felt. It had been a day and a half.

Aron bowed again, but lower. "My Lord!"

Papa groaned. Wallace was worried about him. He didn't look

good. His eyes revealed not only his pain but that he wasn't quite with them, vacant if Wallace were to describe it. He'd not seen Papa like this before. There were also a lot of blood still coming outta him, blood Aron's bandages didn't seem to stem from flowing.

Wallace ached with worry and fear.

Papa couldn't die. He simply couldn't.

"Oh, Aron," Roderick said, relieved, turning Wallace's attention back to him. He held Papa as he listened; what else could he do? The nobleman continued, "It's just brilliant to see you. Brilliant. I've been so stressed and worried, you have no idea. No idea."

Aron stood tall, proud, reaching to hold the chancellor's son's hands, coming face to face with him. Close too. Wallace noticed there were no hugging or kissing in greeting this time. Which somehow made their hand holding seem very intimate, not a common sight since arriving at the city.

Papa winced when Wallace moved within his embrace, sucking air through his teeth in obvious pain, even though he held Wallace back with as much intent and love. Wallace couldn't help but blurt, his vision misting with his emotions, "I love you, Papa," he whispered.

"And I fucking love you, Wallace," was the immediate, heartfelt reply, accompanied by a kiss upon his forehead. Not in greeting, how the Thentathions did it, but with undying, unconditional love.

Although Wallace knew he'd have a bloody mark on his brow from the kiss, he didn't care. He didn't wipe it away, either.

He held his papa tighter.

Aron clearing his throat directed Wallace's attention back to what had unfolded inside the throne room. The gore of battle lay all around them, including a lump of a horse still twitching as it died within a pool of its own blood.

Good riddance ta ya, Wallace thought.

After letting go of Roderick's hands, Aron cleared his throat again. "Did you want me to help relieve some of your tension, my Lord?"

And Wallace knew what *that* meant. Although he hoped Aron didn't get onto his knees and fish out Roderick's willy with everyone here watching. That couldn't be how it was done. Could it?

Roderick adjusted the bulge within his fancy pants. He then smiled, one full of lust Wallace had seen plenty of times. "Why, I think that—"

But to Wallace's relief, Papa—again with hurt in his voice, teeth bloody as much as the rest of him—interjected, "No, Aron will not be relieving your tension, you ponced up little pretty boy. He's fucking attending to me. Go get your cock sucked by someone else and have some consideration for others. There's wounded here, and I'm one of them."

Wallace couldn't help but try and stifle a giggle. He failed. "You're the best, Papa."

"Only because of you, son."

Roderick looked mortified until his mother gently placed her hand upon his shoulder. She said softly, regally, "I believe Lord Hereward, the savior of our fine city, is entitled to have some compensation for what he's done here today. And unfortunately for you, my son, it means you miss out. You'll have to find another favorite, it would seem."

Roderick looked at Aron, then Papa, then back to Aron. He sighed in resignation and flicked his hair. "I *will* miss your skills, Aron."

"As I will miss you, my Lord." But Aron's voice held no interest, and he'd already turned and left Roderick, coming to Papa to quickly begin preparing another bandage. "Where does it hurt the most, Hereward?"

"My fucking heart."

Aron gave a full smile—one Wallace had come to like. He guessed Papa liked it even more, especially that one, 'cause they looked at each other for the longest time after it until Aron averted his eyes, blushing bright red at his cheeks. "That will take a longer time to heal, I'm afraid."

Wallace, feeling the love envelop him, said, "Papa's got all the time in the world, 'cause he's gonna be all right, ain't he?" And with those words, and at that moment—as Aron began tending to his papa once more, carefully, lovingly—Wallace knew Aron were for Papa. And even though the man would never replace Pa, could never, Wallace knew Aron could make Papa happy. And when Papa were happy, he were happy.

Papa just had to realize it himself now.

Epilogue

HEREWARD SHIFTED HIS WEIGHT, uncomfortable no matter which way he moved his arse on the wooden stool. Thank his sword god he had a few ales in him already, numbing him enough. Otherwise, he wouldn't have been able to sit at all. And when drinking, especially in celebration, that was a fucking downer.

Don't drink too much, his sword god said, then chuckled. *You're a lump to move as it is, my love. And when you're inebriated, no one can shift you, not even all the old gods working together.*

She was right, so he didn't reply.

Besides, Abbot Hosho was talking. And talking. And talking. As per fucking usual. "Therefore, it is said, the great war between the dead, undead, demons, gods, and humanity has begun. Ugruthaan will bring about the Purge. It is inevitable, as the universe would say."

"I fucking hate when you talk all philosophical, monk," Hereward said, wiping his chin of ale.

"What else can I do?"

At that moment, Aron came to the table of the tavern they'd found themselves in, the only one within Thentathion Prime that Hereward found to his liking—not too neat and tidy, smelling enough of stale beer and sweat to make him feel at home. Wallace nursed a tankard of goat's milk, talking quietly with Horan, Kieron, and Vash, at the far end of the table. Smiling. Content. Happy. A good sight.

"Do you need another drink, Hereward?" Aron asked, waiting to be looked at before speaking. Full of respect he was. Hereward couldn't help but be enamored by his presence alone and had to be careful; even getting an erection hurt after the battle he'd fought with Vengeance many days ago now.

"If you're buying, I'm drinking." Hereward laughed until his arm hurt where he'd been bandaged. His sides hurt too. Every fucking thing hurt, even though Aron did a good job with his wounds. There were plenty of them, this time.

"Jolly good."

When Aron left to fetch the drink, his musky perfume he always wore left in his wake, as intoxicating as him, Abbot Hosho smiled knowingly. "What?" Hereward asked.

"I see you like Aron."

Hereward shrugged; even that hurt to do so. "Do you mean *like*, as in as a friend, or *like*, as in I want to take him to bed and fuck his brains out when I'm feeling better?"

"I don't think I need to tell you the answer, do I?"

Hereward turned to look at Aron; no matter how fine the clothing that covered it, there was nothing better than to witness a perfectly shaped arse on a man, one Hereward could eat out and then fuck for hours and hours. By his sword god, Aron was handsome, and yes, gave Hereward many, many erotic thoughts. So fucking many, that hurt too.

He sighed, longingly. "Is it that obvious?"

His sword god stayed wisely, and strangely, quiet.

"Again, I think you know the answer to that." Abbot Hosho, also drinking goat's milk, raised the tankard, but paused when it was at his lips. "Aron has given up his Guild membership."

"What?" Hereward was surprised. "Why?"

Abbot Hosho winked. "If we're going to have a conversation where you ask questions you already know the answer to, I'll go talk to Wallace."

"Fair enough." Hereward drained his tankard, wiping his beard. "Aron wants me as much as I want him. There, I said it. Fucking happy now, monk?"

Abbot Hosho leant forwards. "Then what are you waiting for? Let love run its course, oaf. You deserve to be loved."

Hereward paused and licked his lips. His stomach turned in the special kind of way he knew meant he was smitten. But then he hurt all over, again for the same reason. Abbot Hosho's pupil-less eyes boring into him, right to his soul, seemed to peel the truth out of him. A truth he didn't want to admit but had no choice to. He whispered, "I can't love him like he wants...not yet. I'm scared."

"I know you are. But yes, you can. Give yourself permission. Dorgan and Ayrdon wouldn't want you to be unhappy. Wallace doesn't want you to be unhappy. I don't want you to be unhappy either."

The monk was fucking right.

He is right, his sword god piped up.

Again, Hereward ignored her. Ignored the monk. Everyone was a wise arse, all of a sudden. It wasn't as simple as what they thought. Hereward had Wallace to consider, not just himself. Besides, he couldn't mourn another dead lover. He'd mourned too much already.

Too fucking much for one man to bear.

Aron returned, tankard in hand, ale frothing to the rim. He sat after handing it over, his fingers brushing against Hereward's as he did so. A shiver ran through him, and Aron smiled.

Hereward smiled back. "Thanks," was all he could manage, completely caught within the spell of Aron's presence once more.

Abbot Hosho drank his milk, now annoyingly silent.

"What happens now?" Hereward asked Aron.

"I don't know what you mean." That smile appeared again.

"Yeah, and my cock don't get hard thinking about you, either."

Aron blushed again. Strange to see a man so experienced with men, taught how to pleasure them, making a respected living from it, looking as though he was a young man smitten with his first love.

Perhaps he was.

"I think…I believe, I need to learn more about handling a sword. And then we can perhaps go from there, Hereward."

Hereward thought about his words. He was being respectful, letting Hereward come to terms with things before they agreed on anything, a relationship or otherwise. "Sword lessons don't come fucking free."

Aron leant forwards. "And what will be the cost?"

Hereward placed his hand onto Aron's, feeling the warmth, enjoying touching another in such a way again. "I think you need to teach me something in return."

"Oh?"

"Yes." Hereward, unbelievably, felt himself blush. "I think I need to learn how to love someone again, now that my heart might have enough room in it to do so."

Aron gave him that devastating smile. "I accept the terms of our agreement. Where do we begin?"

"Slowly."

That was when Abbot Hosho decided to whisper some of his fucking wisdom. "I have heard whispers of a dead army being raised against us, the Purge Ugruthaan had begun now taking a deadlier, even more threatening turn. I think, being the newly appointed Regent of

Thentathion, Hereward, you should put your resources into the cause, don't you?"

Hereward sighed. "Are you or the universe or the both of you together interfering again, monk?"

"Not at all, oaf." Abbot Hosho sipped from his tankard. "It's got nothing to do with me that Greysen and Novane are heading for Arbour Keep and Dyathian to gain us allies while Kieron and Vash are soon going to do the same in Elemeria and Gateway. Nothing to do with me at all."

"And I'm taking a horse's cock, deep and fucking hard, down my gob."

"I heard it was popular for a while," Abbot Hosho said with a chuckle.

"Ended fucking badly for some, though." Hereward laughed, as did Aron.

Aron then said, "I'm sure Hereward will do whatever is required to aid the kingdoms in their fight against our greatest threat."

Hereward's eyebrows raised. "By my sword god, you're not even in my bed yet and already you're talking for me. You got some balls, Aron. Big fuckers, obviously."

Aron averted his eyes again. "Sorry. I didn't mean to—"

Hereward squeezed his hand to reassure him. "I don't mind." The smile along with the reddened cheeks returned.

Abbot Hosho stood. "Well, I'm glad that's settled then. With your forces joining the others, I do believe those living within the Eleven Kingdoms will now stand some sort of chance against Ugruthaan's Purge."

"I'll drink to that." And Hereward drained his tankard.

Aron took the empty. "Looks like I'm buying another."

"Are you trying to get me fucking drunk to take advantage of me?"

Aron went even redder. "I find that drunken men don't...perform so well. So this ale will jolly well be your last."

Hereward boomed a laugh. Laughing felt good. Again, he watched Aron as he walked away. "Damn, that's a fine fucking arse."

Abbot Hosho said solemnly, "I hope you get to enjoy it often before Ugruthaan strikes. We're not ready for that yet."

"We will be."

"I take it you're itching for a fight."

"Does a deer shit all over the woods?"

Abbot Hosho nodded. "Then I will leave you for a moment to enjoy some serenity with Aron. I have things to do."

"More manipulation of us mere mortals, monk?"

Abbot Hosho said, "I hope to convince a god to help me at least delay things a bit."

"Good luck."

Abbot Hosho bowed his head, looking at Aron as he approached, another frothing ale in hand. "As for you. Be careful. The time for the real war will soon be upon us."

The End

About Kon Blacke

By day I'm a humble physical therapist...and by day I'm also a writer of sweet & saucy boyslove stories (18+). I sleep at night as an old fart like me should. I'm both self-published and traditionally published. Other than that, I live with my partner and two cats and live my best life.

Website: http://konblackeboyslovewriter.com
Twitter: http://www.twitter.com/blackekon

Also from Dreamsphere Books

Gearteeth
Timothy Black

On the brink of humanity's extinction, Nikola Tesla and a mysterious order of scientists known as the Tellurians revealed a bold plan to save a world ravaged by a disease that turned sane men into ravenous werewolves: the uninfected would abandon the Earth's surface by rising up in floating salvation cities, iron and steel metropolises that carried tens of thousands of refugees above the savage apocalypse.

Twenty years later, only one salvation city remains aloft, while the beasts still rule the world below. Time has taken its toll on the miraculous machinery of the city, and soon the last of the survivors will plummet to their doom. But when Elijah Kelly, a brakeman aboard the largest of the city's Thunder Trains, is infected by the werewolf virus, he discovers a secret world of lies and horrific experiments that hide the disturbing truth about the Tellurians.

When the beast in his blood surges forth, Elijah must choose between the lives of those he loves, and the city that is humanity's last hope of survival.

Available now in paperback and ebook

Also from Dreamsphere Books

A Thousand Roads
John Robin

When Jak, a young orphan, arrives at Fort Lasthall, he hopes to find work and a roof over his head. To his great relief, he immediately finds employment as a stable boy, in the house of a stern and reclusive man named Barrik. Although not popular with the other boys who work there, it is enough for Jak that he's found favor with Barrik, a favor that promises more than mere employment.

Jak's life would be perfect—if only he wasn't haunted by the memory of a burning woman; if only his life with Barrik didn't lead to more secrets, secrets that awaken in Jak a longing for the taste of blood, and a distinct awareness that he is being bound to something, becoming slave to a power that stirs under the surface...

Available now in paperback and ebook

Find more great reads at dreamspherebooks.com